A LAWLESS PASSION . . .
A TIMELESS LOVE

Her nearness blocked out the past with its gunsmoke and outlaws. He found her mouth waiting inches away and sought her parted lips, kissing her gently. Norah closed her eyes, choked with excitement.

"Norah, my darling," Mason whispered, putting his arm about her waist, pulling her close, passion heating him.

Their mouths came together again, and lightning lanced through her, surprising her so, she made a sound in her throat. His fingers touched the underside of a breast, and as in the dreams, she longed to open her clothing to him. . . .

Mariposa

Phyllis Leonard

A DELL BOOK

DEDICATION:

Happy thirty-fifth anniversary to my beloved husband, Walter, who made **a vow** in 1948 and never broke it . . . .

> *To love one maiden only, cleave to her,*
> *And worship her by years of noble deeds. . . .*

Alfred, Lord Tennyson,
"Guinevere," *Idylls of the King*

Published by
Dell Publishing Co., Inc.
1 Dag Hammarskjold Plaza
New York, New York 10017

Dell ® TM 681510, Dell Publishing Co., Inc.

ISBN: 0-440-16071-5

Printed in the United States of America
First printing—May 1983

What is life without the radiance of love?

Johann Christoph Friedrich von Schiller:
Wallensteins Tod

Part I

NORAH

> *The joy of love is too short, and the sorrow*
> *thereof, and what cometh thereof, dureth over long.*
> Sir Thomas Malory:
> *Le Morte d'Arthur*

1.

The stagecoach from St. Louis headed for a canyon that twisted and turned between steep walls like the track of a snake in the sand. Seen from a distance the crimson-and-yellow vehicle might have been a galleon on a tawny desert sea.

To the driver, with his nerves and wrists of steel, the coach was his movable kingdom, jammed with passengers, goods, U.S. mail, and now and then a treasure box of gold. He cast a jaundiced eye at the rocky route ahead and sweet-talked the six-horse team: heavy wheelers directly in front of him, medium-weight swingers in the middle, the leaders that were the lightest of all. He called them by name, communicated through each rein, demanded more speed with a crack of his whip above their sweating backs.

The whip popped like a distant gunshot and startled twenty-year-old Norah Carlisle from an uneasy doze. She repositioned her bonnet with trembling fingers. Had they entered the infamous pass described in her paperback guidebook? Had the Apaches attacked? She had but to peek through the canvas curtains to see evidence of past depredations: wrecked wagons, skeletons of draft animals, plundered stores abandoned to the elements, crude crosses over hasty graves.

Dust kicked up by pounding hoofs and iron tires settled on the coach's five passengers, crept down collars and into intimate places, and gritted between the teeth. Stifled by it, Norah pressed a handkerchief to her lips. It came away spotted with blood for the second time since dawn. She gasped and her heart faltered with a familiar terror.

9

"Headed for San Francisco?" The man beside her leaned down to take a small box from the saddlebags at his feet. The emotions that swept across the pale face touched him.

Like the miner, merchant, and traveling salesman on the opposite seat, moving bonelessly as the vehicle rocked back and forth, he did not seem concerned about their dangerous location. Whether their indifference was bravado or confidence lent by past experience, it gave Norah comfort. "No, I'm not going that far. Just to Fort Guardian. Relatives are meeting me there." Arizona Territory. The end of the civilized world. A wilderness of savage men and beasts into which she had been driven like a pariah of Biblical times by the contagious illness that fed upon her.

"What do you know? That's where I'm going, too." He opened the box, which was packed with spice-brown lozenges, and held it out to her. "They're horehound. Take some. Go ahead. I have plenty."

Careful not to breathe on them, she selected four, then slipped one into her mouth. "Thank you. You're most kind."

He had boarded during the night somewhere in New Mexico and until moments ago slept with his hat down on his nose. Drained by sickness, the two-week nonstop journey, bad food, and continually interrupted sleep, Norah had paid little attention to him beyond noticing his wide shoulders silhouetted in the station doorway. Now, however, grateful for his thoughtfulness, she sighed wistfully. Only last year, before she grew white and wasted, she might have triggered a glint of interest in the grave amber eyes that met hers with such polite cordiality. Then Norah caught a flash of silver—a lawman's badge—pinned inconspicuously to the shirt beneath his worn buckskin jacket. He was a native Westerner, no doubt of that: rugged as the mountains, lean and graceful as creatures that prowled them, brown as fine leather.

Mason Fletcher was pleased that the girl's hollow-cheeked features could brighten with a hint of coquetry. She must have been lovely at one time, for she had a wealth of auburn hair, a flawless but too translucent complexion, and dark blue eyes so sprinkled with hazel that they were a new and splendid color. She coughed and edged away, failing to notice his mouth soften with sympathy. Coming West had to be her last stand against the tuberculosis that was consuming her, a final fight for life in the high desert's crystalline air.

He pulled his mind from her with effort, for she appealed to his chivalry and compassion. Seeing that they were now deep in the canyon, he drew one of his two Colt revolvers and rested it on his knee; he pointed its muzzle toward the door while rubbing the walnut handle, already smooth and dark with sweat and usage.

"You expectin' trouble?" the miner grumbled, taking a swig from a bottle in his lap. "Thought all them Apaches was on reservations."

Mason looked up. "Most of them are at the San Carlos Agency south of the Gila River, but we're going through the northern part of the Chiricahua Apache Reservation now. Their chief, Cochise, died last year, and while the majority of his people abide by the peace treaty, there are renegades that spit on it. Better safe than sorry." He patted the weapon for emphasis and gazed out at the bleak walls. The only spring for forty miles in each direction flowed up ahead; it had long dictated this route to nomadic tribes, gold-seekers bound for California strikes, settlers, military and civilian wagon trains. Fort Guardian had been built in 1869 to protect travelers from Apaches, who had until recently ruled from West Texas to western Arizona Territory with blood, iron, and fire.

The other men exchanged glances. They'd been told he was a U.S. Marshal; his six-shooters showed the patina of frequent handling; his companion was a wolf-faced Indian who clung atop the baggage on the roof like a vulture with talons hooked in a carcass. He knew what he was talking about, all right, and by silent, mutual agreement, they checked their firearms.

Norah watched the preparations with apprehension, remembering from her book that this was the most perilous pass on the southern mail and emigrant route between St. Louis and the West Coast. Cold sweat beaded her forehead and upper lip, her breathing quickened, and without realizing it, she moved closer to Mason Fletcher.

"Don't be afraid, we'll come through. There may not even be any shooting." He smiled, suppressing the desire to pat her like a child who sought the safety of his presence.

She nodded with dignity, suddenly ashamed of her fear. Why be so afraid? she asked herself. After all, did the manner of death matter? Perhaps an arrow was cleaner, quicker, and more merciful. Norah coughed into her handkerchief, muffling a scream when a bullet thudded into the woodwork inches from her arm.

"Get down!" Mason pushed her with the flat of his hand between her shoulders. The stagecoach careened around a curve, dropping a wheel in a chuckhole, catapulting her against him. Half fainting, Norah began to slip off the seat. A fierce, unexpected tenderness for this fragile stranger seized him, and he bent, lifted her to him, and at the same time snapped off a shot at an Apache. A lucky hit, Mason thought grimly, as the man fell.

The pungent smoke of black gunpowder filled the vehicle, and the men swore at the ambushers who appeared among the rocks, ducked, then reappeared like a nightmare shooting gallery through which the stagecoach sped. The driver blew his bugle, as was customary before reaching a station, and its defiant notes ricocheted off the walls like bullets of brass.

Troopers from the fort half a mile away arrived at a furious gallop to lend a hand and escort the coach the rest of the way. When the team was reined in, heavily armed attendants at the adobe station grabbed the horses' bridles and tried to quiet the frantic animals. A gray leader

wounded by a flint arrowhead was led to the corral for
treatment or dispatch; Apache barbs often bore poison
concocted from rotted deer liver and rattlesnake venom.

Mail and passengers came next, but Mason was too
anxious about the now unconscious girl to wait. Holstering
both guns, he lifted her in his arms, carefully maneuvered
through the door, and stepped to the ground. He hurried
inside, where the station supervisor helped him bundle her
in blankets against the autumn chill; then they dragged a
straw-filled pallet close to the fireplace and placed her inert
form on it. The merchant carried in a small trunk, hatbox,
and carpetbag, the salesman a purse and gloves; neither
lingered to inquire of their fellow passenger, for ailing
Easterners seeking healthy climates west of the Mississippi
were a dime a dozen.

"Is there a physician at the fort?" Mason asked. "She'll
need one when she wakes up."

"Doc Gates lends a hand now and then if my men get
hurt." The supervisor frowned and shook his head. "She's
ticketed to here and no farther. Where the devil's she going?
I know of a few ranches south of here but none suitable for a
lady this sick."

The men studied Norah, willing her to awaken and tell
them what to do. The thick hair, accidentally released from
pins and bonnet, gave the only sign of life as it curled in rich
disarray, glinting in the light. Mason brooded with a faint
astonishment over his impulse to protect the dying girl. In a
few brief moments this frail outcast had unknowingly
pierced his armor and captured his admiration. He wanted
to see her live.

"If you're going to the fort, get the doc, will you?" the
supervisor said. "I've got people to feed, mail to sort, and a
dozen other things to do. The driver has to leave in fifteen
minutes."

"Be glad to."

"By the way, that your Indian outside? He can't come in
here, but you can take food to him if you want. Lost a man

to the Apaches last week and his friends don't cotton to any Indian."

"He's not 'mine,' but thanks, I'll do that." Mason squatted beside the pallet. If only there were women she might turn to or something else he could do. He adjusted the blankets and carpetbag arranged under her head, coiled the tousled hair as a precaution against stray sparks. He marveled at its silken texture, let it slide over his hand, linger between his fingers. His stomach rumbled audibly, complaining of its last meal hours ago of greasy salt pork and mesquite beans with hard soda bread. Here venison frying and biscuits baking perfumed the air, and his mouth watered.

Mason rose with a lithe movement. After he ate, he'd see that the physician and the girl's relatives hightailed it over here; surely they knew by now that the stage was in. He felt a faint irritation with her people, for he found it impossible to go about his business until she was taken care of. It was like leaving an orphan fawn alone in a forest of predators. She—he didn't even know her name. The girl tugged at his heartstrings, and he vowed to learn her identity before leaving the fort in the next few days. Mason was unable to put a finger on the reason, but he knew he would remember her.

Norah hovered on the misty rim of consciousness, unwilling to surrender the peace of being motionless, and so still she felt disembodied, separate from the damaged husk in which she existed. To stay at rest, a storm-tossed shell cast upon the beach at last, the secret of its life drifting away with the tide—yes, that was the thing to do. She was too tired to try anymore. Norah sighed and opened her eyes.

"Well, at last!" In the lamplight she saw a ginger-haired Army doctor in his fifties. "I was getting concerned about you, young lady. You've slept fourteen hours straight!" He placed a palm on her forehead and took her pulse. "I'm Dr. Theodore Gates, my dear, and you're in the Fort Guardian hospital, such as it is."

"I am dying," Norah whispered. Why did he bother putting the stethoscope to her chest?

He listened with care before pulling a blanket closer to her chin. "No, you're not. You mustn't say that. I've seen many patients in worse shape, some so bad they were carried off the coaches on mattresses, but in time they recovered. It's this wonderfully pure air and sunshine, so don't give up hope. Of course, you'll need months of rest and care, no two ways about that."

A soldier entered with a large tin cup and a wooden spoon. He grinned and whipped off his cap. "Here's the soup you wanted, Doc. Evening, ma'am."

Norah protested weakly. "No, I can't eat." The smell nauseated her and as she turned away, coughing, the soldier's grin faded. He put the cup and utensil down and hurried out.

"You must." The physician raised Norah to a semireclining position on the cot and doubled a bedsack between her and the wall. "I'll wager you didn't have much but cornbread and stew on your trip. That's all I had on my way out here a couple years ago."

Suddenly panic-stricken, Norah grabbed his arm. She coughed harshly and gagged on bloody phlegm. He jumped to keep her from sliding flat, which would allow the matter to rise into her sinuses and cut off all air; once the seizure passed, he gave her a glass of water, then brought a bedpan.

When she was settled again, he said, "Where are you headed? One of the ranches?" He kept his eyes downcast so as not to reveal the pity in them. How was this poor shadow of a thing to manage without proper medical care or amenities?

"My mother's sister and her husband run the—the Double Bar F. I think that's the name. There's a letter in my bag about it."

Dr. Gates dipped into the steaming cup. "Want to try a little?"

She ate most of the soup without enthusiasm, though the

hearty liquid with its beef, onion, and potato flavors warmed her body and raised her spirits. "That was good. I guess I was hungrier than I thought. Thank you."

He chuckled, holding the cup so she might drink the last drops. "Our cook will be flattered. He gets nothing but complaints from us. Now try to nap, Miss Carlisle, and I'll see you again before lights-out."

Norah raised herself up on one elbow. "Tell me the truth. Do you think I'm going to get well?"

His heart melted. He'd been trained to stay aloof, not to get emotionally involved with his patients, but was unable to do so. And, oh, his abysmal ignorance—and that of the profession with its inbred reluctance to accept the new or the better! It depressed him, for what did he know of consumption in a young female, limited as he was to soldiers with syphilis, boils, hangovers, bellyaches, and broken bones?

"Please tell me. I'm not afraid to know the truth."

Ashamed of wool-gathering and of being too cowardly to tell the truth, he made his reply bluff and cheerful. "Of course not, my dear, of course not! You mustn't worry that pretty head. Now get some rest." Turning down the lamp, he left the one-room hospital and closed the door behind him.

Norah stared at the door without seeing it. She had the same symptoms her mother had had, God rest her soul, and they utterly possessed her in all their dreadfulness. How much longer could she endure the fatigue that seemed to dissolve her bones, drenching night sweats and weight loss, a racking cough that steadily worsened, and at the end a hemorrhage that gushed up from dying lungs in a scarlet flood?

She wanted to believe Dr. Gates and the physician in St. Louis who had urged her to make haste in moving to the Southwest. Norah wanted so much to cling to hope, go on fighting, to *live*! Closing her eyes, she burrowed under the coarse Army blankets smelling slightly but not unpleasantly of horses and hay. Their male embrace jarred her memory, and she pictured the man in the stagecoach and how he had clasped her to him almost ferociously as if to shield her from the world.

Norah made a muted sound of longing. Where had he gone? What was his name? The star on his shirt glittered in her mind's eye. Had he helped her because it was his duty to protect a stranger from injury? Had his ministrations stemmed wholly from the desire to serve mankind? No, a bond had somehow been forged between them. Of what dimension or strength she was unable to judge, but it glowed in her heart like a fire in a dark wood.

2.

Cigar smoke floated through the room to cast a veil over the dried mud walls and cobwebbed ceiling of earth and branches. Mason Fletcher and the commanding officer of Fort Guardian, Major Edward Bertram, lounged before a roaring blaze with glasses of bourbon and a bottle on a nail cask between them.

Their thoughts intertwined, for they had been discussing the takeover of Indian lands from the Atlantic to the Pacific. The Army had encountered a myriad of problems in surveying and securing these lands, in forcing tribes onto reservations with a minimum of bloodshed, and in its lesser known role of safeguarding cooperative Indians from the settlers' just or unjust wrath.

Mason cleared his throat. "I wanted to ask you about the attack on the stagecoach yesterday. Do you think those Indians were from the San Carlos Agency? The agent there told me recently that his Apaches are behaving and trying their best to switch from the old ways to agriculture. Says they gathered and roasted more than seventy-five thousand pounds of mescal root this year, for example."

"They could have been young bucks sneaking off to raid in Mexico. The governor of Sonora keeps yelling about the Treaty of Guadalupe Hidalgo that our countries signed after we won the war with them. It stipulates that we police the border—an impossible task!—and pay indemnity for any damage Apaches do down there." The officer snorted with exasperation. "As for Agent John Clum, he had the damned gall to demand we withdraw the Army from San Carlos and let his Indian police take over. He's even organized a native court! Foxes in the chicken house if you ask me."

"Don't sell the idea short, Eddie. The Cheyenne, the Choctaw Nation, the Kiowa, Sioux, and Seminoles have tribal police—have had them long before Clum thought of it. Why not give the Apaches a chance to do the same thing?" Mason held his glass out to the fire, and flames turned the bourbon the color of the girl's hair. He remembered how it had caressed his hand.

His friend grumbled, "That's up to Washington, not me, thank God. I'd put thumbs down."

"Think it could have been Chiricahuas after the coach?"

"Don't think so. Cochise's sons, Tahzay and Nachee, vowed to keep their father's promise of peace. Might be renegades like Geronimo or Victorio, though."

The major refilled their glasses and wondered about the faraway look on his friend's face. He'd always envied Mason's dark good looks, fluency in Spanish, and ability to blend into any situation: such as the way he had masqueraded as a Mexican outlaw, for instance, while working undercover for Wells Fargo in pursuit of highwaymen who robbed company stages. Brother officers during the War between the States, he and Mason had remained in the same units, escorting gold shipments east from California to help finance the Union cause, skirmishing with Confederates along the way, fighting in more battles under Sherman and Sheridan than either wanted to recall.

Lighting a new cigar, Mason pointed at a map on the wall near the major's desk. "Are those the plunder trails I've heard about?"

"All seven." His friend rose to trace the markings that started in the White Mountains in northern Arizona Territory and ran south hundreds of miles to Durango and west to Mazatlán on the coast. "Women and children for slaves, valuable church ornaments, clothing, horses, mules, food— you name it, they took it. Stealing and warfare were their way of life. As you already know, Mexicans and Apaches hate each other's guts, and have for generations."

"Must be hard for the red hawks to surrender their kingdom."

"For God's sake! Don't let the folks around here hear you say that! They've been robbed, burned out, killed, tortured, kidnapped, and scared to death. Sympathy for Apaches doesn't happen to be in their vocabularies."

"I know, I know. But there are two sides to this business. General Crook says you can't expect barbarians to be angels just because they're on reservations now, nor have the sense of honor supposedly civilized people have. Besides, Indians have a very well developed sense of honor—it's different, that's all. In any case, Eddie, I don't plan to advertise my opinions or presence. The men in Tucson would give a lot to know who President Grant has sent to smoke them out."

The major picked up the bottle. "They'll never learn from me. One last nightcap?" Someone knocked as he poured, and Dr. Gates entered, for the two men made a habit of ending the day with a drink, a smoke, conversation, and occasionally cards. Bertram introduced Mason, who shook hands with a smile that said any friend of Eddie's was a friend of his.

"Staying long, Marshal?" the physician said, slumping heavily into the remaining chair, which was made from a flour barrel. He loosened his belt and smacked his lips over the bourbon.

"A few days. I'm waiting for mail from Washington before I ride out." Mason raised his glass. "Here's to home, wherever it may be."

The major watched Theo Gates while he drank. "What's the matter? Your face is as long as a horse's tail. Oh, don't tell me it's another outbreak of clap?" He banged down his glass. "Can't you make the men understand those women are badly diseased? Poor trollops, beaten by their pimp, half starved and working out of a wagon in Apache country."

"I almost wish it were something that simple. No, it's that young woman in the hospital."

"Is she dying?" Mason was startled by the intensity of his dismay.

"She hasn't taken the last step around the bend, but she's close to it. The only decent thing is to see she gets where she's going as soon as possible so she can die with kinfolk. Her aunt is Mrs. James Fullerton of the Double Bar F Ranch in Vista Valley. You know of it, Edward?"

The major groaned and fished in a box full of papers on the floor. "Here's her letter to the Fullertons. It came a month ago, but I haven't been able to spare a courier. No one's come up from there or headed in that direction, either. So they don't even know she's here. Or how sick she is."

The men mulled over the situation. Each was tops in his field—Mason in law enforcement, Edward in Army matters, and Dr. Gates in military medicine and surgery—but none pretended to be expert on women, especially not such a dainty and gallant girl who had risked her life to save it— and was about to lose the gamble.

Silence spun out in the room, broken only by the silken whisper of embers tumbling onto the hearth. Mason left his chair and went to contemplate the map again. "I need to include information on the Chiricahua reserve in my report to the President. If the ranch is anywhere nearby, I'd be glad to—"

"—escort Miss Carlisle to her family." The major finished the sentence for him with a big grin. "What a load off my mind!"

"Mine, too," the physician added. "I must warn you, however, that you face a difficult time. She may hemorrhage to death on the way."

Mason grimaced. "We'll just have to play the cards we're dealt." He put down the empty glass, pulled his jacket on, and settled a worn Stetson on his head. He opened the door, then paused, half in shadow. Edward blinked. His friend had changed from the reckless cavalryman of a decade ago whose derring-do made him a legend among his fellows. Mystery and intrigue now surrounded him, as though his occupation had changed the inner man. The once devilish eyes turned serious and guarded, resting on the major as if Mason read his thoughts; then they warmed and narrowed above a rare and brilliant grin.

"Don't take any wooden pesos, Eddie." With that lighthearted farewell from years past, he vanished, swift and silent as the Apache waiting for him in the night.

Norah remained in the hospital the better part of a week in an attempt to offset the rigors of her journey. She forced down three tiny meals a day, but her appetite did not increase as she and Dr. Gates had hoped. The camp's daily mess was monotonous, but somehow the cook managed to serve Norah rich beef broth, creamy soup, crisp bacon, and hot biscuits, and soldiers dug into personal food caches to contribute evaporated milk, canned peaches, butter, and chocolate.

A pretty girl was a real treat at Fort Guardian, thin and ill though she might be. She reminded them of familiar and beloved places, porch swings on summer evenings, green trees and lawns, ice cream, and kisses stolen beneath flowery hats.

Norah was reading a month-old San Francisco newspaper when Mason entered so noiselessly she was at first unaware

of his presence. Putting the paper down to reach for a
handkerchief, she found him beside her, hat in hand. "Good
afternoon, Marshal Fletcher." She had soon learned who
her rescuer was. The soldier who brought her food knew all
the gossip on post.

"Good afternoon, Miss Carlisle. I hope you're feeling
better." His deep voice sheathed the words in velvet.

"I'm glad you're still here. I wanted to tell you how
grateful I am to you for helping me—and for seeing that I
got to the fort safely."

"I was glad to do it." Maybe his news would cheer her
up, make that mouth curve in a smile. At least the lavender-
brown smudges under her eyes were not as pronounced.
"Thought you'd like to know I've scouted the Double Bar
F."

"Oh, you found it! Is it far?"

"About three days' travel by buggy. It's south of here in a
valley that runs along the western edge of the reservation.
Fine country with grasslands full of game and cattle plump
as hogs."

"How can I get there? Will someone come for me? I
don't know how to ride a horse." Her face tensed. "They
should have had my letter by now. Or—don't they want me
to come?"

"To be frank, they don't even know you're here. The
letter was never delivered. I didn't make myself known to
the ranch house either, because I figured we'd be there soon
enough."

"*We'd* be there?"

"Yes, ma'am. We're going together."

Gazing up at his height from the bed, Norah wanted this
man to take her in his arms again. A fantasy, surely, for she
could expect nothing but a concerned glance and perhaps a
kindly touch. He meant a great deal to her, this booted
Galahad, but to him she was simply a traveler in need. She
smiled, memorizing his chiseled features, then looked down
in confusion.

Mason put his hat on. "If you feel up to it, we can ride out at dawn the day after tomorrow."

The prospect of relinquishing the fort's safety and warmth frightened her, but Norah promised to be ready. Ready for the next step toward exile in an alien place among those who might not grant her asylum.

The soldiers were up early, bearing their farewell gifts: a canvas jacket with a hastily attached rabbit fur collar, fringed Army gauntlets, a box of raisins, an out-of-date almanac, a seed catalog, sandwiches, and hard candy.

Mason moved restlessly on the seat of a dilapidated buggy, eager to be moving before first light. "We must go, Miss Carlisle."

She glanced at the stern profile. What on earth was she doing, heading into nowhere with this inscrutable stranger? What, after all, did she know about him? And his Indian companion, so menacing in the dimly lit yard, dark as mahogany and as impassive. Norah swallowed. Would he murder her while she slept?

Sensing panic, Dr. Gates stepped close to the buggy. "You have a most capable escort, Major Bertram tells me. Marshal Fletcher is an old friend of his and Chico one of the best scouts in the West. Now you'd better get started. You have a long way to go. Good-bye, my dear, and good luck. Good luck," he repeated in a low voice, "and write to me."

"I will. Good-bye. Thank you for everything." Norah's eyes filled with tears. She had found much kindness here.

When the buggy moved forward, there was no unnecessary noise and all lights were doused. Apaches heard grass grow and the bird's wing rustle. Would they hear these wheels and soft clop of hoofs at this early hour? Or did they nestle against the bodies of their women, like all men oblivious to the world when passion pulsed in their veins?

Mason's gray Appaloosa gelding, stabled at the fort while he was in Washington, trotted behind the buggy; Chico's small unkempt pony trudged in back of him. The pony's

unprepossessing appearance, like that of his master, was
deceptive; he could carry a rider for longer periods through
worse country than most bigger horses—especially, with the
exception of Mason's Storm Cloud, those of the white men.

Norah had to ask. "Do you think there are Indians?" she
whispered. "I mean—besides *him*?"

"No," Mason whispered back, "but be quiet. And try
not to cough."

There was no need to describe Apache *hesh-kes*, ritual
killers who prowled these mountains like vicious animals—
nor how their captives suffered. He already discerned much
tension in the shoulder that brushed his, and from the corner
of his eye he glimpsed the white of hers, wide open in an
attempt to pierce the gloom.

No, he wouldn't tell Miss Carlisle anything she didn't
need to know.

3.

Norah sat bolt upright, heart pounding and mouth dry. It
was so dark that Mason, rolled in a blanket with his head on
a saddle, was obvious to her only from the rhythm of steady
breathing. She reached out to touch him.

He turned over, instantly awake. "What is it?"

"I heard a woman scream! Listen! There it is again." She
held her breath in horror. Oh, God! Was some ranchwoman
being tortured?

Mason took the hand that gripped his arm. "It's all right,
Norah. It's only a mountain lion out hunting." The voices
of wildlife were so familiar he had forgotten how alarming

they could be to a city dweller—and to the three horses that moved uneasily, making low sounds in their throats.

He chafed Norah's hands, lending her the comfort of his warm flesh. "We're close to the cliffs where he lives, you see. He's hunting deer, but may have to settle for porcupine."

Norah coughed. "Porcupine? I've seen pictures, but I didn't know where they lived."

Mason drew the blankets about her shoulders again, gently pressing her back upon the ground. "You'll find many animals here. Antelope, bear, fox, javelina—kind of a wild pig—bobcat, coyote, badger, skunk . . ." He paused for a moment. Her hair smelled like roses. "Try to sleep now. You need to rest for tomorrow."

They breakfasted on cold bacon, cold biscuit, and canned apricots, for a campfire might draw unwelcome attention. The trio then angled to the southwest where the great trough of the valley ran between the Chiricahua Mountains on the east and a succession of ranges on the west.

Chico gave mute tribute to Usen, who was Giver of all life, for they had camped near sacred places in the Land of Standing Rocks. Spirits of the dead dwelled there, and their wailing trembled on the night wind and troubled his soul. His eagle gaze swept lovingly across the landscape of autumn grasses belly-high to a horse, blue-green swaths of trees on the mountainside, and the infinite shimmering sky. Far to the south, in golden and violet distances, although he could not see it, the Sierra Madre loomed—Pa-Gotzin-Kay, the Stronghold Mountain of Paradise. There Apache had lived and wandered since long before the Spaniard came with armor, lance, and harquebus.

"Your leg bothers you today," Mason said in Spanish without turning toward the other man who rode beside the buggy.

The Apache's eyes grew hooded in order to hide his wonder. How did his white brother know such things? He might well be a shaman. Yes, the leg ached and probably

always would. He cast his mind back. He had met Fletcher
when he was on the brink of death after going far afield
simply to see what he could see. Like most Apache warriors
he was able to travel ninety miles afoot without stopping.

In the mountains called Santa Catalina northeast of
Tucson he had stepped in a bear trap buried in leaves. The
jaws had penetrated his flesh like hot iron through butter and
had clamped cruelly on the bone. He remembered with
shame that he had fainted from the pain, but regained
consciousness momentarily to see a tall man bent over him.
When he awoke the second time, the leg had been freed and
bound in a soft shirt. He expected death like any trapped
animal, for the man could have slain him while he sprawled
helpless and in agony—as he in turn would have done.

Black Badger—for so he thought of himself then—
despised mercy and compassion as women's emotions, as
did all his people. The two men had stared across the
campfire for a long time, brown eyes and hazel, delving
deep into each other's soul. When they ceased, Black
Badger knew no more than he did before, for the other, like
an Indian, kept secret his inner essence; the only thing the
injured man learned was that Fletcher had spared him
because he chose to do so.

"How long have you known this Chico?" Norah considered the name odd for an Apache.

"Since the fall of seventy-three. Two years ago this
month, as a matter of fact. Found him with his leg in a trap
and freed him. Since then he's been my shadow. I took him
to Washington last winter."

"Whatever for?" Norah coughed hard for several seconds, then discreetly examined the handkerchief. There was
no blood, and her heart leaped with hope.

"So he could tell his fellow Chiricahuas what he saw. So
they'd find out from one of their own how big this country is
and how many people there are."

"And?" Norah considered the incongruity of Chico in
the nation's capital.

He shook his head. "They didn't believe him. How *can* they imagine elevators, typewriters, clipper ships, or carpet sweepers?"

"Does he have any family?" Norah flushed beneath the Apache's frank scrutiny. Her hair, eyes, skin, and clothes— were they as outlandish to him as his were to her?

"No, his wife's been dead a long time. He had no children. Since then he's drifted away from the tribe, Miss Carlisle, caught, you might say, in another trap. He's between two worlds, one that's fading fast and one in which he won't be welcome for a long time to come."

"Last night you called me Norah." She remembered the touch of his hands and the warmth of his breath when he'd bent close to talk and set her mind at ease.

Mason clucked to the horse as it pulled them up an uneven slope and grasses brushed against the side of the vehicle.

"It seemed natural to use your first name. Do you mind?"

"Oh, no, I wish you would! Then I can call you Mason. I mean, after all, we are sleeping beside one another. We don't need to be formal." She flushed painfully, but then laughed.

"I haven't heard you laugh before. You should do it more often."

She smiled pensively upon the valley, so huge and empty, so strangely vacant to the urban eye. Twenty miles wide and seventy long, he had estimated. "I'm afraid I haven't had much to laugh about lately."

"Do you have family? Besides your aunt at the ranch, I mean."

"No, I'm alone in the world." Norah tossed her head, disgusted with the answer. "That sounds melodramatic, but it's true, nevertheless."

Mason made kissing sounds to the horse when it hesitated to cross a rocky dry creek. "Your parents are dead, I take it."

"My father died in a fire two years ago Thanksgiving in his bookstore. It went up like tinder. Then my mother died of consumption this past spring."

He was being polite, but didn't want to hear the whole sad story, Norah admonished herself. She didn't add that she and Mother had moved to cheaper riverfront lodgings, and Mother had slaved in a clothing mill twelve hours a day, seven days a week while Norah sewed in a millinery sweatshop. Norah surreptitiously inspected her short nails and roughened hands. Exhausted by months of nursing care, she had continued in the sweatshop after her mother's death. The backbreaking routine had been a nightmare of boiling handkerchiefs, bed linen, and night clothes in soda and disinfectant; scalding eating utensils; feeding, bathing, and grooming the helpless woman. Then she'd had to get busy on velvet and satin hats to be delivered the next day.

"That's when you got sick and decided to come out here," he urged gently, guessing that talking eased her.

"The doctor said I'd be lucky to last the winter, it was getting so cold and damp, so I sold a family heirloom to finance the trip."

It still pained Norah to think of selling that last link to her father. He had dearly loved the ancient map, an extremely rare third-century Roman road map of the world. But she had had no choice. It had come down to two options: go to the pesthouse to die or take a gamble. She had no longer been able to find work; fine ladies did not want consumptives coughing or breathing on expensive chapeaux.

"Fletcher." The Apache pointed at riders coming from the south. "Gokliya."

Mason paled beneath his tan and swore. He shoved the reins at Norah and grabbed his Winchester carbine. He was not afraid for himself but for his charge.

"What's wrong?" The abrupt change in him shocked Norah, and her stomach fluttered with nervousness. "What did he say?"

"It's Geronimo, a real troublemaker." Mason checked

and cocked both rifle and six-shooter with movements almost too fast to follow. Chico pulled his rifle from the saddle scabbard and cocked it seconds later.

"*Hesh-kes*," Chico muttered. Even his own tribe was wary of this bunch.

"Women don't count for much with Apaches, so let us do the talking," Mason warned. "Now, pull up gently. That's good." The buggy rolled to a halt.

Apaches naked to the waist raced around them, yipping like coyotes and yelling to curdle the blood. After what seemed an eternity to Norah, they reined in and sat staring, every warrior armed. Like goddamned buzzards waiting for a wounded antelope to die, Mason thought, his big Peacemaker trained on Geronimo's belly.

Ravens croaked overhead, their plumage glinting blue in late morning sun as they banked and changed direction. Norah noticed with compassion blood and foam on the lips of Geronimo's horse. The animal opened its mouth, revealing the spade bit that cut its tongue.

She frowned at the horse's sweaty, dusty side, gouged with red furrows dug by a spur strapped across the instep of the Indian's calf-high moccasin. She stared up along the bare, red-brown leg to a dirty white breechclout, and above that a cartridge belt and rust-colored suit coat worn with a calico shirt and checked scarf. Fascinated yet fearful, Norah now looked Geronimo squarely in the face. Her gasp was audible in the stillness, broken only as the Indians' horses caught their breath, shifted under heavy riders, and shook or relieved themselves.

Like most Easterners, Norah had never seen a real, wild, primitive man who made the bowels run cold. She recalled a book of prints in her father's shop picturing Mongols, those terrible little men on shaggy small ponies who had once made the earth shake. They had been yellow, and these horsemen were red, but they could have been cousins.

Geronimo's broad face spoke of cruelty and a life of exposure to the weather; the latter had opened fissures in his dark complexion like erosion cracks in the ground. He grinned, a grimace that lent brutish features a false amiability. "The woman has hair like the sunset," Geronimo growled in Spanish. His voice was rough from years of drinking whisky and *tiswin*, the Apache intoxicant brewed from fermented corn, acorns, and herbs.

Mason swore silently. He had hoped the confrontation would be brief, but a man had to be blind not to admire that gleaming mane. Just their luck she had worn it down. His finger tightened on the trigger.

"That is true," Mason agreed calmly.

Geronimo transferred his reptilian regard to Chico. "Have you seen any boxes lately that carry people up and down in the air?" he asked in Apache. He leaned over the pommel, overcome with mirth at the idea. His comrades joined in the hilarity, shouting derisively that he must have been given a potion that made him see fantastic things.

Chico shrugged. "I know what I saw." He had been to the white man's cities and seen the multitudes, cold eyed and ambitious, numerous as ants. There was no standing against them.

"Is this your man? The one who found you in the trap?"

"*Anh.*"

Geronimo studied the deadly promise of Mason's six-shooter. "He is not afraid," he observed with approval. "And he has eyes like the hawk."

Chico's lip curled. "I would not follow him if he were a coward."

"Who is the woman, old man? His?" Geronimo's bloodshot gaze shifted to Norah, who straightened up and clamped her lips to keep from crying out.

"She belongs to those of the Fullerton ranch to the south. A relative with the coughing sickness."

"That is fortunate. They give us cattle—we give them peace." He motioned to his men. "Let them pass. This time."

The Apaches backed away. Geronimo pointed to Mason's

Colt, which had never wavered from its target. "You don't trust me," he said plaintively.

"Of course I do. As the rabbit does the diamondback."

The ugly face beamed at the comparison. "*Anh,* I like that!" Geronimo wheeled his horse, reaching down to jerk a strand of Norah's hair as he did so. *"Hasta la vista!"*

Norah's exclamation deteriorated into a coughing fit as the renegades galloped away, beating their horses without mercy. Gun still trained on them, Mason took the reins. Only Cochise and the murdered Mangas Coloradas, the great war captains of the Chiricahua clan, had been as cunning and treacherous. God help the settlers if the tribe was forced off their beautiful reservation and moved to hot, arid San Carlos. It was not called "Hell's Forty Acres" for nothing.

Chico said, "They head into high country, Fletcher."

"Good." Mason listened with concern to Norah's coughing. "Chico, I think we'll camp under those oaks over there for an hour, then go on in the early afternoon." He sighed with relief of tension, feeling both his shirt and vest sticking to his back. That son of a bitch could make anybody sweat. Mason holstered the Colt but kept the Winchester on his lap while directing the buggy horse toward shade. Norah collapsed on her blankets spread beneath the trees and fell asleep from exhaustion within minutes.

Norah's nostrils twitched when she awoke, inhaling the familiar fragrance of brewing coffee. But no other part of her moved. Her body had dissolved into the high desert, this almost primeval soil turned fertile by sun and swept clean by wind, never trampled by buffalo or plowed for crops. She compared the pall of soft coal smoke over St. Louis to the valley's unsullied atmosphere. Could it save her? *Oh, God, let it, let it!*

Her eyes opened to find Storm Cloud gazing down upon her. He looked gigantic and Norah shrank from him, as he blew puffs of grass-scented breath in her face. Tentatively she touched the pink muzzle, then exclaimed with delight.

Mason, who was sitting nearby smoking a cigar, chuckled. "Like velvet, isn't it?" There were so many things she did not know. He liked the way she had acted under Geronimo's appraisal—showed she had plenty of sand. But would she be able to survive what she was soon to face?

"How lovely he is. I've never really appreciated a horse before. I looked at them but never *saw* them." The Appaloosa's eyes, liquid as a fawn's, innocent and free of guile, enchanted Norah. "I think I understand now what the poet Walt Whitman meant when he said, 'I think I could turn and live with animals, they are so placid and self-contain'd, I stand and look at them long and long.' "

Storm Cloud moved away on the tether, massive muscles shifting smoothly beneath the dark-speckled gray coat. Mason watched him for a moment, concealing deep affection with casual comment. "He's a good old boy."

Chico trotted back from surveillance of the area and animatedly talked to Mason, who stubbed out the cigar, put the butt in a vest pocket, rose, and spoke to Norah. "We've decided to camp here tonight. It's getting too late to go on, and if there's rain, we can shelter higher in the canyon." He bent down and put a hand on her shoulder. "Are you all right? You look peaked."

"Tired, I guess, nap or no nap."

He held out a hand and pulled her up. "Come on. Chico wants to show us something."

Norah moved toward him imperceptibly. "Are you sure it's safe?" The barbarians' citadel awed and disconcerted her with its somber, haughty majesty.

"Chico assures me it is."

"You trust him?"

"With my life."

They entered a tree-lined canyon through which a shallow stream trickled. Towering rocks dwarfed them, yet Norah rather welcomed the feeling; they comforted and protected, left her less vulnerable to the disquieting spaciousness of Vista Valley. She almost bumped into the

Apache when he stopped. Quiet as a falling leaf, he motioned her and Mason behind a large-boled sycamore, then pointed. Norah looked with surprise at the usually stolid face, now aglow with undisguised pleasure.

Shafts of sunshine slanted through the leaves, and in their radiance a pair of birds fluttered above the water. As the elegant creatures snapped at bugs, the male's emerald head and back, geranium-red breast, and copper-colored tail blazed in burnished splendor. Clad in subtle yet equally exquisite browns, creams, and rosy reds, his mate landed on a branch to rest. White crescents beneath her red-ringed eyes emphasized their ebony brilliance before she joined again in aerial chase. Satiny bodies and long tails created spectacular patterns with each swoop and turn, their reflections in the stream like iridescent fish darting below the surface. Spellbound, their admirers watched until the birds finally flew away.

All at once, too weak to stand, Norah sank to the ground with her back to the tree. Mason squatted down and leaned the Winchester against the trunk between them. "That was the most magnificent thing I ever saw," Norah said enthusiastically. "What kind of birds were they?"

"I think they're trogons," Mason said.

"We call him Rainbow Prince. He is rare. And he is late going south where it is warm." Chico paused, then added softly, "He must hurry."

Norah studied the small Apache, with his wide headband and ragged yellow shirt cinched with a gun belt. He wore the shirt outside baggy cotton trousers which were tucked into thigh-high moccasins folded down above the ankle. A buckskin bag of medicine charms hung about his neck. The *hoddentin*, as Mason called it, included a badger's paw, a dead hummingbird, a splinter from a lightning-riven pine, and pollen from holy plants. He was superstitious, savage, filthy, and aloof, yet had devoted his life to a man of another race and minutes ago had bared a tiny, tender chamber of his soul.

Puzzled by his unforeseen complexity, Norah thanked him for showing her the birds. The sound he made in his chest could have meant a dozen things, and without answering he dog-trotted back to the buggy, shirt-tail bouncing on lean buttocks. "Did I say something wrong?"

Mason smiled indulgently. "I think you just surprised him. Besides, it's time to water the horses. Time for supper, too, and a good night's sleep. We'll be at the ranch tomorrow. You want to be well rested."

Her blue eyes widened, golden highlights accentuated by the sun. "Tomorrow," Norah repeated in an excited whisper.

"We'd better get back." Mason helped Norah to her feet as Chico led Storm Cloud and his pony to drink. "You look tired. Do you feel up to walking? Or would you like me to carry you?"

"I can walk, thank you." But she was at the end of her strength by the time they reached camp, and Mason was forced to support her the last hundred feet, chiding her for wasting her limited energy.

After the evening meal, Norah fell into a restless slumber. She dreamed of Geronimo's men advancing so near that their fierce images blotted out all but the bloody scalping knives with which they menaced her. She woke with a start, the vision so real it did not fade for several moments. It had always been difficult to fall back to sleep, and this night was no exception. Fears and anxieties plagued her.

Suppose the Fullertons didn't like her or want her. She had never met either of them and knew her aunt solely through letters and her mother's fond remembrances. They owed her nothing and might have children; if so, rather than expose them to her disease she would go back to Fort Guardian and take a stage to Tucson.

So little money was left—enough to reach the Territorial capital and live for a while, but no more. Her guidebook advised the town had two breweries, ten saloons, two schools, a photographic gallery, and a newspaper, as well as five physicians, one of whom she could surely turn to for a job such as bookkeeping or sewing until she was well again. Norah began to weep in the dark, afraid and discouraged.

Mason listened, then brought his saddle, rifle, and blanket and lay down beside Norah to shelter her in his arms. He had never married or had a child as far as he knew, but now he instinctively pressed the rose-scented head to his breast, like that of a wife or infant.

"I'm a terrible coward," she admitted, inhaling the sweet male odor of his sleep-warm body.

He located the Big Dipper standing to the lower left of the North Star; the cowboys' celestial clock told him it was close to two in the morning. "I've known big men who ran scared, too."

The virile, steady beat of the heart beneath her ear soothed Norah, and here in this man's arms, she was comforted. How desperately she wanted to live and love in his arms! She now realized they were the arms of the man who meant the world to her.

"It's all right, Norah," he said, feeling the slim form grow tense. "Things will look better in the morning. They always do."

Woman with eyes of sunlit sky, girl with hair like the tail feathers of Rainbow Prince—she had captured his heart. *Let her live, God, let her live*. Mason stared up at the stars, wanting to clench his fist and shake it at the sky like a pagan displeased with his deity. *Do You hear me? Let Norah Carlisle live*. And then he added—*for me*.

4

Chico woke them before dawn, and after a hurried breakfast, they broke camp and resumed the journey. Mason was quiet, and hesitant to disturb him with meaningless conversation, Norah nestled in the corner of the buggy, dreaming of his holding her. He'd introduced her to Western animals and the beauty of the land, and he'd also helped and encouraged her. Most important of all, he had given of himself, strong but unashamed of being tender and caring, unaware of the enhancement of his masculinity's nobility in her eyes.

Soon they began to see cattle in the grass, then the buggy crested a rise, and Mason reined in. "There it is. Your new home."

Home. She peered down at the ranch with a mixture of eagerness and trepidation. Flanked by foothills, the long, free sweep of land which made the buildings seem insignificant was both thrilling and terrifying. Did her aunt like it here? Had it been frightening when they first came, isolated from neighbors, towns, and other women? Was she hungry for company? Would she welcome an ailing relative? Norah wet her lips, squinting in the dazzling light. Her throat tightened with emotion and an almost childish yearning. She had idealized the ranch during the past difficult months, pictured it as the promised land, a place to begin life anew. Now she was here at last.

Watching her narrowly, Chico muttered to Mason in Spanish, "Now the little bird must learn to fly on her own."

Mason's eyes locked with the Apache's. He had become

more involved with the girl than he had ever intended. He guessed they had needed each other for this moment in time, she wanting his strength, confidence, and experience, and he accepting her dependence, ignorance, and weakness with tolerance and a growing affection he was unable to check.

He slapped the reins on the horse's haunch, and the buggy started up again. From the corner of his eye Mason saw Norah adjust her hat, touch the cheap cameo at her throat, and put her chin up.

"You look fine," he assured her.

"Do I? I hope so." She rushed on without waiting for a reply. "I've never met my aunt, you know. She married and went to Texas with Mr. Fullerton while I was still a baby. And . . ."

Mason listened with half an ear, appraising the spread as they approached a whitewashed adobe house with a veranda along its entire length. He saw a cookshack, bunkhouse, blacksmith shop, corrals, a barn, and storage sheds. It was neither a hard-scrabble operation nor a thriving one.

Cowboys hurried toward them on foot and horseback, dogs barked and came running. Mason cautioned Chico to stay close to the buggy to avoid misunderstanding. Gun ports piercing the thick house walls boded ill for any Chiricahua with no one to vouch for him. Neither did the pine-cone wreath painted black that hung on the door bode well for Norah.

"Someone died," he said unnecessarily and pulled the horse to a halt.

"What an awful time for me to come!" Norah pressed gloved fingers to her mouth.

"Maybe it's a good time. You can lend a hand."

Norah clenched her handbag with such anxiety that her comb broke. Just then a tall, slender man of middle age emerged from the house. His costume resembled that of the men who crowded about the buggy: sweat-stained hat and faded bandana, nondescript shirt and vest, dark striped pants and shotgun leather chaps. Spurs strapped to his boots jingled faintly as he strode out to join them.

Eyes brown as coffee berries came to rest on Norah's face after darting to that of each newcomer. He touched his hat brim. "Welcome to the Double Bar F, folks. James Fullerton at your service. Won't you light a spell?" His brows knit. "I know we haven't met, but you sure look familiar, ma'am."

"I'm your wife's niece, Norah Carlisle. She and my mother resembled each other a great deal, judging from pictures I've seen." She craned her neck to look past him. "Is she here? I'm so anxious to meet her."

Jim Fullerton removed his hat, as did the other men. The Texas drawl grew even softer. "My wife is dead, Miss Carlisle. Died of blood poisoning two days ago, God rest her soul."

"Oh, I'm so *sorry*!" Stricken, Norah turned to Mason for guidance.

"My condolences, sir. Mason Fletcher, U.S. Marshal." The men's strong, capable hands met, gripped, and parted. Appraising each other, rancher and peace officer liked what they saw.

"He kindly offered to bring me here, because the major at Fort Guardian couldn't spare an escort. I sent a letter from St. Louis, too, but there was no one to bring it to you." Norah chattered anxiously, then began to cough, more from strain than anything else.

"Rustle up some java, Charlie," the rancher said, and an old man with a flour sack tied around his middle scurried off to the cookshack. "And you boys get back to work."

They drifted away reluctantly, glancing over their shoulders. "You'll have to forgive them, ma'am. Don't see women but once in a coon's age. My wife was the only lady for miles around." Fullerton helped Norah down from the buggy as he spoke.

He led her onto the veranda, then turned. "That a tame

cherry-cow?" he asked, using the cowboys' distorted version of the word *Chiricahua*.

Mason winked at the expressionless Chico, who sat statuelike on his drowsing pony. "I'll vouch for him."

"Good enough. But make sure he stays put. Lots of itchy trigger fingers around here. I don't go along with shooting every Indian I see, but there's others that do." The rancher eyed Chico. *"Comprende?"* he asked in a cold voice.

"Comprendo." Chico dismounted and squatted by the buggy.

Norah and the men entered the house, which was warmed by a fireplace in the center of the far wall. Papers and tally books almost covered a table near the kitchen at one end of a large room; saddles, boots, animal skins, traps, and horse gear were scattered on the floor.

The rancher installed Norah on a chair by the fire and took her coat. Hanging it on a nail, he said, "Coffee should be here soon. Charlie's slow, but the pot's always on."

Norah smiled politely. He seemed like a very nice man, but surely he'd not agree to her remaining. A sick woman with no one to care for her? It was foolish even to think about it. She bit her lip, aware the men were talking in low tones behind her.

"Here you are, boss." The cook backed through the door carrying a battered tin tray loaded with steaming white china cups and a dish covered with a clean cloth.

As Charlie served Norah, his eyes, blue as cornflowers, beamed into hers. "Had a little cobbler left, ma'am. Thought you might find it tolerable. The boys do."

"Thank you," she said, uncovering the dish. "What flavor is it? Honey?"

"Vinegar, ma'am. Vinegar cobbler." He gave her an almost toothless grin. "Make it on roundup, too."

"It must be—unique." Gingerly, she dipped into the taffy-colored mixture while the cook watched with interest. "Why, that's good. How do you make it?" she enthused.

"Be proud to show you, surely would."

When he had gone, eager as any neighbor to describe the
new arrival to his comrades, Fullerton came to stand by the
fireplace. Norah forced herself to eat and drink. What
would the verdict be? "Fletcher says you're a pretty sick
little lady."

There was to be no beating around the bush. "That's true.
The physician at Fort Guardian said I wasn't going to die.
But I really don't know how advanced the consumption is.
None of the doctors do either." Norah put spoon and dish on
a nearby table and laced her fingers about the cup. "I'd be a
burden here. If Mason—if Marshal Fletcher will guide me
back to the fort, I'll take the stage to Tucson."

The rancher sat down opposite her, removing his hat to
reveal black hair in need of trimming. "Don't know much
about consumption, but you're welcome to stay. After all,
you are family even if May is gone." He stared into the fire.
"Lord, she'd have loved fussing over you." He paused,
then he motioned at the untidy room. "You see what I've
got here. You know about Apaches. And if you get real
sick—" He began to feel dubious, recalling his wife's
longing for feminine companionship and the agony of her
death. "I just don't know."

Norah's heart sank. "I nursed my mother. She had
consumption, too, so I know what to do. This air is exactly
what I need. That's what Dr. Gates said." Her voice
quavered, then firmed. "I beg you to let me stay. I won't
bother you. I can cook and sew. And do your paperwork,
too, if you like. I used to do my father's."

Adept at handling men and animals, Fullerton was
usually out of his element with females. Yet he did not feel
that way with this one. Smart and well bred but down on her
luck, she was fighting to survive, refusing to strike her flag.
He admired that and decided not to deny the help she
needed. If it didn't work out, he'd take her to Tucson
himself.

"Well, what do you say we give it a try?"

Norah's face blazed with joy, startling the men with its

fleeting loveliness. "Thank you, Mr. Fullerton! *So* much! You'll never know what this means to me!" She hugged the victory to her. At last, the security of a home, however crude. A haven where her weakened body might bloom again and the hope in her heart be fulfilled.

Bundled in a wool shawl, Norah went onto the veranda to do breathing exercises in air crisp as frost-kissed apples. She had the house to herself, for Jim Fullerton had vacated the bedroom and moved into the bunkhouse. Unaccustomed to the altitude, she puffed and gasped, thinking at first the catch in her throat could be blamed on that. Then she knew it was the sight of Mason saddling his horse, ready to ride out of her life.

The animal danced sideways in anticipation of a run and with the mischievousness horses exhibit on nippy mornings. Mason indulged him but reined him in when they reached the house. "Old boy's feeling his oats today." Resting forearms on the saddle horn, he looked at her with misgivings unallayed by her steady gaze. Was she paler than ever or was it the black shawl? Leaving her nagged at him, yet he had to go about the President's business regardless of any personal tie.

A poignant sense of loss enveloped Norah as she approached Storm Cloud's head and stroked the glossy hide. "I'll miss him terribly." They knew she was not speaking of the Appaloosa. Norah now walked to the stirrup, touching his boot where it wrinkled at the ankle. "I'll miss you terribly, too."

Mason suppressed an impulse to lift her up in front of him, to hold and defend her against her disease and the rigors of ranch life of which she had no conception. Surely nothing but sympathy triggered these feelings—but he had argued with them during the night when sleep eluded him. "The Mexicans have a saying: *Quién sabe?* Who knows? The West is a big place. I'll ride this way again."

"You *must*!" she blurted, and color sprang to her cheeks.

He flicked the brim of his high-crowned hat. "They also say, *Vaya con Dios*. Go with God." His eyes intense, he reached for her hand and kissed the fingertips.

The saddle leather creaked when he did so, and she knew that sound would always remind her of his mouth—and of his going. "*Vaya con Dios*, then," Norah said, proud to catch the silken Spanish phrase so quickly. Then she stepped away from the big restless horse.

"Take care of yourself. Get well." He reined Storm Cloud to the north, the Apache's horse close behind.

"Good-bye," Norah called, and they waved at each other. She stood in the yard until their figures diminished to dots on the horizon. Now she had to come to terms with those secretive mountains swelling high above the foothills that stole toward the ranch, like huge paws creeping out into the grasslands.

Norah glanced in vain at the empty horizon, then hurried into the house and shut the door with its somber wreath. She coughed and tasted blood and her heart raced. The future she had fought for was here—but so were fear and loneliness.

5.

"What's the idea of coming back here to see Rose when you should be riding herd? You're making more work for the others, and I don't approve of this one bit." Jim Fullerton scowled at his son.

The lanky youngster fiddled with a lariat, afraid to look his angry father in the face. "I'm sorry, Pa."

"*Sorry?*" The rancher paced back and forth in the empty

barn where he had chosen to confront his son. "You'll be sorry, all right, if you don't stop this. I won't stand for it, Joel. Damn it, sometimes I wish I had never brought that child home."

Joel could not agree. Seventeen years ago his father had found a Lipan Apache baby orphaned by a flood in West Texas and brought it home to raise. It had grown into a rose-brown, lusciously seductive morsel of beddable womanhood who made Joel Fullerton's knees turn to water and his manhood ache. She stirred a madness in his veins that overcame all modesty, reason, and honor. She had only to flash those huge black eyes in his direction, and he turned into a stallion.

"Honest to God, Pa, I'm sorry. But I can't help it." Joel's face twisted with earnestness. "Ain't you ever felt like that? Like—like you had to have a woman or you were gonna bust into a million pieces?" He bent his head. "Not, mind you, that I ever had Rose."

"You damn well better not!" Jim pondered the questions, torn between compassion and irritation for Joel's lack of self-discipline. It had been many years since he had gone to a fancy house, and after he married there had been no need. To his recollection, he had not at any time suffered a fever such as his only son suffered for Rose. He was not too old, however, to forget the voluptuous mouths and hips as well as dreams that bothered him during long drives up the Chisholm Trail to Abilene. "All right, listen and listen good. I won't have Miss Carlisle exposed to scandalous behavior any more than I would have your ma. Do I make myself clear?"

"Yes, Pa, but what about Rose?"

"Wish I knew what to do about her." No white man in this part of the country would marry Rose with the Indian situation so touchy, even if she was a good-looker. Chances were good she'd marry well if an Apache clan accepted her, but would she accept it? No, only if she were in love. She merited a chief, but truth to tell, he'd hate to give her to one

of those warriors who abused women like horses. Jim
realized belatedly he had made a whopping big mistake
years ago when he failed to take the baby to an Indian
agency.

"You know how I stand, boy. We'll go from there." Jim
clapped Joel on the shoulder, feeling the large bone fit the
palm of his hand. Love flooded his being, and he strode
away to hide what his face must surely show. The rancher
was still angry with his son, but he would give him another
chance, recognizing that Joel's problem had to run its course
like any sickness. As for the men, they had already
expressed disapproval through pranks and dirty jokes; Joel
would have to regain his peers' respect on his own.

Joel leaned against the nearest stall and wiped his
forehead with his arm. Christ, that was close. He loved and
respected his father but feared him as well. Those fists
landed like sledgehammers, and when that Fullerton temper
steamed full blast, you'd better hit the trail a-runnin'!

"Hey, Pa, I'm gonna break that blood bay after a while!"
He followed his father into the sunshine. "Think Miss
Carlisle might like him?"

Jim did not answer immediately, his mind occupied with
the spread that ruled his life. Double Bar F hands worked
seven days a week if they had to, for ranch work, like a
woman's, was never done. Today, a Sunday, had turned out
easy, and a well-deserved rest after roundup found the men
cutting hair, shaving, writing letters, and mending chaps. A
harmonica in the bunkhouse entreated "Buffalo Gals" to
come out by the light of the moon. Most of the cowboys
squatted near, sat on, or rested against the horse corral while
they rolled smokes, told tall tales, and discussed one of their
lives' greatest interests: horses and more horses. Two
Mexican vaqueros twirled sixty-foot rawhide riatas in
friendly competition with a black cowboy who formed
equally intricate patterns with a lasso. Pride coursed
through the rancher. He had been among the first to dare to
bring cattle into Apache country for consumption by the

military, the miners, and reservation Indians. It had been nip and tuck but worth it. His ranch nestled close to tree-covered foothills; artesian wells furnished all their water needs; and he had a truce with the Chiricahuas, admittedly an uneasy one, whereby they took the cattle they needed in return for leaving him and his crew alone.

"Pa, what about the blood bay for the lady?"

"The lady doesn't ride, son." The shock on Joel's face amused his father. The boy had not met many women in his socially and geographically restricted life, but those he did know rode and rode well.

"Don't ride?" Joel shook his head with wonder. "That must be like not eating or breathing."

"Like to teach her? Put her up on Lovey?"

"On Ma's horse?" The young man's eyes suddenly filled with tears, and he blinked furiously to hold them back.

"Can't let the animal stand around and get fat. Can't put her in the remuda with the geldings. And I don't want to sell her, either. She throws good colts." The more Jim thought about the idea the more he liked it. Norah and his son were only a few years apart. He didn't anticipate a romance between them, but this might be just the ticket to get Joel's mind off Rose.

He had not been enthusiastic about Norah moving in yesterday—or about giving up his bed. It wasn't the consumption that bothered him, because there were too many other ways of cashing in your chips down here to worry about a disease that might be curable. What bothered him was the fact that she was now cut off from other womenfolk and medical attention of any sort. Perhaps he'd made another big mistake. On the other hand, he felt about her much as he had about Rose when he brought her home, wrapped in a horse blanket and no bigger'n a button. Norah had no one to turn to, while he had room to spare; also she replaced his wife as a decent influence in a camp of footloose men. His lips clamped with rueful self-criticism. Just as long as nobody suspected he had a heart soft as mush when it came to little lost female critters!

Joel had been thinking. "Reckon I could teach her to ride. Be proud to, once she's feeling better. Never saw a person so white before. That puny, neither."

"She's got to take it real easy," Jim said. "Wish that—"

"What, Pa?"

"Oh, never mind." Jim headed toward the house, stroking the thick mustache that bracketed his mouth. He wished Rose would pitch in and help Norah with the housework, but then she had seldom helped May these past couple of years. His wife had spoiled the girl outrageously and he was now hard put to reverse that.

He stopped at a shed to get flour for Norah. Wrestling with bags of pinto beans stacked in his way, Jim heard the door latch and whirled, gun half out of the holster. This shed had been robbed before and was a favorite target of the Apaches, for it held molasses, salt pork, coffee, canned goods, sugar, and preserves his wife had put up.

"It's only me. I saw you coming this way and I wanted to talk to you."

Jim let the gun go and started to hoist a bag to one shoulder. "You're liable to get killed, surprising folks like that, Rose." Repressed anger left from the quarrel with Joel boiled over. "Where the devil you been since the funeral? With those cherry-cows again? You've been gone four days! You need to have your backside tanned for worrying me that way."

"I'm safe in Tahzay's camp, you know that. When I go there, it's like belonging to a big family. The women teach me things. Apache things. Look what I made!" Rose whirled and in the dimness hundreds of tiny tin cornucopias flashed around the hem of a full buckskin skirt.

"Yeah, that's pretty, all right." Jim's anger faded; he never could stay mad at her long. "Listen, a young lady from St. Louis—your mother's niece—has come to stay with us. You won't be alone anymore. How about that?" He beamed as if it had been his doing. Maybe the girl would stay at home more now that she had company.

Rose made no response, but moved close enough to brush his arm with her breast. She wanted to take him for a lover, and his ignorance of her intent made the plan that much sweeter. While his wife lived, Rose had kept her pubescent desires leashed—except to tease Joel—for she had loved her adoptive mother dearly. Now, however, Jim would need a woman.

She ran a finger down his cheek, brushing the stern mouth she dreamed of feeling on her flesh. He had no idea how much she wanted him. Rose rubbed her body up against him and kissed him passionately.

"*What* in blue blazes do you think you're doing?" Jim dropped the flour in sheer astonishment, missing her feet by inches.

"Kissing you." Rose tried again but without success, for he had seized her wrists and was holding her away, frowning. Enough light entered around the shed door to illuminate her almond eyes and delicate eyebrows, and her waist-length crow-black hair. The hungry mouth pouted in shadow, but light glinted on her moist lower lip. "Let me go," she moaned. "You're hurting me."

"Only if you behave yourself. What's got into you?"

The girl sighed and dropped her head back so the flawless young neck curved defenselessly. "I love you."

"Well, I've known that since you were in diapers," the rancher snapped. "I love you, too. Now quit this nonsense." He released her.

"*James!*" she cried. "I *love* you! Don't you understand? Like a woman loves a man, not like a child." She threw an arm around his neck before he knew what she was about and kissed him again, gently caressing his private parts with her free hand.

Thunderstruck, dismayed by his involuntary physical reaction, Jim Fullerton did what he had never done—struck a woman, not once but twice, sending the girl to her knees.

"Slut!" he growled. "To think that May and I—I can't believe—" Unable to continue, he tossed the heavy bag onto his shoulder, stormed out, then stopped. "You get yourself into the house right now, hear?"

As he stalked off, Rose staggered to her feet, sobbing with pain, frustration, and fury. James often called her his Apache *nah-lin,* his maiden child. But not for long. Not for long.

Jim crossed the veranda and without thinking almost entered his home. Then he stopped to knock, although the door stood ajar. "Norah? You there? You all right?"

Her voice was faint. "Come in."

Shaken by the confrontations with his children, Jim was not in the mood for more trouble. He pushed the door open, saw Norah sitting by the fire, and inwardly sighed with relief. "Something bothering you?" he asked, dumping the flour in a corner near the stove.

She motioned to a dog that rested with head framed by his paws between her and Jim. "This huge animal came bounding in here as if he owned the place and hasn't taken his eyes off me since. I'm half afraid to move!"

Jim chuckled and bent to rub the great cranium. "Is that all? Why, this is just old Baron. He won't hurt you. He was May's dog. Miss her, don't you, boy?"

"You'll think I'm silly, I know, but I never had a dog. And he's so *big!*" she marveled.

"Mastiff, I think. Weighs as much as most of the men. I wouldn't want to tangle with him except with a gun." Jim backed up to the fire to warm himself, while the dog's tail brushed back and forth on the floor; Baron knew they were talking about him.

"Did Aunt May have him as a puppy?"

"No, he showed up one day in New Mexico Territory while we were on the trail with the herd. I think he was with travelers who got into difficulties. Indians, or fever, maybe, wiped them out and left him to make it on his own. Had a bad time of it himself, judging from the scars. You can see them here on his neck and flanks and back."

Norah made a soft sound of concern and the dog cocked his head. She smiled but said, "I wish he'd stop staring."

"He chooses his friends and tolerates the rest of us. You must be okay because I never saw him do this before. Smarter than a lot of folks about making friends, aren't you, Baron?" Jim glanced about with approval. She had tidied the front room and kitchen and washed the dishes. He made a mental note to tell the men to bring her more water and wood.

She fingered a band of ribbon on her cuff, and spoke hesitantly. "I feel selfish putting you out of your own home. I don't need all this space. Can't you sleep in the other bedroom? It might not be proper, but frankly, I'd feel better about it."

"Hasn't Rose been to the house yet? That's her room."

"*Rose?* You mean there's another woman on the ranch? Who *is* she?" Norah's whole attitude brightened.

"Didn't I tell you about her? She's our—my adopted daughter. An Apache," he added a bit defensively. "Rose can read and write, that'll give you something in common." He made a face. "Wish we'd done as well with Joel when it came to book learning."

"I feel better just knowing she's here." Norah's eyes glowed above the smudges marring the pale skin.

"She'll be along directly. Say, you can mend, can't you?" Town women weren't always as handy as country gals.

"Oh, yes, I'm very good with a needle. I make ladies' hats, too."

That struck him funny, and he started to laugh. Norah bridled, then she, too, smiled at the uselessness of such a talent on the ranch. They were still chuckling when Rose came in. The dog lumbered to his feet and trotted out, giving the girl a wide berth. She nodded to Norah and went to stand beside the rancher, hands clasped demurely at waist level.

"Rose, this is Norah Carlisle. She's going to live with us

for a while, and I know you'll welcome her." Jim tried not
to glare but failed. "She's been ill, so you'll have to help
around the house."

"Pleased to meet you, ma'am. Sorry to hear you're
ailing." Her good manners clothed immediate dislike for a
possible rival. Rose's sensual glance slid from Jim to the
bedroom. "You sleeping in the barn, then?"

"In the bunkhouse." He had planned to move into the
barn so he wouldn't cramp the crew's style, but there was
safety in numbers.

Norah sensed conflict between the two and did not speak
but covertly admired Rose's apricot-hued complexion and
firmly rounded flesh, the rich, lush brunette Indian loveliness.

Jim grew uncomfortable. "Got chores to do. I'll leave
you two to get acquainted."

The door slammed shut, and Norah said, "You have no
idea how glad I am that you're here. I thought I was the only
woman from here to Tucson! I'm sure we'll get along." She
was not sure at all, but the initial effort had to be made. She
swallowed and braced herself for the usual rejection. "I
have to tell you though that I have tuberculosis. I'll put
dishes and bedding and silver aside for my use so you won't
be—"

"Is there anything to eat? I'm hungry." Rose interrupted,
opening the pie safe, a wooden two-door cupboard on legs.

"There's stew Charlie brought. It's on the stove."

Rose took a cold beef roast from the safe and cut a large
piece. She complained, "Stew, biscuits, and beans, that's
all he knows how to make." She paused at the door, tearing
at the meat with sharp teeth. "Hope you can do better."

Once she had gone, Norah settled back in the chair. What
a brat! The girl had been spoiled, which seemed surprising
since there was so much work to do. The litany of labor
made her head ache: washing, ironing, making lye for soap,
cleaning, pouring candles, cooking, doing dishes, tending
plants, sewing, baking, and mending. Was there a garden

here? And what had Jim been about to ask her to mend? Her eyes grew moist. Had it been necessary for the girl to be so rude? Should she tell Jim or try to handle it on her own? Norah coughed, feeling the pull deep in her lungs. Stress invariably made her worse; she had to learn to control her feelings.

She walked tiredly into the bedroom and sank down upon the bed made of mesquite poles laced with rawhide; the thick wool mattress was covered by blankets and a quilt with stylized flower boxes in different colors. She lay back and shut her eyes. Her mother had started a quilt before she was forced to work in that dreadful factory. What had happened to it? All she had left of her parents were the family Bible, daguerrotypes of them—thank goodness, she had those—the cameo, a few books, and pieces of lace from her mother's wedding gown.

A wedding gown. Marshal and Mrs. Mason Fletcher. Norah pictured him waiting at the altar in the unstudied elegance of a black broadcloth suit, and fell asleep fully clothed, Mason's image on her mind sharp as catclaw thorn and dear as first love.

6.

Joel saw Rose come out of the house. He had not actually been waiting for her to appear but rather biding his time until he was ready to board the blood bay. It was an estray, an animal found wandering without an owner. Indians had likely stolen it, and the horse had escaped. The owner, if alive, now had no way to trace it.

Estrays were usually advertised, because most ranchers

operated on the principle of doing good unto others. But the Double Bar F was too isolated to put an ad in the Tucson paper. If anyone showed up with proof of ownership, the horse would be released; meanwhile, it earned its keep in relative safety.

"That's a good-lookin' piece of horseflesh," one of the hands observed. "Ain't no crowbait."

"Oh, man," his companion snickered, "look at that sonofabitch lay them ears back. Joel's gonna bust his tail on this one!"

The animal was saddled and bridled and held by men on horseback who had put ropes around his neck. His reddish, lustrous coat shone in the sun, and the trembling of his muscles created little flashes of light. A handsome animal with black mane, tail, and hoof, his fine breeding was evident—as was his bad temper.

Rose wandered toward the corral. Joel hitched up pants and chaps, settled the Stetson tight on his shaggy head, and sauntered toward the horse's side, talking quietly while he checked the cinch.

"Ride 'em, cowboy!" a man yelled.

"Watch that bastard's teeth!" another cautioned. "Took the seat outa Charlie's britches t'other day!"

The men roared as they clambered atop the corral fence and hooked their boot heels on the railing their feet rested upon. "Charlie's Britches! That's his name! Charlie's Britches!"

Joel pulled the horse's head toward him with his left hand, grabbed the saddle horn with his right, put a boot into the left stirrup. The animal shook with rage and fear. He had had a hard time of it since being stolen near Santa Fe, passed from owner to owner, mistreated and ridden by all types of men. He froze, spraddled legged.

"Say howdy to the angels fer us!"

"He's gonna put daylight 'tween you and him, Joel!"

Jim tamped tobacco in his pipe, deciding the estray was a dandy. And his son could ride anything with four legs. His

pleasure faded a trifle when Rose came to stand beside him.
"You get along all right with Norah?"

She spit out a piece of gristle like a fastidious cat. "That
was stringy beef."

"You get better at Tahzay's? He eats *my* beef, you
know."

"We had a doe roasted whole, stuffed with potatoes and
onions and garlic." Rose rubbed her stomach, mouth
watering for the succulent venison.

He snorted. "Not often, you don't. That's a wedding
feast you're talking about. Most times they eat nuts, roots,
agave hearts, and corn-meal mush. Don't kid me."

Rose wrinkled her nose at him and climbed onto the fence
to watch Joel. He'd get a real ride on that *caballo*. She had
no particular affection for horses, but this one appealed to
her. The Apache girl was competent in the saddle but she
knew she used the quirt too often to suit Jim. If it pleased
him, no whip from now on.

"Ready?" one of the cowboys asked.

Easing into the saddle with reins wrapped around his fist,
Joel got ready for hell to bust loose. The blood bay was not
a man-hater in a classic sense—wouldn't try to kill you with
his forefeet or tear your flesh out in chunks—but he did
detest men. Joel went along with his pa in believing that a
careless or brutal cowboy was usually behind a horse that
had gone bad. Charlie's Britches would make a damned
good mount once the edge was off his fear and his revenge
had been taken.

"Let him go!"

What was that noise? Norah raised herself up on one
elbow, frowning in concentration. It was like nothing she
had ever heard. Muffled by thick adobe walls, the wild cry
still penetrated against a background of excited voices. Had
Jim had an accident? Nothing must happen to him. Her life
depended on him! Norah rolled off the bed and ran out of
the house. The commotion came from near the barn, and

she hurried in that direction, not noticing that Baron was loping behind. Approaching the corral, Norah saw Jim, Rose, and a line of yelling men perched on the top rail like crested birds in their high-crowned hats. It had been nothing to worry about, some sport, that was all. She almost turned back, feeling foolish and ignorant. Then, drawn by the squealing and bawling and clouds of dust, Norah looked into the corral.

Joel had lost his hat, his shirt clung to his wet body, and blood trickled from his mouth. The horse's hide foamed with sweat, and although he still pitched and plunged, it was with less and less enthusiasm. As Norah watched, his gyrations and cries ceased, and he stood spent with fatigue, sides heaving and head lowered. Whistles and applause greeted Joel's successful ride. He climbed down, stiff and white-faced, but grinning. The horse snorted, pawed the ground, and tried to bite him. Joel slapped the horse lightly, brought the reins over his head, and led him away.

"Why, Norah, how long have you been here?" Jim jumped down to join her where she leaned against a post, coughing from the dust. "You okay?" His brown eyes grew almost black with worry. "Hey, you okay?" he repeated.

She coughed up phlegm and turned away with her handkerchief. "Yes, I'm all right. But when I heard the horse—I couldn't imagine what made such a sound. It was hair-raising! I was afraid for you." She spoke sincerely, yet burned with shame that her first thought had actually been for her own welfare, not his.

"Thanks, but as you can see, we were just having fun. Let me take you back to the house—you don't look so good."

"I don't think I can make it." Her eyes beseeched him to understand. She had used up her strength running out to the barn.

Picking her up in his arms, Jim was touched to find she weighed little more than a newborn colt. Shyly, she put her arms around his neck and bowed her head to avoid breathing in his face. Neither was conscious of Rose's stony regard.

As they passed the barn, Joel strolled out with an elderly cowboy who wore an eyepatch. His face sobered. "Anything I can do, Pa?"

"No, Miss Carlisle's just plain tuckered out, that's all. Shouldn't be running like she did. Say, that was a good ride, son."

The young man's shoulders went back; he was tired but pleased with his performance. "Thanks, Pa."

The oldster spat. "Brace yuh every time, that un."

Joel worshiped Shorty, a living legend who was blood brother to the Cherokee; he had fought with Houston at the San Jacinto, driven stages and dug for gold in California, guided wagon trains, battled Indians, and knew more about cattle, mules, and horses than twenty Texans put together. "Yeah, but he'll make a good pony, won't he?" Joel asked.

"What's yore thinkin' on that, Jim?" the old man countered. The single eye, still devilish and unruly in a mind decades younger than the creaky frame that held it, examined Norah with interest.

Jim continued toward the house. "Think my boy's got himself a fine animal, Shorty."

Norah heard the words faintly. "Say, that gal's no bigger'n a Mary Posee. No sturdier, neither."

Not until Jim let her down on the veranda did she ask, "What on earth is a Mary Posee?"

Holding the door open, Jim smiled. "How about a cup of tea? May liked a cup when she felt puny." Not waiting for an answer, he made sure Norah was seated before stoking the stove and putting a kettle on to boil.

"'Mary Posee' is Shorty's version of the Spanish word *mariposa*. Means butterfly."

"I see."

Jim found a pot and a canister of tea. "We weren't close enough to hear, but he probably said you were pretty as a butterfly, too."

"I hope so!" Norah adjusted her voluminous skirt to cover every vestige of petticoat. "Oh, Jim, don't use that cup and saucer. Give them to me. You take yours from the cupboard where Rose gets hers."

He rinsed the pot with hot water, filled it, added leaves to steep. "You know, Norah, I'm going to try to find you a milk cow. Maybe some chickens, too. Milk and eggs would be good for you."

"Aren't there cows out there?"

"A range cow will give a bit of milk, but she's heck—pardon me—the pure dickens to milk. You have to rope her by the horns, snub her to a post, tie her hind legs so she can't kick, and then you're lucky to get a cupful unless her calf is tugging and butting on the other side. No, I'll have to see what I can do." Jim poured the tea, handed Norah hers, and sat down on a leather-covered trunk.

"My goodness, all that for a little milk!" Norah exclaimed. "Mmmm, that hits the spot. But I should have made the tea."

"A cowman is an all-around man," he stated with casual pride.

She studied him, the virile, capable pioneer who balanced cup and saucer on his knee as gracefully as any matron at an afternoon party. "I can see that." Norah's gaze fell on the darned pocket of his shirt. "Oh, you asked this morning if I could mend and we didn't go on about it. As I said, I sew very well. I've made garments, towels, linens, curtains, rag rugs—"

"Don't mind working on men's clothing?"

"Of course not. I made most of my father's, even his suits now and then. I may not be bigger or stronger than a butterfly—right now—but I'm determined to help as best I can." Refreshed by the beverage and the prospect of contributing, Norah got to her feet. "More tea, Jim?"

"'Fraid not. Time for supper pretty soon, then bed. I'll have Charlie bring the mending over later." At the door he mused, "You know, your hair *is* kinda the color of a butterfly that lives in the canyons."

"I should have the hang of the kitchen by tomorrow, so you can take your meals with us," she promised, feeling guilty about disrupting his life to such an extent.

His brow furrowed. "Don't do too much right off. You might get sicker than you are. I can eat with the men until you're up to it." Jim waved and walked toward the bunkhouse with his easy, loping gait.

Norah sipped the last of her tea on the veranda, watching him detour to close the barn. Thanksgiving wasn't far away. She'd make it up to him then with the best meal she could put together.

A dead turkey sat on the table, its bare bluish head dangling forlornly, red wattles like droplets of congealed blood. It weighed twenty-two pounds and after having its head and feet cut off, had to be plucked, singed, cleaned out, washed, dried, stuffed—Norah had doubts as to whether she could manage such an undertaking.

She had put her foot in it, suggesting a holiday dinner to vary the unrelenting beef and beans. A fowl had been delivered to the kitchen in short order, for plump wild turkeys roved the canyons, ignored by Apaches, who also scorned bear, pork, and fish. Now, however, Norah was at a loss—and feared her efforts might be in vain. She had a sneaking suspicion that Jim and his Texans preferred steak dipped in flour and fried in a cast-iron Dutch oven.

Lack of experience did not make her hesitate, for she had done the majority of her family's cooking; the barrier was that slim reservoir of strength, already eroded by washing bed linen and hanging it to dry. Singeing the turkey, for instance, just holding it over the flames, required more endurance than she possessed. If only Rose would help. But the girl was intent on herself and stirring up trouble.

Norah smoothed the bronzed, iridescent feathers. She had discovered a situation that disturbed her deeply. It was none of her business, yet it affected her because of the ranch's isolation. Much like a sailing ship, it was populated by those who worked cheek by jowl and depended upon each other whether they liked it or not.

She had gone to the barn to groom Lovey, the mare she would eventually learn to ride. The horse generally roamed the range, but a rattlesnake bite on the nose had caused swelling and breathing difficulties. Her condition was improved, but Lovey had to be confined for the time being. Most of the men were out for the day, and Charlie was busy with dried apple pies and the evening meal. Norah had thought she would be alone in the barn, so searching for greener wisps of hay with which to pamper the convalescing horse, she worked her way around a large stack of it and came upon Rose and Joel lying side by side in the gloom. The girl's dress was unbuttoned and open to the waist. He held a breast in one hand while kissing the other.

"Oh!" Norah gasped without meaning to, wishing she could vanish into thin air.

"Get out," Rose hissed, pulling away from Joel, whose eyes popped open with surprise.

Norah turned on the ball of her foot and rushed outside, where she stood in the cool breeze until her cheeks no longer burned. Returning to the house at a slow pace, she hoped she hadn't called attention to the lovers by appearing unsettled.

That evening after a simple meal of cold meat, bread, and corn relish, Norah sat down with a book. As the illness progressed, she had gotten into the habit of reading before bed; it held the sleep-broken night at bay when coughing and perspiration woke her so frequently. Concentration on the book, a life of Benjamin Franklin, seemed impossible tonight, however. Rose was washing up, throwing dish-water out, slamming pots and pans. Knowing the girl was being noisy on purpose, Norah grimly turned the pages even though she scarcely knew what she was reading; the shocking scene in the barn dominated all else in her mind.

Rose finally finished in the kitchen and flounced into her room. Norah sighed, hoping now for peace and quiet, but Rose reappeared in a few minutes, buttoning the neck of her nightdress. "I don't love Joel, you know."

"You could have fooled me."

Norah had seen things on the St. Louis waterfront no respectable woman should have; Rose's nakedness had not distressed her so much as the implied aftermath. Her Anglo-Saxon mind could not as yet entertain the possibility of a white man marrying an Indian; yet once Joel ruined the girl—which might already be done—the only honorable course was matrimony.

"He's a baby. I wouldn't give myself to him. I love a *man*." Rose bent forward so her long black hair almost fell into Norah's lap. "I love Jim."

Norah dropped the book. "Your *father*?" she cried with repugnance.

The girl made an explosive sound, sending spittle into Norah's face. "He's not my father. I don't know who my father was."

"But surely . . ." Norah stopped, at a loss for words.

"Surely what?" Rose's eyes narrowed. "Surely I've noticed how Jim cares for you like a precious piece of china? Surely I've seen how his face changes when he speaks of you?"

"What are you talking about? He's my uncle by marriage. We're friends, nothing more." Troubled, Norah fingered her cameo.

"He evidently doesn't think so."

"You're imagining things. He's been more than helpful, but that's all."

The girl straightened to her full height, and scorn shone in her eyes. "*You*—what do you know about love? Real love? You've never been with a man, have you?"

Norah flushed. "No, but that doesn't mean—"

"It means you haven't the faintest idea what I'm talking about. But I'm telling you. He thinks of you as more than a friend and I don't like it. Remember, he's *mine*!" she warned, then padded away, bare feet silent on the floor.

Stung, Norah groped for words, then said in a loud voice, "You can have him! Whether he wants *you* is another matter entirely!" Witch, selfish child-woman ready to break Joel's or Jim's heart. Norah wished herself elsewhere, away from the incestuous simmering of this adolescent who had hit the nail on the head. True love *was* a stranger to Norah. Yet pity for Rose intruded on her indignation. The girl was ready for love, hungry for it, and where was she to find it in this godforsaken place?

Every detail of that conversation came back as Norah contemplated the turkey. Since that night, within the limits of her strength, she had bent over backward to do things for herself, for neither Jim nor Rose must believe she had designs on him. When she dreamed of love, her thoughts turned to Mason, not Jim.

Groaning audibly at having to prepare the bird for roasting, Norah donned an apron and sat down. To break the quiet, she sang as she labored. She had plucked the breast and gone through two stanzas of "My Heart's in the Highlands" when gunfire and shouts shattered the morning. Memory immediately called up the stagecoach attack, and she felt the blood drain from her face. Forcing herself up, Norah opened the door. A small brownish-black bear lumbered past the veranda, fleeing to the foothills, grunting harshly in terror, as it plunged into the grasses. Several cowboys soon reined up in front of Norah. "Which way'd he go, ma'am?"

She pointed purposely in the wrong direction, and they thundered away, yelling like boys on the way to the swimming hole on a hot day. Why had she done that? Weren't bears dangerous? Norah walked around back to the outhouse. Maybe adult bears did bring down a calf now and then, but this one had been young and scared. She had been moved by him, for she, too, had fled for her life. She hoped he had made good his escape by now.

Norah returned to the kitchen just in time to see Baron run across the yard with the turkey in his jaws. She started to call him back, then decided against it. He had saved her a lot of work, and cowboy fare was plenty good enough for Thanksgiving after all. She sighed. Suppose Mason Fletcher rode up to share their meal? Any food would surely taste like champagne and caviar! Norah wondered where he was and wished them together.

7.

The guest who drew attention at the traditional New Year's Day reception at the White House was not President Ulysses S. Grant but a man from the state of California. Unknown to most of the motley throng of scalawags, robber barons, grafters, and politicians, U.S. Marshal Mason Fletcher was famous among his peers and held in high regard by the President who had appointed him.

Those familiar with the responsibilities of his position admired him mightily, albeit grudgingly. Marshals had to have many talents in addition to a fast draw to fill the job. They policed the Indian Nations, assisted tribes in resisting white encroachment, protected public lands and property, enforced revenue laws and arrested moonshiners, served warrants, tracked down criminals, escorted prisoners to federal penitentiaries, and safeguarded the mail. The life span of these officers was often short, for they faced constant hostility and danger.

Yet the man who mingled with the reception guests like a tall-sparred clipper ship sailing through a fleet of clumsy barges gave no indication that his perilous duties disturbed him in the least. He was an enigma to the Easterners, who had expected a dime-novel frontiersman with sombrero, buckskins, long hair, ferocious mustache, a Bowie knife in a beaded scabbard, and Samuel Colt's equalizers on both hips. They saw instead a sophisticated cosmopolite like themselves in fashionable garb who knew how to act in high society, knew what silverware to use and which compliments to offer over a lady's hand.

Women's hearts and fans fluttered over the brave and handsome Marshal, but men stepped as carefully as predators sniffing an enticingly baited trap. They exchanged New Year's greetings with him, fidgeting beneath his cool appraisal, then retreated to bottle or buffet.

The President flipped his coattails and sat down. "When do you leave, Mason?" He lighted a gold-tipped cigar, narrowing hard blue eyes against the smoke.

"In the morning, sir. On the earliest train." Mason looked out at a gentle snowfall, wishing he were on his way this very minute.

Grant blew a smoke ring. "Anxious to get back, are you?"

Fletcher was hard as nails, a man after Grant's heart, but he was glad the Marshal would soon be out from underfoot; the man was an embarrassment despite his fine service record. His report on the Indian Ring—or Tucson Ring, depending on the source—had been excellent, both shocking and explosive. The fly in the ointment was that Fletcher had fingered some of Grant's friends among the corrupt federal officials and government contractors who were swindling reservation Indians and forcing them back on the warpath. He studied the Marshal. Not a man to cross. Better see him on his way before he ruffled too many feathers.

"If I may be brutally frank, sir, Washington holds no charms for me."

"You like those wide-open spaces, eh?"

"There are so many things to be done there, from the Sabine River in Texas to the Pacific. Even to Hawaii." The

Californian's face lighted with vision and zeal. "Today is the first day of 1876. A hundred years from now, Mr. President, the West, not the East, will be the pulse of the nation."

"Impossible, young man, impossible! Didn't Kit Carson say the Gadsden Purchase was too worthless to feed a wolf?"

"A figure of speech, sir, I'm sure." Mason had soured on Grant's reception and interpretation of his hard-earned information, ferreted out at the risk of his life. It was unfortunate the President admired rich men no matter how they got that way and brushed aside allegations of criminality among the very ones who brushed elbows with him here at the White House.

Grant also dismissed the thorny dilemma of the Chiricahua Reservation. Mason had tried to impress upon him the importance of allowing these particular Indians to remain on their own land in their beloved Dragoon and Chiricahua Mountains. If these, the most warlike, intractable and merciless Apaches, were torn from their homeland, blood would most certainly flow as it had not done since 1861 when Cochise took revenge for the Bascom Affair at Apache Pass.

Mason signaled a waiter for more champagne. He needed another drink whenever he remembered the President's answer. He shuddered at the consequences for people who lived below the Gila River—for Norah Carlisle, if she still lived.

"The Mexican government has been at me hammer and tongs to get those blamed hostiles away from the border. As I understand it, that reservation abuts against the border and affords excellent sanctuary for Indian bands raiding into Mexico. Let the Indian Bureau handle it. They know what they're doing. You have plenty of other work to do out there."

Glancing at the gold pocketwatch Wells Fargo had presented him upon his resignation, Mason was glad to see how late in the day it was. He sought out Mrs. Grant, a famous hostess, thanked her for inviting him, then returned to say farewell to her husband.

"Take care of yourself, Marshal." Grant grinned around the cigar stub and shook his hand.

"Thank you, Mr. President. And you can depend on me to—"

"Keep that badge shining," Grant interrupted. "Don't let anything tarnish it, my boy."

"I won't, sir. Depend on it. Good-bye. And Happy New Year." A servant brought Mason's greatcoat and hat, and he left to walk to his hotel, welcoming the clean and innocent snow.

Chico squatted in a corner of the hotel room, watching Mason shave by lamplight. "I not come here again."

"Why not?"

"Too cold. All damn time snowing."

Mason ran fingers over a smooth chin. "It's pretty in springtime."

The Apache stared impassively at the striped satin wallpaper. It reminded him of a dress his wife had been fond of. Many moons had passed since he lost her. They had married in the spring, and she died in the spring when colts were being born, trees were coming into leaf, and his heart was breaking.

"You come to ride the elevators," Mason teased, putting away shaving gear and arranging his cravat.

"No, I come to save you from women with big eyes that eat you up. Chattering women with great skirts dragging, hair like bird nests, skin white as a fish's belly."

Humming, delighted to be on his way, Mason closed his suitcase and buttoned his overcoat. "*Bueno*, Chico, *vamos*. Back to where the sun shines every day and a man can see the horizon." He checked out of the hotel, oblivious to muttered comment and muffled feminine shrieks. The

Apache had painted his face and enjoyed scaring people with menacing motions and grimaces.

Mason hailed a carriage to take them to the railroad station. The driver stared at Chico and curled his lip. "That dirty savage ain't gonna ride in *my* rig, mister!"

"I'll double the fare." Mason had run into this before and sighed with impatience.

"Nope."

"Triple."

Suspicious eyes inspected the alien being. "Wal— awright. But he sits on the floor, mind!"

"Awright," Mason mocked angrily, and gestured to Chico, who was already hunching down in front of him.

They drove through the snow-covered city, their exhalations like fog before their pinched faces. Mason reflected on the future of Apaches. Were they always to be the lowest of the low to rough men like the driver, who were not much better? He burrowed his chin into his collar. Damn, how did Washingtonians stand this damp cold?

In late January Norah suffered a relapse. She lay in a coma for two days and regained consciousness only to bring up such amounts of bloody phlegm that in her mind she prepared to die. Jim, who had seen death in many forms, was not sure she would survive either. At his wits end over caring for Norah, Jim was surprised when the old one-eyed cowboy, Shorty, volunteered to nurse her.

"Ain't no good on a hoss no more," he admitted mournfully. "Beat-up hands plain creak with arth-aritis, but by gum, I'm too ornery to catch this here consumption." Shorty patted the worried rancher on the back. "Don't fret, son. She's either gonna live or die."

Jim studied Norah with a heart already torn to pieces by the loss of his wife. How hard it would be to part with this girl, too.

"Thanks, Shorty. I'm grateful."

Shorty could not have laundered Norah's bed linen,

handkerchiefs, and nightdresses had he wanted to. Which
he did not. During the next few weeks he simply saw to it
that she ate and drank, and he matter-of-factly emptied
chamberpots, brought water to wash with, and when the
spirit moved him, rinsed out her sweat-drenched garments.
On occasion, tired enough to be tender and seeing how
much tangled hair bothered her, he brushed the long dark
red tresses and let their ends curl over his knobby knuckles.

Shorty became a tyrant. When Jim or Joel carried Norah
outside to bask in the sun, he bullied her into breathing
deeply and sitting up to do so, even when she half-fainted
with effort. Despite her objections and gagging, he forced
her to drink the fresh hot blood of the cows butchered for
food.

"What did you do before you had me to order around?"
Norah asked one afternoon in late February. Rain poured
down, and they sat by the fire, cozy as fleas on a dog, as he
said.

"Pushed buffler, cow critters, 'n' mustangs around." The
bluish-gray eye glittered slyly. "Mules, too. But ain't
nothin' next to a critter in petticoats."

"Oh, you." She threaded a needle, intent on finishing a
shirt for him. No father could have been kinder or more
patient, or such a taskmaster. Tough old rascal, she loved
him.

"Shorty, what's your real name? I've never heard anyone
mention it."

He spat into a can by his chair, pulled a tobacco plug from
a vest pocket, and gnawed a piece loose. Norah sniffed the
licorice in it, had smelled it often since the old man began
his rough-hewn nursing. "How long you been away from
the East?"

"Not long. Almost five months. Why?"

"Ain't perlite to ask a feller's real name out here. Where
he hails from, neither."

Norah labored over a buttonhole. "Why not?"

"Ain't nobody's business and could be plumb dangerous."

"You mean—he might be wanted by the law somewhere."

"Yep, man could be on the dodge." She was as he pictured his own youngun to have been had he settled down to have one. And he sure wanted a worthwhile woman like her to remember him when he went to meet his Maker.

"Promise you'll keep it to yore own self?"

"Cross my heart." Norah did so with solemnity.

Shorty cleared his throat and said almost bashfully, "Theodore. That's my handle. Theodore Obadiah Peebles."

Norah leaned forward to grip the hands that tended her, gnarled as roots exposed by a flash flood. "I'll never tell a soul. Nor tell what a great softie you are, either." She treasured the compliment paid her, surmising correctly that few had been so honored.

The door flew open to the accompaniment of rain drumming on the wood-shingled veranda roof. Jim hurried in, slicker billowing in the wind, water dripping off his shoulders. Propping a rifle by the door, he glanced with interest at the tableau by the fire: the aged adventurer, solitary eye dewy with affection; the girl, beaming at a confidence shared or secret told.

"What's this?" he inquired, turning his back to remove wet clothing. "Beauty and the beast?"

"What a thing to say," Norah chided, going to the kitchen. "I don't think we'll give him any of that peach pie I made."

Jim approached the fire, rubbing his palms together with a rasping sound. "Good rain, Shorty. Kind that sinks into the ground."

"Plenty of snow on them peaks, too," the old cowboy added, still embarrassed by uncharacteristic sentimentality. "Means a fine melt come spring." He drank the last of his coffee and slowly got to his feet.

"Must you go out in that rain?" Norah objected.

Shorty pulled his hat brim down. "Been wet as a frog more times 'n I can count, sis." He waved and went out.

Norah served pie to the rancher and herself. "Hope you like this. I haven't made any since last summer before I left St. Louis." She felt a maternal pleasure to see his face light up with anticipation when he lifted his fork.

Suddenly the face of Mason Fletcher leaped to mind for no reason Norah could imagine, unless golden darts of flame in the fireplace resembled the color of his eyes. Not that she thought of him often, but now and then he came to her in a dream. Sexually unawakened, Norah blushed to recall a recent fantasy in which they slept side by side beneath the stars. They had awakened and he reached out, put his mouth to her throat, and there among the grasses that murmured so intimately she opened her clothing to him—

"Norah, you'd better move away from the fire. Your face is getting red." Jim put down the empty plate. "That was fine pie. Charlie couldn't have done better." Everyone missed the cook who had died hideously from lockjaw after being bitten by a rabid skunk during the winter.

"What a wonderful compliment." She thought with regret of the dear little man, the artistry of his flaky biscuits, sourdough bread, doughnuts, pancakes, cornbread, and rice puddings. "He must have been the best ranch cook in Texas."

"We thought so." Jim yawned, content to be where it was dry and fragrant with the smell of baking and the scent of a woman. If he was not mistaken, Norah had gained weight. The unsightly discoloration under her eyes had faded to very pale lavender; another few weeks, and it would be gone. He had only awhile longer to wait before asking her to marry him. His eyes flicked toward the bedroom. He had a few years on her, but he was still virile and sinewy; he would teach her all she needed to know.

"Do you," he asked tentatively, "feel up to cooking for the hands until I find a man to take Charlie's place? There's six of us now. And Shorty. A few punchers quit while you were sick, including Sam, the Negro hand. I was sure sorry to lose him. He was one of the best, pure magic with the animals. The men said they'd rather take a chance with Apaches than eat Rose's grub." Jim laughed soundlessly.

Norah tried not to giggle, having developed a hearty dislike for the girl, who in turn made no bones about her animosity. Being friends could have been so nice, so rewarding, with tasks halved, confidences shared, and loneliness assuaged. Norah had not complained but tried to be cheerful, an effort that endeared her to each man, including Joel, who was beholden to her for not tattling about his rendezvous in the barn. Norah was regretful that Rose considered her a rival; the misunderstanding robbed the family of peaceful, productive domesticity.

"I'll take a stab at it, but I'm not completely well, you know. Will the men object?"

"Not if you bake like this they won't."

"The way to a man's heart." She shook her head.

"Tomorrow morning then," Jim said. "About four."

"How will I know . . ."

"Rose will wake you."

"I'll bet she will."

Reluctantly shrugging into the slicker, Jim turned with a hand on the door. "Say, what were you and Shorty so sociable about there by the fire?"

Norah shut one eye and squinted at him with the other. "Ain't nobody's business—and could be plumb dangerous," she intoned in a fair imitation of the oldster's voice.

Jim threw back his head and guffawed. "You varmints ain't gonna tell me a confounded thing, I see." He put the rain-darkened Stetson on. "Remember, four o'clock. No sleeping in."

Norah cleaned up the kitchen, emptied coffee grounds, reminded herself to grind more, and added wood to the fire. Six men plus Shorty, Rose, and herself. Twenty-seven big meals a day and as many plates to wash in addition to pots, pans, cups, bowls, utensils. She pictured dishes barely done from one meal before time to start preparations for the next. Her busy hands slowed. Merciful Heaven, was she up to that?

True, she had gained weight; her clothes no longer hung like sacks. Sleep came more quickly and lasted longer, and the mirror reflected a rosier complexion, brighter eyes, and cheeks beginning to fill. Shorty had said the night she awoke from the coma, the choice was simple as ABC. Live or die. Give up or hang on. Arizona Territory would kill her or cure her, so she'd better make up her mind. There was no physician to consult about the improvement. Desert air and altitude might be responsible, and certainly weeks of uninterrupted rest had helped, as did that ghastly beef blood, sunshine, and a hearty, if plain, diet. Of course, the factors involved did not matter so long as her return to health continued. Whether the work of cooking would undermine this progress remained to be seen. Meanwhile, bread had to be baked, beans put to soak, supplies stocked in the cookshack. She had to prove herself; she wanted to help and pay back.

In bed that night, she prayed as always to be strong. To be normal again. And her mouth curved with satisfaction to think of the *mariposa* about to quit the chrysalis and spread its wings.

The stove had been fired up, steaks carved, and coffee boiled by the time Norah arrived, sleepily apprehensive about filling the stomachs of robust men facing a brutal day's labor. Tin platters stood stacked near the stove; plates, cups, iron utensils, pitchers of lick, slabs of canned butter, and dishes with red jelly marched down the length of the board table. Bless him! She had had a hunch Jim planned to smooth the way for a few days until she got the hang of things. Then the city girl was on her own.

"Good morning." As Norah removed her shawl half a dozen rope-roughened hands reached for it. She catalogued the men swiftly: Jim, Joel, a wiry Mexican called Emedio, the red-bearded brothers Tom and Slim, and grizzled, silent John Smith. And of course, Theodore Obadiah Peebles.

Now she approached the huge black stove, drew a deep breath, and began. Twelve steaks, fifty pancakes, eighteen biscuits, and four pots of coffee later, the cookshack had emptied of politely murmuring men. Norah, exhausted yet exultant, surveyed the breakfast wreckage and wondered where they had put it all.

Her mouth began to water with a craving for meat such as she had never had before. Flinging aside the tarp in which the carcass was wrapped, Norah was taken aback by its size; but hunger—actually more of an urgent need—overcame hesitation. She cut a steak, wielding Charlie's big butcher knife with more eagerness than dexterity, dredged it in flour, slapped the meat in a frying pan, and hungered over it while it cooked.

Unable to bear further delay, Norah transferred the steak to a plate and cut into it, popping a piece in her mouth. She could not chew fast enough—it was as if her body demanded sustenance that very second. Finished eating, Norah slumped onto one of the hard benches that flanked the table. She put her head down on her arms and fell asleep.

The table moved, and she awoke, brushing at whatever was sniffing at her hair. "Baron, stop that. What do you think . . ." Norah's fond remonstrance faded away as she lifted her head to stare into the eyes of a steer with great horns at least five feet across. It drooled on the table, bellowed, and stamped its foot. The sound appalled Norah, paralyzed her. What did the beast want? Was he going to charge, destroy the cookshack—or her?

"Where'd that slab-sided old cuss go to, Pa?" Joel's voice inquired nearby.

"Joel!" Norah cried. "Joel! In here!"

Spurs jingled when he entered. "I was afeared he'd get

here 'fore I did. Did he scare you? Old Sugar led our herd all the way from Texas. Wears this bell, see?''

"What does he want, for heaven's sake? Why isn't he out with the rest of them?'' The animal shoved at the table again. Norah scrambled off the bench and grabbed a big skillet.

Joel laughed and poured sugar into the palm of his hand. He held it out to be scoured clean by the animal's coarse tongue. "Oh, he comes for his treat every day 'bout this time. Charlie spoiled him.''

"*I* don't intend to. Get him out of here.'' Norah glared at the gaunt intruder, whose eyes begged for more sweets.

Joel seemed to feel the necessity of defending Old Sugar. "He don't mean no harm, you understand. He only came in 'cause you weren't waitin' outside.'' He took a flour sack and snapped it at the longhorn's rump. "Git. Go on, you long-legged, fiddle-faced ol' good-fer-nothin', git.'' They watched as the animal deftly maneuvered his horns through the door, halted, bawled as if in protest, then plodded away.

"Anything else to eat, Joel?'' Norah looked at the spot where the longhorn had been to make sure there was nothing to clean up.

"No, thank you, ma'am. Pa's waitin'.''

"Call me Norah, Joel, not ma'am. I thought we settled that.''

He ducked his head like a little boy and grinned. "Norah.''

She followed him out and sat down on a stool against the cookshack wall. Here Charlie used to peel onions and potatoes, keep an eye on things in general, always ready to feed a hungry hand. Jim and his son rode off side by side, the former touching his hat brim to her.

A bond had been forged between her and Joel as the result of her silence about the scene in the barn. Norah noticed he now made an effort to avoid Rose, which was difficult for him because they were constantly thrown together by circumstances, and unquenched desire smoldered in his dark eyes. Rose ignored him, did tasks Jim gave her, and lived in a world of her own. Norah felt sure it was the quiet before the storm.

She studied the adobe house nearby, appreciating the utilitarian design of the frontier fortress. The veranda did not belong; perhaps it had been a labor of love for Aunt May. The residence mirrored the hardship and danger the Fullertons had faced since trekking to Arizona Territory. Other pioneer houses in the vicinity must be similar bastions of defense, Norah thought, yearning to meet the women in them.

What women they must be, she decided with humility. They had not been driven by illness but had chosen to come to this place of peril with their menfolk and children to build anew after the war. They had braved the unknown when their hearts must often have been in their mouths. What had Jim said not long ago? If a thing's worthwhile, it's worth fighting for. Norah gazed about. Oh, yes, she would fight tooth and nail for this if it were hers.

Which brought her to that question with no answer. Once she was completely recovered, should she go home to St. Louis or stay in the West? In San Francisco, maybe, where a well-read, cultured young woman who plied a clever needle could find a niche. Wasn't she still a city person at heart? Didn't she miss the grocery shop, the bakery, the candy store down the block, and most of all, a library, church, and concert hall?

She smoothed the hair at her temples and took a deep breath of sweet, untainted air. Or should she stay here where she had fallen in love with the golden and turquoise days, velvety nights, a spoiled lady horse, a giant dog, and cowboys who ate like lions and acted like pussycats?

8.

Norah's question remained unanswered as the weeks spun into the spring of 1876. The Apaches lived quietly on their reservations, the majority abiding by white man's rules. Their relatives in Mexico, as usual harassing long-suffering Sonorans, had not reappeared in southeastern Arizona Territory.

Signs of spring were abundant as young stock was rounded up for branding; Lovey threw a filly the color of chocolate fudge; the grasslands greened and flourished. Norah, too, bloomed like a plant long dormant, and her clothes had to be let out. Her waxen-hued skin grew creamy and her mouth with its large lower lip, so innocently sensual, was wild-primrose pink. The men could hardly keep their eyes off her as she bustled about readying the cookshack for its new occupant.

His name was Chan Lee. He had cooked for a gold-mining camp near Prescott until prejudice and a fight over stolen gold dust triggered his hasty departure. Sam, the Negro cowboy formerly with Double Bar F, was in camp trying his luck; knowing the Chinese to be honest, he directed him to the Fullerton spread. A friend of Sam's who was on his way to a nearby ranch eventually brought word that a replacement for Charlie was on the way.

"I'll miss seeing your face at breakfast," Jim complained to Norah. They strolled toward a firing range set up for her, leather targets positioned against an earthen bank.

"I won't miss getting up," she replied, "you can count on that! Why, I'll be able to sleep—until five at least."

They were alone except for Baron, who now followed Norah like her own shadow. Momentarily shielded from curious eyes by outbuildings, Jim took her arm and pulled her to a halt. She was ready now for what he had planned for months, and he bubbled with the juices of spring like a creature about to molt and discard its skin.

"I'd sure love to see that face on my pillow every morning." He took off his hat, revealing the untanned strip of skin that ran from mid-forehead to hairline. "Will you marry me, Norah? I'll make you a good husband. As God is my witness, I will."

She flushed with surprise and excitement. His proposal answered the question of where to go, what to do, how to spend the rest of her life. Yet they both knew he was only a friend. Was that a valid reason to refuse such a stalwart, kind individual? Love would develop, come with time, children, shared experiences. But where was the spark, the thrill she dreamed of at night when Mason came to her and loved her so she awoke, tingling? Jim must be a decade older, too.

"My dear—" Norah laid a palm along his cheek.

He reached up, took the hand, and kissed the palm. "I see a long lifeline." Norah smiled, and the man's heart swelled until he could have floated across the valley. Christ, she was neat. Neat as a good cow pony who turned on a coin and gave you change. She was a woman who looked well in broad daylight, for her coloring harmonized with the environment. Her skin was like pearly petals of desert yucca, and her hair was as rich in hue as the blood bay's hide. Eyes—oh, Lord, those eyes—they matched Texas bluebonnets drinking in the sun. Shirtwaist and skirt molded to her newly rounded curves, Norah Carlisle radiated energy and happiness. For an instant—like a flame flaring— the rancher caught the impact of a powerful but undeveloped facet of her personality. The impression faded as she spoke with firmness softened by shyness.

"I am honored, James Fullerton. Truly I am. But I'm not

ready to be tied down again just yet." She wouldn't hurt his
feelings. How was he to know she loved another man?
Loved him purely, hopelessly.

He put his hat back on, puzzled and let down. "Again?
Were you married before you came out here?"

Norah put an arm through his, and they walked on, their
relationship changed forever. "No, no. I've never been
married. It's hard for you to understand, I think. You've
always been so strong and vigorous. If you were ever sick,
it was probably for a short time. But I've been hamstrung,
as you'd say, for more than a year by my consumption."
She broke away and whirled around and around. "But I'm
not going to die now! *I'm not!* You can't imagine how that
feels, Jim. I want to fly! I want to run to the top of that
mountain and shout, *'I'm well, I'm well!'*"

Stopped in front of him, bosom heaving with exertion,
eyes sparkling, Norah glowed with the sheer joy of living.
Delicate beads of perspiration shone on her upper lip, and
taken unawares, Jim had to taste them. Surely they tasted
not of salt but of wild strawberries, juicy and waiting to be
gathered. Hot with desire, he pulled her unresisting to him
and gave her the first lover's kiss on the mouth Norah had
ever had.

"Oh, my," she whispered against his lips. *"Oh, my!"*
Her every nerve vibrated. Flesh beneath his fingers exploded with sensation. This put a different complexion on
things!

Jim reined himself in. He kissed her again but less
passionately so as not to frighten her. Procreation had taken
the upper hand with his dear, departed wife; they had
produced the one child, Joel. In the undefiled Norah he
would plant his last seed as well as indulge in sensual
marital exercise dreamed of but never come to pass before.
"We'd better go on," he suggested.

"Yes, we'd better."

Overcome, she looked at the ground as they went and he
mooned over her, tantalized by long eyelashes that con-

cealed her inner spirit. They walked as in a trance, oblivious to Rose, who knelt hidden behind a tree. They did not see the Indian girl copy the mourning of women of her race, casting dirt upon face and head. What Rose feared in the depths of her being had come to pass. James was lost to her. She might one day tempt him to her bed, but in his heart the white woman reigned supreme.

Rose gasped at the pain clawing her chest and sought surcease in the Chiricahua range behind her, which was the home not of her people but of Apaches related to them so long ago they might have hunted side by side elephant, bison, camel and sloth. Perhaps that was where she belonged, a sister to the wild things that knew no envy or hate or all-consuming desire. Perhaps her place was beneath pine and aspen, along creeks where the water ouzels built mossy nests, in canyons where bighorn sheep, bobcat, and white-tailed deer wandered.

She was a stranger here, wanted by and dear to no one. When the time was right, therefore, she would turn away and go. Go and find her own world.

9.

First Lieutenant Carleton Madison Beatty of D Troop, Fifth Cavalry, swore silently. Scion of an old and inordinately wealthy family in Philadelphia, he had never intended to be in Arizona Territory. Yet here he was riding north through Vista Valley on a warm June afternoon, disgusted at his failure to catch the Apache warriors who should have been on their reservation but instead had been raiding in Mexico. His pale blue eyes squinted to close out the sunshine. Lord

God Almighty, he was sick of sunshine. Wasn't it ever cool and cloudy? He brooded over the deliciousness of soft gray afternoons, pregnant with rain to last the night.

It had been on such a cloudy day that his father discovered him with the older man's mistress. Volunteering for a tour of duty seemed wise at the time, a haven from parental wrath; but Carleton had been horrified to learn he'd been assigned to that Siberia of posts, the Arizona Territory. He was even more distressed when his father, a powerful senator, did nothing to quash the orders. He ran a finger inside his sweaty tunic collar. All this discomfort, inconvenience, and exposure to danger just for a little ass. What a fool he'd been!

He was not without sensitivity; a man had to admit this was truly splendid country. Mountains to the east soared high above the valley, with their cliffs and canyons of muted green, blue, and lilac at varying altitudes. These vast basins and rangelands no doubt made prime grazing land with grass so high it brushed his horse's belly. There was not a tree in sight. Where *was* everybody? Not a community worth mentioning within hundreds of miles, no railroad, no telegraph, no culture, no amenities. Emptiness. Who would choose to live in this magnificent but isolated wilderness? A breed of men with whom he had nothing in common, that was certain.

Larks and quail shot shrieking into the air, disturbed by the hoofs of the cavalry troop. Prairie dogs scolded the travelers impudently while their enemy, the black-footed ferret, and their neighbors, droll burrowing owls that utilized empty tunnels, popped underground to wait until the horses passed. Carleton ignored the local fauna, his gaze sweeping the landscape and finally picking up figures of men on horseback among browsing longhorns.

"Sergeant Mulrooney, find out how far we are from the Fullerton Ranch."

"Yes, sir." Returning within several minutes, he reported, " 'Tis no more than a half hour's ride, sir."

"Excellent." The lieutenant was hot, thirsty, and bored. At least the ranch offered a change of scene. He thought this fuss about Stone Age savages ridiculous. What was so difficult about conquering a few thousand fleabitten nomads? Gallop in and flush them out, he maintained, his Eastern mind ignoring the abundance of strongholds in remote wildernesses where a few could hold off a hundred until hell froze over.

The young officer, like many Americans of the period, was an unabashed racist who believed Anglo-Saxon domination of the continent to be America's manifest destiny. Furthermore, he was ready to help carry the white man's burden: educating and caring for uncivilized peoples met and vanquished on that continent. Once this Apache thing had been ironed out, an exercise of no more than a few months, he had a good chance at desk duty in Washington. He and his father had made cautious truce by mail, for the woman who had caused their estrangement had been cast out for dalliance with younger men.

"There it is, sir." The sergeant pointed.

"I have eyes in my head."

"Sorry, sir," Sergeant Mulrooney mumbled. Like he'd told his wife, there was no pleasin' the fancy Dan. Brave enough he was, but he niver let you close, niver told a man he'd done well.

When the troop trotted onto the ranch grounds, the men in front saw a sight generally confined to saloons and bawdyhouses: women fighting on the ground, showing black hose and petticoats. Riders to the rear pushed forward, eager to be diverted, and if they were lucky, to catch a glimpse of lingerie.

Norah had two strikes against her: Rose's blind fury and Baron's clear intent to hurt Rose. She and the girl had quarreled over a silly trifle—whether to have cornbread or biscuits with the evening meal. Words had led to angry silence, then Rose had started to cry. Norah, hoping to bridge the gulf between them, had hugged the girl, only to find she was holding a slapping, biting, kicking hellcat. Forced to defend herself, Norah fought as best she could but soon became concerned about the dog, who nipped, snapped, and tried to bite the other girl. He despised Rose, who slipped hot chile peppers into his meat scraps, kicked him when no one was looking, and stoned him if he followed her into the woods. Memory of these insults faded, however, beside her attack on the creature he loved so dearly.

Norah heard Baron growl in a different tone, glimpsed boot-clad feet beside her head, and tried to pull away. Her cheeks stung, and Rose had landed telling blows in ribs, stomach, and kneecap. "Rose, stop it! Do you hear? *Stop it!*" Soldiers dragged them apart and tried to hold the Apache girl, but she wrestled loose and ran into the house.

"Hey, dog, don't show them fangs to me." The sound of a gun hammer being cocked was like thunder to Norah.

"Baron!" she gasped, and flung an arm about him. At the same time she managed to brush hair out of her face and to confirm that her dress was still buttoned. It was then that she saw the officer. He was a young god on horseback with a chin cleft beneath luxurious reddish-blond mustaches, a military Apollo whose cool stare examined her with disapproval and aloofness—but also with curiosity and interest.

The sergeant offered the back of a freckled hand to the mastiff so he might not misinterpret an open one for a coming blow. Satisfied no danger threatened his beloved or himself, the dog allowed the man to pull Norah to her feet. "Bit of a scrap there, miss." His homely, honest face showed he found her a charming lady, brawl or no.

"More than a bit," Norah muttered, mortified and swaying from shock and exertion. "Thank you—"

"Sergeant Mulrooney, at your service, miss." He stepped back, face turning blank, as the lieutenant had spurred his horse forward.

"Whom do I have the honor of addressing? Miss Fullerton?"

"No, I'm Norah Carlisle, a relative."

He then identified himself and the unit. "We'd like to water our mounts. We've just come up from the border."

"Of course! The trough is right over there. And you and your men are welcome to rest." The troopers looked tired, eyes red from dust and sun glare, lips chapped and dry.

Carleton dismounted, pulled off gauntlets and a yellow-corded black hat. "They need it. Chasing Apaches is like trying to catch a mirage." He surrendered the reins to the sergeant.

"Sit down on the veranda and cool off, Lieutenant Beatty, while I change. I won't be long." Norah left her guest at a dignified walk but once inside she closed the door and slumped against it, bruised, exhausted, and breathing harshly enough to make her cough. Damn that girl anyhow! Norah poured water in the washbowl and cleaned face and hands before putting on a yellow-and-blue batiste. She checked herself for injuries—none visible now at least—brushed her hair, and tied it back with a blue ribbon. Did she look presentable enough for the urbane officer? She was much abashed to have been found rolling on the ground in such an ill-bred manner. Then Norah tossed her head. If he didn't approve—

She went into the kitchen where the stove, stoked to cook meal or snack, kept water hot, beans simmering on a back burner, bread rising in the warming oven. Perspiration beaded Norah's brow as she cut into an apricot pie baked that morning, poured coffee, and put dishes and utensils on a tray.

The young man rose when she rejoined him and took the tray while Norah positioned an empty crate between chairs and covered it with a green-and-white cloth. "You needn't have gone to so much trouble." He placed the tray on the makeshift table and held a chair for her.

She sat down carefully, only now aware of a sore behind.

"It was no trouble. Everything was ready. Besides, we haven't had visitors for months." He was attractive and charming, but Norah hoped he wouldn't stay long. All she could think of was taking a spoonful of nerve medicine and a nice long nap. She took a deep breath, conscious of a slight nausea and headache in the aftermath of the fight.

Carleton cut into his pie. "Living here must be like living on an island. How do you stand it?" He watched Norah as he ate and liked what he saw. No, adored what he saw! A lovely creature to be stranded here.

"Actually, I like it very much, except for not having neighbors nearby, and Mr. Fullerton—he was married to my aunt, who died last fall—has been wonderful. I was quite ill when I came here, you see."

He smiled and scoffed, "You don't look as if you've been sick a day in your life."

Norah let the subject drop. "Another slice, Lieutenant?"

"Yes, please. It's quite delicious." He watched with idle approval as she rose and went into the house. Moments later he heard voices, Norah's placatory, the other angry. The girl she had fought stormed out, eyes swollen with crying, gave the officer a sullen glance, and stalked off to a barn not far away. He considered asking the cause of their tussle but decided it was not for a stranger to know. Some female quarrel, no doubt.

Searching the pack mule's panniers, Sergeant Mulrooney had found items bound for the ranch and had brought them to the veranda. "Here you are, sir." He grinned at Norah who stood with cup in hand. She reminded him of Irish colleens, she did, with those darling eyes and that mop of red curls.

"Did you get something to eat, Sergeant?" She had seen Shorty go into the cookshack; on days when his arthritis wasn't acting up, he liked to prepare meals.

"We did indeed, miss, thank you." He saluted. "I've sent a man to bring Fullerton in, sir."

The soldier wheeled at his superior's nod and returned to

the unit sprawled under a stand of oaks. The men had quenched their thirst and gobbled down beef sandwiches, and the horses and mules had been watered and now drowsed in the shade.

Norah's delight with her first mail in eight months tickled Carleton. If he were able to visit her now and then, patrolling this area would not be so onerous. After all, the ranch was on a plunder trail that needed constant surveillance—what more logical reason to ride by? Carleton pondered his feelings, vaguely astonished by their strength. Had he been away from women too long—or had love come unbidden in this remote place? The rancher's arrival disturbed the cavalry officer's musings. Carleton had ridden his entire life but realized with chagrin he would never have the natural, easy seat of this cattleman and the younger one who accompanied him. The men shook hands, exchanging names, then Jim and his son hunkered down on their heels to roll smokes while Carleton talked.

"I don't know if you're aware of the situation, sir, but Washington has ordered the Chiricahuas removed to the San Carlos Reservation. Agent John Clum is escorting them there now. Geronimo, Juh, and Nolgee, however, have fled to Mexico with their people. We were on their trail, but they had too much of a head start."

Jim was not surprised. "Knowing them like I do, I can tell you they strangled their dogs so there'd be no barking and killed old and disabled horses that might slow them down." He glanced at Norah, then pressed on. "Sometimes warriors and their women ride off together, abandoning their elderly. Tie them to bushes with their dogs and leave them to die, because they can't keep up on foot."

"How dreadful!" she murmured. Hearing about Geronimo was bad enough. She had never forgotten the terror he inspired in her.

Jim blew a cloud of smoke, disturbed by the news. "Why were they moved? This could cause everybody a passel of trouble. Some might take their vengeance out on us."

"That's why the major ordered me to warn you. So you'd be prepared for any eventuality." Carleton paused, collecting his thoughts. "Is, or was, a Thomas Jeffords Indian agent at the Apache Pass Chiricahua Agency?"

"He was Cochise's friend and responsible in great part for the chief's agreeing to peace in '71. In fact, he took General O. O. Howard into camp to make treaty. What do you mean 'was'?"

"Governor Safford has requested Washington to dismiss Jeffords and close the reservation because Jeffords allowed warriors to hunt in the Dragoon Mountains. Claims there wasn't enough government beef so he let them go after game. Malcontents led by—what's that impossible name?— oh, yes, Pionsenay—went on a rampage, killed two white men, burned houses, stole cattle, and generally raised the devil. Even killed his own two sisters, the savage."

Joel frowned. "Drunk as lords, I reckon. But now they'll all be punished. Ain't fair."

Carleton shrugged condescendingly. "They're all alike, aren't they?"

"I'm no Indian lover, but that's not true," Jim objected. He made a pattern in the dirt with a twig, thinking aloud. "Wouldn't be surprised if Mexico wasn't politicking to get them moved. If we're lucky, the Mexican *federales* might nail Geronimo. They want him so bad they can taste it." He shook the twig at Norah. "We'd better be more careful than ever. That means no more bird-watching out of sight of the ranch, and Rose isn't to gallivant off, either." The men rose as one, sensing that nothing more needed to be said; what had been discussed was enough to fill any man's craw. Jim and his son rode back to the valley, but Carleton lingered to talk to Norah.

"Do come back when you ride this way again." She held out a hand, regretting she had not been more of a hostess.

Enchanted and reluctant to leave, he fumbled for gauntlets and hat, clumsy as a boy, thrilling to her touch. "I'll be back if I have to fight my way through the entire Apache federation," he promised, memorizing every feature of the face upturned to his, drowning in those splendid eyes he'd now see in every sky.

Mulrooney had brought Carleton's horse. It was time to move out. Hearing the lieutenant's vow, he twirled around, ostensibly to check on the men mounting up. The fancy Dan was head over heels!

Cheeks pink with the compliment and the pressure of his fingers, Norah withdrew her hand. "Good luck. Be careful. And please give my best to Dr. Gates."

"I'll be glad to." He donned his hat. "Your pie was wonderful."

"I'll make apple next time. With brown sugar."

"I love apple."

"I'll remember. Good-bye." Norah called to Mulrooney. "Take care of yourself, Sergeant."

He turned. "That I will, miss, Lord bless you." He mounted after Carleton did, and held up an arm. "Forward!"

With the soft thud of hoofs, jingle of bit chains, and creak of leather, they saluted and grinned as they rode by; a few remembered the thin, coughing wraith of the past winter and shouted her name. Norah waved and smiled at the manly veterans who sat cockily in their saddles, hats at a jaunty angle. She had been too ill to watch mounted drill at the fort; this first sight of troopers on patrol in hostile country, therefore, thrilled her with its suggestion of martial valor and battles fought and won.

She sat down to enjoy the mail after they had gone. She had a long letter from Dr. Gates at Fort Guardian with a note from his wife, newly arrived from Delaware; San Francisco, Dodge City, Abilene, and Boston newspapers collected by them from stagecoach passengers; and joy of joys, three books Norah had not read. Elizabeth Gaskell's *The Grey Woman*, Charles Dickens's *Little Dorrit*, and Charles Reade's *The Cloister and the Hearth* had also been gleaned from travel-weary wayfarers.

A packet of letters from St. Louis was tied with string. One from a distant relative advised that her parents' graves had not settled despite an unusually rainy winter; her minister sent a box of Dr. Carhart's Consumptive Powders (which claimed to "Positively Cure Consumption and all other Diseases of the Lung"); and her best friend reported the birth of Christmas Day twins.

Tears blurred her vision. No matter the front she put up, she missed everyone. Terribly! Hugging her treasures, Norah hurried into the bedroom and had a good cry, which made her feel better and relieved her headache. She looked at the bed with longing, for her body felt as if it had been pounded with hammers. It was almost suppertime, though, and Jim would be hungry. Probably Rose, too; she was still growing. She and the girl would never be friends, Norah knew that now; for whatever reason—jealousy, fear, misunderstanding—they had become enemies. She shuddered. Or was she overwrought? That had to be the reason for the feeling that tragedy crouched in the future like a vulture waiting for a kill.

10.

Chan Lee was lost—and afraid.

He had walked almost three hundred miles without serious mishap, but now he was adrift in an ocean of grass, a solitary wanderer in an empty landscape. Sitting down to pull off his boots, Chan Lee examined sore and blistered feet and wished for thick-soled felt slippers in his pack. To avoid undue attention, he had worn white men's clothes for this odyssey, including a slouch hat beneath which his plaited queue was coiled. Apaches found Chinese easy to scalp, because their hair was shaved close to the crown—or so they said.

He wriggled his toes, massaged his arches, and pulled the boots back on. What should he do? Sleep here? Did it matter? As far as Chan Lee could see in any direction, there was nothing but grass, grass, grass. Mountains, of course, chunks of amethyst and jade thrown upon the earth. But where was the ranch to which he had been sent? Awe shriveled his stomach, for he was small and the American countryside enormous. He had traveled through Phoenix, stunned by the valley's furnace heat, on south to Tucson and then to Tubac, where he found kindness, rest, and directions as well as warnings of death at the hands of Apaches who had long controlled southern Arizona Territory.

Should he have returned to Tucson to work in a grocery, laundry, or restaurant? No, he had not left his ancestral village, never to see his family again, only to turn tail and run. He trudged to San Francisco from Mazatlán, Mexico, where he and fellow Chinese had disembarked, had tamped dynamite for the Central Pacific Railroad, swung a pick in Wickenburg mines, and washed laundry in the Colorado River at Yuma. Before settling down, he wanted to see what was on the other side of the hill, if the grass—oh, the irony of it!—was greener there. Americans were not the only ones with adventure in their souls. At this particular moment, however, all he wished for in life was a place to rest and work in peace.

Shouting erupted behind him, startling in the sunny silence. Chan Lee panicked. Grabbing his pack, he ran, stepped in a prairie-dog hole, and fell with a twisted ankle. Big men on big horses surrounded him within seconds, faces shadowed by wide-brimmed hats. Chan Lee cringed involuntarily and despised himself for doing so, despised them for inspiring such fright. He labored to his feet, biting his lip in pain.

"I'll be goddamned if it ain't a Chink!" The speaker was

heavy and muscular with pale green eyes, silver sideburns, and large predatory teeth. "Say, you speakee English? What you doee on my land?"

Chan Lee fumbled in his pocket and gave the man a paper; he understood English but spoke it seldom. He glanced furtively at the others. Like this one with tiger's eyes, they had broad shoulders, long strong legs, large hands. He was a cricket at the feet of elephants.

"This here's a note from a waddy named Sam. Says this Chink's an honest man and a fine cook and we should pass him along to the Double Bar F."

One of the West's early cattle kings, Eli Martin was not unkind, but gazing down at the slight yellow stranger, he felt a twinge of contempt and dislike. The foreigner was not welcome on Eli's hard-won, bloodstained land. He gave the note back and pointed. "You go that way."

He pointed to infinity, as far as Chan Lee was concerned, but the Chinese bowed in thanks. He would ask for nothing but find the way himself somehow. As he bowed, he froze. Disturbed by the horses' hoofs, a rattlesnake had crawled between his feet and now poised there with black forked tongue flicking in and out. Chan Lee gasped, and the serpent shook its tail, making a sound like dry leaves that turned his blood cold. His knees began to tremble.

"Stand still, you savvy? Still like Buddha statue." A rider with his arm in a sling drew his gun, aimed, and fired.

Staring at the writhing body, Chan Lee saw that the bullet had blown the rattlesnake's head off, missing his feet by inches. He broke into a cold sweat, fighting with great difficulty the urge to relieve himself.

"Since when have you handled a shooting iron with either hand?" Eli wanted to know.

Mason Fletcher grinned. "Lots of things you don't know about me, amigo."

They laughed as people will who know each other's past. Eli motioned to his cowboys, who reined their mounts toward the Fullerton ranch and spurred them into motion.

"Wait a minute. We can't leave him here," Mason objected. "Poor bastard's hurt his ankle, and I'll bet a dollar to a doughnut he's lost. After all, we're going to the same place. You lost, Chan Lee?"

Chan Lee tried to retain his dignity, badly damaged by the snake incident, his aching ankle, and the possibility of being abandoned. "Yes," he said in a shaky voice.

"Climb aboard." Mason removed a boot from the stirrup.

"Let him ride with Chico back there," Eli suggested, motioning to the Apache who wore a bandage beneath his headband.

Mason chuckled. "*I* couldn't ride with him today. He's got a hangover big enough for six hombres." Seeing the Chinese was unable to reach the stirrup, he seized the upraised hand and lifted Chan Lee off the ground and onto the horse's back behind the saddle.

"Thank you," the man whispered, weak with fatigue and his ordeal. "Thank you." Cautiously, he took hold of Mason's belt. "Okay, kind sir?"

The man swiveled his head to stare into his passenger's eyes, and Chan Lee bowed his head in respect. Eyes like purest amber that held no evil. A good man. "Sure, it's okay, kid. You'll fall off otherwise." Mason grunted and mumbled to no one in particular, "Shoot, he can't be more than nineteen."

Eli had ridden on and now yelled impatiently, "Come on! Jim's always got some Kentucky bourbon kickin' around. Besides, I want to meet this pretty little redhead you told me about."

Mason spurred the Appaloosa into a slow trot. He sure hoped that pretty little redhead was still alive.

It was the custom to call out when approaching a ranch so as not to spook its occupants; those who failed to advertise their presence occasionally met with a load of buckshot from someone who fired first and asked questions later.

Norah heard the whoop of the incoming party and hoped it wasn't Carleton. Not on washday! She looked askance at her faded gray calico and soiled apron. Her hair, worn in a confining bun for work at the outside fire, flew in every direction. For pity's sake, she wasn't dressed for company.

Because Norah's mind was still partially that of a city dweller, it had not dawned on her until too late that the ranch was running out of soap. In St. Louis she bought it in a store; here she had to spend the entire morning making a supply. First, she had to make lye water by boiling hardwood ashes in water, skimming away scum that formed, letting it stand to form sediment. This was then boiled with grease and stored in a dry place to set; the latter step kept the soap from dissolving too quickly in laundry water.

The day had been most irritating so far. Sourdough stored in a tin container had turned green. The last of Aunt May's jam had disappeared at breakfast; this meant berry gathering under armed guard before she could put up more. Mending waited—a veritable mountain. She had forgotten to add sugar to the apple pies, and to top everything off, her time of month came during the night. Norah stirred the steaming clothing with a stick and sighed with resignation. If it was Carleton, he'd just have to remember how nice she had looked last year in her apple-green cotton.

Jim emerged from the barn, where he was treating his best cutting horse for a tendon sprain. He shook hands with the visitors and directed Eli's men to their friends working out in the valley. Chan Lee slid gratefully to the ground and waited for the cessation of greetings, boisterous and typically American, so noisy and discourteous beside those of his race. Some distance away he saw a woman agitating her wash in a large iron kettle that squatted over a fire.

"How goes it, Jim?" Eli clapped his neighbor's shoulder. He respected him and coveted his property, principally for its artesian wells. "Had any trouble with cherry-cows lately?"

"No, those renegades step lightly around here." Jim shook Mason's hand. "Glad to see you again, Marshal. Norah will be, too."

"She's—all right?"

"More than all right. See her over there? Introduce her to Eli while I show Chan Lee the cookshack and where he sleeps." Jim beckoned to the Chinese leaning against the barn, who was plainly ill and on his last legs. "You better get off that foot. Come on. Cook's here, Norah!" he called, and grinned at her mime of exaggerated relief.

Chan Lee followed his new employer, mind fixed on a pot of hot tea. Put him in a shack. Put him in a corner. But please, Kuan Yin, goddess of mercy, let him have that tea before he fainted.

Two men left Jim and strode toward Norah. She looked, then looked again. *Mason. Mason Fletcher!* Her pulse raced, and there in the sunlight she could feel his arms around her that night when the dread of dying had banished sleep—his mouth upon her hair, their hearts beating as one—

"Norah! I'd never have recognized you!" Mason seized her moist, chapped hand and squeezed it like a boy. "I can't tell you how glad I am to see you." How many times I've dreamed of you.

"Why, you've been hurt," she said in a low tone, nodding at his arm.

"It's nothing." Lines of pain on his face belied the words.

The world faded away and they stood entranced, seeing what they had loved months ago, tasting with their eyes new and wonderful aspects. A missing piece of Norah's life fell into place. Mason's face glowed. Subtle electricity thrilled through them, and Norah turned molten and quivery inside. She glanced at Eli and smiled, including him in her joy.

"Howdy, ma'am," he said, touching his hat brim. "My *friend* here—guess the cat's got his tongue. I'm Eli Martin, your neighbor. Pleasure, ma'am." The rancher's green eyes smoldered in the tanned and powerful visage of a man accustomed to having his own way.

"I brought you something." Mason walked back to his horse and unbuckled a saddlebag.

"He still has Storm Cloud. He was the first horse I got acquainted with," she explained to fill the lull.

Eli lighted a cigar. "That's a good pony. Duns, buckskins, and grullas are best for here, though. They can take this country 'cause they're native born. I've got a buckskin with black points who'll do anything you want and then tie a bow on it."

As Mason approached with a package, Norah suggested Mrs. Martin ride over one day. "I'm not much of a horsewoman yet."

He rolled the cigar between thumb and blunt forefinger, openly appraising her rich beauty, which was emphasized rather than diminished by dishevelment. "Ain't no Mrs. Martin. Yet."

"Here. Hope you like them." Mason gave her the package.

"Thank you!" She dried her palms on the apron, stepped away from the fire, and untied the string. A *Godey's Lady's Book,* jet earrings, and a box of rose-scented soap.

Soap! Norah started to laugh. "I've slaved all morning making soap, and here you pop out of nowhere with more!"

Mason's face fell. He had bought the gifts in Washington, hoping against hope Norah was alive. Now she scoffed at the expensive presents he had carted around for weeks. Eli chuckled at his friend's discomfiture.

"Oh, Mason, I'm sorry.. I love it! I love everything! It was so thoughtful." Norah put the gifts down, dashed a bucket of water on the fire, and then took them up again. "I'm going to use the soap this minute." She fled toward the house, hair falling out of its bun, calling over her shoulder, "You're staying for supper!"

Eli sighed. "Here's one old boy who'd like to court that filly."

Mason grew cold and distant. He was uncomfortably aware of the shortage of women out West, of his own gypsy existence, and of Eli's geographic advantage and material wealth. "All's fair in love and war, I guess," he said stiffly.

Eli peered into the other man's eyes, hard and dangerous as his own. "Ah, goddamnit, I ain't horning in. Let's go get that bourbon. Jim ought to be through with the Chink by now." Mason grinned sheepishly, and Eli pretended to punch him in the ribs to smooth over the awkward moment.

They went to find Jim, who was blissfully unaware of how their destinies were joined to Norah's.

Once supper was over, Mason and Norah left the house. The two ranchers raised eyebrows at their departure but continued the discussion of government stupidity, rain, horses, silver mining south of the Dragoons, blooded Durham bulls from Illinois that Henry Hooker was breeding to longhorn cows. They smoked and drank, comfortable together despite Eli's fortune and Jim's much more modest means. It was a tenet of the West that any man was as good as the next had he but a dollar in his pocket.

Outside in the moonlight, the couple strolled back and forth, content not to speak. The swish of skirts and petticoats, her fragrant nearness, tender shadows between her breasts—these were at once alluring and alarming to Mason. He had unintentionally gotten attached to her last year, and seeing her again had jolted him like a bucking bronc.

"How did you get hurt?" Norah settled on a log with its top side planed flat for a seat. She was a study in black and silver, light flashing on the earrings' facets when her head moved.

Mason joined her, pleased with the private spot near the blacksmith shop. "To make it short, I was chasing a murderer. I followed him across the Red River into the Indian Nations, and we tangled north of the Canadian." Unconsciously, he caressed the shattered arm hanging helplessly in its cradle. The missionary doctor at the

Seminole Agency said he had come within a hairbreadth of losing the use of that arm.

"Did you kill him?"

He glanced at her sharply. Did she enjoy talk of death? A few women did. Or had she been so close to it in her struggle for life it seemed a familiar presence? "Yes. He tried to ambush me, but it didn't work. I wanted to take him back for trial in Texas, but he preferred to shoot it out."

"You don't like to kill, do you?" She watched the bats swooping, dipping and darting like thoughts in a tired mind.

He pondered the answer. It was, in an odd way, a very feminine question. Women had no way of understanding a man's feelings about a gun. It could be his best friend in a pinch. It slew poisonous snakes and game to eat; dispatched injured animals; protected those he loved; signaled for assistance; and, yes, on occasion killed a man. That was when the gun became a deadly enemy, when you had another human being in your sights and for an instant, you were God. In a strange, inexplicable way your weapon was an extension of masculinity. Disciplined men leashed their primitive instinct, however, controlled the violence burning like lava below civilization's veneer. They leaned on guns for succor but holstered them otherwise. He had blood on his hands. It was part of his job. But he had never experienced any satisfaction at killing, abhorring it instead.

"No, Norah, I don't. No decent man does. Sometimes it's necessary, though."

She leaned against his shoulder and tapped her heart. "I knew you didn't. Right here."

For Mason, her nearness blocked out the past with its gunsmoke and outlaws. He found her mouth waiting inches away and sought the parted lips, kissing her gently. Norah closed her eyes, choked with excitement. Since Jim had kissed and held her, she had been prey to seductive fantasies about Mason. Her body had responded to them in ways that shocked yet titillated her there in the darkened bedroom.

"Norah, darling," Mason whispered, pulling her close with his good arm, passion heating him.

Their mouths came together again, and lightning lanced through her groin, surprising her so she made a sound in her throat and thrust her tongue into his mouth. His fingers touched the underside of a breast, and as in the dreams she longed to open her clothing to him, to lie naked and hungry before his desire.

He broke away, aroused and breathing hard. "You're like a forest fire!"

"I—I'm sorry. That was bold of me. Don't know what came over me."

Mason laughed softly. "I do. You've grown up since I saw you last. I'm the one who should apologize." He kissed the tip of her nose. A muffled giggle interrupted his words, and Baron, dozing behind Norah, growled and leaped to his feet. "Was that a girl I heard? I didn't know there were any women here!"

"That was Rose, Jim's adopted daughter," Norah replied in an annoyed tone. "Baron, stay here." That minx, spoiling such a romantic moment. Now they were even for the time in the barn.

Mason glanced about. He was irritated, too, but mostly with himself for not realizing someone had crept so near. A rueful expression crossed his face. How could a man think of anything else with this enchantress in his arms?

The dog came to sit in front of them, great shoulders rolling like a bear's as he stepped around the log. He rested his head on Norah's knee. "Oh, that weighs a ton," she objected as she always did. Kneading behind his ears, she chuckled at his grunts of pleasure.

"He's a fine animal." Mason reached out to contribute a scratch or two. "Not very friendly though. Still, that makes a better watchdog."

Baron rested his grave gaze first on Norah's face, then on Mason's. He made a decision and transferred his head to the man's knees.

"That's a real compliment!" Norah exclaimed.

"You're right. It does weigh a ton." Honored by the dog's acceptance, Mason put his nose close to Baron's and muttered unintelligible endearments that inspired furious tail-wagging. Mason loved dogs but had not had one since before the war; his life left no room for a pet.

"I take him bird-watching with me," Norah said, rising and dusting off her skirts.

Following suit, Mason sucked in a breath of pain when his arm bumped hers. "You don't go far from the ranch, do you? There might be—"

"Yes, I know. There might be Indians. I'm sick of hearing about them."

They headed for the ranch house at a snail's pace, arms about each other's waist. "You and everybody else in Arizona Territory. But Norah, remember, this was their land. They fought each other, then the Spaniards, then Mexicans, then us. Most of them are now on reservations, many of them far from home. Surely you must know how it feels, being cast into a hostile place through no fault of your own?"

She stopped. "I hadn't thought of it that way. I was lucky, wasn't I? I've worked from dawn to dusk since I've felt better, but I've been happy. The ranch is like a friend to me, and Jim—" Norah resumed walking.

"—is more than a friend." Mason finished her sentence morosely. Not just Eli, but Fullerton, too, was close where he could court her. Near the barn they heard horses snorting and blowing, men cussing them casually. "How much more?" he prodded. She was marrying age, past it, really, held in check by illness. The ranchers would be utter fools not to try to win her.

"He asked me to marry him."

"And?"

"I refused. He's a dear, but he's just like my uncle." *You are the one I love.*

Eli hailed them when they came into sight. "Got your

horse saddled. If you're comin' with us, get a move on. Ain't got all night." He had planned to spend the evening feasting his eyes on the redhead and was piqued with Mason for monopolizing her company.

"You'll come again?" Norah asked once Mason mounted Storm Cloud. She tried to make it sound as if the invitation included them all.

The riders loomed above her, silhouetted against a starry sky, faces dim under hats and sombreros.

How she loved it here, among men like these! As a woman, she was not part of their world, but this moment with them finalized her resolve not to leave the Arizona Territory. *Mariposa.* The name galloped into her mind. Her own ranch. Norah Carlisle's Mariposa—hers and her husband's where she and Mason would ride to the top of a hill each morning to inspect their domain.

The cowboys tipped their hats, said thanks and farewell before drifting into the night. Eli reined in beside her. "Nice meetin' you, miss. Keep your powder dry, Jim."

"You, too, Eli. And don't forget about those chickens."

Mason chuckled. "I'll bring them over next week and ride shotgun."

They all laughed and said good night, and the men trotted away, stirrup to stirrup, Eli's cigar tip a firefly bobbing up and down.

Jim slid an arm around Norah, whisky on his breath and a little loving on his mind. He didn't stand much of a chance with the Marshal around; she'd made that clear, but it didn't hurt to try. "Want to take a walk in the moonlight?"

She yawned and slipped away. "Not tonight, Jim. I have to clean up the kitchen before I hit the hay."

He lounged against a hitching rail after she'd gone in, smoking and thinking. She was so young and desirable, who did he think he was trying to compete with Fletcher and Beatty? It wasn't as if he were madly in love, though he certainly loved her. Ten years from now—were they married—he'd be an old man and she in her prime. Maybe

just being friends was the ticket. Women needed special
friends as much as, or maybe more than, a lover. Being near,
guiding, helping—that was love, too. Jim ground the stub
of his cigarette underfoot and saluted the house. Good
night, dear Norah. Adios, my youth.

11.

The red-faced warbler jerked his tail sideways, peered at the
figure below, and resumed a liquid song that slurred upward
on the final note. His glowing red face and breast contrasted
sharply with black crown, white nape, breast, belly, and
flanks, a pearl-gray mantle, and darker gray and white wing
bars.

Back braced against a pine, Norah studied the bird with
field glasses borrowed from Jim. She was playing hookey,
dangerous hookey, for she had traveled far from the ranch
on foot with only Baron for company. Summer rains had
turned sun-bronzed grasses to emerald green, stupendous
cloud castles formed overhead, and restlessness flooded her.
She wanted to do something different. There were plenty of
chores—giving the house a fresh coat of whitewash inside
and out, for instance—but Norah had rebelled. Jim and
several cowboys were on a short drive, delivering cattle to
Fort Guardian. Men, always able to be on the move. She
had wanted to go also, but as yet her horsemanship left too
much to be desired.

Norah was not afraid to be here in the canyon. Geronimo
and his band were supposedly raiding northern Mexico and
southern New Mexico Territory, which was a long way off.
She'd be back on the ranch by early afternoon with no one

the wiser; the creek she'd followed in led right out to the valley again, so it was impossible to get lost. The warbler flew away, and Norah turned the glasses on large pigeons with yellow bills and iridescent shoulders. She had hoped to see the Rainbow Prince again, but perhaps that was a once-in-a-lifetime privilege. The day she saw him was the day she came to the realization that she loved Mason, her own special prince.

"It's a blue-throated hummingbird!" Baron glanced up from digging. Finding he had not been spoken to, the dog returned to excavation, for his nose assured him of a treasure buried there. Norah ducked involuntarily and backed away, marveling at the bird's audaciousness. It buzzed her again in defense of its minute nest that clung to a fern nearby.

A book about birds of this area—had one ever been compiled? Surely not, for would it have been worth an ornithologist's life to roam Apache haunts? Why not write it herself? Ridiculous! Women didn't write books, especially without scientific credentials. But she was here, and the scientists were not. Her list of descriptions—she had no way of knowing birds' names—already totaled sixty-two. Norah's gaze wandered up the mountainside where there were trees, flowers, and birds she hadn't seen yet. A book! Nonsensical to entertain such a notion, yet the challenge enticed her.

Baron trotted past with a dirt-covered bone in his jaws. How the mountain lion would growl with fury when he found his cache raided! Norah thought with a shiver of the scream that had awakened her on the way to the ranch last year.

Having grown uneasy, Norah quit the canyon more swiftly than she had entered, and soon sighted valley and ranch. Not far away, the riders were returning from the drive with Old Sugar, the Judas longhorn, in the lead, while ahead of them a cavalry troop cantered, small figures in sky-blue pants and dark-blue blouses. Carleton. She smiled.

Suddenly a loud rustling in the bushes, high, piping calls, and low grunts filled the air. Norah grabbed Baron's collar, unsure whether to flee or stand her ground. The mastiff had his own problem: he could hold the bone or drop it in order to bark. It was solved when at least a hundred coatis of various ages burst into view. Baron released his prize and roared. The droll rusty-brown animals resembled raccoons but had long upturned snouts and vertically held tails ringed from rump to tip. They screeched to a halt at the sight of the woman and dog, then scattered in a storm of protest.

"Norah! Where are you? *Norah!*" She heard more crashing in the brush, hoofs ringing on creek bedrock where the stream had dried up. Jim and the cowboy John Smith pulled up a few feet away. "We heard the dog. Are you all right? What are you doing here, anyway? Kee-rist! Didn't I make a special point of your not being out of sight of the ranch? Boy, I wish you wouldn't go off half-cocked like this." Jim stopped for breath.

"But you should have seen the—"

He gestured with scorn at the field glasses and notebook. "Bird-watching again, I suppose. What you find so dog-gone interesting about that gets me. Let me tell you, young woman, you're lucky some 'Pache brave wasn't bird-watching with an eye for that red hair! Now get yourself up here behind me and let's go home. I'm tired and hungry."

His eyes blazed with anger, and Norah dared not refuse. Putting a toe in his stirrup, she swung up behind, sitting with both feet on one side. The cowboy followed without a word, seeming to mock her obedience with his silence. Norah had not liked him when she met him, and she did not like him now, with his cold gray eyes and thin lips. "John Smith" indeed. His picture was on a wanted poster somewhere, Norah felt sure of that, but ranchers hired men without asking about their past. As long as a man knew cows and minded his business, no other information was necessary. Holding onto Jim's waist, Norah discovered he had a little paunch starting. Wrinkles cut deep into the back of his neck, and white hair sprouted there. "What did you say?"

"Ought to be spanked. Spoiled, that's the trouble."

Norah moved impatiently. "Oh, Jim, for heaven's sake, have a heart. I get sick of housework every blamed minute. There aren't any Indians in here, you said so."

"How do we know?" he shot back. "They camouflage themselves like part of the landscape. Walk past a greasewood bush, and there they are, buried next to it." The rancher swore to himself. He had never spoken to her like that, or cursed before her either; deeply relieved to find her safe, however, he had let his tongue and temper run away with him. Likely nobody was up the canyon, but he didn't want to take chances on anything happening to her. Not to his Norah.

She was thinking about her final decision not to marry Jim, and about her enormous gratitude for his taking her in. Impulsively, she hugged him and he snorted with surprise and pleasure, caught unaware. "That's because you're such a nice guy," she said in his ear.

He stopped to let her slide down in front of the house, where Carleton waited, wavy dark blond hair disheveled in the breeze. "Now, *please* do what I tell you until we're sure it's safe."

"You're liable to wind up in some filthy ranchería on your knees grinding corn on a stone metate." Carleton was alarmed to find that she had deliberately put herself in danger.

Jim dismounted, and said as he led his mount away, "Absolutely right, Lieutenant. Maybe you can put some sense in her head."

"Truly, my dear, you mustn't go off like that. I—I couldn't bear to lose you. Nor could your other friends," Carleton hastened to add, taking notebooks and canteen from her hands.

They sat on the veranda and she showed him her descriptions and drawings, shyly confiding her ambition to write a book. He blinked, impressed with what he saw, and offered to send the manuscript to a museum curator in Philadelphia.

"You'd do that for me?" Norah visualized the book printed, bound, and with her name on the cover.

"These might help." Carleton gave her a heavy package.

She smiled, saying, "What now?" He brought a present each time he came by, even if he had only enough time to water his horse and ride on. "Oh, these are *just* what I wanted! But they're much too expensive! I can't accept them. A hanky or a book or a lace collar—I'm delighted to have those, but *these*—" Norah put the streamlined binoculars to her eyes, adjusted the focus, and swept the ranch, picking up minute detail. "Wonderful!"

He edged closer and tucked a strand of hair into her chignon. "If they give you pleasure, I want you to take them and forget the cost. The merchant in Tucson assured me they were perfect for bird-watching." He studied the line of her throat, her strong yet feminine jawbone curving up to the ear. Carleton was unable to resist kissing the lobe, whispering, "I love you."

She continued to hold the glasses in one hand, concentrating on a hawk that circled lazily over the chicken coop, but held out the other. "Now, Carleton," she admonished affectionately. His ardor increased with each visit, and glorying in her new-found power to attract men, Norah made no effort to dampen it.

He seized the proffered hand, clasped it between his own, and put it to his lips. It smelled of pencil, dog, leaves, and rose water. It was that of a woman who had much child in her yet; it was the most precious object he had ever held. She laid the glasses in her lap and a hand on his forearm. His heart leaped like a trout hooked and fighting to get away. Unlike the fish, Carleton wanted never to escape.

After sweeping the earthen floor, Rose sat down to put in a hem. She adored vivid colors, intense hues of purple, orange, cardinal-red, sunflower-yellow, lime-green. This dress was pale pink with cinnamon-brown flowers, and she detested it. "I don't like this," Rose grumbled, deliberately taking big, ugly stitches.

"I think it's pretty," Norah countered. "And pink is lovely with your skin." She spoke with care, for Rose had been cooperative lately, showing no more enthusiasm for work than ever but at least helping when asked. That Rose's turnabout coincided with the appearance of romance in Norah's life had not dawned on Norah. She attributed the change to her efforts to reach the girl. "See? I have a ribbon for your hair that's an exact match." Norah set about looping a bow.

"What are you dressing me up for? Who's going to see me?" Rose's face tightened and she ceased to sew.

"There'll be beaus."

"Oh? Where will they come from? The reservation?" Rose leaped to her feet with a catlike movement. "I am Apache, but I am *mansa*. Tame. No warrior wants me. And white people hate all Apache. So who will marry me?" Her eyes flashed with an old anger and despair. "I wish I were dead! I wish he had thrown me into the river to drown with the rest of my family!"

"What did you say?" came Jim's whisper. He was in the doorway with a small table Norah had asked him to make.

Rose rushed to him, so close her breath was warm on his lips. "I said I wish you had thrown me—"

"Honey, I couldn't have done that!" Memory flashed back to the raging torrent, the butterball baby with wet black lashes and a rosebud mouth.

"I'd have been better off. You don't love me." They both knew what she meant.

His face turned red. Thank God, Norah had gone into the bedroom and closed the door. "Watch what you say in front of her."

"She knows."

"You *told* her, for Christ's sake?"

A whoop outside distracted Jim. Glancing out the door, he saw Mason leading a mule with two crates of chickens tied to it. "Norah, your chickens are here."

Norah hurried past the unhappy pair without looking at them, calling, "Mason! You really did bring them! Oh, how lovely! Now we can have eggs for breakfast. What a treat!"

Mason grinned, teeth gleaming in the lean, brown face. "Listen to them! They've scolded me every inch of the way."

Jim slammed the door. "Listen, Rose, this can't go on. You've got to get hold of yourself, girl."

She wound her long hair around one wrist. "I don't care. I can't help it."

"It's just not right. I'm old enough to be your father. I *am* your father!"

She sank to the floor, put her arms around his knees, her head on his thigh. "I'm going crazy, don't you understand? I want you to love me—*make* love to me." Tears trickled down to moisten her ripe mouth. "Please. Take me."

Jim stared at her. His monkish existence, not unusual among widowed or bachelor pioneers living far from the towns, left him raw to the quick, open as a fresh wound to the sex Rose offered. His manhood hardened, and alert to the change, Rose pressed a cheek to it. She pulled herself up by clinging to pants, belt, and shirt so her body never left his.

"Kiss me," she whispered, pressing against him so he could not help but thrust below her pubic mound.

Jim shook his head, brain spinning with desire. It had been months since his wife died, since he had entered a woman. Years since he had pierced a virgin.

"We—are—not—related. Remember that. *We are not related.*" Rose kissed him, holding his face between her hands.

When their lips finally parted, he said huskily, "I asked her to marry me."

"But she does not love you as I do." She cannot have you.

"I could make her love me as a wife and the mother of my sons."

"No, James, you are mine. And I have wanted you so long. Come."

Rose led him, finally unprotesting, into her room where she closed the door and began undressing him. "You are so handsome," she crooned, running her hands across his chest and down to his loins, where he waited for her. There was no more conversation then, only the rustle of clothing and the sounds of love.

"Put them in the barn, Chan Lee, so they can cool off and calm down. Give them plenty of water, too. We'll get them into the new coop as soon as Shorty's through making it." The Chinese nodded and carried the crates into the redolent gloom.

"Have you eaten, Mason? Chan Lee can fix you something."

"No, thanks, I'm not hungry. But how about a ride? It's a nice day."

Norah looked toward the house and wondered how Jim was handling Rose. Surely, he'd have no objection to her riding with Mason. A girl could not ask for a better guardian, and Chico would keep an eye out for trouble. "All right. I can always use the practice. Just for an hour, though."

He pulled a gold watch from a vest pocket and consulted it. "I'll count every minute and have you back right on time, Cinderella."

He pointed at peaks soaring thousands of feet above them as they rode through the valley. "Been up there?"

"Not yet." She reined the horse left in order to avoid a burrowing owl that staunchly guarded his tunnel entrance. "I'm not a good enough rider yet. And I still get tired so fast."

"Small wonder, all the work you do, a little thing like you. You were at death's door only months ago. You do too much. Can't you move to town, live like a lady should?"

"How would I earn a living? The only thing I can do is make hats, and that means I'd have to be in a big city in order to develop a clientele." She motioned to the grasslands. "Besides, I don't think I can live in a city again. I'd miss all this space. This wonderful light. Being able to see for fifty miles."

He squinted into the distance, thinking of Eastern cities, always cold or hot, humid and crowded. "I'm with you. This is God's country."

Norah tried to get more comfortable in the sidesaddle. "If I used a man's saddle, I think I'd get the hang of this better. You know, get the feel of the horse under me. This horn chafes my leg."

Mason reined the Appaloosa to a halt and glanced about. They were alone except for Chico. "You mean that?"

Norah's eyes shone with mischief. "Yep."

He dismounted. "Come on, then." She jumped down from Lovey's back and dropped the reins of the pony, trained to be ground-tied.

"He's too tall!" she said, gauging the height of Storm Cloud's stirrup. "I need a rock to stand on."

"I'll help you. Put your foot in the stirrup—whoa, boy— and lean on my shoulder. No, the other one. Wish I could lift you." He still wore the sling and was concerned his arm had suffered more damage than had originally been diagnosed.

"Okay, there you go. Watch it. *Watch it!*" Norah grabbed for the saddle horn but missed it, her weight falling onto him, her boot slipping out of the iron stirrup. They fell backward into the cushiony grass, laughing like children. "You'll never make a cowgirl that way!"

"He moved. On purpose!"

"She can't talk about my horse that way, can she, S.C.?" The horse lowered, then raised, his eyelashes almost flirtatiously, whinnied, and showed long, yellow teeth.

Norah giggled. "You males do stick together."

Mason settled into the fragrant green, hat tipped over his nose. "I love to hear you laugh. When we met, you were so serious. Of course, you had every reason to be. Wherever I was after that, I used to think about you and hope you were alive."

She lay back beside him, pondering cloud banks moving in stately procession. "There's a sheep and a witch's hat. And a rabbit. And the head of a pelican. See its beak?" Norah turned on her side and shoved his hat up. "Look!"

"You have the most marvelous eyes," he murmured. "Did you know there are little sparkly glints in them?"

"Yours are marvelous too."

He put his uninjured arm around her shoulders, and she snuggled up to him. Her hair tickled his chin, and she smelled of his gift soap, crushed grass, and indefinable female fragrances that made him a trifle dizzy. They sighed at the same time, content and at ease, aware in mysterious ways they could not have explained that they belonged together. Before she dozed off, Norah listened to his watch ticking against the counterpoint of his heartbeat. She had once believed danger impossible, and death unthinkable in the shelter of his arms. There was no reason to change her mind.

Mason let her sleep, feeling tender and protective, soaking up the warm softness of her. When she awoke, he would show her the ancient cliff dwelling he and Chico had discovered not long ago. The Apache had been surprised to find it, even though his ancestors had lived in the mountains since the coming of White Painted Woman, Mother of all people. It was not literally a cliff dwelling like those the Pueblo tribes had built much farther to the north. This would more likely be called a cliff refuge. High, dry, skillfully constructed, it had perhaps been a retreat for the sick or diseased, for those seeking dreams and their meanings, for those exorcising personal demons, for the newly married. From the stone shelter nestled beneath a rock overhang, you could see the many ranges that marched down into Mexico and dissolved one by one into the horizon's deepening azure.

He kissed the top of her head. Extraordinary girl. Norah had conquered death, coped with a strange and difficult environment, and come to terms with herself. She possessed admirable qualities: courage, determination, intelligence, a sense of humor, compassion, and a talent for homemaking. Everything a man could want and then some. Mason bit the inside of his upper lip. He knew what was happening. *But, damn it, love had no place in his life now!* A U.S. Marshal did not discard his position lightly, nor did the job make for long engagements or happy marriages. Wait a minute. That good-looking cavalry officer buzzed around her like a bee in a sugar bowl. Maybe she was more interested in him.

"Goodness!" Norah sat up and smoothed her hair back. "You shouldn't have let me sleep so long!"

"It's only been fifteen or twenty minutes." Mason let her go.

"Really? I feel as if I'd slept for hours. I'd better get home now."

"I wanted to show you something."

"Hush. You're a Pied Piper as it is." Norah put fingertips to his mouth. He kissed them, and she flushed to recall their other kisses and his caresses. "I have lots to do yet today." Norah scrambled to her feet and straightened her skirts. Someday she'd wear pants, they looked so comfortable. Retrieving Lovey's reins, she reached up to rub Storm Cloud under his forelock. "We'll try that again sometime, big fellow."

When Mason told her about the cliff house and how to get there, she answered with enthusiasm, "That sounds interesting! Maybe we can go there next time." If there was a next time. She hated to think of his going, it made her heart ache. She wanted his arm to mend so he'd not be in pain, but he'd be leaving when the wound healed. "How's the arm?"

"I'm taking it out of the sling tomorrow to try some exercise. I'm sick of having only one wing."

Riding back to the Double Bar F, close enough to reach out and touch each other, they chatted about whatever came to mind. Norah had never felt so well nor Mason so young and carefree. Their infectious laughter and joie de vivre affected Chico, too, so he spoke more kindly to his unkempt pony.

"Is Eli Martin an old friend? Is that why you're convalescing at his place?" She had not liked the man, thinking him a touch coarse in his inspection of her. If Mason liked him, though, she might have missed something. It was difficult for a woman to understand male relationships. She had been amused to learn that some horses, much like men, ran in pairs for years, while others changed their companions often.

"I met Eli during the war. We were full of the devil then, he, Eddie Bertram, and I. What times we had! He saved my life at Chickamauga and I returned the favor at Chancellorsville. When the war ended, we rode back to California together. His father had made a fortune in real estate between 'forty-nine and 'fifty-five, but Eli didn't like being indoors and fooling with papers. He took his inheritance early and got into the cattle business. Turned out he had the same Midas touch his father did. You ought to see his house. It's palatial."

"Would you think badly of me if I said I wasn't sure I liked him?"

Mason chuckled. "Oh, Eli's all right. You have to get used to him. He's just a bull in a china shop when it comes to women."

They approached the hitching rail, where they saw Emedio, Chan Lee, and Shorty—an unlikely trio, Norah decided—gaping through the corral fence. Dismounting, she and Mason joined them to find that they were watching a fight between Joel and Jim. The last time she had seen Joel in the corral he had been breaking the estray, Charlie's

Britches, and blood had been trickling from his mouth. This time blood was flowing from his nose, staining his entire shirtfront, as he and his father traded blows so brutal the spectators heard teeth crunch.

Norah put a hand on the gate, but the Mexican vaquero held it shut. "No, señorita, you can do nothing. When men fight over a woman—" He shrugged expressively.

"Come on, I'll take you up to the house. He'll unsaddle for you," Mason said.

"Of a certainty, señorita," the vaquero assured them, taking Lovey's reins.

"No, wait, I—" She winced as Jim took a blow to the chin that sent him onto one knee. This must have been building up for weeks. Would they get Rose out of their systems? Joel waited, feinting with big fists. Jim staggered to his feet and held up both hands with the palms out, speaking softly so no one heard his surrender. When the men walked out of the corral, the rancher glanced sheepishly at his audience before plunging his head into the watering trough. He held it there a moment and came up dripping, a wet bandana pressed to his battered lips.

"Anything we can do?" Mason asked.

Jim shook his head, clearly preferring to be left alone. Norah took Mason's arm. "I'll fix some coffee." She'd better get the liniment out, too; Jim would be stiff by nightfall.

Going into the house alone, Norah saw blood on the girl's bed linen and hastily pulled the door shut. Joel must have come for Rose and found her in bed with his father, glossy with voluptuousness and fulfillment. Norah's hand tightened on the knob. What was it like to have a man inside you, a man you wanted? Strange tremors played between her thighs, and she walked briskly out of the house, away from the place of deflowering and desire.

"She in there?" Mason was picking burrs out of the mastiff's coat.

"No sign of her. Wonder where she is?" Norah was

annoyed to hear her voice shake at the sight of his graceful hands.

"Probably hiding until the fight's over." He frowned and gave the dog's ear a tug. "Bad business, the three of them living in each other's pockets."

Keeping busy was the best remedy when she was upset. "Think I'll make a pudding. I found two squares of chocolate and a little nutmeg Aunt May must have put aside for a special occasion. Want to stay and have a dish?"

He took her hand, curled the fingers within his. "No, I'm sweet enough already."

"Oh, you!" Norah laughed.

"Will you come for another ride? Say, the day after tomorrow? We'll go to the ruin I told you about. It's not too far. You're getting to be a better rider each time out."

Having spoken on impulse, Mason promptly regretted it. He was far from immune to what had happened here today. He had no idea which man Rose had chosen, but one bedded her and the other had gone crazy. He looked at Norah from the corner of his eye, thinking of her undressed, of her being bare and gorgeous under him, of her expressive face as he went into her. He wanted to be the first, the man a woman never forgot.

He had no intention of actually dishonoring her, however, spoiling her for her husband, whoever he might be. For a treacherous moment Mason wondered if it was at all wise to continue seeing her. They had been attracted spiritually and intellectually for the most part and until now had gone no further than playful kisses and friendly embraces. But this could turn into serious stuff. It needed only the right moment in the right place to blaze into uncontrollable passion.

Norah rose on tiptoe and kissed him chastely on the cheek. "The day after tomorrow, then. About one. I'll be waiting."

He could not have refused had his life depended on it.

12.

It had been a miserable patrol in a July downpour, and the men looked forward to stopping at the Fullerton ranch. Carleton in particular was eager to reach it, weary of the frequent forays on which he was sent. In any event, the young officer had thought of little else but Norah lately.

Married before coming West, he had lost his frail spouse to pneumonia not long after the honeymoon. Being a husband appealed to him. He liked being waited on, deferred to, and obeyed; loved flesh adorned with lace, jewelry, and satin; doted on perfume in moist, secret places; lusted for the nights when he was master. Hedonist and sensualist, Carleton required a woman in his life.

Norah evidently didn't come from the sort of family from which a suitable society wife was ordinarily chosen. Despite her beauty and spirited personality, this was a strike against her, although being upper crust did not necessarily mean you were a thoroughbred such as she was; a lot of plow horses wore diamonds and controlled empires. Cruel in their own cunning ways, society matrons with old bloodlines would try to make her feel out of place, inferior and gauche, unaware Norah possessed strengths they had no conception of. How Carleton knew this he had no idea, but he sensed it and unconsciously yearned for a strong woman to lean on. That public self-command and private obeisance mixed like oil and water did not occur to him.

Now, sitting on the veranda with left ankle on right knee, he was rather put out. Norah had gone bird-watching! Rain lashed at the roof, and he slapped his boots with his gauntlets. Bird-watching, for Christ's sake. No affectation about his darling diamond in the rough!

Jim opened the door and waved a half-empty bottle at him. "How about a little firewater, Lieutenant? Take the chill from your bones." A black and badly swollen eye bulged out of his cut and battered face.

"No, thanks. We'll be on our way as soon as this lets up."

"Not gonna wait for Norah?" Jim took a long swig.

"I hardly think so. My men are tired. I want to get them back to the fort."

"You're right. Absolutely right. She's gotten a bit wild lately since she learned to ride so good. God knows where she's holed up in this rain." He shivered and went inside.

Wild. An exciting word to apply to Norah. Carleton glowered at the closed door with disgust. He did not like to think of her living here with these barbarians. This white trash. Sergeant Mulrooney was approaching with a tray covered by a slicker. More trash. Not long from Ireland, the man tolerated anything, like a mongrel dog that took what it got and thrived on it.

"Here, sir. Stew and fresh cornbread. There's a Chinee cook now. Ain't bad." Wet as an alley cat in a drizzle and just as indestructible, the sergeant grinned at his sullen superior. "The men have eaten, sir. We're ready to move out."

Carleton was hungrier than he'd thought, and the food smelled delicious. "Soon as I eat." Alone once more, he wolfed down the meal. He had so wanted to see Norah. Feel her out about getting married. Hear that bubbly laugh, lose himself in those magnificent eyes. His girl—soon anyway—off for an outing. Independent, a touch unruly, free as the wind. A thrill jolted him. Wild. Untamed. Ready to be bridled. He felt movement in his groin and swore. Throwing on the slicker, Carleton donned hat and gloves and plunged into the rain, yelling for his horse.

* * *

The smell of fresh coffee mingled with the distinctive scent of wet pine needles. At six thousand feet the crisp, damp air made a campfire welcome. Norah and Mason drank and chewed jerky in companionable silence, cozy and dry in their cliff house. Chico napped with one eye open at the foot of the cliff where he and the horses sheltered in a cave mouth.

Mason realized he should not be here. The injured arm was well enough now, despite the fact his draw did not yet equal that of the other hand. He had no reason to linger, had in fact mailed a report saying he was ready for duty. For what he had dreaded—yet wanted—had occurred. He and Norah had fallen in love. The past weeks had been spent in paradise. They rode through mountain meadows ablaze with wildflowers, Norah crying out in dismay to see the horses' hoofs crush them. They devoured sandwiches beside crystal brooks that cascaded down granite canyons and cantered through parklike glades where cinnamon-red ponderosa pines soared above browsing deer and freckled fawns.

Norah had been right about using a man's saddle; it made all the difference in the world. She had altered a pair of Joel's pants, taken tucks in an old shirt, and borrowed a pair of Shorty's boots that fit quite well; like many cowboys he had small feet in which he took great pride. Mason had also taught her to ride bareback, and she felt the bond between animal and person that came from the pounding of the horse's heart against her leg, its warm body blending into her own, its smell. Mason told her when you came to know a certain animal, you found it had its own odor same as a human being.

He let her ride Storm Cloud, now and then, to experience the strength of a powerful, high-strung mount, of brute force controlled and guided solely by will and bit. She resembled a young boy in the saddle, he thought, hips slender, legs long, back straight, only high breasts revealing her sex.

"You're getting to be a good rider," he complimented her.

"There's so much to learn about horses," she said. He had described the one-man horse, the man hater, and the fighting outlaw that was so unwilling to be servant to man it did not hesitate to commit suicide. "And just like you said, that scrub John Smith bought at Fort Bowie didn't look worth a plugged nickel but knew cow like all get-out."

"Smith knew what he was doing. And when you buy horses, Norah, don't fall for one that's knock-kneed or pigeon-toed or splayfooted, no matter how pretty he is to you. 'Marble' or 'glass' eyes in a white face are a bad combination, too. Could mean poor night vision." Mason was on safe ground with this subject, distracting him from her. "And remember, too, the long hairs on lower lip and jaw are essential for locating feed and water, 'cause a horse can't see the end of his nose. And sometimes you can cure lameness by putting the animal on soft pasture without shoes. You'll learn. You've got the touch for horses."

Mason stretched, then folded his arms, content to look at Norah watching the rain. Shorty's most disreputable hat was perched on the back of her head.

"Know what I feel like?" Norah mused, blue eyes brilliant in the gloom.

"Shoot."

"An onion."

"An onion? You don't smell like one, do you?" He nuzzled under an ear. "No, not an onion. More like a flower."

"I feel as if layer after layer is peeling off. I seem to change every time I turn around." Norah jammed cold hands into her canvas jacket pockets. "You have to admit I'm not the same person you met last October."

"Nope, different gal entirely." He reached out and clasped her to him. "I love her even more," he murmured against her eager lips.

"And I love you."

A hermit thrush landed on a ledge of the cliff house, brown back, reddish-brown tail and spotted breast blending with the old stones. Oblivious to the intruders below, the singer known as the American nightingale poured out his simple heart to the forest. Haunting, flutelike, the bird's music floated about the lovers.

"What's that, bird-watcher mine?" Mason kissed her cheeks and brow.

Norah sighed, intoxicated by the matchless moment. "Where is he? He sings like a tiny angel." They lifted their heads to see the little troubador and absorbed the glory of his song. When he took flight, she fished in a pocket for paper and pencil, jotting down form, color, bill type, size of eye, approximate size. Mason watched with fond amusement, grateful for the interruption. His iron self-control had been badly warped by the heat of their kisses. He wouldn't bring her here again.

"If only I could identify them. Did you see them today before it rained? Hawks, hummingbirds, crows, turkeys, woodpeckers, swallows, robins—why, these mountains are a garden of birds! You know, Dr. Gates might be able to get me a bird book from Tucson. I'll write and ask him."

Mason had to bite the bullet, disliking himself intensely for getting hopes up and then dashing them, for encouraging dreams at the expense of her feelings so he might luxuriate in her dearness until the last moment. Now the time had come to tell her, and the words were bitter in his mouth. "Don't bother. I'll send you the very best bird book I can find. The newest and biggest."

She recoiled as if slapped. They had discussed his departure, but gently. This inference had bite, an ominous sign that meant dedication to his work took precedence over the love between them. "Where will you send it from?" Norah poured water from the canteen onto the ashes, stiff with hurt, acting on the need to do something other than sit stunned and rejected. Late afternoon sun cast a golden glow across his dark face, and in the rain's aftermath, trees drooped beneath millions of droplets flashing the colorful magic of refracted light.

"The first city I come to that has a good bookstore." He tried to keep the answer casual.

"That means—you'll be far away."

The anguish in her voice and eyes undid Mason, and he seized her to hold her tight. "Darling, try to understand—"

She pushed him away violently. "I understand. Perfectly! You love that damned job more than you do me!"

"Now listen," he flared back. "I've explained before. The law is my life. My appointment is by the President and was confirmed by the Senate for four years. It's nothing to throw away like a—a hat that's not in fashion! I do love you. Surely you know that. But I swore I'd never marry while I was a Marshal. I've seen it happen with other men. They were fine officers. Their wives—and children—begin to see them as hired killers. I couldn't stand that. I couldn't do that to you! It would destroy us."

She made an aimless motion. "When are the four years up?"

"October 1878."

"Oh, God, more than two years of wondering where you are and if you're dead in some coulee or alley." Norah got to her feet. "No, you're right. I couldn't fight that, knowing you chose the badge over me."

"It's not a matter of the badge over you. I have an obligation to enforce federal law wherever and whenever necessary for a specified period of time. Oh, let's get out of here," he said brusquely, seeing her mouth quiver. "This is madness to torment each other."

They climbed down to join the waiting Chico and rode through the woods, blind to its splendor. At the ranch she dismounted and waited beside the horse, gripping the bridle so hard her tendons showed. "Will—will you ever ride back this way again?"

He had considered the inevitable question from every angle over the miles they traversed. Honor and conscience, duty and accountability were only words, fleshless, cold, and ghostly in the night, compared to Norah. But for now a gold band on her finger would mean an iron band of fear constricting her soul. No, better to cut the tie woven of summer flowers, birdsong, laughter, and unawakened kisses. It had been an enchanted time, but she'd get over it. Other men would woo her and she'd love them all until the right one came along. She had to be set free to find the future she deserved, a husband with roots and a tomorrow, young, ambitious, with semen full of sons.

"I doubt it."

She leaned on the horse, coughing and white as when he first saw her in the stagecoach. Filled with his own distress, Mason saw her struggle for command and achieve it. Another layer of the onion. She'd get along all right, he counseled himself. But would he in the lonesome years ahead?

Norah even managed a smile. "Good luck then, Mason. *Vaya con Dios*."

The tears in her eyes—he wavered, then responded. "Good luck to you, Norah." Trotting into the setting sun, he did not turn and wave, for the temptation of her might shatter his resolve.

She unsaddled and unbridled the mare and wiped the sweat off her back. To get "bloom," Mason said, you brushed and rubbed in the same direction as the hair grew. Norah wept as she used the curry comb.

"Saw you comin' back, sis. Get wet?" Shorty appeared and ran a palm down Lovey's back. "Good ol' girl, ain'tcha?" Then he noticed Norah crying. "What in tarnation? Say! That Fletcher feller didn't—"

Norah threw herself into his arms. "No, that's the trouble! He's going away. And I love him, Shorty, I love him!" she sobbed.

The old cowboy patted his youngun's back. Tears seeped through his shirt and underwear onto the skin. He remembered long ago. A body never forgot, that was the pure truth of it. Oh, Christ, yes, a broken heart hurt like hell.

Jim cut the steak into little bites. His teeth bothered him since the fight last month, but they were the least of his worries. He had not only lost, he had damaged his son's respect, much of his own pride, and Norah's esteem and affection. He glanced shyly across the table. Since the clash over Rose and Mason Fletcher's departure, Norah had changed. Sunday dinner, once the week's highlight, no longer sparkled with smiles and quips about her mishaps and triumphs of the week before.

"More biscuits, Jim?" She held out a plate.

"Thanks. Believe I will." He took two. "More gravy if there's plenty."

Norah went to the stove, ladled gravy into its boat, set it on the table. "There you are."

Jim heard himself chew and swallow. "House sure looks nice," he remarked desperately.

She had gone through the place like a whirlwind, painting, sewing, cleaning, and rearranging. New burlap curtains, dried grass bouquets, horseshoes nailed in a decorative pattern on the pie safe, a quilt started, mattresses restuffed, stove polished to a fare-thee-well. Even Lovey and Fudge shone like burnished wood.

"Guess I broke my plate with you, Norah." Might as well ask straight out, these wordless meals gave him the willies.

"I'm afraid you did." The large and glorious eyes studied him a moment then softened. "But you're my friend and always will be. My best friend."

"Whew! That makes me feel a heap better!"

"I just don't understand why you did it."

He sopped up the last of the gravy with a piece of biscuit. "Don't think I can explain. It's a—a—"

"A man's affair? You must know by now, women feel passion, too." She gestured toward the bedroom where

Rose napped, tired from a trip to Fort Guardian to have a tooth pulled.

Jim's jaw dropped, and his face reddened. "You—you telling me you and Fletcher—"

"Oh, for heaven's sake! I'm trying to say—and not very well—that I appreciate how easily Rose could tempt you, and how hard she'd be to resist. What beats me is where your brains were. Suppose she gets pregnant? Joel will never forgive you."

"Think I'll get some air." The rancher's stomach churned, and he pushed back from the table. "Norah?"

"Yes?" Her schoolmarm voice. She stacked dishes and put salt cellar and vinegar cruet aside to fill.

"About Fletcher. A man has to do what he has to do."

Norah said a word the cowboys used.

Jim reeled mentally but stood firm. "Not many men will do what he's doing. You've never seen a trail town when the herds are in, or outlaw hangouts where your life isn't worth two cents. Or met the gallows birds up in the Nations. He's the best there is. You can be proud he loves you."

"Not enough to marry me." She fussed at the stove so he was unable to see her face.

"He knew better. Didn't want to hurt you." Jim relaxed on the veranda. A baby didn't bear thinking about, his and Rose's. God forbid she was with child. He'd had a deuce of a time doing it—kinda disappointed her—so maybe his seed hadn't taken. One thing for sure, it wouldn't happen again. This misery wasn't worth it. A whoop sounded, and Jim yelled to Norah. "Hey, that cavalry lieutenant's coming in with his sergeant and a few men. Must be a social call."

"I'll be there in a minute." Norah removed her apron and smoothed down the skirts of her blue checked dress. Outside, Jim had already diplomatically departed with Sergeant Mulrooney.

Mustaches waxed, uniform immaculate, Carleton towered over her, overwhelming with spit-and-polish masculinity. "Norah, what a treat to see you! I prayed you'd be here today."

"Sundays I seldom go riding. I just write letters and catch up on my reading. Why, is today special?"

"Can we go for a walk?" he asked, bent on getting her alone.

"All right. Let me change my shoes first." Fixing kiss curls in front of her ears, Norah also applied a smidgen of rose oil behind them. The lieutenant had come courting again and deserved a little scent for his efforts.

They strolled to the artesian ponds, glinting in mid-August light. Carleton lifted her onto the seat of a wagon under an oak tree where sun-dappled shade spangled her richly colored hair. Every tendril wrapped about his heart, intensifying his adoration. He came right to the point. "Norah, will you marry me? I love you so much!" He held her hands, silently vowing they'd no longer be raw and chapped, but silken, creamed, and pampered.

Norah looked at his mouth, parted and vulnerable. Why not accept? She was fit as a fiddle. She no longer needed the ranch. Her contributions to it wouldn't be missed; she could be replaced by Rose, who would eventually marry Joel, Norah was sure. Furthermore, she honestly was fond of this suitor who fixed his gaze so worshipfully upon her face. Getting married—would it erase the misery of losing Mason?

"Say you will, dearest. Say yes! I'm wealthy in my own right. You won't want for a thing in your life." His fair skin, always sunburned, turned even more ruddy with emotion.

"I—I'd like to think about it."

He brought her down to him. He was no ninny, he knew he was catching her on the rebound, but Carleton wanted her so much he'd take her any way he could and worry about the consequences later. He'd *make* her love him. "I wrote my parents and told them to send the family rings."

"Pretty sure of yourself, aren't you?" She was both nettled and amused.

"When will you give me an answer? How soon?"

She looked at the valley, shimmering in the heat. She had learned to be direct like the Westerners among whom she lived. She didn't want to hurt this young man whom she might learn to love and again might not. Wasn't she being immature to think he could never replace Mason in her heart? Especially after the passage of time? "Come for Sunday dinner next week if you can. I'll give you my answer then."

He touched her as if she were breakable. "Would you think me awfully bold if I said I've dreamed about you like this, close enough to—" He kissed her again, more thoroughly.

"We all have our dreams. Some come true and some don't." She smiled and he chuckled as if he thought her observation clever.

After refreshments he cantered away with his men, his final remark ringing in her ears. "I'm going to be the luckiest man in the world!" But would he? It depended on her.

Charlie's Britches moved up the slopes at a ground-eating pace. Norah had taken a chance, riding the skittish gelding instead of the slower Lovey. Fast becoming an accomplished rider, however, Norah anticipated no trouble. She knew him—he loved to run more than anything else.

She had to make this journey, for it was a final visit to the place where she and the first man she loved had known happiness. She had wanted to dare, be reckless, throw caution to the winds—such luxuries would be denied her once Carleton slipped those rings on her finger. The blood bay surged mightily under her, great muscles carrying them to higher altitudes, lungs laboring to accommodate reduced oxygen. Her long hair, loose and free as the horse's mane, bounced and blew back in a mass of mahogany and gold.

The wind was rising, shoving titanic dark clouds before it. Thunder muttered, and birds cried out in alarm, hurrying to refuge. Gray foxes flashed by, reddish-orange sides and throats vivid in the dwindling light. Baron, loping effortlessly at the horse's heels, dashed after them, changed his mind, and resumed his pace.

She tied the bay securely to a tree by the cave mouth where he would have shelter and told the dog to guard. Norah scrambled up the incline to the cliff house, over the ledge, and down into the pitlike enclosure. She gasped and almost screamed, confronted by a man crouched with a hand on his gun butt.

"Norah! What are you doing here?" Mason held a large package wrapped in oilskin.

Her eyes feasted on him, and as Mason stood tall, something turned over inside her. She wanted to slap him, scratch him, hurt him—touch him, lie beneath him, know him in her.

"You might call this a sentimental journey," she answered flatly. "I may get married next month."

His mouth thinned. "Congratulations. Who's the lucky man? Jim Fullerton?" He jerked his head around. "It isn't Eli Martin, is it?"

"He's Carleton Madison Beatty of Philadelphia. A cavalry officer at Fort Guardian."

"You didn't let any grass grow under your feet." Jealousy and anger barbed each word.

"How dare you say that?" she snapped. "You're the man I wanted. You didn't want *me*."

Lightning cracked, and Norah jumped. The horse whinnied in terror as a white bolt lanced into a pine, setting it on fire, the flames quickly doused by rain.

"That's not true, Norah. And I apologize for what I said. The news startled me." Mason proffered the package. "Here's your bird book. I wanted you to find it here." He rubbed his hands together. "How about a fire?"

"No, I'm not staying." Not a minute longer in proximity

to those eyes, that wide mouth, those broad shoulders she had visualized naked and rippling with muscle in her fantasies.

The skies opened up with such a violent explosion of sound that the earth reverberated under their feet. Then the rain settled into a downpour. "We're not going out in *that*," Mason declared. "The horses could slide right off the mountain." He set about kindling a fire and soon its warmth reflected off stone walls and lent a false glow to their faces. As they stared at each other, Norah's eyes glittered with unshed tears.

"Ah, don't cry. For God's sake, don't cry!" Mason strode around the fire pit, grabbed her and shook her, kissed her eyelids, tasting salt. "Don't *cry*, Norah!" He buried his face in the abundance of damp hair smelling of roses and pine, a fragrance he knew would haunt him for years. His mouth traveled over her soft cheek, and thunder echoed in the impact of their kiss.

Tongues touched and caressed, hands reached for and found what they hunted for. They needed no words. Their bodies spoke for them, divested of clothing, satiny, gleaming, flesh on flesh berry-brown and yucca-petal ivory, lips glued together, primeval storm ancient as the mountain. Tumult and desired pain, sweet urgency, tempests to equal that which rocked the forest, cries of climax that rose and vanished on the howling winds like birdsong.

Norah rested, her face hidden in her hair. Surely she was like the pine riven by that lightning bolt. Mason, excited by her innocent seductiveness, took her once more. "My wild flower," he murmured.

Wanting him but too shy to say so, when he touched a bare shoulder and curve of breast, she shuddered and collapsed, letting him enter her again and deliver them. "Stay with me," she whispered. "Don't go. We could be so good, you and I."

"Norah, stop it."

She sat up and put her back to him. "Go then. Get out. If there's no way I can hold you I don't want you."

He slowly dressed then strapped on his gunbelt. Humility and tenderness swept Mason when he saw blood on her inner thigh, and he knelt beside her. "Let me take you home, Norah. You can't stay here alone. The storm's died down but it might start up again."

She wanted only to remain where she was. Yet night was coming on, she had no food, and there were animals to consider. Then, too, the men would be searching for her in the bad weather if she didn't return. She dressed hurriedly, and they descended to their horses without speaking, the dog frolicking about them.

Not far from the ranch gate, hunched in slickers and wet hats, they came to a fork in the road where he hoped to stop and talk. He pulled rein. "Norah, I was wrong. Maybe we ought to—"

She trotted past with only a single sad glance for him. Her horse was anxious for the barn and she for a place to lick her wounds, a place where Mason was no longer welcome.

"Norah?" he called after the fleeing figure, waiting in vain for her to halt. Mason considered going after her then decided against it. What was to be gained? It was really over for good now. He shook his head—it might be over in this time and place but never in his memory. Cold and solemn, the Marshal headed out.

She entered the house and then the bedroom, walking in a daze of delayed shock and euphoria. Rose, washing beans, stared in astonishment as Norah passed. Removing the wet male riding garments, Norah towel-dried her new body. She touched the kissed, possessed, lovingly violated parts. The journey, the joining—they had a dreamlike quality belied by the stranger's form she now inhabited, for the lovemaking had happened so fast it melted reason. What had he said once? *You're like a forest fire!*

He'd remember her. She had triumphed over him, bound him even more tightly to her, despite their leave-taking. As for Carleton, had she betrayed him? Or was she not her own woman and no one else's, surrendering what was hers to give? She'd chosen to give herself to one man, yet would devote her life to another. Neither was a small thing.

Placing the unopened bird book on the bedside table, she slipped a nightdress over her head and climbed under the covers. She was a different person. A different woman.

The butterfly—*La Mariposa*—had left the chrysalis.

When Carleton came again he had rings in his pocket and a growing impatience tempered with tolerance for female notions. If Norah wanted to be married at the fort, not Tucson's best hotel, so be it; if she refused to accept money for a wedding gown but would make it herself, he understood; if she brought one of Fullerton's horses, that was acceptable, though Carleton looked askance at the bear of a dog she refused to leave behind. Too deeply in love to care how frequently he deferred to her, he was not so dense as to overlook a new and thrilling *something* about her that excited him. He patrolled and paced and waited.

Jim put aside his tally book one afternoon and lit a cigarette. He inhaled and blew smoke out his nose. "Norah, aren't you a little hard on the lieutenant?"

"What do you mean? There are so many things to think about, that's all." She avoided his knowing look; the accusation was just. She'd been taking her anger with Mason out on Carleton because he let her do so, thinking it bridal jitters.

"Can't say I've ever been crazy about him, but he sure as heck is crazy about you. Give him a chance, honey, a fighting chance. Things may work out a lot better than you think."

Sticking her needle in a pincushion, she folded a tablecloth with its neat patch. "You're right. I don't really mean to do it." But Carleton need have no worries on that score. Norah planned to make him an exemplary wife.

Part II
CARLETON

She lov'd me for the dangers I had pass'd,
And I loved her that she did pity them.
                                        Shakespeare:
                                        Othello

13.

"*A tent?* We're going to live in a canvas *tent*?"

Norah was torn between laughter and tears. A crude sign above tied-back flaps proclaimed it Honeymoon Haven, and calico bows festooned the tent pole. Inside iron cots crouched with their legs in water-filled tomato cans to outwit the ants; other furniture included straw-filled bed-sacks covered with sheets and Army blankets, a camp table with a candlestick, two chairs with rawhide seats, and a big metal trunk.

Carleton fidgeted, mortified at his inability to offer better accommodations. "I'm sorry, Norah, it's the best I can do. The roof of the officers' quarters hasn't been repaired yet. The summer rains literally washed it away. It's mud, you know. They're all living in tents. But just as soon as—"

"You never mentioned a tent. I didn't have the slightest idea we'd be living like this. Why, the ranch is a mansion next to—"

He took her by the arm, led her inside, and closed the flaps. Afternoon sun had made the tent a furnace, and perspiration sprang out on Norah's body. She complained when he took her in his arms. "It's too warm in here for—"

He kissed her temples, her throat and eyelids. "Too warm to let me do that?" Carleton lifted her chin. "Or this?" He kissed her mouth, pouting and provocative. "We *are* being married tomorrow, you know."

Norah already regretted her outburst. Life on a frontier Army post was no bed of roses, and being a poor sport wouldn't help. It had been a shock nevertheless to discover the lack of privacy there for bathing, dressing, and disrobing—she had disrobed only once before a man, and her heart lurched at the memory of Mason's hands reaching out for her.

"I'm sorry, Carleton. Truly I am. We'll get along fine here once we're settled." She fussed with a uniform button right under her nose. "It will be a lark, and someday we can look back and smile about this."

"When I leave the Army, you shall live like a queen. Clothes from Worth in Paris. Jewels from Tiffany. Servants. Furs. You'll forget this abominable tent ever existed." He ran a finger inside his collar. "It *is* warm in here."

She put both arms loosely around his waist. "It's not entirely the weather, Lieutenant." Norah tried to blank out the vision of Mason by the campfire. It was Carleton's happiness that mattered now. Standing on tiptoe to kiss him, she took pleasure in his shaving lotion, his silky mustache, the thickness of his hair, and the sweet hardness of his lips.

"Mmmm, I liked that."

"Don't you think we could step outside? It's an inferno in here!" Norah raised both hands to tidy her hair, and he leaned down swiftly to kiss the breasts that lifted with her gesture.

Her face flamed. "Carleton! Please!"

He flushed in turn. "I'm sorry. I got carried away." He raised her left hand between them. Adorned with a pearl and diamond engagement ring, it would soon symbolize his possession of her. "I love you, darling. So much."

"And I love you." The words came easily, and Norah assured herself they would soon be true. She opened the round gold watch pinned to her waist, a gift from Carleton's mother. "I still have hours of sewing on my dress. I'd better get busy."

He embraced her a final time, backed up, and swore under his breath. "Almost fell over this monster." Carleton stared at Baron without enthusiasm, and the dog returned his scrutiny with no sign of friendliness. "He should have been left at the ranch."

"He'd have followed us. Besides, he'd give his life for me. That's why he's always underfoot." She patted the scarred head.

"That's the only quality I like about him." No need to lay down the law now, but that animal was *not* going to Philadelphia.

Norah left to work on her wedding gown while Carleton searched the quartermaster's storehouse for a second tent to hold luggage, belongings, and wedding gifts. They would meet later when they dined with Major Bertram and Dr. and Mrs. Gates at the Gates's residence where Norah was staying.

The bugle had sounded afternoon stable call, and Norah veered to walk toward the corrals. Lovey had remained at the ranch after all, for a mare would cause havoc among Army geldings. Carleton, therefore, casting about for a wedding gift appropriate to temporary surroundings, settled on a riding horse, a blue roan with black mane and tail. Norah had named the splendid creature Steel; his color was like a finely blued rifle barrel. She exchanged greetings with the men busy at daily tasks: blacksmiths forging shoes; saddlers mending bridles, harness, packs, gun slings and saddles; farriers, early-day veterinarians, attending ill or wounded horses and mules. Cavalrymen—officer and enlisted man alike—groomed personal mounts upon which their lives depended in the field, polished their gear, and cleaned stalls.

In the ammoniac gloom Norah made out Steel's noble head turned toward her, his muzzle a deep rosy pink. Edging in beside him, rubbing his rump, she talked to him, fed him brown Mexican sugar, and combed his forelock with her fingers. She blew gently into his nostrils, a tactic Plains Indians used when taming a horse, according to Sergeant Mulrooney. Despite the tragedy at the Little Big Horn this past June twenty-fifth, Mulrooney admired the Sioux and Cheyenne when it came to horsemanship.

"Oh, you're a dandy boy!" she complimented Steel.

"We'll have good times together. Do you realize that tomorrow about this time I'll be Mrs. Carleton Madison Beatty? What do you think of that? I don't mind telling you I'm a-flutter!" Steel vibrated his lips and made her chuckle. She gave him the rest of the sugar and departed the stables. Crossing the small barren parade ground, Norah noticed two men dismounting in front of the adjutant's office. One was bandaged and manacled, the other wore buckskins and a dark Stetson. A sensation close to agony tore at Norah's midriff. *Was that Mason?* She came to an abrupt halt in dust and glare.

The lawman's back was to her, and she almost fainted at the sight of glossy black hair when he removed his hat and mopped his brow. Every good and honest intention to forget Mason fled. Then the man turned a stranger's face to her, and Norah took a breath of relief and disappointment combined. She continued toward the doctor's quarters. Suppose it *had* been Mason? What would she have done? Was she going to get the vapors every time a line of cheekbone or a hazel glance assaulted her heartstrings? She tried without success to keep from crying.

When she entered the modest adobe dwelling, Lollie Gates met her with a cup of tea. Tiny but full bosomed, pert and bustling, the white-haired woman reminded Norah of a mother bird. "You shouldn't be out in the sun without a hat, child! You want a peaches-and-cream complexion when you go back East. That's what's fashionable. Heavens, they'll think you're part Indian. Here, I just made this. Why, dear, have you been crying?"

"I—stubbed my toe," Norah lied. "These kid slippers aren't *any* protection. A rock was sticking up and I didn't see it in time."

Lollie shook her head and suggested Norah put her foot up. "Lucky you didn't break the toe. I did once, exactly the same way. Forts are male places for cavalrymen with big boots and horses with iron shoes. But we ladies brighten the corner where we are, don't we?" She beamed at striped serape curtains, rag rugs on a well-swept dirt floor, barrel chairs cut to shape, cushioned, and covered with chintz. Mattresses and blankets piled atop packing crates made a comfortable lounge, and a rolltop desk shared space with a treadle sewing machine in one corner.

"It's so cozy, Lollie. I can hardly wait until we move into our own quarters. I don't know how I'm going to manage in that tent!" Homesickness for the ranch attacked Norah, leaving a lump in her throat.

"You won't notice a thing. For a while at least." Childless Lollie wondered when the first baby would come. She sighed. Oh, to be young again and know what she knew now.

Norah got busy inserting detachable sleeves in her wedding gown. Carleton had told her not to bother; there would be no necessity to alter the dress later for everyday use. Her wardrobe would be extensive, reflecting the many activities of a wealthy aristocratic wife, with gowns for walking, sports, breakfast, dancing, visiting, driving about at watering places, the opera, and traveling abroad. By contrast Norah had lived a life of thrift and periodic deprivation, of make do, and waste not. The sleeves were going in—just in case.

For a time she had despaired of having a dress ready, for none of her aunt's garments lent themselves to being bleached and tinted light coffee, the preferred color for nuptial wear. Not only that, the nearest store was in Tucson—which might as well have been on the moon; getting material from there could take weeks. Resigned to wearing one of the dresses she already had, Norah had clapped her hands with glee the day Jim lugged a brass-bound trunk into the ranch house.

"There's bound to be something in here you can use," he had assured her, panting. "I'd almost forgotten this was in the storeroom."

They opened the lid and were met with a little gust of

sandalwood and violet. "White brocade, fans, gloves, lace, ribbons—why, Jim, this must be her trousseau."

He touched the feminine frills as if they were glass. "May didn't have a chance to wear such pretty things after we left Texas."

Norah put a hand on his arm. "She wouldn't have had it any other way."

His dark eyes met hers with affection. "I miss her. And I'll miss you like the very dickens!" He cleared his throat. "Okay, let's see what we've got here. We want you to be the best-dressed bride in the whole Territory, even if I'm not there!"

Joel and Emedio escorted Norah to the fort with the mastiff and a pack horse loping behind. Jim had elected to remain home so as not to make the spread short of men; at any rate, a young buck like Joel would have more fun at a wedding. Before she departed, Norah had kissed them upon hearing that father and son had shaken hands after Jim stated candidly that Rose remained a daughter to him and nothing more. What the girl's opinion was they didn't know, for she had retreated into one of her black moods.

"There," Norah murmured, clipping a thread, and bringing her mind back to the present. "One more row of lace and they're done."

"What an exquisite seamstress you are! And this is the most adorable bonnet!" Lollie held up the confection with its sapphire blue satin flowers in beds of ivory lace, artificial pink roses and ostrich plumes of a brighter blue that curled down to brush one cheek.

"Just a little bit of this and a little bit of that." Norah studied the hat with a practiced eye. It would be smart tied under her chin with an ecru bow to match the gown. "I'll be happy to make you a chapeau if you like. I worked in millinery once."

"That's obvious. Norah, seeing how handy you are, I want to give you some material I bought in Wilmington." Lollie vanished into the tiny alcove that served as a bedroom. "This was on sale. I shouldn't have bought it—it was so expensive—but Theo and I had had a spat, and I was going to show *him*!" Lollie unwrapped a length of silver-gray serge and held it up to Norah. "The color is perfect for you! And here's the pattern. Actually, a riding habit like this was much too daring. The town would have ostracized me had I worn a divided skirt to ride cross-saddle in!"

Cross-saddle meant astride, Norah remembered, a word considered bawdy in the East. Yet Shorty had told her about Spanish women in California who rode like men in vaquero saddles, and he vowed they had been modest and ladylike. She rubbed the material between thumb and forefinger. "A divided skirt, Lollie, what an interesting idea. It's so practical. But I won't take this unless you let me design you a hat."

"I don't know where I'll wear it, but that's a bargain." Lollie clapped her hands in consternation. "I wonder if those canned hams got here. I'd better check, because we'll have to change the reception menu if they didn't."

Content to be alone, Norah sipped the cooling tea and fingered a strip of lace saved from her mother's wedding gown and now inserted in her own. She pressed it to her lips, her throat thickening with familiar grief. If only her parents had been alive to share her happiness! For she was going to be happy. How could she not? Handsome, stalwart, and brave, Carleton was a man any wife could be proud of. A rich and cultured gentleman, he had chosen her over sophisticated, better-schooled, and generously dowried prospects awaiting him back East. Filled with pride, Norah promised him in her heart to live up to his expectations.

Lollie soon returned with her spouse in tow, his ginger-colored hair a trifle thinner and grayer, paunch a bit heavier. He greeted Norah with an affectionate kiss. "What do you think of this young lady, Mother? I can't get over it. Came out here this time last year looking like death warmed over—"

"Theo! What a terrible thing to say," his wife scolded.

Norah nodded. "He's right. You should have seen me."

"—and now she'll be the most beautiful bride west of the Pecos!"

"Oh, yes," Lollie agreed, "oh, yes, she will indeed."

The older woman poured freshly made tea for her husband, and Norah asked if he had finished his rounds. Plumping down on the lounge, he replied, "Ah! That hits the spot, my dear. Yes, I'm through, but there wasn't much doing today. I treated a wasp sting, set a broken ankle, and prescribed for the runs. A quiet time, really."

"Sometimes he's so busy, Norah, I don't see him until bedtime. Why, last week—on one day, mind you—he cauterized a rattlesnake bite, amputated an arm, saved a soldier who tried to commit suicide, treated an alcoholic with delirium tremens, and removed a bullet from the tailor's leg."

"Don't forget the splinter I took out of your finger."

His wife smiled at him fondly and said, "That was the biggest operation of all."

"It gets hectic when there's Indian activity." He emptied his cup. "Thank goodness, there's none of that right now."

"Do you still take care of stagecoach passengers?"

Theo shook his head. "Stages don't come this way anymore, Norah. There's a new road farther north that's a lot easier. Little towns springing up along it. Nothing down here but the fort now, and we have our own transportation, although a wagon comes over from Lordsburg now and then. Matter of fact, it came yesterday with the preacher. He'll marry you tomorrow, hold services Sunday, and then go back."

Norah made the final stitch. "Did the canned ham get here?"

"Oh, I forgot to tell you. It did, and so did a case of plum pudding. Where it came from I can't imagine," Lollie said.

"Some quartermaster in Washington wanted to get rid of it," Theo grumbled, "that's where. You'd think they'd send decent supplies to these posts out West. Half the time they act as if we're in a foreign country, and the other half they forget us completely."

Lollie patted his knee. "Now, Theo, you know it's the same at every fort. The Army's the Army. The pride and despair of career officers. Besides, I think plum pudding with vanilla sauce will make a nice dessert even if it isn't Christmas."

"I'd rather have ice cream."

She threw up her hands. "Land's sakes, Theo, ask for chocolate mousse!"

"Would it do any good?" he asked with a mischievous grin. His wife was a culinary artist, and Army provisions drove her wild with their monotony, poor quality, and irregular delivery.

"Of course not! Who can get baking chocolate, butter, and orange liqueur in this out-of-the-way place? Or ice to chill it?"

"In that event I shall console myself with a predinner nap." He kissed her cheek. "You are sweeter than any mousse."

She waved him to bed and drew the floor-length curtains between alcove and parlor. "He's a rascal," she said with a laugh.

"I hope we have a relationship like that when we've been married as long as you two have. But today I'm—well, to be honest, I'm afraid this may not be the right thing to do, after all."

The other woman nodded. "That's only natural, my dear. Everyone gets jumpy. I lost my voice two days before our wedding and didn't get it back until two days later. Theo says he's never been that lucky since! But don't worry, this time tomorrow you'll have a husband to love and protect you 'until death do you part.' "

Norah hoped that would not be for many years and shrank from a premonitory shiver that went down her spine.

14.

Coyotes yapping and howling woke Norah in the middle of the night. She listened while their harsh music faded, and she could picture the little wolves running so swiftly in the moonlight their paws hardly touched the ground. Intense longing to be in the open seized her, and she rose from the makeshift bed. Putting on slippers and a wrapper, Norah went outside; sentries stood on duty but weren't near enough to see her. She breathed deeply, soothed by the wine-dark night. Mountains loomed sooty black against star-dusted infinities while clouds scudded north, silvery-blue phantom galleons on an ocean of air warmed by the Mexican terrain to the south. Perched on a camp stool, Norah carefully covered her upper chest and neck against the breeze. It constantly amazed her how hot the desert could be in daylight and how deceitfully cool after dusk. It was easy to catch cold, and she had to be mindful of her lungs for the rest of her life.

This time last year she had been coughing her guts out, as Shorty so succinctly put it; now she experienced only occasional pain as if healed tissue was stretching. That was physical, but Norah bore other scars no physician in the world could heal. *Where are you tonight, Mason?* Rolled in a blanket beside a campfire? Dozing like a big cat, amber eyes slitted at the slightest sound, strong hands on your weapons with a lover's touch? *Ah, I hate myself for it, but I can't stop loving you!*

"Can you use company?" Theo whispered. "Or would you rather be alone?"

Norah looked up. He was rumpled, sleepy, and dear, a father to her in a way. She held out a welcoming hand. He squeezed it, then brought another campstool and sat down beside her. For a while they listened to great horned owls conversing gravely, to the poorwill's song repeated so steadily and for so long it seemed the high desert's pulse. Far off the roar of a bear brought Baron to his feet, sniffing the breeze.

"I'm rather glad you're here. I need to tell somebody something. I don't want you to think ill of me, though," Norah began hesitantly.

"I never could." He had heard so many confessions over the years. Hers would be mild as milk.

"I don't want to burden you."

"Physicians are confessors."

"I can't keep it bottled up any longer. I've done something I shouldn't."

Theo sighed. "Who hasn't, my dear?"

Her hands clenched. "I've—I've done with another man what I'll do with Carleton on my wedding night. It didn't seem to matter before, but now I feel I've robbed Carleton of—oh, I don't know how to phrase it. Of being the first man, yes, but—of something else that isn't at all physical." She glanced at him. "Are you shocked?"

"It would take a great deal to shock an old war-horse like me. I must admit I'm surprised, but certainly not offended. You are too good a person to shock me." Theo crossed his legs and studied the moon.

"You have no idea how many times I've heard this story or a version of it. Naturally you feel guilty and ashamed, but it's not the end of the world." He wondered who it had been; he knew Norah would not give herself to just any man.

She hunched over as if in pain. "What makes things worse is—I did it after accepting Carleton's proposal."

"Do you still love this man?"

"I think I always will."

"Do you love Carleton?"

"More each day."

Theo rose and folded up the campstool. "Norah, you have a wonderful life ahead of you. Just be the best wife you know how. That's the best thing to do."

He bent to kiss the top of her head, and Norah caught his sleeve. "Can you love more than one person at the same time? Is it possible?"

"Oh, yes, I'm afraid so."

A cloud obscured the moon then, and Norah sighed, anxious for her wedding day to arrive.

The ceremony turned out to be far nicer than Carleton had anticipated. The preacher conducted a dignified service in the major's parlor, which had been cleaned, aired, and decorated with pine branches and ribbon. Music was furnished for Norah's walk to the altar on Dr. Gates's arm by a flute-playing blacksmith and a cook, who produced surprisingly professional melody on a battered violin. The cowboys, including Fullerton's son, behaved decorously. They had even shaved and washed their shirts for the occasion.

Carleton had tended to look down his nose at preparations for Fort Guardian's first wedding. At home his mother would have arranged teas, dinners, and lavish parties for the engaged couple; Norah would have been up to her pretty ears with shopping and fittings. A formal ceremony at the high Episcopal church his family had attended for more than a century would have been followed by a reception at his parents' Georgian mansion.

Here nothing was elegant except the bride, and their guests were rude soldiers and boisterous settlers instead of Philadelphia society. They had Caucamonga wine instead of champagne; canned ham, venison haunch, and plum pudding instead of French dainties; and his wife wore a hand-me-down wedding dress instead of a pearl-encrusted work of art from Paris.

Yet when the time for the ceremony came, Carleton was not able to resist the warmth and sincerity of his comrades and commanding officer, nor that of Lollie, who had worked so hard to make the occasion festive for two young people far from home. She had even arranged to have the soldiers attach their twenty-one-inch-long bayonets to their Springfield rifles so the lieutenant and his lady might proceed from the makeshift desk-turned-altar beneath a canopy of military steel and a shower of rice.

"A toast," Carleton said, holding up his glass. "To Mrs. Gates—who has made something very special out of very little."

"Hear, hear!" her husband applauded, gratified to hear the usually aloof officer compliment his wife. Lollie colored with pleasure.

Norah hugged her bridegroom's arm. "That was lovely."

"Not as lovely as you," he whispered. "When can we go?"

"I heard that! Not until she waltzes with me once more. Rank has its privileges, you know." Major Bertram bowed, and Norah stepped forward to place a gloved hand on his blue-clad arm.

She floated over the parade ground like a twilight flower, full skirts belling out as they danced. Carleton lighted a cigar, amazed to find himself willing to lend other men Norah's smile, her laugh, her slim waist. Oh, she was a love! What a stroke of luck to have found her blooming here, a tiger lily in a cactus patch.

The party lost steam when the newlyweds made their farewells, and everyone watched as they strolled away. The bridegroom's fair head bent down; the bride's face, an ivory blur in the early evening, lifted to his. The music faltered and ceased. Within an hour the fort had returned to normal, taps were blown, and night wrapped the outpost in loneliness and shadow. Sentries saw the light go out in the tent, and their sighs blended with wind from the mesas.

* * *

Carleton had stepped outside while she undressed, a lengthy process of removing hat, dress, bustle, corset, petticoats, undergarments, stockings, shoes, and jewelry. She then put on her best nightgown, refurbished with blue ribbons, and brushed out her hair, washed this morning in Lollie's tub, which was half of a vinegar barrel painted pink. Anointing herself with the last of her perfumed oil, Norah called out, "You can come in now."

Carleton put revolver, matches, and a water carafe on the table and lifted the candlestick. "Shall I?" Not trusting herself to speak, she nodded, conscious of his gaze on her body beneath the covers. He blew out the candle and lay down beside her. Norah felt the swollen manhood thrust through the cloth of his nightshirt, and inadvertently stiffened. Carleton ran a hand over her gently but quickly as he might a frightened horse.

"Nothing to be afraid of, my darling." He kissed her, ran his tongue into her mouth experimentally, then retreated. He buried his face between her breasts and reached under her nightgown so he might caress them.

"Oh, Carleton!" When he raised the garment, he moved his also so his member rested on her, for he dared not touch her entry so soon.

It was more or less accepted that lovemaking was not conducted in the nude, but Norah was ignorant of that intimate code of behavior. Thinking to please, she pulled the gown over her head and dropped it to the floor. He sucked in his breath, then discarded his as well.

"Wicked girl," he breathed against her mouth. "Wicked, seductive girl from the wilderness."

"Take me back if you don't want me."

He shoved a pillow under her hips. "I'll take you!" His hard hands caressed every joint, every bone, every fold of skin.

Norah moved to shift under his weight. She and Mason had not hesitated but come together in a frenzy of passion. Mason. Damn him! Let her not think of him but of this young husband whose tongue probed, whose fingers crept into her, testing and exploring. His breathing hoarsened and quickened to find her moist and welcoming.

"I—can't hold back, Norah."

She arched her back when he went in, big and hard and wonderful, and her tissues imprisoned him so that they locked together in glory.

The bugle blew reveille at sunrise, but Carleton made no move to get up. Today belonged to him and Norah. He spread her hair out in a fan on the pillow. "I'm glad you don't crimp or frizz your hair."

Norah agreed sleepily. "I tried it, but it ruins the hair."

"Do you know how gorgeous you are in the morning? Most women aren't, do you know that?"

"You're the expert."

"Hair like melting copper. Eyes like sun-flecked pools."

"How poetic! Tell me more."

"And your skin—" Carleton worried at her neck with his teeth and made a small hemorrhage. Like branding a milk-white mare. Desire flooded him, and he took a nipple in his mouth, ran a hand between her thighs.

"Wait a minute. Please." For Norah, the night had been both revelation and disappointment, a time of naps interspersed with lovemaking when he fed his hungry body with hers. That he was good at what he did was no surprise; after all, he was a man of the world, but that made it the more puzzling that he didn't take her need into consideration.

"Carleton, *wait*." Norah tried to pull away, but the narrow cot left no room for maneuvering.

"What for?" he muttered, on fire as he had never been. He had had her all night, yet this was like the initial entrance.

She couldn't fight the disloyal memory that Mason took her with him, wanted her to know the joy of making love. She would have to be bold and assert herself. "I want you to wait because I want—to come, too," she finished in a rush.

"My dear Norah!" Dumbfounded, Carleton stared down at her. "That's—why, don't you know that isn't ladylike?"

She analyzed the past several hours and started to laugh. "Are you joking? Very little of what we did seemed ladylike." Norah struggled up on one elbow, piqued and mystified by his disapproval. What went on between married people was no one else's business, was it? And if she wasn't ladylike in the dark, who was to know?

"Why, I—I never thought about it. That's just the way it is. Ladies don't—uh—only men—uh—"

"Would you have married me if I weren't a lady? Would you present me to your parents if I weren't?"

"No, but—"

She stretched. "Then be quiet and do your duty, Lieutenant."

"Well, I'll be damned!" Carleton could not remember being spoken to like that. But he kissed her, slid to the foot of the cot, and parted her legs.

"Whatever are you—" Norah gasped when his tongue touched her, then slid into the opening. As he loved her, thrills traveled up her inner thighs, and she began to quiver with desire. Or was it lust? Did it matter? All she wanted was him, in and out, the silk and iron rod, branding its memory in nerves and flesh. Norah came, and molten honey spread outward from the seat of sensation in waves that conquered mind and body, made her move in ways she never had, ways that drove him crazy.

Spent and sweaty, he retired to his own cot and collapsed. Norah closed her eyes, replete with sex and an awareness of self. They were on the brink of falling asleep when a voice brought them back to reality.

"Breakfast, Lieutenant and Mrs. Beatty. Courtesy of the officers."

Carleton looked at Norah. "Ten minutes sooner—" She laughed and pulled the sheet up to her chin.

"Beg pardon, sir?"

"Put it in the other tent, soldier. I'll get to it in a minute."

Carleton pulled on longjohns, trousers, and boots but left his torso naked. Pouring water into a basin, he washed, then kissed her, his face stubbled but cool and fresh.

Their eyes locked in tender secrecy, and he went to fetch their breakfast. Norah arranged the pillows in back of her. Seldom had she been so pampered. Once they had their own home, she could indulge herself. Carleton had promised they would have so many servants that she'd need not lift a finger.

How ironic to be one of those distant, richly clad women for whom she had once created hats, their patronage her single barrier against starvation and the workhouse. One thing was certain. When ordering hats, gowns, lingerie, gloves, or shoes, she'd remember the sick, penniless girl she had once been, and be kind and generous.

"Say, this isn't bad." Carleton backed in with a tray. "I think I see the hand of Mrs. Gates." He put it on his cot, cleared the camp table, and set dishes on it, giving Norah the tray to put across her lap.

"Baking powder biscuits, butter, hash, eggs! Wherever did she find these things! Those sweet frijoles I like, quince jam, and chocolate!" Norah beamed. "When we get to Philadelphia I want to send her the nicest gift I can find."

"My mother has excellent taste. She'll take you to the proper shops, and you may buy whatever you like. Mrs. Gates deserves it."

"I love the watch your mother sent me." Norah leaned forward, the sheet sliding down a fraction to reveal cleavage. "Do you think she'll like me?"

He choked on his biscuit and washed it down before answering, eyes glued to the sheet. "How can she help it?"

"I get nervous thinking about meeting her. What about your father?"

Carleton addressed himself to the last of the hash. "Don't worry about him. He'll worship you."

"When will we go back East?"

"I came in for a five-year stint, as you know. Family

tradition and all that. Time's up next July. I could resign
before then, but it's a matter of pride. Have to prove I'm a
chip off the old block.'' He set about cleaning his teeth with
an ivory toothpick; secured on a gold chain, it was kept in a
tiny pocket below his belt.

Norah suddenly realized there was a great deal about her
husband she did not know. ''What will you do then? I mean,
how will you make our living?''

He laughed and chucked her under the chin. ''I won't do
anything, pet. I have a trust fund from my grandfather that
came to me when I was twenty-one.''

''A trust fund?'' Norah repeated with awe. Such assets
meant nothing to her. She could only think of her father
wrestling heavy boxes of books that brought mere pennies;
her mother fainting from fatigue after a twelve-hour
workday; herself mending over mends, fitting cardboard in
shoes when soles wore through.

She pondered the idea of being wealthy. It had no reality
here in a tent in the middle of nowhere. ''How did your
grandfather get so rich? And your father—is he a—a
millionaire, too?'' She expected him to correct her. Not a
millionaire. Not that well off.

Carleton poked his head out of the tent. ''Where the
devil's that orderly with my hot water? I want to shave.
How did Grandfather get so rich? He dabbled in railroads,
canals, banking, textiles, steel—nothing to interest a woman, really. And Father parlayed his mother's small estate
into a fortune after he left the Army. He's a senator now,
incidentally.''

The orderly arrived with a can of hot water and took the
dirty dishes away. Carleton hung a small mirror on a nail in
the tent pole, poured the water into the tin basin, lathered
his face, and started to shave. ''By the way, Norah''—he
worked the straight razor under his mustache—''be sure to
give me your money later in the day.''

''What?'' His sentence startled her out of inertia.

''Your money, I said. Give it to me later in the day.''

Norah frowned. "Why should I do that? It isn't much, but it's all I have left from the sale of Daddy's antique map."

"Women don't know how to handle money, you sweet goose. When you get married, your husband takes care of money matters and gives you what you need."

She sat erect, the full lower lip thrust out. "I'm quite capable of handling my own money. I've done it for years. Since I was a child, in fact. My mother taught me so people couldn't take advantage of me." Her eyes blazed despite a friendly tone. "I—I don't *like* the idea of having to ask for my own money!"

Carleton rinsed and dried his face, slipped his arms into underwear and shirt, buttoned them, and pulled suspenders over his shoulders. "How much do you have?"

"It may sound like chicken feed to you, but I have two hundred and one dollars and thirty-eight cents."

"Know it to the penny, do you?" he teased, shrugging into the uniform coat.

"Of course, I do! I'm very careful with money." Norah started to say something else, then changed her mind. They shouldn't start their married life on a sour note. "Are you going to check on the horses?"

"Brownie got kicked in the left knee the other day, remember? I'll have to break another horse for patrol."

"Patrol?"

He gazed at his reflection with satisfaction and smoothed one side of his hair. "That's what we do most of the time. Ride mile after endless mile to make sure those savages at San Carlos haven't sneaked away to Mexico."

"I think the preacher said services were at ten, Carleton," Norah interrupted, not liking to think of him confronting renegades. She caught her breath. Mason had to bring men like that to justice. Wrenching her mind from him, she pictured Carleton in a velvet-collared overcoat and top hat riding beside her in an upholstered carriage on their way to dinner and the opera.

"Why don't I meet you at the adjutant's office? It's after nine now, but that will give you plenty of time to dress."

"All right. I think I'll wear my—"

He sat on the cot's edge and ran his hand down her bare back to the swell of buttock. "It doesn't matter what you wear, you luscious baggage." Her husband nibbled her ear. "I feel like kissing you from head to toe."

She put her cheek to his for a moment. "Shoo. I want to freshen up and dress, and I don't know how long it will take. I'm not used to tent living."

"I'm going. But you'd better get started. I might forget about the horses and come back to spend the day in bed."

"Really! This *is* Sunday." Norah pretended indignation and pushed him away. "Get out!" After his departure, she peeked through the flaps to make sure he had indeed gone to the stables. Yes, there he went, ramrod straight, unconsciously a bit cocky after his wedding night.

Norah washed, braided her hair, dressed, and put their belongings in order, careful to shake out shoes and garments that had been on the ground in case scorpions had crawled into them. Then she stepped outside, feeling fresh and renewed. Birds flitted about in juniper trees and sagebrush, and Norah had a pang of regret to think she'd not write that book now. A crimson flash heralded a cardinal's arrival, then a black-and-lemon-yellow oriole winged past, followed by a bumblebee that echoed its colors. Norah patted the mastiff's side as he pressed lovingly against her leg. She sighed with contentment.

Her whole life lay ahead like an endless sea, the past a distant shore behind her soon to be forgotten. She saw her husband waiting outside the major's quarters and waved her hat—the ribbons moving in the air like a trogon's tail—then walked purposefully into the future.

15.

Mason watched Norah hungrily from a window in the parlor. She wore blue and carried a white, lace-trimmed parasol beneath which her skin glowed like pearl. The large eyes roved about the compound, and Mason guessed she was bored. He chuckled in spite of his melancholy, recalling her energy and curiosity.

"Still got it bad?" Edward Bertram asked. He rested on the bed in shirt-sleeves, tired and muddy-skinned from a summer dysentery he was unable to shake.

"Head over heels. Didn't know it could hurt so much. And listen, Eddie, I don't want her to know I'm here."

His friend yawned. "I know, I know. You riding out early tomorrow?"

"Before first light. And not looking forward to it, either. It's a long way to the new Territorial Prison at Yuma and still hot as the hinges of hell between Tucson and the Colorado River. That sheriff from New Mexico did a heck of a job bringing the prisoner in. I'm going to chain that murderer's feet under his horse's belly so he knows I mean business. I don't want to be chasing him through those big sand dunes."

"A real bastard?"

"Murdered three men and a woman on a ranch near Tubac, then set fire to the buildings and accidentally killed a young boy asleep in the barn. Thinks it's a big joke."

The major went into the next room to use the chamberpot and returned to fall back on the bed. "God, I wish I could get rid of this. Theo's given me every medicine he's got."

"Is she happy, Eddie?"

"How the devil do I know? The wedding was only four days ago. Ask me next year. If they're still here—which I doubt. He's rich. He can take good care of her. Women want security. More than love sometimes. And it's not as if he's a career officer, waiting for a promotion that might take ten years."

Mason left the window and sat down in a chair near the bed. "When was your last promotion?"

Bertram rolled his eyes and then shut them. "Six years ago."

"Too damned long," Mason complained sympathetically. Rank came slowly in the Indian-fighting Army, out of the sight and mind of Washington, where an Apache was the same as a Sioux, primitive men of valor to be treated as children with little regard for cultural differences.

"Do you know what I have to do in the near future?" Bertram's eyes opened and he stared at the ceiling. "I have to punish a deserter. An Irish immigrant who likes to sing and dance, a youngster who can't stand life without grass and rain." His voice dropped to a grim whisper. "I hate the smell of live flesh burning. It stays in my mouth for days."

Mason went back to the window. He would rather escort an unrepentant killer to prison with death at his elbow than brand a fellow human being. He had seen it done: the D-shaped brass harness ring, heated red hot, was imbedded in the white softness of each buttock. He was always amazed by how white they were though the man might be brown as toast elsewhere. He shook his head to rid himself of the vision. "He has to be made an example of," Mason comforted, knowing his comment was no help at all. "You know that. You've done it before."

"Yes, God help me, I've done it before. But we can't keep good men when we punish them like that. The regulations must be changed." The officer turned on his side to try to sleep.

Mason frowned. Dr. Gates had tried every remedy he

knew, but Eddie's diarrhea and malaise had grown worse and more debilitating. He had an idea, but—what the hell, Eddie had nothing to lose. Striding to the back door, he called out.

"I am here, Fletcher." The Apache came from a corner in the kitchen where he had been meditating.

"Can you get some herbs for Major Bertram?"

Chico showed tobacco-stained teeth in amusement. "White man's medicine no good for the shits?"

Mason ignored the jibe. "You fixed me a tea once, remember?"

"The summer of the great thunder."

"Do those shrubs grow nearby?"

The man fingered the bag of *hoddentin* hanging from his neck. "Hour's ride maybe."

"Get going, then. I'd like to know he's feeling better before we go in the morning."

He resumed his vigil by the window, but Norah did not reappear. Mason sighed, saw that his friend was sleeping, if uneasily, and tiptoed to the kitchen to brew coffee. He brooded over the next day's journey—and the woman he loved who was now lost to him.

The three men rode west from the fort before dawn, and Norah heard the horses' hoofs on the hard ground. Alone because she insisted Carleton sleep in his own cot after lovemaking, she raised herself up to listen. He snored steadily and not too noisily, a good sign of the deep sleep he needed before going on patrol in a few hours. She kept an eye on his food and rest, anxious he remain well under the pressure of days in the saddle and an inadequate field diet.

Retrieving her slippers from under the blanket, Norah put them on, groped her way to the tent flaps, and untied them. She stepped into what she thought of as tender darkness, seeing the riders fade into nothingness with only a spark from an iron shoe striking rock to reveal their momentary position.

Accustomed to rising before or at first light, Norah had come to cherish this time of quiet and privacy. She liked twilight, too, but the fresh, dewy day especially pleased her. At the ranch she had often timed the song of the canyon wren, a white and chestnut-brown mite who heralded the coming day. *Catherpes mexicanus* was somewhere nearby now, a melodic alarm clock caroling to the sun.

Light crept gradually onto the mesas and into arroyos and canyons. Mountains grew in size as sunlight ascended their slopes. Textures varied with distance and ground cover; some resembled crumpled paper, or folded velvet; a few thrust toward the opalescent sky like what they were— brutally honest rocky crags.

A trembling sigh left Norah's lips as she pictured a crag where a cliff house slept snuggled in the pines. She stepped into the tent and studied her husband. She could not picture him there, hunched by the old fire pit. No, he was as alien to it as porcelain and china were to rough clay pottery.

Unable to do any chores in the small confines without waking him, Norah sat outside in her wrapper. What were they doing on the ranch right now? Wasn't it time for fall roundup? Chan Lee would have fed the crew by now and given Old Sugar his daily handout. Jim, needing a haircut as usual, was no doubt going about his daily routine, and Joel had taken the crew into the valley, and dear Shorty was probably grousing about not being in the saddle with them.

She missed the Double Bar F much more than she had anticipated, and aside from the men, whom she loved like brothers, what she missed most was her freedom. Norah had not put the feeling into words before; in fact, the word *freedom* popped out of nowhere. But that was it—liberty, elbow room, being on her own hook. There would be precious little of that for the wife of one of Philadelphia's leading citizens. No bareback rides in men's clothing, no doing what she damn well pleased after work was finished. No rolling in dew-sweetened grass and wildflowers like a colt intoxicated with life. Bird-watching, yes, that genteel hobby, but not in the wilderness she had grown to love so much, remote and splendidly dangerous.

"Norah? You out there?"

"I was watching the sunrise."

"I need my morning kiss."

"Only one? Are you tired of me already?" She went back into the tent, tying the flaps behind her.

Now their lives revolved around bugle calls: reveille at sunrise, guard mount before breakfast, in mid-afternoon, and before taps, sick call, officers' call for orders, stable call, fire call, and Norah's favorite, retreat. When taps were blown, the bugler turned to the four points of the compass, the silvery notes easing into lilac skies, across vermilion cliffs and down the tawny distances.

Ten days after the wedding Norah saw her husband off to war. Indian depredations had increased of late. Roving bands of Chiricahuas, disgusted and discontented with inferior and meager rations, angered by disagreement between military and civilian authorities, broke out of San Carlos. They raided and stole livestock, burned and killed—it was the old way of their ancestors. Some joined Geronimo, Juh, and Nolgee, operating out of Hot Springs Reservation in New Mexico where they rested and got supplies; others rode in loose, constantly changing groups, elusive as campfire smoke. These bad apples, contaminating the whole barrel, had to be captured and returned in irons. Or be left to rot in the sun. It was their choice.

The trumpeter sounded assembly. Horses had been saddled and packed, and troopers carefully inspected each buckle, canteen, and weapon. Anything overlooked could mean the difference between life and death. Carleton led his mount to where Norah stood alone in front of the physician's quarters. "Don't know when we'll be back, darling. Take care of yourself." He drank in her image to sustain him in hours of boredom and peril.

"Carleton, I'm afraid for you!" She held him close and they kissed.

"You're afraid I'll find another pretty girl on a ranch somewhere," he joked. "Now, don't worry. I'll be back before you know it."

"The roof will be finished this afternoon. Maybe our 'house' will be ready by that time." Norah was determined to send him off with dignity and pride in her self-control. "After I've unpacked, you'll never recognize the place."

He glanced at the picket line and mounted. "Looks like we're ready to go. Good-bye, my sweet." Carleton could not resist a final kiss.

"Good-bye." Her response was a whisper, but she smiled and waved as he joined his men. The guidon on its lance rose up against the burning blue sky and the cavalry moved out at a walk. As was customary, it departed to the strains of "The Girl I Left Behind Me," rendered by the blacksmith's flute and cook's fiddle in the absence of a military band.

Norah felt Lollie's presence beside her and was grateful for her support. They watched until the column was little more than a trail of dust illumined now and then by flashes of sun on metal. Norah cleared her throat and wiped her eyes. "That was hard. And so soon, too." He meant more to her than she had realized.

"You did very well. A real Army wife." Lollie linked arms with her. "Have you had breakfast?"

"I couldn't." Norah put a hand on her abdomen. "It's still churning."

"In that case, come along," the older woman ordered. "Keeping busy is the ticket. We'll have a bite and then tackle the floor in your quarters. Why, you could sleep there tonight if we work hard."

"Oh, I'd like that! I feel so vulnerable, so—exposed in the tent by myself."

Norah took a last look over her shoulder. Nothing showed on the horizon now but a haze that might have been dust devils swirling across the earth, tornadoes in miniature. For an instant she thought of how she had watched Mason disappear from the ranch into the distance. *Vaya con Dios,* he had said. Carleton, dear husband—and all your men—go with God.

"We need another one here, I think." The blacksmith crawled to the spot Norah pointed at and drove an enormous spike to anchor the carpet which had been laid upon canvas to cover the adobe floor.

"That should do 'er, ma'am." He got to his feet, towering over the women, brawny and muscular.

"Thank you so much. You did an excellent job."

"Pleasure, ma'am." He gathered his tools and was gone.

Clasping her hands, Norah bounced up and down in place, so excited was she by the prospect of being mistress of her very own home. "Carpet, curtains, a bed, and a tiny kitchen, too! It's darling!"

"Listen, I'll requisition a few strong backs to cart everything over from the two tents," Lollie decided. "Then you can put things away. Can you manage with that muslin while I'm gone?"

Spiders, scorpions, and centipedes inched across the mud ceilings and necessitated the hanging of the thin, unbleached muslin Mexicans called *manta*. It sagged like a big hammock but caught the creatures if they dropped. She had seen them at the ranch, of course, and they were exhibited in alcohol with tarantulas and snakes at the sutler's store where officers played billiards and cards, and enlisted men bought beer. Standing on the trunk, Norah tacked the muslin firmly to the rafters. The mere idea of such horrid things landing on her while she slept gave her goose bumps!

By nightfall the one-room adobe had a decidedly homey atmosphere. Norah sat in bed, asessing her handiwork and the labors of Lollie and the soldiers who had leaped at the chance to carry boxes and packages for the beauteous Mrs. Beatty. She had paused in her letter to Jim and now continued.

. . . the carpet is Turkey red! A real find from Lordsburg. The trader also had a bolt of red, white, and blue print I have made into curtains, and the whole effect is not only patriotic but cheerful and charming. At least to my prejudiced eye is it! We have a small fireplace, a plank table, a stove of adobe brick and cast iron in the cooking hut to the rear, two lamps, books, and—Oh, I'm sure you don't care what furnishings we have, men seldom do, but rest assured I am safe, happy, and comfortable. (But how I miss the ranch!)

I want to thank everyone again for my wedding gifts. As I wrote earlier, Shorty's best spurs and the horsehair quirt Joel brought come in handy every day. Carleton bought me a horse—Steel, I call him. Would you have imagined me riding a big animal this time last year?

I often wear the garnet brooch you sent, Jim, and you'd have been pleased indeed to see what a nice dress came out of Aunt May's brocade. The gold coin from Emedio and jade butterfly from Chan Lee were great sacrifices for them to make, and I will treasure them.

Thank you, dear friends—and Rose, too, for the embroidered petticoat (I had no idea she was getting so artistic and clever!). I shall cherish each gift as I cherish each of you. Forever.

Love to all,
Norah

P.S. Am sending tobacco, canned milk (you were running out, as I recall), tea, and violet-scented hair pomade for Rose. Did you have a good roundup? By the way, Baron likes it here very much. The soldiers spoil him. He even acts puppyish sometimes!

Putting letter and pencil on the bedside table, Norah blew out the lamp and slid down under the covers, the new straw-filled mattress rustling in a friendly way. Did other women feel like this? she wondered. Did they miss their husbands yet secretly revel in a brief respite to themselves?

Baron leaped onto the bed and curled himself into a ball near her feet. Norah wriggled her toes against his bulk. Carleton would have a fit if he knew, but she liked having the dog close. He was afraid of nothing.

She said a prayer for her husband's safety and then—as she would do many times in years to come—said one for Mason Fletcher.

Please, Lord, keep the men I love safe from harm.

Exhausted, dirty, and irritable, Carleton tried not to glare at Lollie Gates. It was not her fault Norah was nowhere to be seen. He had reported on the troop's fruitless two-week patrol down one side of the Chiricahua Mountains and up the other with frequent forays after Apaches who disappeared into the landscape like prairie dogs into holes. Now he wanted nothing but a bath, a decent meal, and his wife's attentions.

"She's not riding alone, is she?" Little hellion. Norah ought to know better. After all, she had lived in Arizona for over a year now.

"Oh, no. Lieutenant Gray and Corporal Jamison are with her. We would never let her go out there—" Lollie waved vaguely at the unfriendly land she herself seldom visited. "Alone that is," she concluded lamely. What would his reaction be to the riding habit with the divided skirt that Norah wore, that daring garment she found so comfortable and convenient?

"You look very tired. Why don't you get some rest? She ought to be here any minute. They couldn't help but see the dust from the column riding in."

Carleton rubbed his forehead and sighed. "You're right. Thank you, Mrs. Gates."

"You're welcome," she murmured, not knowing what he

was thanking her for. Perhaps it was for the assurance that his wife was even now galloping back to be at his side.

She saw the officer walk wearily to his quarters. Norah was going to have trouble if she didn't hurry! Just then three horses cantered into the fort with Steel in the lead. Norah's graceful figure was an integral part of the animal as she reined him in, instinctively secure in her mastery over him. She dismounted and was about to lead Steel into the stables when Lollie hailed her, trotting across the parade ground with skirts lifted off the ground.

"Carleton's back, Norah! Didn't you see the column coming in?"

Norah put a hand to her mouth. Her first reaction was one of joy, the second consternation, for she had not planned to spring her unconventional riding habit on him so soon. "We were bird-watching on the other side of the cliff. A bunch of noisy quail. Thank God he's safe!" she said, and left at a run. "Unsaddle Steel, will you?" she called to her escorts, who motioned assent. Norah burst into the house and threw herself into her husband's arms, almost knocking him over. "You're home! I'm sorry I wasn't here!"

"I'm all dirty," he warned, holding her at arm's length.

"I don't care!" She snuggled against his chest, smelling sweat and dirt and woodsmoke in his clothing. "Mmmmm, hold me close. Closer!" He held her, rocking her slim form back and forth. Then she bent backward in order to see his face and stood on booted tiptoe to kiss his chapped lips. "Are you all right? Didn't get hurt or anything?"

He shook his head and pulled the curls tossed by wind, looking into the beloved face flushed beneath its golden tan. "Well, you aren't, after all."

"Aren't what?"

"No, you aren't. Too bad."

Norah shook him. "What *are* you talking about?"

Carleton stared down solemnly. "You aren't any prettier. You're absolutely breathtaking!" He crushed Norah to him, kissing her almost frantically as if to draw her substance into him. To moisten parched flesh, fill the hollows of fear and frustration, bathe in the warmth of her love and concern.

She drew him toward the bed, but he stopped her. "No, there's no time. Major Bertram has put me in command of punishing a deserter. It's to be done this afternoon. As soon as possible, in fact." He unwound Norah's arms with reluctance. "Dr. Gates feels the man has suffered enough waiting so long for punishment. But he must be made an example of. Otherwise, you'll have cowards running off any time they—" He paused. "Norah, what is that you're wearing?"

The time had come. She held out both sides of the voluminous, ankle-length garment. "It's a divided riding skirt." She pirouetted.

His eyebrows went up. "I forbid you to wear it again. Ever! And certainly not in the presence of other men."

"But I don't like sidesaddles," she wailed.

Carleton stripped to the buff, discarding filthy clothing worn for fourteen days. He dumped a bucket of lukewarm water into the vinegar-barrel tub Norah had acquired and sat down with a groan of pleasure. "Get me some hot water, will you? And change into a dress. I won't have you wearing pants and that's all there is to it. It's common and vulgar."

"Yes, Carleton," she agreed in a meek voice and brought a bucket from the stove in the cooking hut. Pouring it into the tub, Norah asked, "Doesn't the house look nice?"

On entering, Carleton had gotten the impression of brightness and coziness. Now, glancing about, he commented on Norah's decorating skill and color scheme. He noticed a corner for him: a chair, a crate for a hassock, her wedding gift—the leather-bound trio of *The Count of Monte Cristo*, *Two Years before the Mast*, and *The Three Musketeers*—on a table with cigars and ashtray. "Don't get too attached to this. If an officer who outranks me gets assigned here, we'll have to move."

"Move?" Norah froze in disbelief, long legs bare after removing the skirt.

"That's the way it works. Instead of musical chairs, it's musical houses." He stood up, dripping and refreshed. "Heard of a fellow with a family who wound up living in a hallway. Then he got ranked out of the hallway and left the Army in disgust."

"I don't blame him!"

Carleton toweled himself and felt an erection begin. "I think we'll take the time, Norah. Lock the door."

She undressed swiftly in the bedroom alcove and held her arms out to him. He joined her, skin damp and fragrant with health and cleanliness; there was no need to talk. Norah offered herself, and Carleton took her in an explosion of ecstasy. Then he rested and took her again, but only after making sure she was ready. He had learned. It was better that way.

"Must you go?" she said after a while, walking through his chest hair with her fingertips.

"Yes, and right now." He kissed her mouth and nipples and got out of bed, taking clean hose and underwear from a chest. He donned full-dress uniform with saber and scabbard, white gloves, and the Prussian-style helmet with brass decorations and plume. He turned at the door. "Please stay inside, Norah. This is nothing for a woman to see."

"What will happen?" she asked in a hushed voice, awed by his authority and responsibility.

"Special formation with men in dress uniform, including the prisoner, then the reading of orders. He is held while I tear off every button, the crossed sabers on his collar, the brass shield signifying the Army from his cap, and the yellow stripes from his trousers."

Carleton adjusted his scabbard with a trace of nervousness. "Then I order the saddler to brand the deserter with the letter D on each hip. When he can walk, he'll be escorted to Tucson where the Army washes its hands of him."

"I'll stay inside."

Norah dressed, stored the riding habit in her trunk, and remade the bed. She emptied the bath water, dried the tub, sopped up water he had dripped on the carpet, and bundled the soiled uniform and underclothing for delivery to a laundress on "Soapsuds Row." Busy as she kept herself, the scream of agony that rent the air so unexpectedly made her scalp crawl. She retched at the second shriek and had to wipe away tears.

Carleton returned at the end of the afternoon, face strained and ashen under the sunburn. They had a light supper, and he read for an hour without discussing passages in the book as he ordinarily did. The branding had cast a pall over the fort, and no one called about joining in a stroll, playing cards, or drinking wine and perusing photo albums. When they went to bed, they did not make love but held each other like children whose companion had been chastised.

"I hated doing that," he said, "whether the boy was a coward or not."

"I'm sorry," Norah whispered, heart aching for him and the deserter, who was only a homesick immigrant boy.

"I thought about resigning most of the time I was on patrol. This isn't a normal life, and it's not as if I were a career officer. I'm tired of being a chip off the old block. I've decided to resign as soon as a replacement can be arranged." Finally relaxed by his decision, Carleton fell quiet and slept.

Norah listened to the subtle night sounds. She knew living in a city again would take getting used to. No more sunny stillness. No singing reaches of countryside alive with wildlife. She wondered—would these images eventually fade? All this be lost to her? No, she would never forget.

She moved closer to Carleton, his buttocks nestled in her loins like cup and saucer. Life was a stream of negatives and positives. Loss and compensation. Memory and forgetting. Hurt and joy. Whatever came, Norah knew she was strong enough to handle it. To survive.

16.

The Apache put an ear to the ground, eyes glittering with anticipation. Then he leaped to his feet and shook a rifle overhead in triumph. The cavalry troop was coming.

Fellow *hesh-kes*, the ritual killers, signaled in return from each side of the mountain gorge where they crouched in hiding. They glanced at each other with satisfaction, then they settled down to wait, patient as diamondbacks beside a rodent burrow.

The Indians knew these soldiers were not responsible for the recent deaths of several Apache women; likely it had been greedy men searching for silver. Still, a white-eyes was a white-eyes, and someone had to pay. Their loud bugle calls and big, heavy mounts put the brave soldiers at a distinct disadvantage, for their fleet adversaries could leave them behind as mountain goats did a lame bear.

Sergeant Mulrooney held up a gauntleted hand, bringing the unit to a halt. Hair on the back of his neck prickled with suspicion, a sixth sense, and the savvy old mule he rode pointed his ears forward and grumbled nervously.

Carleton pulled rein beside his sergeant. "What's wrong, Mulrooney—"

"Sorry, sir. It don't feel right, sir. And look at Stonewall. Mules can smell Indians, sir. Guess you know that."

His superior regarded him with an expression bordering on disgust. "That mule is not in command. I trust you understand what I am saying." The superstitious Mick.

"But, sir . . ." Mulrooney had been blooded early in the wars with Plains Indians. Something was very wrong here. He had never had the "sight" his mother did, but he would bet his life on this.

"I expect every man jack of you to follow me through that damned canyon. If you do not, you will each walk the fort perimeter with a heavy log tied to your shoulders and do without beer for a month. This route cuts twenty miles off the patrol and I intend to follow it." They had been out for several days and it seemed a year. He was anxious to be with Norah, who was planning a Halloween party the night of his birthday.

Mulrooney glanced at the tight-faced young troopers, a mixture of Irishmen, Germans, Englishmen, and Swiss. They were paid thirteen dollars a month to face death, and he received eight more for training them to do so. He shrugged with Gaelic fatalism. "All right, boys. Keep your eyes peeled!" Mulrooney pulled his saddle carbine and unfastened the holster flap on his sidearm. The troopers imitated him, moistening dry lips as they did so. Stonewall brayed and bucked. "Shut up, you sonofabitch," the sergeant growled fondly. "Don't you know Apaches love mule meat? You'll not even be dead when they cut it off you, either."

Carleton listened with half an ear, aggravated by the futility of his many patrols and by the fact that no one had as yet been assigned to the fort to replace him. Surely his father had received his most recent letter and was exerting influence at the War Department. God damn it, he wanted to go home and have Norah settled before Christmas! As a gentleman and an officer, however, he could not bring himself to resign and leave Major Bertram shorthanded while the man was still so sick.

An odd *thunk* brought an abrupt end to his musings, and Carleton shifted in the saddle to look behind him. Yanking in vain at an arrow imbedded in his throat, eyes starting and incredulous, a trooper vomited blood as he toppled to the ground and strangled to death. *"Back! Back, you bastards! Get a move on!"* Carleton cut short the recruits' moment of horror and galvanized them into action. They were jammed in a narrow passage between walls rising slate-smooth to their summits where the ambushers had concealed themselves behind an edging of boulders, but the youngsters rallied enough to fire at the invisible enemy and retreat in a semblance of order.

Outside the passageway, sweaty and excited, the men realized they were short one more. "Who's missin', for Christ's sake?" Mulrooney demanded.

"Dewhurst, sir," a trooper told him, gasping. "He was right beside me a minute ago—hey, there he is, sir. Oh, my God—*he's going the wrong way!*" The men yelled, whistled, and shot in the air, but the panic-stricken soldier continued to gallop in the other direction and soon vanished around the bend.

Fingers shaking slightly, Carleton reloaded, mouth brassy and dry. It was his fault the boy was in there, and it was his job to get him. "I'm riding in."

"You can't go alone, sir!" Mulrooney objected, and the entire unit gigged their mounts forward, mouths grim despite the turmoil in their bellies.

"Hola, señores! Soldados!" The sibilant words snaked their way down from above. Spanish was the Apache's second tongue, but few white newcomers spoke or understood it. A language barrier did not matter now, however, for no one had any difficulty understanding the sight of Dewhurst stripped naked with hands bound behind his back, bare feet dancing painfully on the hot rock.

"Oh, *Christ!*" Carleton muttered. Why had the boy run like that? There was little likelihood of saving him now, He gripped Mulrooney's massive arm. "Is there some way we can get up there?"

"Have to go 'round the whole range, sir, and come up the rear. Take two hours, maybe three." He lowered his voice.

"Boy'll be dead by then, God willin'." Carleton gave him a sharp look but said nothing further.

He bit his lip, wondering whose son this was and how he'd feel if the boy were his and Norah's. A friend of Dewhurst's sobbed in boyish fury and aimed at an Apache, who yanked the long blond hair so cruelly the boy shrieked. *"Cuidado,"* another Apache warned, and cut a bloody cross on the boy's chest with a knife that flashed in the light.

Dewhurst screamed in agony, and his knees buckled, but he was held upright by his hair. His comrades swore terribly and clenched their weapons, raging with impotence and grief. They heard laughter; then somebody shouted *"Hasta luego."* Until later. Words to fray the nerves and quicken the imagination.

They stared, fascinated and appalled to see their friend jerked backward and out of sight. His faint cry might have been that of a rabbit crunched in a fox's jaws. The men chafed at their helplessness, and the boy whose aim had inspired the cutting was inconsolable. Were the tales of torture true? What would they do to him, poetic, shy Dewhurst, only months from Bristol, seeking adventure in the American Indian-fighting Army?

The troop struck a gloomy camp that night not far away. Supper was the standard field mess of hardtack, beans, bacon, and coffee. Much of it came back up when a horse lumbered into camp with its eyelids sewn shut with rawhide. Whinnying in pain and fright, the animal carried a stained sack stuffed with Dewhurst's remains. The message was clear as rain water: *dah-eh-sah.* Death.

Norah had found that Carleton was usually gone ten to fourteen days. He swung north, then east, then south along the mountain range to the Mexican border where he joined with other units intent on the same goal: netting Chiricahuas who prowled from one country to another like coppery mountain lions. Barred by international etiquette from crossing the border, Army men saw many a chase end in frustration and fatigue while Apaches rode safely into Sierra Madre strongholds.

One morning the first week in November, Norah awoke thinking of the Halloween party canceled in Carleton's absence, and then of the ranch. The fort was a temporary abode and the Philadelphia mansion nothing but words, and she was like a horse who considered his birthplace his home—his *querencia*, Emedio called it. She had been reborn on the Double Bar F and she hungered to poke fun at Shorty's tall tales, discuss the calf crop with Jim, eat Chan Lee's chocolate cake, see what Rose was up to, feel the rhythm of ranch life revolving around the herds that gave it meaning, purpose, and a future.

Dressed in her prettiest pink cotton and blue-feathered bonnet, Norah visited Major Bertram, but her feminine wiles were ignored—if in fact they were noticed at all—by the ailing officer. "I'm very sorry, but we're much too short-handed to provide you with an armed escort." He was in uniform and performing administrative duties, but his yellow eye whites and complexion clearly revealed the ravages of jaundice.

"Furthermore, dear lady, your husband was adamant about your remaining here. I have good news for you though." He tapped a paper on the cluttered desk. "I just received word that a West Point graduate has been assigned to replace Lieutenant Beatty. He should arrive by the end of the month. So you see? You'll be presiding over your own stylish household during the holidays and will soon forget all about us out here on the frontier."

Norah's face glowed. "I will never forget! Last year when I was carried from the stage station to your hospital, I was more dead than alive. I found kindness, concern, and affection here that I will always treasure."

He nodded, pleased and touched. "You have repaid us by being a sister to us lonely fellows."

"I do hope you feel better soon," she said, walking toward the door.

"My medical leave has been authorized, thank the Lord. Dr. Gates can do nothing more and wrote a strongly worded letter to Washington that did the trick. The new commanding officer arrives tomorrow, and I catch a stage for the East the day after." He opened the door for her, getting a whiff of cologne. "I am sorry I could not accede to your wishes."

"I understand your position, and you're no doubt right." Norah leaned forward and kissed the yellow cheek lightly. "God be with you."

He took her hand in its crocheted glove and kissed it, then leaned against the doorjamb to watch her cross the parade ground like an inverted flower blown along by the wind. Had he been less struck with Norah's beauty and more his old keen self, he might have recognized resolution and decision in the set of her shoulders.

She sank onto the bed and removed her bonnet. So Carleton's replacement would be here soon. All the more reason to go to the ranch now. Once in the East, she would never see her friends again. She had to visit them a final time, had to say good-bye.

Norah ate with the Gateses when Carleton was away, but this time begged off from the after-dinner card game. Pretending she was indisposed, she returned to quarters early and made preparations for the ride to the Double Bar F. She estimated the distance aboard the gelding, remembering that a good horse like Steel could cover eighty miles in twelve hours. The ranch lay approximately fifty miles south, which meant he could deliver her there by early afternoon if they started at dawn and ran into no trouble. Norah fully realized that the trip she contemplated might be dangerous, but she tingled with anticipation.

Up well before departure time, she drew the curtains tightly so the lamp could not be seen. She ate a hearty breakfast and fed Baron well before dressing in the divided riding skirt, boots, flannel shirt, and a felt hat tied on with a scarf. At the last minute she checked her field pack: blanket, jacket, hardtack and jerky, extra shirt, lariat, and canteen, with a shelter tent in which these items were rolled to be strapped in back of the saddle.

Her heart fluttered with excitement when she buckled on her gun belt. She was ready. Norah then pulled on gloves and blew out the lamp. In her mind's eye she reread the note to Carleton propped against his books. Norah visualized his reaction, but firmly put it out of her mind. With luck she would be back before he was.

It seemed an omen of good fortune that no one was on duty at the stables, although voices sounded from the barracks mess hall not far away. Quickly she bridled and saddled her horse, tied the pack on, suspended field glasses and canteen from the saddle horn, and led him outside. She mounted, regretting there was no way to avoid the gate sentry, who could easily see she was equipped for a journey. He was, fortunately, a new recruit who didn't know her.

"Halt! Who goes there?" The sentry peered at the slight rider. Norah moved closer, and the man exclaimed, "Ma'am! You—you aren't going off post alone, are you? I'll have to report."

She gave him her most dazzling smile. "Oh, Sergeant . . ."

"Corporal, ma'am," he corrected automatically.

"I just can't keep those chevrons straight." Norah looked about in a conspiratorial manner. "I know a gentleman like you can keep a lady's secret. A rather silly secret, mind you. But they laugh at me." Which was a fib. The fort's intellectuals approved of her hobby. Isolated posts such as Fort Guardian often boasted members who passed their spare time with such amateur studies.

The soldier admired the line of thigh under the scandalous riding skirt, knowing as sure as he stood there he would do what she asked. "I wouldn't laugh."

Her voice dropped to a whisper. "I know you won't. You see, I'm going bird-watching. Right over there where the cliff swallows have their nests. They're difficult to observe because they're so fast. There's a bird called a swift, too, that's a cousin, I do believe." Norah chuckled as if sharing a joke and gazed absentmindedly toward rock-ribbed hills overlooking the fort.

Poor lady, the sentry thought, admiring her dark red hair and classic profile. He had heard of a post where the colonel's wife had gone insane from boredom, loneliness, and worry about her husband, who was in the field almost constantly against the Shoshone. What harm could come from bird-watching? The hills were right within range of vision, and he would tell his relief to keep an eye on her.

"You go along, ma'am. Have a good time. Just don't go too far, will you?"

Norah's face lit up. "Oh, I'll have a good time. Thank you." She gave him a mock salute, touching her quirt to the plumed hat, then spurred Steel into a slow trot.

The soldier heard her singing to herself. The trio made a pretty picture in the growing light: the great brindle mastiff running beside the dove-gray figure on the black-maned blue roan. Then he cursed. She wasn't headed for the cliffs at all! Goddamn it, she had turned south and was galloping out of sight as if the horse had salt under its tail. The sentry sighed and kicked the gate hard enough to hurt his toe. Women! He was in hot water for sure thanks to those sultry blue eyes.

Norah threw her head back and cried out with joy as Steel sped through the morning. In the distance, mountains cloaked in sunlit emerald and plum-dark shadows beckoned, and the grasslands lifted their jade arms and sighed their welcome.

She was free and coming home!

The Apaches saw her before Eli Martin did. He had been combing the range for a prime yearling bull with more wanderlust than was good for him, while the Chiricahuas had slipped into the southeastern corner of Arizona Territory to steal horses. Halfway into the journey, Norah had made a rest stop, and not until she was back in the saddle did she notice riders approaching from the south. Grabbing the field glasses, she focused in on them. A dark, feral face leaped into view, and Norah almost screamed aloud. *Geronimo!*

She jammed the spurs in so hard her astonished horse reared and pawed the air before launching himself to the west with Baron racing at his heels. The Apaches yipped with triumph and the thrill of the chase, their cries chilling Norah to the marrow. Much too far now from the fort to make a run for it, she had to gamble on reaching the spread that belonged to Mason's friend. The Indians would hardly shoot Steel. He was too superb to risk injuring, a chieftain's horse worth a fortune. Chances were they would not shoot her, either, but an Army wife knew she should put a bullet in her brain rather than let herself be taken. Norah risked a glance over her shoulder and gasped with alarm to see how close Geronimo and a younger warrior had drawn; a belt made of gold and silver watchcases taken from dying men glinted around the older warrior's midriff.

Steel flew past a handsome yearling nestled in the grass, whose big eyes widened with surprise. Hope surged through Norah then, as Eli Martin and his cowboys suddenly galloped into sight, pounding in her direction. The Apaches slowed and angled back the way they had come. They had no taste for combat with hard-bitten sharpshooters like these; facing a hail of bullets was foolish, whereas ambush and deception had worked for centuries. They also recognized the supreme irony at work here. The Army was under orders not to kill them if they surrendered and settled down to raise crops, regardless of what crimes they had committed. White settlers, on the other hand, many of whom had been victims, operated on a different principle: an eye for an eye.

Norah pulled rein with the last of her strength. The rancher and one of his hands thundered to a stop on either side while the other men galloped on, shooting at her pursuers. *"You!"* he exclaimed, reaching out to steady

Norah as she swayed half-fainting. Dismounting hurriedly, he lifted her down, hands around her waist.

"Hey, Slim, get that whiskey outa my slicker. I don't want to let her go."

"Don't blame you," the cowboy said with a cheerful grin. He unwrapped the bottle and reached across Norah to give it to his boss. Baron snarled and bit at the man in warning. Eli put a hand on his head. "We won't hurt her, son."

The cowboy took his hand away from his holster. "That's the darndest thing, the way you do that."

"He'd have my throat torn out by now if he didn't sense I was trying to help her," Eli said, putting the bottle to her lips. Norah choked on the fiery liquid, but it brought her to life. She coughed and drew away, eyes streaming.

"Sure didn't expect to meet up with you this way." Eli took a swig himself and offered the flask to Norah, who shook her head. "Where you headed?"

"For Jim Fullerton's ranch." She recovered enough to run a hand down Steel's legs and examine his ankles.

Eli squinted at the sun. "You better not go on with them hostiles nearby. You're closer to my place than the Double Bar F anyhow. Have dinner and stay the night. Be proud to have you."

"Thank you, but I must go on." She had forgotten how dominant a personality he had and how striking he looked with those green eyes, dark as an icy forest pool, set deep in the tanned face. He had grown a mustache, brown and silver like his collar-length hair.

"No, you *ain't* goin' on. Might be more cherry-cows 'tween us and Jim's. Put the whole Arizona Territory in a tizzy if they got hold of you! Can't let you have an escort either, 'cause a bunch of my men are up at Hooker's Sierra Bonita racing horses."

"Well, in that case—"

"Got a Chinee woman cook and a German housekeeper. You'll be chaperoned."

Norah's rings flashed when she removed her gloves to pin up disheveled hair and pull her hat on tighter. "My husband will be glad to hear that."

Their eyes met for a long moment. Strong as she was, he was stronger and not about to indulge her high spirits. "All right, then, I accept your invitation. With luck my husband and his unit may ride north tomorrow from the border and I can join them."

Norah remounted, and Eli took her ankle in a snug grip. "Ain't no need to keep tellin' me about your husband. Heard you got spliced not long ago. Congratulations."

His men cantered back, and he vaulted lightly into the saddle. "Okay, *vamos!*" he called and led the way toward the EM Ranch. Eli Martin smiled to himself, looking forward to an interesting evening.

17.

Mason leaned back in the chair, lifting its front legs off the floor. "You think Chico's herbs made you worse, Eddie? He'd feel bad about that." He was visiting his old friend in Washington's Army hospital.

"No, no. Theo said the jaundice had advanced too far for them to have had any effect. They tell me here it's an excess of bile from the liver. I'm one funny color, aren't I?"

"Well, partner, I have to admit you're not the most edifying sight I've seen lately," Mason joshed.

The patient rubbed his forehead and yawned. "Speaking of edifying sights, Mrs. Beatty came to see me before I left. About a month ago. Wanted permission to ride down to that ranch. I didn't have any soldiers to spare and thought I'd persuaded her to stay on post, but doggone if she didn't ride out the next morning on the pretext of bird-watching, and the sentry fell for it."

Mason's chair thudded to the floor. "You sent men after her?"

"Couldn't. I never had more than forty men, you know that. Beatty had twenty on patrol, eight were sick, six were hunting in the Dragoons. I had no choice." The major chewed his lip. "She did have a Colt, a cartridge belt, and supplies. And we know she can shoot. She was also riding a great horse, a blue roan that runs like glory-in-the-morning. She's bound to have been all right."

Mason strolled to a window and gazed out at the darkening afternoon. "Wish they had telephones out there."

"What?"

"Telephones. Haven't you heard about them? You talk into this instrument, and the person on the other end hears you and talks back. Alexander Graham Bell demonstrated it at the World's Fair this past summer. I understand the emperor of Brazil held it to his ear and said, 'My God, it talks!' "

"You don't think it'll come to anything, do you?"

The Marshal remembered hundreds of weary miles ridden for nothing, of being too early or too late. Of criminals gone before he got there. Of floods and storms he might have avoided en route to pick up prisoners or chase down outlaws. Of the many, many times he'd have given everything he owned to speak to Norah. To hear the beloved voice, to persuade her to wait, not to marry until they discussed what they meant to each other.

"The telephone will revolutionize the world, Eddie." Mason returned to the bed and found his friend asleep, eyelids twitching as if dreaming. Turning off the light, he advised the nurses, then walked out into an autumn evening. He strode through the streets to his hotel, impervious to prostitutes' invitations, rejected as prey by

hoodlums who knew trouble when they saw it. There was
nothing in the world he could do for her. Whatever had
happened had already happened. Turned cynical by his
work, Mason Fletcher nevertheless prayed Norah wasn't
lying crumpled in the grassland with a bullet through her
breast.

Eli and his guest carried wineglasses along as they toured
the grounds. He had an hour before dinner, ample time to
display the heart of his empire, planted squarely and
arrogantly on an Apache plunder trail.

"And this here is my little zoo. *Mein tiergarten,*
Gretchen calls it. My animal garden." Eli made kissing
sounds near a cluster of miniature corrals and cages.
Pandemonium broke loose instantly, and baby animal
voices clamored for his attention. Antelope, deer, and elk
butted against the bars, and a black bear rose up on its hind
legs in order to see better. A young mountain lion paced in a
pen near a gray wolf and coyote, both of whom barked for
attention. Eli paused to speak to each creature and scratch
the ears of gray fox, jackrabbit, pack rat, and limpid-eyed
ringtail.

"Why, this is wonderful!" Norah exclaimed. "Mason
never told me—" The rancher glanced at her but did not
pick up the thread of conversation. He pointed instead at
two tiny peccaries, grunting and rooting together. Norah
giggled, put down her glass, and scooped up a cottontail to
cuddle.

"Ever seen a porcupine?" Eli dipped into a can and
shoved pine needles in to the ponderous, quill-covered
animal. "Won't bother you if you ain't botherin' him. Just
like skunks."

"You have skunks? Isn't that asking for trouble?"

He held his nose. "Would be. Don't have badgers or
weasels, neither. Those two smell bad and act bad." He
walked on. Norah replaced the rabbit, then followed him.
"You seen coati?"

"Oh, yes, they're funny!" She described meeting the large pack in the mountains, noisy as children let out of school. They watched a coati and two raccoons playing before going into the large adobe barn. Here small cages hung on a wall at eye level, allowing Norah to peer in at the tiny inhabitants: cactus, pocket, kangaroo, grasshopper, and white-footed mice. Smiling at their antics, Norah asked, "What's your favorite animal? After horses, of course." He failed to answer, and she turned to repeat the question.

His face was slightly flushed. "You're gonna laugh."

"No, I won't." She considered Eli coarse and forward, but his obvious love for wildlife now triggered a warmth toward him.

Eli shuffled his feet, then said somewhat aggressively, "Mice."

She smiled sweetly. "A man can still be a man and like mice, Eli. Even roses or poetry. All kinds of people like delicate things."

He shook his head. Eli had socked more than a few chins over his weakness—which was what it was in his book—but still he melted when it came to baby animals. "You hungry?"

"Starved! All I had today was a little jerky and bread."

"Come on, then. My stomach thinks my throat's been cut."

They strolled back to the ranch house which was built four-square around a courtyard with a well. It had no outside doors or windows. Walls two feet thick, an adobe parapet pierced with rifle loopholes, and heavy gates leading into the courtyard reflected the owner's determination to hold and defend what he had fought for.

Dinner was served with china and crystal at a damask-covered table: vegetable soup, steak, fried potatoes, fresh green peas, bread, butter, raisin pudding, coffee for Eli, chocolate for her.

"I sure like to see a woman eat. Not pick around on her plate."

"It's so delicious!" Norah helped herself to more peas, then said, "I had no idea your ranch was so handsome." Her gaze roved approvingly over oil paintings and the rosewood sideboard, then into the living room. A man-high stone fireplace, maroon leather furniture, sky-blue Navajo rugs woven from cast-off soldiers' trousers, a varnished plank floor, bookcases, a mammoth desk, and a variety of chairs created a comfortably masculine yet sumptuous decor. Baron sprawled in front of the fire, bigger than, but accepted by, Eli's three hunting dogs.

"They look decorative there," she said.

"That monster of yours likes it here, don't you, boy?" Baron's tail moved back and forth, and Eli grinned.

"Where *did* you find potatoes and peas? I can't eat enough of them! Fresh vegetables are so hard to get at the fort." Norah smiled up at the German girl as she served more portions.

"Mary has the—what is it you call the thumb?" Gretchen snapped her fingers in frustration with the phrase.

"Green. A green thumb," Norah said. What a nice girl. It was a marvel she had not been snapped up by a wife-hungry settler. She said as much when Gretchen returned to the kitchen.

"I'd give a lot to keep her permanently, but she's just working till her husband's enlistment expires. Company commander refused to give permission for him to marry so they did it on the Q.T. That's insubordination, so she's here and he's up north at Fort Whipple near Prescott."

Norah put her spoon down. "The Army! It thinks it's so high and mighty. Telling people whether they can get married or not. Do you know wives and children are considered *camp followers*? Only the laundresses are recognized as part of the Army. They get quarters, fuel, one daily ration, and surgeon's services."

"Army's more or less patterned on the British. That's the way they did it, and when the Army gets an idea in its head—" He rose and suggested having wine by the fire.

He added kindling and saw Norah snugly ensconced in a chair beside him, and on a table between them he set port wine, fudge, and walnuts. The mastiff rearranged his big limbs and sighed with contentment. Norah studied him and bit her lip.

"What's wrong?" Eli said, leashing an urge to pull her to her feet and crush her close, kiss her until she cried for mercy. He was no longer surprised that Mason had stayed drunk for three days—or was it four?—when he and this woman had parted.

"I need a favor." Her face was serious.

"Name it." He'd give her the moon, for Christ's sake.

She slid out of the chair and took Baron's head in her lap. "My husband doesn't like Baron, and the feeling is mutual. When he resigns and we move to Philadelphia, I don't think Carleton will let me take Baron along. I'd like you to have him. He'd be happy here with the animals, and you could give him an excellent home. He's been through so much I can't bear to think of him being hurt again. Jim thought maybe he'd been abused, and had escaped and lived in the woods. See the scars here?"

Eli leaned down so their faces were inches apart. His eyes glowed with ardor. "That all? Don't want the world on a silver platter, nothin' like that?"

"No, nothing like that." She scrambled back to the safety of the chair. "Just take care of my friend here. We should be leaving in early July, I think."

"It's a deal. I'll come get him. What about the blue roan? Sure like to race him against one of Hooker's nags."

Norah shook her head. "I'm taking Steel with me. Carleton says we'll do a lot of riding."

"Not in divided skirts, you won't!" Eli guffawed. "Ain't your husband the son of Senator Beatty of Pennsylvania? Yeah, I know the old man. Pompous old sonofa—"

"I beg your pardon," Norah objected stiffly. "You're speaking of my father-in-law."

"Met him yet?"

"No."

"Then watch your bustle, honey. He's a pincher."

Norah had to laugh, and her host grinned. Then he sobered. "Now, about your goin' to Jim's. God, girl, you shouldn't be out alone like that! Don't you know Jim's shorthanded? He can't spare one man to ride you back to the fort. You been spoiled, runnin' free as a summer breeze. This place won't be no picnic till 'Paches are underground or sent somewhere. In the morning you can head for the fort with ten of my boys."

"I am going to the Double Bar F!" Norah's eyes flashed.

"No, you ain't!" His stubborn nature locked horns with hers.

"I want to see everybody before I leave!"

"Don't care who you want to see. We ain't runnin' an escort service." He patted Baron who came to them, concerned by the agitation in their voices, then slammed a fist on his knee for emphasis. "You're goin' back to the fort, and you'll have to take Gretchen with you. Gossip travels like a brush fire. If you don't go back with a lady in tow—a new friend, maybe, who needs medical attention—why, girl, your reputation on that post is ruined!"

Norah snapped a walnut meat between her fingers, incensed by his tone and adamant refusal. She did not plan to go on alone; her narrow escape had been frightening enough. And, yes, now that she examined the situation in more detail, Norah saw that her reckless action could cause Carleton embarrassment. No doubt she had worried her friends and gotten the sentry into trouble, too.

"I hate to admit it, Eli, but I was wrong. All I could think of was being out in that valley with a fast horse under me, the wind in my face, and nobody to answer to."

He nodded, eyes hooded to conceal emotion. This would have been the woman to help him build yet another empire! Too bad he hadn't lassoed her first. "I know." Eli got to his feet. "Better hit the hay. Told Gretchen you wanted coffee and hot water at five. Breakfast's at half past."

"Spoiled, am I? Look who's doing it!"

He gazed down, tracing the curve of hip as she sat curled up in his chair. "If you were my woman, I'd certainly spoil you beyond redemption!"

That night Norah stretched out, hands clasped behind her head, wondering what mail had reached the fort, and how she should dress to ride in the stagecoach. But her thoughts kept returning to the feeling that had filled her when she was galloping away from the post. *She was free and coming home!* The exultation had welled up almost as overwhelmingly as sexual climax.

The unexpected stab of sorrow was so keen it hurt; she had really wanted a little spread of her own one day. Horses and cattle and being her own boss. *The Mariposa,* her own brand, stamped on hides, saddles, gates, spurs, clothing— burned into her heart.

Norah tried to picture herself instead in the hothouse climate of high society: acting the fashion plate, observing proprieties, being a mistress of punctilio. That was not quite fair, of course. She would have many advantages, principally wealth and position. And how could she prejudge her reactions when she had never had one nickel to rub against another? She and Carleton loved each other. Things would work out. Memories faded. Didn't they?

The smell of cigar smoke brought Norah to a sitting position, heart beating faster. Eli was outside her bedroom door. The floor creaked when he shifted his weight, and she tensed. Then he walked on, but Norah lay awake thinking long after.

It seemed impossible that the events of twenty-four hours could restructure one's life so completely. Norah returned to the fort to find herself restricted to quarters by the new commanding officer; vaginal bleeding necessitated an examination which revealed she was pregnant; and the remnants of Carleton's patrol trudged in at dusk without him or Sergeant Mulrooney, both of whom had been captured by Apache renegades.

"Oh, my dear!" Lollie said in a stricken voice. "You must be brave."

Norah was too proud not to keep her chin up in public, but in the privacy of their rooms she died a little each day she had no news. Where had they taken him? What were they doing to him? Had they killed him? Had he suffered? Like other Army wives, she agonized over his pale-skinned body blackening in the sun without the dignity of burial. Oh, how she hated those savages! What made her think she ever loved this place? In the back of her mind other questions tormented her. Was this a punishment for deceiving Carleton, for being willful and selfish? For being unchaste before marriage?

Six days after her return Carleton staggered into the fort alone—gaunt, parched, raging with fever. When the cry went up at his return, Norah rushed across the compound to embrace the ragged figure, weeping, coughing, and laughing. Jubilation on the brink of madness gleamed in his eyes at the sight of her, and without speaking, he collapsed at her feet, grasping the hem of her gown.

Theo ordered them to the hospital. He later told Lottie that Norah and Carleton had each plunged into personal hells unappreciated by the other. Time, breeding, and their love would dictate their psychological recovery. Watching Norah tend her husband devotedly when she herself was ill confirmed the physician's diagnosis. Love was the great healer, and it was busy at work.

18.

Carleton had little to say about his wife's escapade except to order her not to·do it again, especially with a child on the way. He did not seem impressed by her pregnancy, one way or another, for other matters seemed in his troubled mind to have greater import.

"Was it—was it very awful?" Norah said, smoothing his hair with maternal affection. His head rested between her breasts, and her arms were wrapped around him so he might hug when need or inclination so moved him.

"Can we talk about it later?" Carleton kissed the hollow of her throat. "I have to go again. You're sure it's all right?" It seemed as if he could not get enough of her. He entered, came to a quick and shuddering climax, and soon grew hard again. Yet she didn't sense the happiness that might be expected after a long, perilous patrol.

"Dr. Gates said so." Actually, Theo had discouraged lovemaking, but Norah could not find it in her heart to refuse her husband. Theo had diagnosed pregnancy at least three months along; she was firm and tight as a melon, but there was to be no more reckless riding. Norah remembered vividly how the blood had drained from her face in shock at his words then rushed back. She felt a joy such as she'd never known. *She was pregnant with Mason's child!*

Could Theo be wrong? He had never delivered an infant or treated women; he frankly admitted his experience had been restricted to men's ailments and accidents. Perhaps he was wrong about this. Much as she still loved Mason, this *had* to be Carleton's baby! Norah set her mind on that as if an effort of will might change the physical reality of Mason's seed planted in virgin ground.

Carleton rolled away, hair damp and body wet. "I'm sorry," he apologized, rubbing his temples. He suffered from vile headaches, although he had not been hit or wounded in the head.

Trying for a light moment, Norah said, "It's a good thing I'm already pregnant, or I would be today."

He smiled weakly. "You're the best girl in the world."

"Thank you, sir. Now, what do you say we get dressed and take a stroll?" Norah hopped out of bed before he could object and reached for stockings and undergarments. "This November weather is so cool and invigorating. Such a relief after the summer!"

He watched her, bedecked in ribbons, flounces, and laces, and attempted to enter into the spirit of things. "At least you're not restricted to quarters now that I'm back. You might have withered up and died in here if I hadn't made it."

Norah stopped in the process of hooking her corset. "Oh, don't say that even in fun! I don't know what I'd do if you—"

"I have a hunch you'd get along."

"Not without you to cherish and love me." She came back to the bed and leaned down to kiss him. He reveled visually in the milky flesh of her breasts, the full lower lip he loved to suck on, the eyes that stayed with him in a vivid image when he was away from her.

"Your replacement must surely be on his way," she went on, "and I hear twenty more men are en route from the San Francisco garrison. They won't be shorthanded here anymore. Why not go ahead and resign?"

"No!" He sat erect and his face turned crimson. "No! I'm going to hunt down that bastard and kill him! Murder him like he did Mulrooney!" Tears of corroding guilt and stress shimmered in his eyes. "Inch by fucking inch!"

"Carleton!" Norah was aghast at his vehemence and vulgarity.

"It was my fault. I didn't listen. Thought a Philadelphia dandy knew more than an old Indian-fighting cavalryman. More than that damned *mule* of his. Know what they're calling me? Bad-luck Beatty." He grabbed his head in both hands. "Oh, Jesus, why didn't I listen?"

"Who is this bastard?"

It was a sign of Carleton's distress that he paid no attention to her use of the word. "I don't know his name, but I'd recognize him anywhere. As big as I am. Bad teeth and one eye. I'll never forget him!"

"Why? What did he do that was so—so—dreadful?"

Ordinarily, Carleton would not have continued, but the outpouring of hate, failure, and self-disgust now swept away common sense. His eyes rolled and his body shook. "A monster, that's what he is. I want to kill him, do you hear? *Kill him!*"

"You're hurting me, dear. Please." His fingers were digging into her arm. There'd be bruises tomorrow.

"I'm sorry." Carleton flopped back on the bed to stare at the *manta* drooping from the ceiling. "We'd lost two men the day before. Good boys. One got an arrow in his throat and the—the other was killed after capture and sent back tied to his horse. Mulrooney warned me the next morning we had to hightail it out of there, that a large band was in the area, according to the hoofprints. But I was so sick of the whole situation I told him to shut up. Even when I saw the smoke signals I did nothing but order a canter." Carleton ran a hand through his mussed hair and his voice rose. "I must have been temporarily insane. There's no other answer.

"And you know what they say about Apaches not attacking at night? About night being sacred to the gods and if they killed a man at night their souls would walk in eternal darkness? That's a bunch of bull! Unless this one is a half-breed and doesn't give a damn about custom, because they jumped us while we ate that evening. Crept up on the sentries and choked them to death.

"We tried to regroup, but when they drove our horses through camp the men scattered like quail, trying to find cover where they could defend themselves. Mulrooney and I got separated from the others. It didn't take more than five minutes, I swear to God, before they got us both."

"And then?" Norah was sickened by what was coming. Still, she could not deny her husband this emotional catharsis.

"They tied our hands and led us with ropes around our necks. It's a miracle we didn't break our legs or ankles stumbling through the dark. At their camp they bound us to trees, and I remember thinking, 'Thank God, their women aren't here!' They started drinking *tiswin*, and pretty soon they'd stripped us naked. Then one of them brings Stonewall, and he brays to Mulrooney like he's talking to him. Like he's scared.

"I can't—no, I won't—tell you what they did to that animal. They knew he was Mulrooney's mount, and he's sitting there, tears pouring down his homely Irish face, swearing at them in a steady monotone."

Norah cleared her throat, unable to speak. She patted him as she might a child.

"After they got roaring drunk and passed out, I managed to get loose and throw on my clothes and almost had Mulrooney loose, but his wrists had swelled up around the thongs and I couldn't get the knot. That one-eyed bastard woke up and yelled and I had to run. It was light by then and I went back to our camp to find a weapon, but no one was there. My men were only a mile away, but I didn't know it." Carleton hesitated, swallowing hard.

"I crept back to the clearing and Mulrooney saw me in the rocks above it. He kind of smiled and shook his head and then never looked in my direction again. They—kept him—alive for two days." A wild expression convulsed

Carleton's face and he retched, wiping at his mouth with a handkerchief.

"You stayed there all that time? God in Heaven!"

He gripped her hand. "I had to stay! It was my fault, don't you see? At least he knew he wasn't alone. We never liked each other, but *I had to stay.*"

What had Major Bertram told her once? That it was characteristic of professional soldiers to fight without hating but characteristic of short-term volunteers like Carleton— and of recruits and vigilantes—to become emotionally involved and act irrationally. Her husband had courage and was following family tradition, but he was not a military man. What a dreadful experience it must have been, keeping the deathwatch when he himself remained in constant danger of discovery.

Norah nestled down beside him and drew him close. "Of course, Mulrooney knew you were there. And you did the right thing. The honorable thing."

Tears trickled down his cheeks, and he dashed them away angrily. "I won't forget his screams, Norah. Not as long as I live."

"Yes, you will. Believe me, you will."

They lay quietly then, both spent, and Norah slept from nervous exhaustion. When she awoke Carleton had calmed down and suggested taking the stroll Norah had proposed earlier. While they dressed, Norah described how nerve-racking the wait had been; how she had worried about him, about having the baby, about what to do if she were widowed. "They were concerns we hadn't talked about, and they frightened me! I'd hate to suffer through days like those again!"

"Norah, I want you to go and stay with my parents. Because you may have to face days like that again. I intend to track that killer down before I leave Arizona." His voice quavered with repressed fury.

"You can't carry on a personal vendetta, Carleton!"

"No one will know. Just you and I." Carleton polished

the brass buttons on his coat. "I want you to go to Philadelphia where you can have the baby in a civilized environment. I'll join you as soon as my time is up."

"I won't do it," Norah replied quietly. "I'm staying right here with you."

"But the baby's due in early summer, and it's so hot here then. Furthermore, Gates isn't a woman's physician. That bothers me most of all." He was just realizing how wan she looked.

"Lollie will help. And one of the laundresses is a good midwife, Theo says."

"A laundress!" Carleton was incensed. "A creature like that delivering our child? Why, I won't allow it!"

"You'll have to allow what's necessary at the time, my dear. As a matter of fact, I doubt if you'll have a thing to say about it." Her chin went up, and she unconsciously put a palm to her abdomen.

Touched, Carleton put an arm around her waist and kissed her nose. "You're a stubborn lady, aren't you?"

"A stubborn Army wife, that's what!" They laughed for the first time since his return, and he buttoned the back of her dress, joking with her about its not fitting anymore.

They walked toward the stables to visit Steel, the dignified and virile officer with his parasol-protected wife. Carleton held a gloved hand over Norah's where it clung to the crook of his arm, nodding, saluting, exchanging greetings. He was abnormally aware of his clothing rubbing his genitals. The Apache had played with him, squeezed his sac until he screamed, poked into the penis with a reed and cut an ominous pattern around the scrotum.

The Indian's one eye had gleamed with sadistic pleasure in the campfire's light. After an hour or so—maybe more— he had begun practicing psychological warfare, promising to geld the prisoner. Send the white-eyes home to his wife a different husband indeed. Carleton died a thousand deaths before he got away but failed to escape the dreams in which calloused fingers degraded and hurt him, castrated his self-respect.

Norah winced with pain as her husband's grip crushed her knuckles. She said nothing to him, but exchanged greetings with the sentry who had been on duty the day she rode away. He had long ago accepted her apology, sweetened with a plate of sugar cookies.

She nodded agreeably to those they met, caught up in a wondrous feeling that was hers alone. No matter that her mind refused to recognize the fact, Mason's child had moved in her womb. Gazing up at Carleton's profile, Norah hugged his arm in a confusing mood of delight and contrition. He smiled down at her.

"Feel better?" she asked.

"Much. And you?"

"Oh, yes!"

They were both lying, but a new tenderness and respect rose in each of them for the other, and a maturity neither had possessed before imbued them with melancholy grace. The lieutenant and his lady walked on, he in blues and she in muslin the color of lavender sagebrush, and onlookers nodded with approval at the handsome couple. Obviously they didn't have a worry in the world.

"Carleton, this has got to stop! That's the third one this morning on an empty stomach." Norah frowned as he poured the cavalry officer's eye-opener: whisky, water, bitters, and sugar to be tossed off shortly after 5:30 A.M. reveille.

"I can handle it." He combed the full beard grown to protect his face from the sun.

"That's what they all say."

"Who says?"

"Men who drink too much."

"Are you inferring I'm turning into a drunkard?"

Norah made a sound of disgust and curled up on the cot to give him as much room as possible. "Of course not. But whisky dulls your appetite, and you're not eating properly. Besides, I don't like the smell of it on your breath."

He brushed his mustache, peering critically into the small mirror. "'There are five good reasons we should drink: good wine—a friend—or being dry—or lest we should be by and by—or any other reason why.'"

"Oh, *bother*! I don't know what's got into you lately." Or did she? Things had gone so well through the holidays and into the new year of 1877. Then a series of incidents had hit them like a landslide.

The murderer Carleton sought was discovered at San Carlos Reservation, safe and contentedly receiving rations. Norah and Carleton were ranked out of their quarters in April by an insensitive senior officer and forced back into a tent. And the fact that she was well along in pregnancy and no longer slept with him tended to put him on edge. To cap the problems, his parents begged him to come home; his father had fallen seriously ill and needed help managing family affairs. Unable to comply because Norah was so close to confinement, Carleton found himself in that unenviable position of an only child torn between spouse and parents, a position exacerbated by his growing obsession with revenge, now his ruling passion in life.

He seized any chance to go on patrol, for Apaches still sneaked off to join relatives in Mexico despite Geronimo's capture in April by Captain Clay Beauford. Carleton felt sure the one-eyed hostile who had tortured Mulrooney to death would bolt from San Carlos eventually—and he would be waiting.

"How about a bite of breakfast, m'dear?" Carleton kissed her in an aura of whisky and bay rum.

"Do you mind eating with that friend of yours from Yale? I'm not up to cooking, and Endicott won't be here for a while."

She could not imagine how they would live without Endicott, their striker, an enlisted man who worked for them when he was off duty. Norah considered him worth much more than seven dollars a month, for he cooked, cleaned, gathered wood, emptied slops, filled water containers, pressed uniforms, polished boots and shoes, and generally made himself indispensable. Endicott was a godsend, and she wished they paid him more. Carleton certainly could afford it! Norah had finally surrendered her money after much pestering, but unknown to him, kept a sum aside for a rainy day, as did any canny wife. Had the secret little hoard not been so treasured and hard won, Endicott might have enjoyed an occasional reward from Norah.

Annoyance rippled across Carleton's face, which then softened just as quickly. Living in a tent again was much worse for her than for him; somehow he had to get better quarters. She had been deeply depressed at relinquishing that miserable shack with its red carpet, print curtains, and fireplace. No better than the servants' lodgings in his parents' home.

"Are there twins in there?" He rubbed her abdomen gently; the child was due any day.

Norah groaned. "I'm sure it's a baby elephant."

They chuckled, and she studied him with open concern. "Please eat a good breakfast? And no more eye-openers?"

"I promise." He paused with a hand on the tent flap. "Will you be under the tree today?" A large oak nearby cast welcome shade where Endicott daily set up a lounge chair, table, and pillows so Norah might escape the tent's confines. "Some of your admirers want to bring their banjos and guitars."

"I'll be embroidering this bib." Norah shook her head so the long hair fell back of her shoulders. "Any serenade will be listened to with appreciation, tell them. I'll furnish lemonade and applause." It was the sole element of the Army Norah liked—the chivalry and camaraderie, the familial yet socially and militarily correct relationships that made living in such close quarters bearable.

"Lollie's lining the tent with green cambric today to cut down the glare," she added, "so I'll be right here." Indeed, where else would she be? She rose and washed, muttering aloud at the inconvenience of having no closets or shelves and being forced to store everything in boxes or luggage. At the ranch she had at least had a room to herself. It would be good to be at the Double Bar F now, where there were trees and birds and water. Jim had driven cattle to the fort not long ago and brought her up to date; things were pretty much the same, he allowed, except that Rose and Joel had been married by an itinerant preacher. They fought a lot but Jim reported that they seemed happy enough.

Norah now parted her hair down the middle, braided and coiled it over each ear, put on a loose blue robe and pearl earrings. Where were those slippers? Her ankles were too swollen for shoes. She turned and blanched at the sight of a foot-long lizard waddling over the tent floor in her direction: a Gila monster with beaded charcoal-black and pinkish-orange skin. Falling onto a cot, she lifted her feet up and screamed for help. The lizard stopped right beside her, black tongue flicking in and out of a lavender-lined mouth.

The striker burst into the tent, pulled his revolver, and blew the lizard's head off. "Oh, Endicott!" Norah started to cry.

Long and slim as the Kentucky rifle he had learned to shoot with, Endicott fussed over the woman he worshiped. He pulled her slippers on and took the liberty of giving her arm a pat. "Critter's daid. Don't carry on so! You'll bring the baby!"

"I wouldn't mind! Get me out of this blamed tent, Endicott! Take me to the chair under the tree, will you? I don't think I can walk. My knees are shaking as if I have the ague." Norah put her arms up to him, and the man braced his legs and hoisted her up in his arms.

"Sakes alive!" His face grew scarlet with effort.

She giggled through the tears. "I'm sorry I'm so heavy."

"T'aint you, it's me. Gitting puny on Army chow!" Endicott backed out of the tent and almost bumped into a man hurrying toward it.

"Heard a shot. What's wrong?"

The mastiff barked, a rapid series of friendly sounds. Norah lifted her head from the striker's shoulder and stared into the face of the father of her child.

When the men had settled Norah in the chair, Mason covered her legs with a shawl, and the striker rushed to get her hot tea. She wiped her eyes, unwilling to face this man she loved, after making such strides in replacing him with Carleton. "What are you doing here? Don't you think it's cruel to show up now?"

He crushed the crown of his Stetson between both hands. "I'd never hurt you. Never! I heard the shot, that's all. I didn't even know you were still here. I just got in. And I sure didn't know you'd be living in a tent, for God's sake!"

"It's the best he can do," she answered, flaring in defense.

"I'm sorry, I'm sorry. I didn't mean to—"

"To what?" she snapped, anger disguising the weakness she felt at his nearness.

He sat down at her feet and hung his head. "—to love you and leave you. It wasn't until later that I realized what an idiot I'd been, what I'd done to you and how selfish I'd been. Suppose I'd left you with child! If it means anything, Norah, you're the only woman I'll ever love." Mason caressed her every feature with his eyes, lingering on the round belly and enlarged breasts. "If I'd had a lick of sense, this would be our baby you're carrying."

"It is, Mason." Her voice broke as she made her joyous yet bitter confession. "It—it *is*, darling."

His heart jumped, and he was filled with a thunder of elation that was quickly stifled by a strange grief welling up inside him. "Does your husband—"

She shook her head, first in answer, then in warning. Endicott approached with a tray and unloaded teapot, dishes, utensils, and cookies, waved away their thanks, and trotted off to attend to his housekeeping. Mason poured and they ate a few bites in silence, both devastated by what might have been, aching with forbidden love.

"Mind a cigar?" he asked when they were through.

"No, as long as there's a breeze to blow the smoke away." She watched him light the thin, brown Mexican cylinder, eyes narrowed, face muscles tensing as he drew in the smoke. Christ forgive her. Simply to trace the outline of his body, gauge the leanness of his waist—it made her sick with longing and regret, scourged her with shame that she should want him so in her condition.

"I left you a double burden, then, if you've had to lie," Mason accused himself. He ran a finger under the mustache he had grown, black and full above a mouth she remembered with crystal clarity. "Can you ever find it in your heart to forgive me?"

She leaned forward to cup the back of his head in her hand, its curve tingling in her palm, the neck muscles tightening beneath her fingertips. Mason's scalp prickled, and he moved away.

"I once asked Dr. Gates if it was possible to love two men," Norah said. "He assured me it was. In fact, his words were, 'Oh, yes, I'm afraid so.' Perhaps he loved two women at the same time once, I don't know. But he was right. I love you both—and I forgive you, Mason, because I see now that you were doing what you thought best for me."

She struggled to keep from crying. "We'll be going to Philadelphia soon. His father has been ill and needs him to manage the family assets. They're very rich." Norah gasped, put a hand to her body, and smiled tremulously. "He must know you're here. He's eager to be born!"

"When's the baby due?"

"Any day." Their eyes locked, each brain computing, recreating.

Mason sprang to his feet and strolled a few feet away. In another second he could not have restrained himself from touching her abdomen, putting his ear to it to hear his child move within her. "Are you frightened?" he asked tenderly. Childbirth under these primitive conditions would petrify most women.

"Very. But Dr. Gates thinks I'll be all right." Fear flashed across her face, belying the words.

"A lot more all right than the girl I took to the ranch a year and a half ago."

"Have you been to the Double Bar F? I miss them all so much."

"No, but I've been to Eli's and he told me about your visit. That was a crazy thing to do, riding down Vista Valley by yourself." Then he chuckled, leaning against the tree trunk so as to appear a casual visitor to any curious eye. "Eli thinks you're the most beautiful woman to come down the pike. Which you are. Says you spoiled him for any other filly."

"Do you know what his favorite animals are? Mice! A big, rugged cattle king like that! My opinion of him really changed that day. And the way the animals came to him was something to see. I've asked him to take Baron."

"It will break his heart when you leave him."

"I can't help it." Tears rose in her eyes again, and each knew they spoke of both man and dog.

He picked up his hat. Officers with guitars had emerged from their quarters and grouped together, strumming chords and harmonizing. The sight puzzled Mason until he realized this was Sunday. He lost track of time while traveling and counted time like an Apache: that summer when rain turned to white pebbles; the winter the horses starved; the spring when birds that had forever eaten insects fed on hummingbirds; an autumn when white men's fever killed the children. Now he had another date to summon up as he rode the lonely land: that month when his child was born—to the wife of another man.

"I know you can't help it. The fault was mine, dearest," he said, kissing her with a glance. "One that ruined my life. I hope to God it hasn't ruined yours."

"Will I see you again?" She gripped the chair arms so hard they hurt her hands. "I—I always seem to be asking that."

Mason found it hard to answer. It would serve no purpose to continue hurting each other, yet knowing he was here might comfort Norah in her coming travail. Mason realized, too, that he *had* to see his child at least once. That child of haste and a love that had transformed his life. "Do you want to?"

She choked and coughed. "Yes, oh, yes, I do so want to know you're close! Will you stay until your son is born?"

"Nothing on this earth can keep me from you. I'll be nearby."

The officers called out then, and she waved for appearance's sake, but Norah was steeping herself in his very essence. Her heart did not have to tell her she would continue to love Mason Fletcher until she took her last breath.

19.

Nora's labor had been long and difficult, not unusual for a woman delivering the first time, Theo assured himself. Nevertheless, he worried from the time her amniotic sac broke during the afternoon until three in the morning when she delivered.

"Should I give her more chloroform?" His wife stood poised at Norah's head, face taut with responsibility and nervousness.

"No, that's enough. We mustn't interfere with the contractions. Push, Norah! Push! That's the girl. There.

There it comes, Lollie! *There comes the head!*" He supported the soft skull as it emerged. "Look! Look! Isn't this splendid!"

"You're not doing any of the work, Theo," Lollie said tartly.

Norah screamed as the infant slowly left the birth canal, then she lay gasping, quivering, worn to a frazzle but exultant. "What is it? Boy or girl?" After fourteen hours of labor Norah had just enough strength left to turn her head.

"A boy, my dear. A perfectly beautiful boy." Theo placed the infant in her arms, wrapped in flannel that had been warmed in an oven and rushed to the hospital from the kitchen. "He must weigh nine pounds if he weighs an ounce! Looks about twenty inches long. He's going to be a big fellow. Congratulations, Norah." Theo kissed her moist forehead.

"Where's Carleton?" She held her son in the crook of one arm and delicately placed a finger within the minuscule hand.

Observing the immemorial pose, Lollie paused in her work to ponder the sight. "That hair is *so* black! With that red face he's a regular little Indian!" She sighed over the baby.

Lollie missed the glance between mother and physician. Norah had naturally wondered about the child's appearance; it was possible she had conceived on her wedding night, a month after she and Mason made love. Norah vacillated between delight with newborn Andrew Carleton Beatty and sorrow that she must deceive her husband, for there was absolutely no doubt in her mind now whose son this was.

Despite the hour, men were clustered outside the hospital, smoking and talking. They were fond of the lieutenant's high-spirited lady and in any case had found it hard to sleep through her muffled cries. Endicott strode back and forth, and his comrades teased him about being more excited than the father. Which inspired the question: Where the bloody hell *was* the father?

A muted cheer went up when Theo opened the door to announce both mother and child were doing well. "Where's her husband? She's asking for him."

Endicott's horsey features tightened. "I'll git him. Tell the missus we're plumb pleased fer her."

"A new father's entitled to a few drinks, you know," Theo called after him. "Think I'll have one to celebrate *my* first baby!"

Carleton had wandered to the sutler's store early the previous evening. He played billiards, sent an enlisted man to the hospital for news every hour, and drank steadily. Dr. Gates had ordered him to stay out of the way, and Carleton was content to do so. He disliked women's illnesses, the blood and odors, malaises that robbed them of looks, vitality, and availability. Having a child must be incredibly messy. He loved Norah more than anything in life but was glad husbands were not involved in birthing.

Had he not drunk so much, he would not have had such a scare, but stepping outside in the gloom to relieve himself, Carleton inadvertently voided on Mason's Chiricahua companion. Like a rattlesnake rearing up to strike, the Indian shot to his feet with urine dripping off his long unkempt hair. "Goddamn," he hissed, "*goddamn!* You pee on me I cut it off!" Chico sliced viciously at the other man with his Bowie knife. Carleton yelled and stumbled backward. The dread of castration that tormented him with nightmares now drained him of strength, and he fell heavily and noisily into a pile of empty tin cans. The blade flashed again, and material ripped. Shocked into momentary sobriety, Carleton yanked his revolver, cocked it, and had rolled to one side ready to fire when his wrist was seized in an unbreakable grip.

"Chico! Stow that knife! And you, Beatty, holster that gun. What the devil's going on here? You son of a bitch, your wife's having a baby and you're rolling around in the garbage drunk as a hoot owl." Mason gestured with disgust at the trash around him.

Carleton struggled to his feet and holstered his weapon. "Dirty, thieving Indian attacked me." He glowered at Chico and fingered the rip in his pants.

The Apache dug into the rich manure of obscenity in the Anglo-Saxon language which his own Athabascan tongue lacked; borrowing from freighters and stagecoach drivers who were masters of the art, he showered the drunken man with abuse.

"That's enough, that's enough," Mason growled. "What happened?"

"Jackass peed on me."

"Didn't see him," Carleton declared, "but might have anyway. Jus' on general principles."

Mason motioned to Chico with a thumb. "Dump a bucket over your head. A bath won't hurt you anyway."

"No like get hair wet," the Apache answered, snarling.

"Stink like a polecat then. Just don't get upwind, understand?"

"Buy you drink?" Carleton suggested, holding the doorjamb to keep from falling.

"Haven't you had enough?"

"Whatteryou? Brother's keeper? My business how much I drink."

Mason stepped forward so they stood toe to toe. "Drink yourself to death for all I care. But your wife will want to see you—"

"You're damned consherned—concerned—about *my* wife, mister."

Mason edged past the other man knowing nothing was to be accomplished with a souse like this. Then he wrinkled his nose in disbelief. "You shit in your pants!"

"Jus' like a baby. Jus' like *my* baby. Gotta change pants," Carleton chanted as he staggered into the night. "Jus' like a—" Endicott caught him as he crumpled to the ground, out cold. The striker grumbled but carried Carleton to the tent, dumped him on a cot, and threw a blanket over the inert figure. He spat with disdain and hurried back to the hospital in case the new mother needed him.

Weary but unable to sleep, Norah meditated with eyes closed. God had indeed been good to her; He had made her well, given her the hearts of two fine men, blessed her with the miracle of a child. Her son slept beside the bed in a hardtack box converted to a cradle by the fort carpenter. When a hand enveloped hers, Norah did not start, so immersed was she in love and the profound aftermath of the birth experience. She didn't need to open her eyes, for her feelings for Mason ran so deep his presence in the room had registered before he touched her. "My sweet," she whispered, the smile on her lips including him in her happiness.

"I shouldn't be here, but I thought you should know your husband celebrated too much and passed out. He wanted to be here, though." Mason fought the impulse to gather her to him, kidnap her and his child, gallop into the night with them, keep them for himself throughout eternity.

"Something's bothering him, but he'll be here in the morning, I'm sure." Norah's gaze was candid now upon him. Would Andrew be as handsome as his father?

"What are you thinking?" He sat down on the side of the bed, careful not to jar it.

"Give me your son to hold." She rearranged the covers so he caught a glimpse of a blue-veined breast.

"You mean pick him up?" He peered into the cradle with a slight frown.

She laughed deep in her throat. "He won't bite."

Mason lifted his son gingerly but proudly and placed him beside his mother. "Half-pint," he whispered, dropping to his knees, kissing each finger, flower petals in his own brown ones. He looked at Norah, who clutched her throat at the heartbreak shimmering in his unshed tears.

With a final kiss he got to his feet, feeling old and burned out. "I'm only making it worse for us, being here. You have your life to live. You'll be all right. At least you'll have him."

She reached up and seized his wrist with astonishing strength. "Don't go. *You're* my husband in my heart and soul! *Mason, please stay!*" Her face turned wild with impending loss and she sobbed, grasped the baby, and feebly tried to get out of bed.

"Stop that!" he ordered. "Stop it this instant! You're too weak. You'll hurt yourself." Mason bent and kissed her mouth quickly, holding woman and child for an aching moment that destroyed what composure he had left. "Good-bye, love. The Lord keep you and Andrew." He turned and almost ran from the room.

The door closed and Norah cried out in anguish. The infant murmured sleepily and moved its head so the thatch of black hair rested under her chin as if to offer comfort. Norah dried her face on his little blanket and studied him in the shadows cast by the lamp. She'd look for Mason in him as he matured, this boy born May 25, 1877, named for her father and her husband but resembling the lover without whom life had lost much meaning.

"I ought to be shot for not being here when Andrew was born!" Carleton kissed her cheek, then sat down next to the bed. He grinned at the baby. "He is a grand chap, isn't he? Nine pounds, Dr. Gates told me. A big boy! Must take after my father, he's the one with black hair. And you're all right? Perfectly all right?"

She reached out to pull a button through its hole. He did not look as well turned out as usual, and his hands trembled. "I'm okay. And he *is* beautiful, isn't he?"

They beamed at Andrew, and Carleton noticed but lent no importance to the big tears rolling down his wife's cheeks. Women had moods at times like these. He brushed them away and half-rose to kiss her cheek and pat her shoulder.

"I almost resigned today," he said, sitting back down with caution. His hangover was monumental.

"Almost?" Norah frowned. Now that she was anxious to take the babe and flee her past, why *almost*?

"I forgot—if I ever knew—that the minute you're out of the Army, you're out of shelter. You must give up your quarters right then."

"Our canvas mansion," Norah said scathingly.

"In any case, this means I can't resign until you and the child can travel. There's simply no place in the area to stay. We might try Tucson, but what I hear isn't encouraging. Besides, that adds more distance to be traveled going back. It's too bad the Southern Pacific Railroad comes no farther east than Yuma on the Colorado River. I don't like the idea of your being bounced around on a stagecoach."

Norah retied a blue bow at the end of one of her braids. "I don't know how long it will be. That's up to Theo."

He rubbed bloodshot eyes, thinking a little hair of the dog might help. "You mustn't worry, but I'm going out again tomorrow. It's only to buy horses from a rancher. They can trust old Bad-Luck Beatty to do that, at least."

Her mouth pursed with distaste at the odious nickname. "Don't."

Carleton pressed his lips to her forehead. "Hurry and get well."

"I'll try." When he left the hospital, Norah wondered if he was headed for a drink. She hoped not—but knew better.

By the end of the second week she went back to the tent, although several officers offered to surrender their quarters. Norah thanked them for their chivalry but chose to remain where she was. It would only be a matter of days now until her full strength returned; then they would depart in the Army ambulance for the stage station.

Theo was loading her up with cod liver oil and iron, and Lollie saw that her surrogate daughter had the best and most nutritious food possible. Norah complained good-naturedly one day when Lollie brought beef pie, canned tomatoes, frijoles, and applesauce cookies. "I can't eat all of that!"

"Sure, you can." Lollie tossed the mastiff a bone and blew the sleeping Andrew a kiss. She rushed off. "Can't stay. Theo needs help. Passel of soldiers down with fever."

Norah was surprised at how much she did eat. Storing the cookies for later, she lay down to nap. It seemed no sooner had she closed her eyes than he cried, and she changed his diaper and settled down to feed him. "Are you hungry, sweetums?" Norah gave him a breast with the poignant memory of her mother calling her by that very endearment. She hoped her parents somehow knew about their grandchild. Then sad thoughts disappeared, and she chuckled in amazement at the baby's sucking power. "It's a good thing there's plenty more where that came from, you little pig!"

Engrossed in the sensation and pleasure of delivering food to her boy, admiring his coloring—red, white, and black like a red-faced warbler or a painted redstart, Norah decided facetiously—she did not notice the man. The mastiff did, however, and sprang across the entrance with fangs bared in warning but not in threat. She glanced up to see a familiar Chiricahua with a package. Blushing furiously, Norah turned her back.

"Pretty picture, lady. No shame in feeding son." Chico crouched a respectful distance from the dog, who had recognized him and returned to his bone.

"Do you have a son?" she asked over her shoulder while she burped Andrew.

A short silence ensued. "No," finally came the terse answer.

Norah dropped the subject. "Did you—have a message?" She prayed for one, yet cursed the fatal weakness that allowed her to do so. *That was all over, Norah, that was all over!*

"Present for baby," Chico said, and removed rope and burlap from around a wooden box. He pulled out a worn flat velvet jewel case and several objects wrapped in black cloth. "Case for you." He handed it to Norah, who had fastened her dress and carried Andrew outside. She tried to juggle him and open the gift at the same time.

"I hold baby?"

Norah studied the small, grimy man and saw a hunger that twisted her heart. She knew he would die before harming Mason's son. "Be careful," she admonished unnecessarily when she laid the child in his arms.

The Apache laughed aloud, exposing damaged and missing teeth, and began gurgling and cooing. Norah and the baby both laughed. Chico lifted him high overhead. The baby reached for the golden light that poured down from the sky. Then the Indian held him low to the ground and pointed him in four different directions. Putting Andrew on a chair, Chico opened his bag of *hoddentin* and withdrew a pinch of pollen, which he sprinkled over the tiny body. Norah opened her lips to object, but changed her mind and allowed him to complete the ceremony of drawing signs in the dirt with a stick and dotting dust on the rosy cheeks.

"Thank you, my friend," she said solemnly, noting with relief that Andrew seemed no worse for wear after what she assumed had been a blessing and prayer. Norah was equally if not more relieved that Carleton was not home to witness the scene. "I'll just put him down so I can look at the presents." Inside the tent Norah cleaned the infant's face with a damp cloth and brushed the pollen off. He yawned and she covered him lightly, pushing hair back from his translucent brow. She remembered the cookies and took them to her visitor, who grabbed them with a glance skyward in unspoken thanks. He bit into the sweets without delay.

"These are magnificent!" She held up an intricately carved gold necklace with flower petals of opal, emerald, and pearl and a pair of long earrings to match. "Are they Mexican? I can't get over such workmanship!"

"Aztec. Old, old. No white men here when these made."

"Where did he get them? They must be worth a king's ransom!"

Chico shook his head. "Baby cup, see? Baby knife, spoon, and fork and plate." The dark eyes shone. "All silver. Very nice."

"*Very* nice," Norah agreed, studying Andrew's name and birthdate on the cup in ornate letters and numerals. "Please thank Fletcher for me." She used the last name as the Apache did. "And I thank you for bringing these gifts. You must have traveled far. You are a good man."

Chico placed a fist on his chest. "Fletcher send great love to woman and son. Until the sun shines no longer." His features softened for he knew what it was to lose love. She repeated his gesture but did not speak. For a few moments they stood together in silent rapport, then he trotted into the waning afternoon. Soon his figure was no more than a mote of dust. He had melted into the high desert earth that had once belonged to Those Who Came Before, then to him and his tribe—earth that nourished them and at the last accepted them when life was done.

20.

It was their first serious quarrel. There had been sharp words on his part about tardiness, flirting, and overspending and protests from her about untidiness, gambling, and drinking too much. But these were minor irritations compared to the argument that now set them apart.

Norah sat under the tree, six-week-old Andrew in his cradle beside her. Her skin itched with perspiration on this breathlessly hot June day, and she hated every needless article of clothing women were forced to wear. In fact, at this moment she despised the whole Arizona Territory with its hot wind, relentless sun, and high temperatures that lingered into the early evening hours. Most of all, however, she was furious with her husband, who slouched in front of her.

"Do you mean to tell me we aren't leaving the day after tomorrow, after all? That Baby and I have to endure this hell until the next stagecoach comes just so you can chase an Indian?"

"Ah, Norah, you don't understand." He was out of uniform now, shirt and longjohns unbuttoned to show damp chest hair. He could do what he wanted, unhampered by regulations.

"I certainly don't. Here we are, all packed and ready to go. Theo's been living at the hospital with a bunch of sick soldiers to make room for us since your resignation. It's hotter than Lucifer's pitchfork, and *you're* riding into that furnace on a fool's errand. No, I *don't* understand!" Norah shooed flies away from Andrew's face. "We waited and waited for that officer to replace you, and now that he's here you won't go. I am flabbergasted!"

Carleton watched the soft dress material fall away from the upper part of her left breast. He sighed and walked to the tent where he slept, courtesy of the commanding officer, who bent the rules in view of the fort's isolation. Oh, God, he was so unhappy! He waited for his erection to recede. It would have angered Norah even more—she never seemed to believe it was involuntary. Didn't she want him anymore? How many months had it been since they went to bed? Did she think he was a monk? He ground his teeth with frustration.

"Can you hear me, Carleton? I said I'm going on the stage without you! And your parents aren't going to know what to make of this, either!" When he failed to answer, Norah made a sound of exasperation with her tongue against the roof of her mouth. She picked Andrew up to nurse him. Blast that cowboy, anyhow! Why hadn't he kept his big mouth shut?

It started when a California crew stopped for the night outside the fort, full of stories about trailing a drought-stricken herd to rangeland north of the Double Bar F, and about a brush with lone-wolf Apaches, including a one-eyed warrior with teeth like cinders. Carleton collared a cowboy for more information about the Indian, but Norah wondered what Jim and Eli thought of livestock from another state competing with theirs for feed. Still, there was grass enough for many herds.

Carleton slumped on the cot, hands hanging between his knees, a faraway expression on his face. Norah was struck by the contrast between this wretched, disheveled man and the vigorous officer who had courted her. Settling the baby in an open trunk atop shirts and socks, Norah joined her husband.

"Please," she began, putting an arm around his waist, "please give this up. Someone is bound to kill that Indian eventually. Or he may die of natural causes. You don't *have* to go after him. You are no longer Army. You paid your debt to Mulrooney and did all that can be expected of you. Let it go. *Let it go!* Think of being home again, of how wonderful it will be." Norah believed, and with reason, that the desert heat could drive people mad. Had he been so affected and she so engrossed in motherhood that she failed to notice?

He embraced her and kissed her neck, immediately intoxicated by the fragrance of skin and a faint odor of milk. "Norah, I need you so." He bent her backward, unresisting, on the cot. "Let me make love to you. It's been so god-awful long."

Carleton undid her dress and chemise, cupped an engorged breast in his palm. She seemed in a trance, eyes sleepy looking. His face slowly turned dark red, and he pressed her hand into his groin. "Is there some left for me? Or did he take it all?" He tugged gently at a nipple.

"No, darling, you mustn't. You—" But how sensual that was, the lips and tongue creating currents of excitement.

She, too, had been hungry for love, but her son had taken precedence over all else.

He drew away long enough to tie the tent flaps, lift her feet onto the cot, and open their clothing so as to expose them both. His fingers touched her vulva, and Norah cried out. "Did I hurt you? Didn't mean to." He returned to the nipple, moaning in his throat over this erotic experience he had never known.

She laughed tremulously. "No. You—surprised me. It hasn't been used for so long. That way, I mean."

"Norah, where do you hear such expressions? In the stable?" Carleton could not remember being so big and hoped it would not cause her too much distress. He touched her again to see if she was ready. There was no time to play or tease.

She gasped and instinctively tightened to defend herself, but inflamed by primitive lust that brooked no contradiction, he plunged into her. She gasped at the joining, the pain part of the pleasure. They kissed as he began the rhythm, and their lips did not part during intercourse, which was short and indescribably sweet. They climaxed simultaneously, both crying out in ecstasy as she dug nails in his shoulders and he arched in convulsion.

"I love you," he whispered as he lay upon her, limp and sated. "Oh, God, how I love you!"

Norah seized on the moment. "And I love you. But if you *really* love me—I beg you, Carleton—come with us."

He shook his head in obstinate refusal. "I've got to get him."

"He—whoever he may be—is more important than I am, is that it? Why, that wasn't love just now!" she exploded. "That was nothing but lust! If it were love, you'd do what I want."

Their glares locked inches apart. "You seemed to enjoy it as much as I did."

"I'm only human, aren't I? Oh, Carleton, look at me. Look at Andrew! We're dying in this heat. What can be more important than your wife and—and child? I wasn't fooling. We're taking the stage without you."

He rolled off, straightened out her skirts, stood with bent knees, and yanked up his trousers. "All right, you win."

Relieved, Norah said no more, but put a palm to the canvas overhead. "It must be ninety degrees in here! Maybe more! Poor Andrew," she exclaimed. She fastened her clothing and picked up the baby, who had begun to fret. "I'll take him to Lollie's and give him a bath. She keeps their water in those clay ollas and it stays fairly cool."

Carleton kissed her lips, then Andrew's. "By George, he is hot. Better run along and get him into that tub."

"Do I look all right? Is my hair coming down?"

He chortled. "No, you're enchanting. You look like a wife whose husband just made love to her."

"Carleton, you're scandalous! I'll feel as if everybody's staring!" She returned to the tree for her parasol and baby things and was soon on her way. She stopped once to motion for him to put on his hat, not to stand there in the sun like a ninny. Men! Bad as children sometimes.

When she mentioned it, Lollie nodded sagely. "Are they ever! Theo used to sulk like a little boy. Do everything but put a thumb in his mouth. Of course, I did, too." She giggled like a girl, rocking back in the chair, and lifting her feet off the floor. "When we were young, making up was the best part of the quarrel."

Once Andrew was bathed and powdered, he fell asleep while Norah fanned him. Lollie said it was catching and stretched out on the lounge to doze. Taking pitcher and basin into the alcove, Norah removed dress, corset, and drawers and washed, wincing now and then. She hoped Carleton had not made her pregnant again, but if he had, the second baby would be born under the safest and most luxurious circumstances. She yearned for a rich wife's luxuries: bathtubs, beds without dust or insects, milk, vegetables and fresh fruits, seafood, cool, dim rooms to which maids brought glasses tinkling with ice.

She sighed and powdered her damp body. There was a time when she would have been happy with much less as long as Mason Fletcher came home to her every night. But fate had decreed otherwise, and now she was increasingly anxious to pick up the strands of life in a civilized environment. Norah dressed again, then lay down on the bed. After tonight and tomorrow night they would be gone—ready to start a new life.

In a way Carleton was sorry to lie. Yet, he hadn't actually promised *not* to pursue the renegade; he had simply said he would depart with her the day after tomorrow. Which he would. He had nothing to do in the meantime, however, and a little ride down to Eagle Creek, where the cowboys had exchanged shots with the Apaches—why, that distance was nothing for his horse and would kill time besides. He waited until dusk, when it was not so hot, in order to spare his mount, for Carleton had grown fond of the animal that had carried him so many miles.

Mountains turned deep smoky blue as the sun went down. What color did Norah compare them to? The great blue heron, that was it. He planned that she continue bird-watching to her heart's content and grinned to think how her eyes would sparkle to see shorebirds on the Atlantic beaches.

Carleton cast a jaundiced glance at the full moon, red as molten metal, enormous and sailing low on the horizon. An Apache moon, the Mexicans said, crossing themselves. Bright and crimson with blood the Apaches spilled. He sniffed. Rain far down toward the border. Moist tropical air rolling up from Mexico to trigger summer rains. He sniffed again. Smoke from a campfire.

Then it dawned on him how foolish he had been, riding along outlined against that damned moon. His brains must be addled by the heat! Carleton promptly dismounted and led the horse to the entrance of Eagle Creek, where he tied the reins to a sapling. He took the rifle from its saddle scabbard, removed his spurs, and drew the Colt .45. This had to be an Indian broiling stolen beef over the fire. Carleton could smell the meat now. Yes, it had to be, because no white man in his right mind would set up camp in this vicinity. Chances were good the man he hunted was still here, confident of seclusion and off guard.

He poised to listen, keenly aware of feeling slim and fit, refreshed by evening coolness, buoyed up and relieved by the afternoon's lovemaking. A small mammal ran through the grass near his feet, causing him to crouch and follow the trail of sound with both gun muzzles. All extraneous thought was erased from his brain, purifying it for the primordial killer instinct that welled up inside him. With a last touch on his horse's neck, Carleton began the stalk.

The big Apache was tired, and as usual his rotten teeth ached. Why Usen had cursed him with a mouth full of pain was beyond his comprehension. He beat his wives, true, and had cut the nose off one for adultery, but so did all the men. He beat his horses, too, but again that was not out of the ordinary. He prayed, followed custom—why, he did whatever a good Apache was supposed to do! Which made it hard to think of any reason why he should be singled out for such misery. *Ek!* They hurt! He would be lucky if he was able to chew the cow meat that smelled so good; more likely he'd be sucking juices from it like a toothless old crone.

He put fingers in his mouth to wriggle a loose stump. The agony that shot through his jaw made him gasp, and tears sprang to his eyes. Like most red men, he took immense pride in his capacity for pain, to bear it without complaint, even without facial contortion. But in the absence of his comrades, who were camped on the other side of the mountain, he let himself go and wept.

Then his dog-faithful pony tossed its hammer head and blew its lips in agitation. The Apache leaped to his feet but remained in a crouch, wiping tears away with his shirt. He tilted his head to listen. A bear? A mountain lion? The great spotted cat from Mexico? Or a creature more dangerous than any of those—a certain white man intent on revenge? Rumor of him blew like dead leaves before the storm. Yet he cared not. A famous warrior, he had killed many men in his lifetime. One more meant nothing.

Carleton stopped to catch his breath. His heart pounded. In the silence he heard blood pulsing in his brain. His pupils, already accommodating to the darkness, enlarged even more. Not far ahead a tiny glow betrayed the Indian's location. His nostrils flared as they drew in air redolent with pine and wild primrose. Apaches were far too canny to be surprised, yet they, too, grew old and tired, slept soundly. Carleton saw a form some distance from the fire, wrapped in a serape: his quarry, resting while the meat cooked. He eased the trigger back.

The knife blade actually brushed his ear before thudding into a tree trunk, and Carleton threw himself to the ground and fired at the shadows from which it had come. No one was there. He swore under his breath and remained perfectly still. Let his enemy find him again.

A hush fell upon the woods as if wildlife sensed death in the air. Then a bird a few feet away launched off its nest with shrill cries of alarm. Carleton grinned and aimed in that direction.

When the buckskin moccasins with their hard elk-hide soles slammed down upon his arm, he shouted with pain, thinking it broken. He lost his grip on the revolver and then the man was fighting him, stinking of bear grease and foul breath. Carleton was forced to relinquish the rifle as they grappled, first one on top and then the other, well matched in strength and stamina.

The struggle raged through the woods: grunts, breath rasping, unintelligible words hissing between clenched teeth, involuntary breaking of wind. They staggered to their feet, growling like animals. Each fought to strangle the other, knee him in the genitals or gouge his eyes. The pony stepped back and forth nervously as the fight approached and swung wide to avoid the men near his unshod feet.

Carleton grabbed a piece of burning wood from the campfire and tried to bury it in the Apache's good eye. In so doing he inadvertently bashed his opponent in the jaw and dislodged the rotten tooth. The Indian bellowed, fell back, and yanked a dagger from his belt. He plunged it to the hilt in his enemy's breast just as a bullet from Carleton's large caliber boot Derringer blew a hole between his eyes.

When dawn broke, Carleton regained consciousness. His life's blood had drained into the ground beneath him. He knew he had only minutes to live. Flat on his back, he searched tree and sky for the birds Norah loved. His Norah, whom he loved as he had never loved a woman before. The sun climbed higher, and its warmth seeped into him. Behind his eyelids a scarlet cloud soft as dust kicked up by horses' hoofs ballooned and exploded. His last breath mingled with the morning breeze a moment before the hermit thrush alighted on a nearby branch. The bird opened its beak and filled the air with incomparable song, heralding a new day—a rebirth.

21.

Men from the Fullerton ranch brought the body in; they had almost buried the stranger before Jim showed up and recognized the bearded face. He now stood in the Gates's parlor, turning a disreputable hat in his hands while his cowboys squatted outside the open door rolling smokes.

"By God, Norah, I'm plumb sorry to bring you this news."

She looked past him, eyes swollen with crying. "I was all ready to go." She gestured at luggage piled beside an Army ambulance parked near the gate. "He promised he'd go with us, didn't he, Andrew? He *promised*!" The baby frowned at his mother's agitated voice and waved his fists.

"You taking the stage anyhow? You know you're always welcome at the ranch." Jim craned his neck to identify the riders dismounting outside. "That's Eli Martin. What's he doing here?"

Norah fought for control, to bring order to the chaos in which she was whirling. "Eli? Why, he's come for Baron. But he doesn't have to take him now, does he? Baron can stay with Baby and me. Carleton—doesn't—care—any—more." She broke down in a storm of weeping.

Eli strode into the room and removed his hat. He reached down absentmindedly to touch the mastiff who came to greet him. "Heard about your husband. Anything I can do, Norah, name it." He and Jim shifted from boot to boot, at a loss as to how to comfort the woman who meant so much to them both.

Theo and his wife entered and motioned the ranchers outside. Lollie had to smile at the big, awkward hulks usually so capable and confident, yet so helpless when confronted by a petite female in tears. "Go on, go on. We'll let you know when she feels up to talking."

The physician mixed powdered tranquilizer with water. "Drink this, honey, it will help you rest." He led her into the alcove and made her sit on the bed while Lollie loosened her clothing.

"The baby—"

"He'll be all right until you wake up. Now, lie back. That's it. Shhh, shhh." Lollie perched beside Norah and held her hand. She wished Norah were small enough to rock, poor, unhappy girl. Once she fell asleep, the older woman returned to care for Andrew but found his cradle empty.

"Pretty as a speckled pup, ain't he?" Masculine voices, muted as befit the occasion, rumbled with amusement while the baby was passed from man to man.

"Hey, button, you 'bout ready to take the edge off that bronc of mine?"

"Nah, he ain't gonna be a bronc peeler. He'll go to some fancy eastern school. His ma'll see to that."

"*Qué muchacho bonito.*" Emedio smiled. "You will be so handsome!"

The infant had no fear of the big people who held him and dangled pocket watches before his hazel eyes or tickled him with rope-calloused fingers. He sputtered and bubbled, eyes not yet focused.

"Cute little cuss, ain't he?" Eli beamed at the child in his arms. The longing for a son of his own burned fiercely in him. He had met but one woman fit to be his wife and bear his children. And she was a widow now, ready to be wooed and bedded and spoiled.

"What on earth—!" Lollie rushed at them in a flurry of skirts, clucking, they agreed later, like a bitty white bantam hen. "Keeping him out in the sun! Getting him all dirty! As if she doesn't have enough to worry about!" She seized Andrew and marched back into the adobe coolness. The men chuckled, unabashed. Sun and dirt didn't hurt boy babies. Shoot, the boy'd see to it his own self pretty soon.

Norah awoke in early evening. The muslin ceiling reminded her of droopy diapers, which immediately brought her alert to Andrew's needs.

Theo peeked in. "Thought I heard you moving around. How about a cup of tea?"

"I should feed Andrew!"

"He's asleep. There's time to freshen up and have a bite before you feed him."

She swung stockinged feet to the floor and sat staring at them. "I'm not hungry."

"No, but you haven't had a thing since five this morning. You need to keep up your strength for the baby if not for yourself."

Norah mulled that over. "I'll be out in a minute." Her mind worked slowly, her hands were clumsy, her mouth dry. The tranquilizer had worked, but nothing would help her forget Carleton's body being lifted off the horse, stiff as a board with rigor mortis.

Tears slipped down her cheeks and seemed to keep on coming. She went to the bureau for a handkerchief from her purse and recoiled from the image in the mirror: pasty skin, half-moons underneath the eyes, pale lips. Some of this might have resulted from the drug, some from grief, but Norah battled the effects of both. Decisions had to be made.

Carleton—she whispered his name aloud and gripped the bureau to keep from falling. She grieved for him despite not having given all of herself, not surrendering that inviolate part that belonged to Mason. A letter—as soon as things were straightened around, she'd write Mason a letter. As soon as her time of mourning was done. But first her husband had to be buried, and she had to find a place to live and decide whether to stay with Carleton's parents for a while or remain in Arizona until Mason came for her.

And so the meal passed in a blur. Tasteless food and drink entered her mouth; she swallowed, knew a fullness in the stomach. She fed Andrew in a trance, his pulling and emptying in innocent greed a physical link with reality. The awful reality that had to be faced tomorrow. Theo had not meant for her to hear, but Norah had: it was impossible to put Carleton in a coffin because of his outflung limbs. He would be wrapped in canvas, therefore, and interred quicky before decomposition set in in earnest.

Norah rocked Andrew back and forth long after he had finished nursing, breast bare and gaze blank. The Gateses, worried about her long absence, found her swaying to and fro. She refused to surrender the infant but drank the tranquilizer without protest. They propped her up with pillows, covered her nakedness, and stayed with her until she dropped off, mouth going slack and arms limp.

Lollie tucked the baby into his hardtack box and put him on a chair next to the bed. "Poor lamb. I wish we could help her more."

Her husband pulled her close. "Don't worry, sweetheart, she's tougher than those men out there."

"I wish I could believe that. What do you think she'll do?"

"Probably go back to the ranch."

Lollie's voice quavered. "I wish she were ours, Theo."

Remembering miscarriages and stillbirths, he hugged her tight. "She is, very much so. And now let's have a dish of your berry cobbler."

When they reached the kitchen, he put a finger under her chin. "I love you, woman. I could not have loved you more had we had children. Now! When I retire from the Army, what do you think of finding a place near Norah where I can practice medicine and we can watch Andrew grow up? Along with Norah's other children. Because, mark my words, she'll be married again this time next year."

"That would be a dream come true! You deserve two helpings of cobbler!"

Norah's sleep was restless and plagued with dreams. Toward midnight she rose up on one elbow in a haze of confusion, thinking at first she was in St. Louis and her mother had not yet come home. Then quiet laughter drifted in from the parlor, where the older couple so dear to her kept vigil. Her child slept peacefully within arm's reach. Jim, Eli, and their men were snoring outside beneath the stars. Norah gave a great sigh and relaxed for the first time in hours.

Everything was going to work out, for love was all about her.

*   *   *

Fort Guardian's commanding officer conducted the burial services. Despite its not being a military affair, officers and numerous enlisted men attended in Norah's honor. Three officers sent written condolences and sympathetically phrased proposals of marriage; a woman with education, pluck, and looks was a rare find on the frontier.

At the late-morning collation which Lollie served, Norah thanked all the men for being with her at this difficult time, particularly the striker, Endicott. She expressed appreciation to the commanding officer, offered regrets to the prospective suitors, arranged for a wooden headboard on her husband's grave, and asked when the mail patrol was leaving so she might send a letter to Carleton's parents. Had she had an address for Mason she'd have written him also; that was another problem—did she reach him through President Grant?

"You're doing awfully well." Theo poured more tea into her cup, lacing it with brandy and sugar.

"They expect it of a brave cavalry officer's widow," she said, wan and hot in borrowed black. "I understand Elizabeth Custer put aside her own grief, threw on a shawl, and immediately went to comfort each wife widowed at the Little Big Horn. The least I can do is keep my chin up in public."

"Good girl! But it's just about over. Sit down, why don't you?" Drained and gaunt, she was acting the trooper Theo knew she was.

Norah eased into a chair, feeling brittle enough to break and woozy from the brandy. Her mouth curved upward as Jim approached with spurs jingling. He squatted down beside her, smelling of horse, leather, and tobacco. The familiar and unpretentious odors made up her mind then and there; she'd be a maverick that never browsed with the herd in Eastern society. Here she knew who and what she was.

" 'Bout ready to head out, Norah. Anything you need before we go?"

She touched his arm. "May I come home? At least for a time?"

Pleasure flooded his weather-beaten features. "I—we—was all hoping you'd want to. Rose, too." He ducked his head. "And you don't need to worry none. I know we're just friends."

"The best," she said. "The best. How soon should I be ready?"

Jim got to his feet. "How soon can you be ready?"

She removed the hat with its suffocating veil and dropped it in her lap. "I have to write a letter to—to Carleton's mother and father and pack the few things I've been using."

"I'll take care of the luggage and your horse." He thanked Lollie for the hospitality and for taking care of Norah, invited the couple to visit, then hurried away to attend to his errands.

Norah thought of the grasslands, the sky and mountains that were so much a part of her now. Her son would love them, too, grow strong and tall there on the range. Her heart lifted. That was where she belonged. It was the place she and Mason would build their dynasty once he put his badge aside.

"You goin' to Jim's?" Eli loomed over her, eyes intent and hungry.

"For the time being." She fiddled with the hat, for he made her nervous. He exuded power and sexual attraction, this man who did not tolerate defiance or rejection, both of which he'd ever find in her.

He glanced about, wanting privacy for his declaration. "Reckon you know how I feel about you. I'd be right proud if you'd marry me, Norah. Give you anything you want."

"The world on a silver platter?" He seemed the genial host no more but a ruthless empire-builder intruding on her grief.

"On a gold platter if you want it."

"In return for a son?" Motherhood had sharpened her senses.

Eli's mouth thinned. "What's wrong with that? Ain't a man entitled when he gives——"

She rose and stepped behind the chair, putting it between them. Her initial dislike returned in full force, and red spots glowed on her cheekbones. "I am not a brood mare, Mr. Martin. I suggest you remember the word 'love' the next time you propose to a woman." Whatever made her think he was sensitive? That he loved a bunch of juvenile animals meant there was a chink in his armor, but she was not interested in peering behind it.

"Don't be so high and mighty," he said through gritted teeth. "I can tell that's Mason's kid."

Norah turned away and called to Theo. "Will you get Mr. Martin more refreshments before he leaves? I must write that letter and get it to the adjutant's office right away."

Eli donned an expensive new Stetson and snugged down his gun belt. "We'll see each other again, Norah. The valley ain't that big."

"Good-bye, Mr. Martin."

He glowered at her for a moment, then wheeled and strode away. A few minutes later the cattle king who had everything but what he wanted most cantered away with his men.

"Think he'll give you trouble?" Lollie asked in a worried tone.

Norah's eyes flashed. "Nothing I can't handle."

At the last minute Theo decided Norah must not ride so soon. She would be far from his care and guidance and had to be cautious of tissues still mending from birth travail. Jim borrowed a wagon and horse, loaded the luggage into it, and by early afternoon the party was on the trail. He drove with her beside him, his mount and hers tied to the tailgate. Riders fanned out and took the point, eyes squinting against the sun, hands ready to seize their weapons.

"I feel like a queen being escorted through enemy country."

Jim slapped reins on a shiny haunch. "That's about the size of it."

"Tell me when we get to Eagle Creek."

"Can't stop, Norah. Sorry. Want to push on so we'll be home by twelve or so. Full moon means we don't have to camp overnight."

"I don't want to stop, just to know where it is." He nodded, mind occupied with a multitude of chores left undone during his absence.

When they passed the canyon from which the creek emerged, he pointed. "One of the boys saw an Army mount tied about where that tree with the lightning blaze is. Three of them rode in and found your husband and the Apache. Did the valley a favor killing that one. *Ojo Muerto,* they called him. Dead Eye. More ways than one."

Her vision blurring, Norah said nothing. Carleton's obsession had cost him his life and drastically changed her existence and her son's. Sincerely sorry to have lost him, she was nevertheless honest with herself—she felt a growing anticipation at the prospect of being with Mason. The wagon drew away, and Norah prayed for her late husband's soul and for forgiveness for having deceived him. Young and passionate, they'd found love for a brief moment—she'd remember their good times and let it go at that.

It was about one in the morning when they rolled into the ranch, Norah and Andrew asleep on a mattress jammed between two trunks, and covered with blankets against the cool air of the higher altitude. Norah opened her eyes to see friendly faces peering in at her from both sides. The baby started to cry, and Rose reached in to take him but hesitated at his mother's sharp glance. Then Norah relented and transferred the small body to her.

"Hello, Tom! Slim! Oh, Joel, how good to see you!" The young man hugged her as he lifted her down. "Chan Lee, you're getting fat! Hello, Mr. Smith." She had not changed her opinion of that man. "Where's Shorty?"

"Comin', Norah, comin'!" He hobbled toward them, pants pulled over longjohns like the other men, feet in Mexican huaraches.

She pressed her cheek to his bristly one, not wishing to embarrass him with too warm an embrace. "Why, you're a regular old porcupine!"

"Give a feller a little warning, will yuh?" he complained with a grin.

"Awright, folks, let's hit the hay. We'll meet ourselves getting up at this rate. Besides, the doc at the fort said Norah has to have a lot of rest. She'll be here to talk to tomorrow. I mean today! And the baby, too." Jim kissed her on the way into the house with her bedding. "Welcome home and—aw, Norah, don't cry."

"I'm sorry. It just feels so good to be home!"

The men smiled, said good night, and began to disperse.

Rose had already changed the baby, using a towel for a diaper, by the time Norah came in. She tried without success to soothe him, black eyes soft and thoughtful. "Is he hungry?"

"I'm sure he is. I'll feed him in just a few minutes." Norah had to clear a path to the bed, for her old room was stacked with kitchen supplies. "How have you been, Rose?"

"All right, I guess." The girl brightened a trifle. "Joel and I have our own house now. Down near the colt pasture. It's not big, but it's ours."

"Congratulations. I hope you'll be happy. And I hope you'll like the wedding present I brought."

"What *is* it?" Rose's maturing beauty glowed at the prospect.

"You'll see in the morning." Poor child, no doubt her only gift. A set of six cranberry crystal goblets was hardly practical, but they were the type of thing that became a housewife's pride and joy.

Norah pushed the mattress onto the rawhide strip supports, threw pillows and blankets on top, and then took the baby. "My goodness, you're tuckered out, mad, and hungry as all get out, aren't you?" When the infant assured his mother he was, Norah said good night and closed the door. Unbuttoning her dress, she sat down and put the baby to breast, eager to shed her clothes after the long day and dusty ride. This day had begun with a burial and ended with the feeding of her son—the past and future.

Andrew's rosebud mouth pulling at her nipple reminded her of Carleton doing the same, and she wondered drowsily if she was really pregnant. A month or so would tell. And if she was? Then Carleton lived on through her, and she was glad of that.

"How about a brother or sister?" Norah asked her boy. He yawned, showing his palate. "A lot you care." She tucked him into his cradle, placed it between her and the wall, and stripped down to her undergarments, in which she'd sleep.

There! Far off but audible to a keen ear was the musical humming of the grasslands she had once been afraid of. In her mind's eye the grasses rippled and billowed, black and satiny, in the night wind, ebbing and flowing like life itself.

Life and death. Antelope and prairie dog listened tonight as did mouse and burrowing owl, for predators might approach undetected under cover of the great rustling. Faint and silvery, the howl of a wolf rose to the stars, and Baron shambled to the door protectively, finally crumpling there in fatigue.

Norah caressed the Aztec necklace she had worn beneath her blouse. Her talisman, it was a magical piece of jewelry touched by his hand. Her mind emptied of doubt and depression simply by resting where her soul was content, and Norah tried to reach out to him whom she had always loved.

Her thoughts entered the night and wafted over vast distances like nocturnal birds crossing the heavens. *Mason —beloved—I am free. Come to me—come to me!*

Part III
ELI

Heaven has no rage like love to hatred turned . . .
William Congreve:
The Mourning Bride

22.

Carleton's daughter arrived on a blustery March day while thunder rolled sullenly over mountains greening with spring. Rachel Jeannette Beatty, named for her grandmothers, caused Norah more pain and suffering than Andrew had—which was to typify their relationship in years to come. Small and fidgety, the new infant required more care, time, and patience than her brother ever did. Andrew was quiet and good-natured, often grave and curious, and always the apple of his mother's eye.

Rocking Rachel, crooning to her, Norah frowned with worry. The infant had been fed and should have slept but instead whimpered and moved restlessly. "She's never still! Do you think she's sick?"

"Give her to me. Maybe she needs changing." Gretchen Baumgartner had come from Eli's ranch to help during Norah's confinement, and the young women had become fast friends. "Come, my dumpling." She lifted the baby and cuddled it on an ample bosom. "Rachel is our darling, aren't you, *liebchen*?" Singing a German lullaby, she left the bedroom, and soon the sewing machine treadle click-clacked as she continued making a supply of diapers quilted from shirttails. She was childless as yet but came from a huge family into which a baby had entered annually. The oldest girl, she had helped to feed, dress, and discipline younger members, and she handled Andrew like a tiny brother. Now, for instance, he sat in a muslin swing she had suspended between two posts beside the veranda; the men often detoured to speak to him, and Baron dozed at his feet, lifting an eyelid now and then.

Norah coughed several times. That sharp pain under the ribs! What could it be? Had the second pregnancy on the heels of the first drained her strength to the point of exposing her to infection? To an old enemy she thought had been defeated forever? God forbid! How she missed Theo. Despite the lack of knowledge he readily admitted, he had been a comfort beyond telling. The fact that he was fifty miles away and no other physician was closer than Tucson had weighed upon her mind once her water broke. She was worried to death until Gretchen bustled in, although she and Jim had discussed earlier what had to be done. He hadn't told her he was appalled by the idea of delivering her child. And he couldn't say how much help Rose would be.

"But you've seen colts and calves born!" Norah had tried to keep panic out of her voice. "And you told me you help the mothers sometimes."

Jim turned mottled red, thought of reaching into the vaginal canal to wrestle a membrane-encased creature into proper position. *Christ!* Suppose he had to do that for Norah! Wild eyed, he had turned for the stable. "I'll get that housekeeper of Eli's!"

"I hardly know her! Maybe she doesn't know about babies. Suppose she won't come?" Norah plunged her hands into the pockets of her apron so she would not openly twist them in despair.

"Of course she will! Don't worry!" Jim and three cowhands had galloped out of the yard, not sparing the horses.

Gretchen had come, and after a long but normal delivery, the women held hands and gave thanks to God.

Norah was soon back on her feet, although she had to rest at frequent intervals and did not recoup her energy fast enough to suit her. The morning her friend was to depart, they lingered over breakfast.

"*Ach, Gott,* the house will be a mess. And he has worn his last clean shirt, I am sure." Gretchen shook her head and smiled, partly with fondness, partly in exasperation, as women will at a man's helplessness.

"Can't he wash one out himself? Or is he too big and important to do that?" Norah moved her daughter's cradle with one foot, a real cradle of ironwood her Aunt May had brought from Texas.

Gretchen's bright blue eyes twinkled. "You like him, yes?"

"I like him, no! He's insufferable and conceited."

"He thinks you are *wunderbar*—ah, wonderful."

"We didn't part on very good terms at the funeral. He's pretty puffed up about himself."

"I think he loves you. It is hard for him to say."

"Well, he might be all right once you know him. A friend once said he was a bull in a china shop when it came to women." Norah's mind strayed from the conversation. "I'd better notify Carleton's parents that they have a granddaughter. Will you mail my letter?"

"Mr. Martin can take it to the fort the next time they drive a herd there." Gretchen rose when Jim popped his head in the door.

"You 'bout ready to go?" He smiled at Norah, who was too damned peaked to suit him. "How's the baby?" A thin cry answered him. "Sorry."

"You didn't do anything," she said tiredly. "The slightest little thing wakes her up. Oh, Gretchen, how can I ever thank you for what you've done?" The women hugged, and Gretchen kissed the children.

"Hurry and write your letter. We will take my things out. You have my horse, Mr. Fullerton?"

"Thor is sure a big fellow. . . ." Their voices faded, and Norah hurried into the bedroom for paper and pencil.

She sealed the envelope, pleased to think of the grandparents' joy. Norah had postponed again and again the task of telling them Andrew was not their grandson, that until

Rachel came, nothing remained on earth of their beloved only son. They had written several times urging her to visit, but she had put them off, unwilling to break their hearts. Another problem loomed, too. Money from Carleton's estate was piling up in Andrew's name at a Tucson bank—funds she'd never touched, of course, but which should be transferred to his sister.

Standing beside Andrew with Rachel in her arms, she waved and waved until Gretchen was no longer recognizable. Suddenly Norah had the feeling she was about to be buried under an avalanche of a thousand chores. She ached, trembled with fatigue. She couldn't do it. *She simply couldn't!*

A tugging at her skirts interrupted Norah's attack of anxiety. Andrew had his fingers splayed before his face, playing peek-a-boo. Sunlight gilded the glossy black hair, and his eyes shone with fun at the game Gretchen had taught him.

Norah laughed in surprise and copied him, talking to Rachel, including her in the game. Going into the house for a cushion, she brought it out and sat down with Andrew, whose attention had now settled on a black beetle. The late morning was too balmy and pretty to bother with breakfast dishes, Norah decided.

The men came and went at ranch duties, saw and heard the serene young mother playing with her children. Each had his own thoughts, for some were fatherly men and some were not. But ever after in the barren loneliness of cowboy bachelorhood, they carried glowing in their memory the image of Norah with her infants, a Western Madonna.

After laboring over the spring tally, Jim grinned, teeth startling white against nut-brown skin. "By darn, that's not bad. A good profit on the hoof there."

Norah pursed her lips in thought and entered the last figure for him. "Jim, I'd like to go into the cattle business in a small way and maybe have that spread I've talked about. Raise the children there."

"Don't see why not. Made up your mind, have you? Not going to wait any longer?" Jim handed Andrew a toy made from empty thread spools on a string.

She shook her head. It had been almost a year since her first letter to Mason, directed to a Washington address provided by the governor's office. Either he was dead or no longer interested in them. Norah couldn't believe the latter and tried not to think about the former. Whatever his fate, her children's futures had to be planned for. She coughed with nervousness. "No, you've been so good, supporting us since Carleton died, I thought I'd invest what funds I have so I can start paying you back."

"Whaddya mean? I don't know what I'd have done without you all these months, now that Rose has her own household. You've earned what you've gotten. You're not beholden to me for one penny. 'Sides, I like having the three of you around. But if you're really serious about that spread—"

Norah folded her arms. "Never more so."

"Okay, then, here's what we can do. Down on the border south of here there's an old abandoned Spanish hacienda called the San Bernadino. Emedio says a Mexican Army lieutenant bought part of it in the 1820s, but the Apaches got so bad he gave up during the thirties. Most of the big ranchers south of the Gila River did. Naturally, thousands of cattle ran wild, and we pick up their offspring during roundup. Mavericks, we call 'em. What do you say I give you half the number that comes in and you brand your own herd?"

"That's kind of you, Jim, but they'd compete with your animals for forage."

"Why, there's enough for a hundred years out there. Don't worry about that." Like his fellow ranchers, Jim believed the range's capacity to feed cattle was limitless.

She sat up very straight, a bargain struck, the initial step taken to independence. "All right," Norah said, shaking his hand, "it's a deal. In return I'll pay you a percentage of the sale price for handling."

Jim chuckled. "Spoken like a cattleman." He went onto the veranda and carried in a long object which he dumped in her lap. "Here. You have to have this."

"It's so heavy! What on earth—" She removed the burlap wrapping and shouted with delight. "A branding iron! *My own Mariposa!* The outline of a butterfly on top of a horizontal capital N. Is that the Mariposa Lazy N?"

"Sure is."

Iron in hand, Norah rushed around the table to kiss Jim on the cheek. "What a sweet man you are!"

Jim laughed, sharing her pleasure, content to be her friend, nothing more. "I'm real glad you like it."

"I love it!"

"I designed it and John Smith welded it. Kinda like it myself."

She praised the design enthusiastically, holding the iron up to the light. "Thanks for getting me started, Jim. I think I'll keep a step-by-step record of what happens on fall roundup so I can refer to it later. Which reminds me—have you seen my bird-watching records? Oh, Lord, don't tell me I left them at the fort. I put them away when I got so busy with Andrew."

The rancher rose and stretched. "Think they might be in that big trunk in the shed?"

"I was sure I unpacked everything, but maybe I didn't."

"Let's go look. Hey, Andrew! There you go, *way* up in the air!" He swung the boy overhead, and Andrew chortled and reached for the ceiling. Walking toward the shed, Jim said, "We must look quite the family, each of us with a baby. By golly, it feels good to hold one, don't it?"

"You make a good father."

"There were times in my life when I wondered if I did." Jim abruptly turned, hand on his gun. "Who's that coming?

Look, Norah, somebody's bringing a milch cow. I'll bet a dollar to a doughnut Eli Martin's sent it for the children!"

The lanky rider leading the cow approached at a leisurely pace. He was familiar to Norah and she hurried forward. "*Endicott!* What are you doing here? Where'd you get that Holstein? Aren't you in the Army anymore?"

He grinned at the spate of questions, dismounted, and shook hands with Jim. "Nope. Done left the Army. Missed my li'l feller." He patted Andrew's shoulder. "And this ol' gal? Got her at the EM Ranch. Stopped for directions and Mr. Martin ast me to bring Rosebud 'long to you. Hyar's his letter."

"Thank you, Endicott. My, it's good to see you!" Norah shoved the letter into an apron pocket. When the cow mooed plaintively, she went to it and patted the sweaty neck. "Hello, Rosebud. Welcome to the Double Bar F. See, Rachel?" The baby bawled, and Norah returned to the men, trying to soothe her daughter. "Big animals frighten her. She cries when we get close to them, but Andrew wants to kiss them."

"Light a spell and come to the house." Jim gave Andrew to her, took the cow's rope, and started toward the barn.

"You by any chance lookin' for an extra man, Mr. Fullerton?" Endicott called after him. "Ain't too much with cattle, but—"

"He can do anything!" Norah said.

"Don't pay much," Jim warned. "But you get three squares a day and a decent place to sleep. I've got men for range work, but Norah and the cook need help with heavy chores—chopping wood, emptying laundry kettles, doing repairs—"

Endicott held out his arms to Andrew, who came, bubbling and laughing. "Jest tell me what to do."

"I'll get the cow settled and be up to the house directly," Jim said. He was glad to hire an extra pair of hands for Norah; his wife had been old before her time.

Norah was exuberant. What a stroke of luck! Putting

Rachel to bed with a sugar teat, she prepared a snack while
Endicott sat on the porch, bouncing Andrew on bony knees.
"Ride a cockhorse to Banbury Cross, to see a fine lady on a
white horse; rings on her fingers and bells on her toes, she
shall have music wherever she goes." Rendered in his
Kentucky accent, the nursery rhyme acquired fresh charm.

"Can you milk a cow?" she asked through the door,
mentally crossing her fingers.

"Why, shore. I can put milk in a cat's mouth at six feet."

"Don't have a cat. How about Baron's mouth?"

"Put the whole cow in that mouth!"

Norah put Andrew down with another teat, then joined
the two men after pouring more coffee. They were quiet and
pleasantly tired, each content with what the day had
brought. A summer breeze tripped through the oak leaves,
rustling them like swatches of deep green taffeta. The aroma
of baking bread stole from the oven. Butterflies and birds
decorated shrubs and trees. A mare and her filly paused to
regard them with demure curiosity, then ambled on to the
artesian pond. The lowing of cattle, turned velvety by
distance, melted into the waning afternoon like honey
warmed by the sun.

Endicott put his fork on the plate without sound as if
reluctant to disturb the holiness of nature. "What a place to
see the day come down! By God, you got a bit of heaven
here."

Norah's eyes met Jim's. No one had ever said it better.

"I have to get out of the house!" Norah slapped a quirt
against one leg. She wore the divided riding skirt, boots and
spurs, a flannel shirt, and a gun belt.

Jim stopped in midstride between corral and barn,
carrying a dutch oven. "Where you going?"

"*I* don't know! Nearby. Anywhere! Another hour doing
that damned housework and I'll lose my mind!"

"Okay, okay, simmer down." If Norah swore, she was
really on edge. "Don't go too far, that's all. The men have

spotted Apaches herding horses out of Mexico. Must be headed for San Carlos to sneak them to friends and relatives. They give us a wide berth, but they'd be after a lone woman like wolves on a lamb."

Norah remembered her heart jumping that instant when Geronimo's visage had leaped into focus. "I promise to stay along the foot of the mountains so I can ride home quickly if I have to." The children had been fed and were sleeping, and Endicott was sharpening knives and telling Rose tall tales about Davy Crockett. Bread was rising, beans soaking, gingerbread cooling. All was right with her domestic world this October afternoon. Her nerves were another matter entirely.

"Take Steel, then. Isn't a horse in Arizona fast as he is." Jim put the oven down and took her shoulders in his hands. "We love you, you crazy bird-watcher. Don't want anything to happen to you."

"Okay, okay, simmer down," she mocked, covering his right hand with hers. "When will the Army get them under control?"

"When they catch 'em. Now get out of here," he growled, fighting an impulse to slap her on the rump. "And be back before dark, hear?"

Steel trotted across the reddish earth, farting occasionally and snorting with satisfaction. At least that was what she thought he was doing. After all, why shouldn't intelligent animals have some of the emotions human beings had? Steel liked to travel, just as a person did. Norah scratched his shoulder with affection.

The red-haired brothers hailed her as she went by, and Emedio, farther off, waved a gauntleted hand. Though the herd roamed free, the men scouted constantly for rustlers who might steal cattle for food to sustain them in their marauding. Norah identified the different animals: black and white, brindle, buckskin, and calico cows from Mexico; fleshy, buffalo-colored chinos, the curly-haired animals from Texas; gaunt longhorns of mixed color with white

patches, the poorest in salable meat. Jim planned to buy
Devons or Herefords from the Midwest when he could
afford to upgrade his stock. Most cattlemen nurtured a
similar ambition, but meanwhile enjoyed the continuing
demand from military posts, mining communities, and
government buyers for the reservations.

Norah searched as she rode, eager to spot the Mariposa
brand, but saw only Double Bar F marks. Because Jim's
range was very large, he had isolation pastures, including
one where new colts were nursed, close to the ranch
buildings. Her mavericks—weaned but not branded—
usually grazed there until ready to mingle with the other
animals. She made a note to ride home that way and count
her herd increase. Her children had been sick during full
roundup, and Norah had been unable to keep track. Jim
would have the count, though, right down to the last
notched ear. But time for that later—

Spurring Steel to a canter, yet taking care to avoid prairie
dog holes, Norah headed for a canyon that opened on the
valley and offered fast escape. A family of woodpeckers
that nested there were brown, white, and red, whereas most
others she'd seen were black, white, and red. Theo and
Lollie had written to say they had met Captain Charles
Emil Bendire and Colonel Bernard J. D. Irwin, surgeon-
naturalists; most of their time was devoted to collecting
specimens of birds, reptiles, and plants in Arizona Territory.
They had been intensely interested in Norah's "studies"—a
thrillingly professional word—and suggested she send skins
and data to natural history museums avid for information on
bird life in the Chiricahua range. The area was like the other
side of the moon to Eastern scientists.

"*Skins!*" Norah said aloud with indignation. She dodged
a branch. It would be a cold day in Hades before she killed
and skinned birds. Red-tailed hawks screamed overhead,
and Norah reined Steel in. She loved the eagles, hawks, and
falcons—they symbolized the very spirit of freedom to her.

Dismounting by a cottonwood tree, Norah dropped the

reins to delve into a saddlebag for the journal labeled WOODPECKERS: ORDER *PICIFORMES*, FAMILY *PICIDAE*. Her journals on Arizona species now filled two large boxes and contained in many instances more specifics than did her bird book.

She had taught herself that a bird's name consisted of two parts: the genus and species. For example, genus *Apheloco-ma coerulescens* was the species Woodhouse or scrub jay, discovered by Dr. Samuel Washington Woodhouse during the 1851 Sitgreave Expedition that surveyed northern Arizona. The bird belonged to the family *Corvidae*, which included crows, ravens, and magpies; according to her book, the term possibly derived from the word *corvine*, first referred to in print in 1656 in Blount's *Glossography*.

Pride surged through Norah to think——despite her spotty knowledge——she might contribute ornithological informa-tion about species of a relatively unknown region. Her scalp prickled at the very thought.

Certain bird names made her laugh: baldpate, booby, bufflehead, coot, cuckoo, bristle-thighed curlew, loon, ovenbird, pewee, tattler, wagtail. Who chose such names? What fun the boys in the bunkhouse would have with them!

Not a single rat-tat-tat disturbed the quiet. The woods were more silent than she had ever known them to be. After a quick scan with binoculars turned up nothing but squirrels and sparrows, Norah settled at the foot of the tree and soon was engrossed in an illustration of a bird's anatomy. Suddenly she looked up. "Baron, what *is* it?" He had leaped to his feet with an explosive bark. Both mastiff and horse appeared to smell trouble, and Norah jumped to grab the reins. Steel whinnied, showed the white of his eyes, and backed away from under the tree, dragging her with him.

The dog put his head back and growled deep in his chest. Norah followed his gaze and froze, lips parted in fright as well as fascination. Greenish-golden eyes glared down at them. Leopard! No, *jaguar! El tigre* of which Emedio spoke with such respect. The great cat of the Americas that was to the New World what the lion was to the Old. His eight-foot, 250-pound body, heavy neck, large paws, and bared fangs testified to his potential for death and destruction.

The jaguar had fed well during the summer in the deserted Chiricahuas, his menu much the same as that of the mountain lion: deer, rabbit, peccary, and wandering cow. He had roamed far from Mexican haunts, and now, sensing the coming of winter, was traveling down the mountain cordillera toward home. At the time these three creatures stopped below him, the big cat had been waiting for afternoon prey, crouched motionless on a branch, his coloration blending with the yellowing cottonwood leaves. Jaguars did not attack human beings except in utter desperation, and this one wanted nothing to do with the dog, either, but the wind had shifted and blown his scent the wrong way. He snarled soundlessly at his canine adversary who dared him to descend. Thundering challenge, Baron reared on his hind feet and clawed furiously at the tree trunk, hackles straight up from the nape of his neck to the base of his tail.

Norah drew the gun she had yet to fire in anger or defense. The jaguar was a danger to Jim's herd and her mavericks, very likely to any person or animal. It would be easy to shoot him right between the eyes, through the skull that held the magnificent face with its black rosettes, coarse whiskers, and broad nose. But his fierce vulnerability swayed Norah as she cocked the trigger, aimed, and fired. Bark flew, and the jaguar spat in anger. Leaping at least twenty feet to the ground, the animal sped away while Baron raced away in pursuit, ignoring Norah's frantic calls to come back.

"That was a pretty poor shot after all I taught you."

Norah's essence concentrated on the voice behind her. Her mind reeled, for knowing he was here at last was like staring into the sun, being blinded by its light, consumed by its heat. She whirled and ran into his arms, the reins slipping through her fingers. The badge pricked her breast.

It was a welcome pain! She cried out unintelligibly, returning his kiss with a hunger honed by many months.

"A terrible shot," he murmured against her lips, the flat of his hand splayed across her buttock cleavage, straining her to him so hard her feet were off the ground. Ah, God, she tasted divine. He smelled perspiration, no doubt from fear of the jaguar, mixed with lily-of-the-valley. She had changed her perfume.

Putting her head on his chest, Norah wept with joy, the tears penetrating the shirt to his skin. He put her away from him for a moment, took the revolver that dangled from her hand, and holstered it. She held on to his waist, aching to touch every inch of him from the hair on the crown of his head to the tiny curls surrounding his privates.

She leaned back in his arms and traced his mouth with a fingertip. Words held in for what seemed forever poured out. "Mason, you'll never know how much I *love* you! Or how much I've *missed* you. Every time I look at Andrew I see you. Don't ever leave me again! I don't think—I could stand it." Her insides hurt, and she moaned softly.

The sound stabbed him to the heart. He yanked her back to him, kissing her brow, pushing her Stetson off so he might run his fingers through her hair, delighting in the full breasts flattened against his chest. "Woman, woman, how many nights I've held you to me like this and hated the man who made love to you. I've taken you so many times and caressed you—and then woken to emptiness. I don't want to do that anymore."

They stood with arms wrapped around each other. The horses browsed and snorted companionably from time to time. Leaves fluttered to earth, brown, beige, and lusterless green. Baron trudged back, tongue lolling, limping with a bruised pad. The woodpeckers returned, calling raucously, a noisy, impudent family.

Mason lifted her chin so that they were looking into each other's eyes. "Norah—Norah, my darling darling—say you'll marry me."

Ascending slowly to higher altitudes, the jaguar paused to cock his massive head. A cry rang out behind him, faint and sweet upon the wind. The golden gaze turned south. The memory of his mate registered hazily in the brutish brain, and *el tigre* hastened his homeward pace.

23.

"What do you *mean*—you're *leaving* in the morning? I—I thought you were here to stay." Norah came to an abrupt halt, empty meat platter in hand, laughter dying in her throat. They were alone and the children in bed, replete with much kissing, cuddling, and cooing from both adults.

Mason carved patterns in the tablecloth with a spoon handle, hating to disappoint her, which was why he had not broached the subject on the way back to the ranch a few hours ago. They had had much to talk about, and he had been able to avoid upsetting her until now. He certainly didn't want to head south, but there was no way around it. The hunt couldn't be called off.

"I'm after a highwayman wanted for holding up a stage and killing the passengers. It was just coincidental he ran this way."

She put the pot back on the stove. "Let me get this straight. You didn't know Andrew and I were here?"

"How could I? I thought you were in Philadelphia by this time."

"You didn't get my letters? You didn't even ask at the fort?" Her shoulders stiffened in hurt.

He got up and put his arms around her. "I see what you're driving at. I never got the letters and I didn't ask at the fort because I didn't pass by that way. If I had, I'd have been here so fast it would have made your head spin! I came from the west and then headed south this time. The man escaped from a jail wagon headed for Yuma, you see, then he picked up a horse and weapons in Tucson and holed up near the ruins of that old Jesuit mission south of Tubac. That's where Chico and I flushed him.

"And we'd have had him if he'd ridden a bit farther into Pete Kitchen's territory. Ever hear of Old Pete? He's a legend, one of the greatest fighters in the West. During the Civil War, after federal troops were withdrawn, there were only two places in Apachería where you were safe: the walled town of Tucson and Pete's place on Potrero Creek. He'd have blown that murderer to kingdom come and saved me a lot of trouble."

Norah's eyes moistened. "Where is Chico, anyway?"

"He's on the trail right now. I'll pick him up in the morning."

"Can't he bring the man in?"

"It's not his job, darling, it's mine, and there's no time to lose. The fugitive can coast right down Vista Valley into Mexico. There isn't a mountain or a canyon he has to cross. If I don't catch him now, he could slip into the Sierra Madre, and it'll be a real problem getting him out. He's half Apache, which almost surely means they'll give him refuge."

Norah disengaged herself and sat down. "Somehow I get the impression that if you hadn't reached the ranch in the afternoon when it was too late to chase this outlaw any longer, you wouldn't have stopped."

He towered above her, the badge glinting in the lamplight. "That's right. But don't forget—I had no reason to stop. I didn't know you were here."

"I *hate* it."

"What?" He joined her, sitting so close their thighs touched, and she edged away.

"That." Norah pointed at the star as if it were a loathsome insect on his garment.

Mason scowled and peered down at it. "I'm proud of it. And of what I do, too."

"More proud of it than of Andrew and me?"

"That's not fair, Norah."

"I'm sorry. Tell me why it'll be so hard to get this man once he's in the Sierra Madre."

He pictured the geography in his mind. "Distances go on forever. You master one mountain and there's another one to climb. After a while you feel as if you're climbing the same one over and over. Vertical cliffs thousands of feet high. Brutal, horse-killing, man-killing country. Pa-Gotzin-Kay, the Apaches call it. Stronghold Mountain of Paradise.

"Chico and I were on the Nacozari River last July. I could hardly touch my rifle barrel or Colt, they were so hot. My boots wore out. My mount collapsed and had to be shot. And I swear rattlesnakes thrived thick as grass. Cactus, flash floods, dust storms, earth tremors—I think they only call it Paradise because there aren't any white men."

She rubbed his knee under the table, thinking not of the danger he faced, over which she had no dominion, but of their coming together, of his entering her, of his shout of release and ecstasy when he expelled his seed, clutched her breasts, kissed her, tongue dueling with tongue. Norah shifted her weight, aware of dampness in her undergarments. She removed her hand, rose, and walked back to the stove.

". . . you didn't hear a word I said!" Mason accused her. "In fact, you missed a most momentous announcement."

"What was that?" How handsome he was! The Lord help her, she could eat him up! Nibble at his earlobes, nipples, lower lip and penis, the flesh of his inner thighs. Norah's face flamed, but she didn't care. That's what she wanted to do!

"I *said*, I've decided to turn in my badge once I deliver

this prisoner. If I'm lucky, I'll be back by the end of November. Maybe sooner."

"Mason, do you really mean that?"

Lithe as the jaguar, he came to her with the graceful stride she hoped his son had inherited. "I love you too much to live apart from you any longer. I'll turn it in and we'll get married and raise—" He pulled her to him and buried his mouth in her hair.

"Raise what? Cattle? Horses?" God in heaven, how marvelous he felt against her.

"Both, although I prefer horses. But more important, we'll raise the most marvelous children you ever saw. As soon as you're well from having the last one, I'll take you in the bedroom and make love to you till the cows come home." Mason grabbed the hair at the back of her head and pulled down. His eyes gleamed as he kissed the exposed hollow of her throat, parted her bodice, and kissed the upthrust flesh.

"Not here!" Norah objected. "Someone might walk in."

Rachel wailed, and Norah stepped away and refastened her bodice. She touched his pants where they bulged with his erection. "You make me act like a fallen woman." The baby cried louder, and Norah hurried to the bedroom to change and comfort her daughter. She saw that Andrew had turned onto his side but had not awakened—solid sleeper, unruffled child.

She turned to find Mason in the doorway. He stepped into the room, locked the door behind him. A tide of blood suffused Norah's cheeks, and her knees shook. He knelt and tried to kiss her groin through thick skirts, reached around to hold her buttocks, but was frustrated by the bustle.

"Darn things," he muttered, "take 'em off."

She was melting. "Go ahead. Make love to me until the cows come home."

"Here? In front of the children?"

Norah laughed and was amazed at a note of hysteria in her voice. "They won't know. Besides, there's no other

place.'' Nowhere else secluded, safe, or decent. Only the
woods or the barn. She recalled finding Rose and Joel in the
hay—no, she didn't want it that way.

He stood and welded her tightly to him. ''I don't want to
get you pregnant, sweetheart. I might not come back.''

''Don't *say* that!'' she commanded with a catch at the
heart.

''It's true. You have to face facts in this business.''

She began to unhook her bodice. ''I love you. I want you.
I'll have your baby and be your wife before it's born.''

Mason's nostrils flared, and he slid both hands inside her
clothing to cup her breasts. ''There are ways—''

Bodice and skirt fell to the floor, followed by corset,
bustle, and petticoats. ''Just love me.''

''What will the men think of me being here all night?''

She tossed her head in Andrew's direction. ''Is there any
doubt he's your spitting image? Jim and the rest of them
know we're going to be married.''

Mason glanced with a smile toward his son's crib, dug a
hand into his back pocket, and gave Norah a small package,
which she dropped. He picked it up and held it in his palm.
''I've carried them around for a long time, hoping beyond
hope. Let's take these off first.'' He removed her engagement and wedding rings, placed them carefully on the
bureau, and then unfolded the tissue to reveal a sapphire
ring set in diamonds and a brooch to match. Mason slid the
ring onto her finger.

''Does it fit? Will you marry me, Norah Carlisle Beatty?''
What a delicious girl in ribbon-threaded camisole and
drawers, hair tumbling down, stockings wrinkled at the
ankle.

''Yes, yes, oh, yes!'' She threw herself into his arms,
holding her hand out behind him to admire the sparkling
proof of his love. She had implied she did not care what the
men thought, but she did. Very much. The ring put a seal on
Mason's intentions, regardless of how much she trusted

him; the men knew they'd been lovers, yet they'd not think too ill of her with a wedding in the offing.

They kissed then until both were dizzy and breathless. He lifted her in his arms, carried her to the bed, undressed, and kissed her. Mason removed his clothing, drinking in the loveliness of the woman with whom he planned to spend the rest of his life. She reached for him. "Hurry! Hurry! It's been so long! *Too* long!"

He climbed in beside her and pulled the covers over them. Their bare bodies touched from throat to toe, tingling, burning, shaking. They breathed raggedly in purest pleasure and anticipation, so ready for one another that little preparation was needed. Mason took something from the bedside table and put it on himself.

"What's that?" Norah asked, wide eyed. Carleton had never used one.

"It's to protect you," he murmured with eyes closed. She was so soft and fragrant. Mason did not need sight. He had pictured her night after night, dreamed of thrusting into moist, hot silkiness. But he had promised himself not to leave her with child again. He had an odd foreboding about the pursuit of the half-breed. Chico, too, had expressed misgivings about plunging into the wilderness this time.

"Why do you have that?" The significance of his carrying contraceptives had not escaped her. Irrational anger boiled up in the question, and for the first time she pulled back, physically and mentally.

Mason shook his head. "Didn't your husband explain things? I suppose not. He wasn't the type. But you ought to know a man needs physical relief now and then. It isn't done with love, and the women know that. I'm sorry if the idea upsets you.

"The worst time is after I kill a man. It's as if I somehow have to emphasize my survival to myself, prove that his death hasn't killed me, too. Do you understand? And sometimes, Norah, she has red hair and blue eyes and I pretend it's you for a few hours." He pressed his lips to the

engagement ring. "I swear on Andrew's life that I will
never touch another woman once we're married."

"Promise me you won't be with anyone until then!"

"I can't."

"Why not?" she flared. "*I* won't be with anyone."

"That's different."

"*Why* is it different?" She tried to move out from under
him, but Mason seized her waist, thumbs digging into soft
tissue. Hair fell over his forehead, and his dark face
tautened with anger. Norah shrank from him, fear mingling
with love. How dangerous he looked. In an erotic way it
thrilled her. She opened her mouth to speak, but he stopped
it with his own and wrung a groan of desire from her.

"What's the matter with you? I love you heart and soul.
Isn't that enough? You've got to take me as I am, Norah.
You can't dictate what I do when we're apart."

She fought as he positioned himself. "*Goddamn* you and
your badge and your whores! I hate you! *I hate you!*" Norah
wanted to kill him. Strike him. Punish him. She beat at him
with clenched fists, bit his shoulder, tried to knee him. Then
he was on top of her, thick lashes down over sultry eyes, his
manhood, long and heart-stoppingly large, penetrating to
nudge the womb. She gasped with fury at his invasion but
with rapture, as well, at the dream come true at last.

He told her he loved her with every thrust until the pace
grew too furious and the sensations that seized and
dumbfounded them hurled the lovers to a climax such as
neither had experienced before. Flesh still vibrating with
ecstasy, she helped him bloom again in her hand and mouth
and Mason showed her other ways to make love—ways
they found almost as satisfying as body within body.
Gradually then, like a storm that had blown across mesas,
buffeted trees, and scoured mountaintops, their desires
lessened and sleep overtook them.

"Still hate me?" he asked before they drifted off.

"Absolutely." They chuckled and kissed, asleep in
minutes, lip close to lip, limb intertwined with limb.

Norah woke just before first light, brain instantly alert and body refreshed, sleek and supple after months of celibacy. She was going to prepare her man a breakfast to end them all: flapjacks with butter and lick, a big steak, eggs, frijoles, biscuits, and jerky gravy. She'd pack a huge lunch, too, with enough for Chico. She wriggled toward the middle of the bed, then exclaimed with dismay at its emptiness. Mason gone already? There was only one consolation. The earlier he was in the saddle the sooner he'd return. She punched the pillows into a nest and wrapped her arms around them. Outside an early flock of scaled quail reproved her for being a slugabed. *Callipepla squamata,* their breasts, bellies, and backs a pewter-gray pattern of scallops, white topknots nodding like the seed-plumes of the cliffrose.

Swinging her legs over the side of the bed, she lighted a lamp and dressed. Andrew awoke while she was fixing her hair and smiled widely to see her near. "Let's see where Daddy went," she whispered, wrapping him in a blanket. She carried him outside in time for a sunrise spectacle.

To the west, suspended like a smoke-stained pearl above a ridge, the moon waned and retreated. To the east in peach and champagne glory, the sky introduced the sun, which stained the ridge scarlet as if in warning to the moon. Norah pointed out the quail to Andrew, busybodies at a kaffee-klatsch near the pond. Nearsighted tarantulas venturing from silk-lined holes teetered across the ground in search of beetles; Norah stepped back but made no move to harm the hairy spiders, for like many misunderstood species, they were both beneficial and shy.

In any event, she couldn't kill a fly today. Norah felt magnanimous and forgiving of all creatures, for Mason had found her at last, and her heart overflowed with love.

24.

Standing on a narrow rock ledge halfway up a steep cliff, Mason and the stone-gray mule glowered at each other in mutual hatred and exhaustion. A crack in the trail from a recent tremor separated them. Far below a river boiled and snarled, swollen by a cloudburst upstream.

"Get over here, you mean and stubborn son of a bitch," Mason said wearily, yanking on the reins. "I'm sick of fooling with you."

The mule was big, at least five feet at the shoulder with ears fourteen inches long; spirited and more intelligent than some men, he was at the moment sick and tired of working. He had been named Grendel by his classically inclined owner, a friendly New Mexico rancher entrusted with Storm Cloud until Mason's return. Grendel's name—that of the monster slain by Beowulf—reflected his disposition, but like most mules he possessed surefootedness, great endurance, and powers of recuperation the majority of horses did not have.

"Shit," Mason sighed. "I'd follow old Beowulf's example, but I'm too damned tired. Here." He dropped the reins. They dangled below the mule's jaw, and Grendel peered down at the river, then at Mason. He snorted several times.

"That's right. It's a very long way down. But I'm through. Stand there for the rest of the year. I don't care." Mason turned and trudged up the trail. Chico, his tireless pony, and a pack mule waited in a recess carved from the cliff. Mason was painfully aware Grendel did not have room to turn around; this meant he eventually had to jump and might trip on the reins. Despite his profound exasperation, Mason would feel responsible for the animal's death. But even more important, losing him would put Mason afoot.

"We will sleep. He'll be along." Mason stretched out, one hand dangling over the edge of the crevice. He accepted the peril of their situation with almost Indian stoicism.

The Apache nodded. Had he been able to pass the mule and crouch above its dangerous back hoofs, he would have knifed it in the haunch and anus until it leaped in desperation. But there was nothing to be done. They were not in jeopardy from the outlaw they pursued; he was ahead of them. Nor were other Apaches near; Chico could smell an encampment a mile away. It would be good for the four of them to slacken pace if only for an hour.

Chico did not close his eyes, although he relaxed throughout his body. He saw that Fletcher slept and sat with knees under chin between the sleeping man and the chasm. Fletcher, his brother, might move in slumber and fall to his death, a sad end for a man about to take his first wife.

La espina del diablo—the devil's spine. That was what the natives called the Sierra Madre range that stretched—so Chico had been told—the entire length of Mexico. He knew only certain geographical areas: seasonal rancherías where women roasted mescal plant hearts to make intoxicating liquor; where jerky was cured in the sun for warriors' pouches; where fugitives fled for succor and provisions. He studied the mountains reaching into infinity, each hazier and more insubstantial than the last. It was as if the sun was drawing up their essence. And was his life not much like that? He grew old and his flesh went away, leaving naught but a leathery envelope that encased bones and innards. So did wind and rain wear away stone, sparing only the inner core.

He wondered how he would die. He wanted to go out fighting as befitted an Apache. How repulsive to decay and disintegrate on a pallet in a brushwood hut, to be fed mush like an old baby and cleaned of defecation. A golden eagle flew past him, the rustle of rich dark-brown feathers distinctly audible. Its untamed eye was tranquil in innocent savagery; ruthless yellow feet clutched a squirrel. Chico got to his feet, took a deep breath, and raised his arms in thanks to the gods. The bird had been a sign. He would die as the eagle flew. In nobility and bravery, regard set upon the sky.

Behind him Grendel suddenly brayed and jumped the gap, skidding to a stop a few inches from Mason's feet. Bleary eyed, Mason rolled over and said, "You stupid bastard, I told you you could do it. What took you so long?"

The map was not only inadequate but undoubtedly inaccurate. Engraved in 1864 under Emperor Maximilian's imperial license, the watercolors had faded, pages were badly smudged, constant creasing had obliterated some detail. Mason rubbed bloodshot eyes, gritty from a dust storm. He was not surprised that the map failed to reflect the country they were now traversing. Who would have any interest in charting this tortured landscape? It offered little to ranchers, miners, or farmers and burdened travelers with an abundance of hardship: dry rivers or flash floods, scarce game, insurmountable rock walls, extreme temperatures, poor trails, Indians and Mexican bandits as venomous and pitiless as the reptiles and arachnids infesting the land. Little soft or fragile survived here except the rare mockingbird or covey of blueish quail scattering before you with sweet shrill cries.

His shoulders slumped. Nothing had gone right on this chase, and once again foreboding darkened his thoughts and weighed heavily on his spirit. In primordial places like these, a man sloughed off civilized veneers, became open to mysteries, superstitions, and apprehensions as he never was in town. What difference would it really make if he returned to Norah, let the fugitive escape, failed to do his duty?

Ah, duty. Honor. Self-respect. Each virtue impaled upon the silver points of the badge President Grant had admon-

ished him to keep shining. Did it pay to be virtuous? Did it
pay to be bad? Did it matter?

"The map, Fletcher. You see our steps?" Chico considered maps astonishing things. By merely looking at a
paper covered with a series of meaningless symbols, you
knew where your moccasins were planted on the earth. He
touched the map with a dirty finger. "Here?"

Mason glanced at him sharply. He could not remember
seeing Chico's hand quiver before. Excitement? Hardly. He
had no nerves. Exhaustion? They had found a spring,
bathed, refreshed themselves, and eaten. Age? Chico getting old? The idea startled Mason, for his friend seemed
indestructible. Yet why not—everyone grew old. Wasn't
that one reason he himself was quitting in order to build a
life with Norah? Dearest Norah. How odd—what came to
mind was not her beauty alone but a picture of her shooting
at the tree trunk instead of the jaguar. A jewel, his many-
faceted Norah. He had a special affinity for her love and
respect for nature.

"See this line?" Mason traced it with a pencil stub.
"Think of our journey as a horseshoe with the ends pointing
at the United States, Chico. We've come down the
cordillera on the west, crossed to the east, and now—I
think—we're close to the Yaqui River. This hombre is
slicker than a greased pig. I figure we've gone five hundred
miles and caught nothing but a whiff of camp smoke."

Chico grinned. "He is part Apache."

"Why don't you find him then? I'm about worn out."

"Part white, too. Cunning as a coyote."

"He's an Artful Dodger, all right." Mason addressed
himself to another of the fish he had been fortunate enough
to catch. Baked in ashes, they tasted delicate and sweet, but
Mason did not offer to share them. Apaches did not eat fresh
fish, although they enjoyed it from the can; it was not an
approved food, for fish were believed to belong to the snake
family. They did not partake of bear meat, either, the souls
of their dead being in the bears' custody. Chico had trapped

and killed a rabbit, however, and dug up tubers near the spring that satisfied him. Neither went hungry, but both grumbled at having run out of bacon.

They left the shade and water next morning. Uneasy and alert to the slightest sound, they had a gut hunch their quarry was not far ahead. Though tough and savvy, he, too, had to be suffering from bone-deep fatigue and constant thirst, had had to lead his animal, wear out his Indian boots. Apaches on foot were capable of seventy miles a day week after week, while a horseman covered but twenty-five in normal travel, less in harsh terrain. Mason recalled an old saying: an American rode a horse until it gave out—a Mexican beat ten more miles out of it—an Indian wrested out an additional ten before the animal collapsed, after which he cut its jugular, sliced off a steak or two, and used the intestines for waterskins. Poor animals.

Glad to have left Storm Cloud in New Mexico, Mason was grateful for Grendel's strength and steadiness. Despite the mule's orneriness, he had become fond of him and planned to buy him. Among other things, he was a good watchdog. They approached the channel through which this section of the Yaqui River flowed, its sullen roar loud and threatening below. The tumult impaired Chico's hearing but not Grendel's. The mule laid his long ears back and blew through his nose. Stepping sideways without warning, he shoved his rider into a cactus that jutted horizontally from the rock. Spines penetrated Mason's right shoulder like hypodermic needles, and he cursed with pain.

Chico pulled his pony to a halt a few feet from the precipice that plunged down to the river. He was used to danger, for it was as present as air. *"Qué pasa,* Fletcher?"

Mason pointed at a cactus pad that dangled from him like a bizarre purplish-green growth. "Get this damned thing out of me. Those barbs are like fish hooks!" He had edged Grendel forward when two shots rang out, one brushing the mule's neck, the other plucking at Mason's sleeve. The mule backed up, unhurt but wary.

"Look out!" Mason yelled. His warning was in vain. The ambusher's third bullet hit Chico in the heart, the fourth dead center between the pony's eyes. For breathless seconds they poised there motionless as a dusty statue.

"Chico! Black Badger! NO!" Mason's cry of grief accompanied the Apache to his death as the pony crumpled and slid over the edge. Chico slipped out of the saddle, and sunlight sprayed him with gold. The speed of descent swept back the graying hair so he flew like an eagle, his regard set upon an endless horizon. When he struck the river and was seized by the current, his soul had already joined those of his ancestors.

Mason cursed in Spanish and English, yanking the rifle from its saddle scabbard with his left hand. His shoulder was on fire, but he had no time to help himself. Dismounting, fighting the urge to peer down at the river, he crept up among the boulders where the shots had come from. Where was that miserable excuse for a human being? Mike Ward was his name—a vicious murderer who shot down women and old men in cold blood. Rage warred with heartache, and Mason saw red. Panting, he breathed deeply and pulled himself together. Emotion played no part in this game. His foe was much too comfortable with death.

A hammer cocked a few feet away. "You lookin' for me, lawman?"

The bullet ricocheted and particles of rock stung Mason's cheek. "You better believe it, Ward. You just killed one of my best friends."

"You travel in damned lousy company," the half-breed sneered.

Mason hugged the wall behind him. The cactus pad, still protruding from his arm, struck an outcropping, and he swore at the pain. Unable to seize its thorny surface without stabbing his hand, he tried unsuccessfully to strike it off with the revolver barrel. Finally he pressed the pad against a boulder with the gun butt and jerked himself free, although numerous spines remained imbedded. Mason now went about his manhunt in blood, fury, and sorrow, berating himself for having let the criminal get the drop on himself and Chico. They had scouted ahead and finally seen Ward well in the distance, but the man pulled a fast one by backtracking and ambushing them.

Mason halted. A trickle of dirt, caused perhaps by mole or lizard, dribbled down a slope in front of him. He jumped back seconds before a rock slab thundered down where he would have stepped moments later. He strangled in the dust, and somewhere Ward also coughed and spat. The river muttered loudly in the stillness. Down on the trail, Grendel and the pack mule tongued their bits, thirsty and tired. Mason fought down hatred that rose like bile; a lawman was not judge or jury and did not perform his duty properly when motivated by revenge. Yet it was impossible to brush aside his friend's cold-blooded murder.

"Give up, Ward. You can't escape." Mason strained to pinpoint the source of the reply.

The other man laughed. He recognized the impasse, too. "Who you kiddin', Marshal? I got 'Pache kinfolk a whoop an' a holler away. You think you got trouble now, wait till they get here!"

Mason realized he had to act fast, for unless he took Ward hostage, he was done for. Every trick he knew, each ounce of strength, all the senses he possessed, poured into a distillation of cunning and dispassionate purpose. Until now their struggle had been man to man, but Ward's reinforcements gave him the whip hand. The outlaw had to be captured without further delay.

A pebble fell at Mason's feet. Ward was so near, yet out of reach. How the devil could he get up there without being wounded? Or could he lure Ward down? That might take too long, Mason decided. He'd have to go in shooting and hope for the best. Ward was one of the cleverest criminals he had ever hunted; despite his heinous crimes, Mason felt a reluctant admiration for the man's ability to evade him.

Moving with a cat's stealth, Mason ran noiselessly to the

rock slab which canted sideways and raced up the smooth incline. Reaching the exposure point, he hunched down to aim at his quarry through a natural aperture created by cactus and boulders. "Drop it, Ward." Nervous sweat broke out on Mason's body.

The outlaw straightened up from a crouch, caught unaware. Then he saw it—the promise of eternity in the muzzle of the Colt. What unnerved him even more was the cold amber eye sighting at his heart. Ward had an urge to urinate, and his intestines loosened.

"You heard me. Drop it." Mason held his breath. Gunfire would draw Apaches and mean two lives wasted— his and Chico's.

Ward's hammer was cocked, and his finger tightened on the trigger. He was trapped, but a shot would bring relatives from the ranchería to avenge him. His shoulders hunched as he prepared to shoot.

"Don't do it," came the warning whisper.

The words breathed of the grave. Gooseflesh rose on Ward's skin. The black muzzle of the .45 hypnotized him, for it seemed to grow in size the longer he looked into it. Then he knew he wouldn't fire. He wanted to live too damned bad. Besides, it was a long way back to Yuma, and who knew what might happen. Ward dropped the gun and put up his hands.

Mason stood and motioned with his weapon. "Let's go. Follow me, but make one mistake and I'll gut-shoot you. You'll take your own sweet time dying." He started to back down the rock slab.

Ward paled. The agonizing abdominal wound was dreaded by all men who wore a gun. It was almost always fatal, and here, with no medical care, it would assuredly be so. "No mistakes, Marshal, honest to God."

By the time they reached the trail, Mason's head ached with tension. "Turn around and face the river. Drop your gun belt. Now your pants."

"What the hell—"

Mason gritted his teeth and jammed his gun into the man's spine. "Drop those fuckin' pants around your ankles before I lose the last of my patience!" The undignified position had kept many a prisoner from trying to tussle with him or run away.

"Well, Christ, let a man take a pee first, willya?"

Hearing water spatter on the ground inspired Mason to relieve himself, too. He unfastened his fly and sighed with relief as his bladder emptied. Buttoning up again, he growled, "I'm telling you one more time and then I'm going to break open that hard skull with my gun butt."

"Hold your horses, Marshal, I'm droppin' 'em. Hey, that feels pretty good, lettin' it hang out in the breeze. Now what?"

Mason took handcuffs off his belt. "Hands on your head." He clamped one brace on and was bringing that hand down to the small of Ward's back when the prisoner executed a whirling jump that brought him face to face with his captor. He swung the loose manacle and hit Mason on the nose. Fierce joy thrilled through Mason as blood spilled out his nostrils. He holstered the Colt, took his gun belt off, and hung it from Grendel's saddle horn. "I changed my mind. Pull up your pants. I'm gonna beat the shit out of you, hog-tie you, and haul you back to Arizona to hang."

Ward buckled his belt and fell into a half-crouch with arms outstretched. He grinned, showing unexpectedly fine teeth at odds with his cold black eyes and long dirty hair. "That's what *you* think."

They circled each other on the ledge, well matched in weight and strength, colliding like rutting bulls and falling back dazed before returning to the attack. Mason soon forgot his own identity or what his mission was, knew only that this man had killed Chico and that he was now his friend's instrument of revenge. Ward staggered at last and crumpled onto one knee. Mason kicked him under the chin and the man fell backward. "Get up, you bastard."

Grendel whickered uneasily and moved toward them.

"He smells 'Pache," Ward gasped with satisfaction. "They'll skin you alive inch by inch."

Chest heaving with exertion, Mason grabbed the man's torn shirtfront and dragged him to his feet. "You'll never see it." Swinging his fist in a long arc, he delivered an uppercut so devastating that Ward's opaque eyes crossed and rolled up into his head before he collapsed.

Transferring supplies to Grendel and lashing them fore and aft of the saddle, Mason quickly tied the unconscious prisoner to the pack mule, then fitted on his gun belt.

The first bullet struck while he was fastening the holster thong to his thigh. It broke his right shoulder, spinning him around and into Grendel. The second shattered the collarbone and knocked him to the ground. The third missed and hit the pack mule in the rump. The animal brayed with pain and fled along the trail, its hapless human baggage jerking back and forth with every step.

On his side near Grendel's hoofs, Mason pulled the Colt with his left hand and fired at an Apache running across the cliff top. Graceful as a bird, the Indian plunged over the edge, clutching his breast. Another took his place, hair and loincloth blowing in the wind, and exchanged shots with Mason.

Drawing upon supernatural strength as adrenaline poured into his bloodstream, Mason pulled himself to a standing position by holding onto Grendel's bridle. He aimed carefully and shot the new arrival through his scarlet headband, felling him unseen among the boulders. The shock lessened, and agony clawed at Mason. Almost sobbing, he holstered his gun, took the reins, and slid a boot into the stirrup. His knees buckled and he grabbed the saddle horn to pull himself aboard, but the pain from the ruined collarbone was so excruciating he fell again and landed on the broken shoulder.

Mason writhed in the dust, a perfect target for the Apache woman, who had accompanied her husband from the ranchería for a little jaunt only to see him killed. She grabbed his Winchester off the ground and jacked a shell into the chamber. *"Netdahe!"* Mason heard. White killer. Blindly judging where the speaker stood, for his sight had dimmed, he pulled the trigger at the same time she did.

The woman plummeted to the ledge beside Grendel and the now thrice-wounded Marshal. Her added weight placed too much stress on the ledge weakened by rain, wind, and temperature extremes over the years, and it began to break away from the cliff.

Grendel felt the shelf go and tried to scramble to safety but failed. Legs flailing, the mule plunged into the gorge flanked by the gravely wounded man and dying woman. Through sheer luck neither Mason nor the mule landed on their bellies. The Apache did, and the sound of her abdomen bursting was that of a melon dropped on a hard surface.

Mason struggled weakly against the current, unable to swim or protect himself from being hurled into boulders and carried downstream. The world was composed of sky and foam and a roaring amplified by the high walls through which the Yaqui River thundered. Battered and close to insensibility, Mason Fletcher saw what was coming and held out his good arm as though to ward off almost certain death. The mule, helpless in the current's grip, hurtled toward him. Grendel's big hoofs aimed right at his face— and the last thing he remembered was their impact on his forehead.

After that, there was nothing but blackness and quiet and a primeval return to the water.

25.

Eli Martin climbed onto the corral fence, hooked boot heels on a lower bar, lighted a cigar, and unfolded the letter. Eyes narrowed against aromatic smoke, he reread Norah's thank-you for the dozenth time. It was distant yet friendly, cool but appreciative with no hint of the woman.

The cow, Rosebud, had arrived safely, and everyone now enjoyed milk and butter. He had been most kind to send such a valuable animal, and she would consider Rosebud a loan until she was replaced and returned. Norah also expressed thanks for hospitality extended to her friend Endicott.

He clamped down on the cigar with strong teeth. What a fool he'd been to act as he had at the funeral. She had wanted—needed—tenderness and a delicate touch. What she got was a mean-tempered boar with about as much finesse as a studhorse! No wonder Norah had gotten huffy.

Oh, well, he'd always been rough with women, never cruel but boisterous and rowdy like an overgrown kid not dry behind the ears. He didn't quite know how to handle those soft voices and places and so blanketed insecurity and shyness with bravado. Most of 'em liked his style, he'd say that—but then they weren't Norah. Proud, independent as a hog on ice, so gorgeous she made him catch his breath—she wouldn't put up with being mauled. In fact, that queen would most likely demand her rights in bed. Yeah, and he'd give 'em to her!

The rancher stared into the distance, the letter dangling from his fingers. No denying it, he was deeply in love. But

259

what should he do about it? Take the bull by the horns? Okay, but gently, gently. Tread careful as a mountain lion on a rotten branch. Woo her. Not so much with gifts but with respect, consideration, and affection. Let her know how precious she was. How highly he thought of her, not as a brood mare—her words—but as partner, lover, and friend. They'd sail to Europe if she wanted. And how his friends in the financial world would drool! Eli envisioned her in elegant ensembles fashionable in Washington, San Francisco, and New York. God, she'd been born to wear them.

Sure! He jumped to the ground. Why hadn't he thought of it before? He'd invite Norah and the Fullertons for Christmas dinner. No cooking or cleanup. That ought to please her! He rushed into the house, plumped down in a chair at the huge desk, and took a sheet of paper and envelope from one of the neatly arranged drawers. Christmas was a week away. Norah might not have started preparations yet and therefore could look forward to a more relaxed holiday. He wrote slowly but confidently, kissed her name once the ink was dry, and then hurried to the corral to find a fast-riding cowpoke.

The messenger returned that afternoon with an invitation to Gretchen, Mr. Martin, and his men to join the Double Bar F on Christmas Day. Again Norah appreciated his thinking of her, but bringing the children was too much of an undertaking. The family would expect them the night before or the morning of the twenty-fifth and looked forward to seeing them.

"Oh, it would be good to hold the babies again!" Gretchen exclaimed. She prayed for them every night as she did for the end of her husband's five-year stint with the Army. *Gott!* Would it never end? She wanted a family, too, but not until they had a proper home in which to raise *kinder*. "But I will stay here."

Eli frowned, knowing she was thinking of Mary, the cook, being alone. "She don't celebrate like we do."

"No, but I will not leave her by herself. We have already

decided on rice cakes and sauerkraut, with beef ribs and maybe apple kuchen.''

"My God." He chuckled and shook his head.

"Mary misses sea snails and dried frogs. Pig livers, too.''

"I'm gonna throw up if you don't quit. What happened to good ol' steak and beans?''

Gretchen shrugged and vigorously polished a desk corner. "Do they eat those in China? I will have to ask. But you *must* go to be with Norah. She likes you.''

He looked gloomily out a window, making a mental note to raise hob with whoever had hung the garden gate crooked. "No, she don't.''

"Yes, she does. I think she isn't aware how much. And you love her very much, *nein*?''

Eli nodded, then swung around. "Whaddya think Norah'd like for Christmas?'' They put their heads together over a list of gifts to take to the Fullertons'; the employer-employee relationship had long been blurred by gentlemanly conduct and good wages on his part, genuine concern for his well-being and scrupulous performance of duties on her part.

Eli paced back and forth and at last paused in the dining room in front of the sideboard. He opened it, removed a silver tray, then put it back. She'd have to polish that. What would a good-looking female really like? "Does she have a mirror? How 'bout the rosewood-frame mirror from the small bedroom?''

"Oh, she will love it! She told me how much she missed having one.'' Gretchen beamed. A perfect gift, so thoughtful and romantic.

He grinned to think of Norah fixing her hair, fastening a brooch, trying on a dress or hat. "Can't think of anything better. Now. For the younguns. Any ideas?''

Christmas morning found Eli and four top hands headed for the other ranch with a pack horse on a lead rope. The men exchanged amused glances to hear the boss man bellowing "Believe Me, If All Those Enduring Young Charms."

"Happy as a pig in a mud puddle," said one.

"Gonna spook them cows if he ain't more keerful," another grumbled.

"Wish he'd dry up. Sounds like he's got a bellyache," the third cowpuncher complained.

"*That* ain't where he aches," the last man laughed.

They whooped and spurred their horses to keep up with Eli, who rode as fast as was safe for the mirror lurching behind him. Antelope bounded away in the distance, and conversation turned to food: would there be turkey or venison or beef? They reached unanimous agreement before their destination came into view—whatever Mrs. Beatty and Chan Lee cooked up would be well worth the ride.

"'. . . each wish of my heart would entwine itself verdantly still!'" Eli bawled to a finish.

He knew he sounded like a wounded buffalo, but singing helped him forget that Norah had been madly in love with Mason since they first met in the fall of 'seventy-five and had even had a child by him. Eli had not heard from his friend in a coon's age. Not that he didn't wish him well, but the rancher hoped Mason was long gone and far away.

Baron signaled their arrival and ran to meet them, trotting alongside Eli's horse, barking his welcome. Dismounting in front of the house, the visitors removed their hats when Norah appeared, followed by Jim, his son, and the elderly cowpoke Shorty.

"Merry Christmas!" Jim yelled, shaking hands all around. He stared at the pack horse. "What'd you bring, Eli? The whole house?" Everyone glowed, looking forward to a pleasant day.

Norah put out a hand and smiled. She had decided to be cordial despite her dislike. The man had, after all, tried to make amends, and if he had no manners, she did. She also felt it would be easier for Jim, once she and Mason had their own outfit, if no hard feelings existed between the neighboring ranches.

"A very Merry Christmas, Eli. Come in, please. We have punch and hot toddies. We even have a tree!" She greeted the cowpunchers by name, and like their boss, they absorbed her loveliness with greedy eyes. Her Christmas dress was white with green sleeves and skirt ruffles, and she had pinned a red cloth flower to one shoulder. Crimson with health and cold, her lips matched the flower, and there wasn't a man present who wouldn't have given a year's wages for a kiss from them.

"My goodness, what *do* you have?" Her eyes sparkled, and she came to stand opposite Eli, who was having difficulty with a knot in his diamond hitch. "Here, let me help you," she offered, seeing that the riders were busy flapping their jaws, as Shorty would say.

Eli had tied and untied more knots than he could shake a stick at, but her nearness flustered him and made him awkward. It had been a spell since he saw her last. "You'll hurt your hands," he objected.

"No, I won't. They aren't that fragile."

The mirror came off first, carefully wrapped in blankets and burlap. "This is for you." He was holding it in his arms, face red with excitement and anticipation, when he noticed the engagement ring. Startled, he blanched and almost dropped the mirror. Had Fullerton proposed and she accepted? No, the ring was too ornate and expensive, for Eli was well aware of Jim's financial position. "Fletcher?"

"Yes," she whispered, touched and sincerely distressed by his reaction. Had he come thinking to reestablish a friendship leading to matrimony? Obviously, he had not known Mason was here in October. "I'm so sorry. There's no way you could have known. He stopped on the way into the Sierra Madre, trailing an escaped convict. He promised he'd be back before the end of November, but he's a month overdue." *Where in God's name was he?*

Eli hesitated, then put the mirror down, leaning it against

his legs. "Wish a woman loved me the way you love him. Hope he's okay." His comforting and graceful acceptance of the situation surprised Eli as much as it did Norah. Why had he said that? Because it was true. He loved this woman and did not want her hurt. He sighed and picked up his gift. "Let's get this inside before I break it. Bring that sack with the rest of the presents, Jim, and don't drop 'em!"

The house was redolent with holiday aroma: pine, turkey, whiskey, beef, coffee, mincemeat, tobacco, a hint of furniture oil, and starch. Despite disappointment and hurt, Eli perked up in the festive atmosphere. Better than a lonely day at the EM, even though he and the men would have hoisted a few and maybe played cards.

"This is—this is exquisite!" Norah had unwrapped the mirror. Softly, so as not to hurt him, she said, "I can't accept such a valuable gift. It must be an heirloom."

"It was my grandmother's. She brought it from London."

"You must keep it, then." She stroked the deep carving of daffodils and ivy, conscious of wanting the mirror more than she'd have thought possible. All she had to work with now was a scrap large enough to see her face in.

He removed the Stetson he wore in the high-crowned style that made men look taller, particularly in the saddle; he was actually short, just a few inches over Norah's height. Regardless of size, Eli radiated virility and power, and facing him, she felt slightly faint and trembly.

"I want you to have it. I'd like to think of you reflected in it. Of—" He stopped for a moment. "I have no children to pass it down to, and my brothers are rich and don't want it. Please. Take it. With my love."

Norah flushed. "Thank you. From the bottom of my heart."

"Hey, Martin, you may be a funny-lookin' Santa Claus, but by God, you sure act like the real McCoy!" Jim joined them with a bottle of Kentucky bourbon in each hand. "Thanks for these, compadre! You know what the Mexicans say: *Mi casa es su casa*. My house is your house," he translated for Norah.

Joel chimed in with his thanks for a new saddle blanket, Shorty for his *Police Gazette*, and Rose for a length of pink velvet from Gretchen. Eli reached into the sack and brought out two small boxes. "These are for the kids. Where are they?"

"It's about time to get them up. I put them down for naps so they wouldn't be cranky. But let me open their packages first." She murmured appreciatively over a beaded buck-skin doll and cubes of pine with letters of the alphabet branded on them. "You've been so generous I can't begin to thank you."

He had never thought of her as a mother but rather as a highly desirable woman with children tucked away some-where. In fact, Eli had steeled his heart against Mason's son after Norah's rejection of him at the fort. Consequently, the rancher was not emotionally prepared for the tiny girl she held nor for the sturdy boy who toddled from the bedroom, clinging to her hand.

Patting her son on the back, she said, "Shake hands with Mr. Martin, Andrew."

His love for baby animals overcoming his reserve, Eli bent to envelop the boy's hand with his. "Mighty happy to make your acquaintance, Andrew." Brilliant golden eyes behind black lashes assessed this new personality with rapt attention. Then Andrew's grin grabbed Eli tighter, as he would later admit, than a pony roped to a snubbing post. The man swept the boy up in his arms and motioned to Norah to give him Rachel, too. She drew back from the stranger and opened her mouth to cry, but decided not to and wrapped her arms around his neck instead.

"They love you!" their mother cried.

He bounced them both and pretended to eat Rachel's ear. She giggled and hid her face in his shoulder. "I'll take you home and feed you to my mice!" he threatened. "They'll nibble your toes—"

"Oh, how are your mice?" Norah accepted a glass of sherry from Joel, who, like the others, was openmouthed at this demonstration of the cattle baron's domestic side.

"Nice," Eli replied, and they laughed, thinking of their day together. He released Andrew to her, but Rachel refused to be let go. Privately he considered the girl a Plain Jane with her silken, sandy hair and washed-out blue eyes. Norah's son, now—he'd be a big, handsome devil like his daddy. The rancher's nostrils flared with jealousy, but it was impossible to stay moody for long in the fragrant, talk-filled room.

"I'd better get dinner on the table. Watch Andrew for me, will you? Maybe he'd like to play with his new blocks." She ran a finger across Eli's back as she walked past, not knowing that her touch gave him gooseflesh and a tingling in his loins.

No one minded the hodge-podge of dishes and cutlery surrounding the centerpiece of pine branches tied with red, green, and white ribbon; it was what they were accustomed to. Eli thought it marvelous that Norah did so well with what she had. By the time steaming food reached the table, the men had had too much to drink, but they bowed their heads for Shorty's prayer while the children chewed on raisin bread.

The old man cleared his throat importantly. "Cain't say I ever ast for much in life, Big Feller, but I ast you now to bless us 'n watch over us. Keep these younguns full 'a piss—uh, keep 'em good 'n healthy. See to them what ain't hyar today. *Gracias* fer the feed and fer bringin' Norah to us. A-men."

She swallowed, throat tight, recalling other Christmases when death attended the feast. All was so dear to her here— the men with cheeks pink and hair slicked down, the children of men she loved. Rose, content for once between father and son, and Eli, seeking love and warming himself at the fires of friendship. At the bunkhouse Endicott and

Chan Lee handed out whiskey and smokes to cowpunchers loyal as family. Only one beloved face missing—

"Wal, we gonna eat or not?" Shorty grumbled, tucking a bandana under his chin. "Stop that snivelin', gal, and dish it up."

Norah dried her eyes with an apron corner and scolded, "You dig in the spurs too hard and I'll tell them what your real name is!" She grinned to assure him she was joking.

He shook his head sorrowfully. "Pass them frijoles, Jim. That gal's gittin' harder to handle 'n a filly on loco weed. Why, I recollect jawin' with ol' Sam Houston 'bout women onc't down at the San Jacinto and he said to me. . . ."

Talk flagged while the gathering polished off full plates, then it started up again over second servings. The women were up and down filling cups, slicing meat and fowl, whisking biscuits from the oven, dishing up crock beans, cutting pie and cake. Andrew and Rachel sampled most dishes, drank milk, and had taffy to suck on afterward.

Eli helped clear the table, scrape and stack the dishes, and carry the sleepy children into the bedroom. When they were settled, he said, "Where do you want your mirror? I'll hang it for you while I'm here."

She clapped her hands. "That would be grand! Let's see. Where do I want it?" Following her instructions, he moved a wooden chest and repositioned the children's beds. He then held the mirror at different heights until she was satisfied and had her mark the wall.

"When they wake up, I'll get a hammer and nails from Jim," Eli said.

"I want to take candy to the bunkhouse and wish the boys a Merry Christmas anyway. We can go by the barn and get the tools you need." She took a shawl off a hook and went to the kitchen with Eli close behind. "Where's the sugar we set aside for the horses and the cow, Rose? Never mind, here it is. By the way, did I tell you how pretty you look today?"

The girl shook her head, well aware the snug red dress

complemented her but eager for approval nevertheless. "Thank you for the necklace, Norah. It's like a rainbow." She held the crystal beads out from her chest and rolled them to see the colors change.

"I'm glad you like it." Norah kissed her lightly on the cheek. "See if anyone wants more dessert, will you? Eli and I are going to the bunkhouse and the barn. Can't forget our four-footed friends on Christmas, can we?"

He followed her out into late afternoon sun that sparkled on her hair. They chatted about ranch affairs, enjoying the fresh air and invigorating temperature. Warmly greeted by well-fed men who had settled down to poker, craps, and tall talk, Norah left bags of fudge, silk handkerchiefs for Endicott, and a hair brush for the cook, who kept his queue immaculate.

At the barn she fed generous handfuls of sugar to Steel, to her first horse, Lovey, big again with foal, to Rosebud, and to Jim's favorite mount, Pepper, in from the range with a bad cut in the sole of his foot. Eli was rummaging through a can of nails when she dusted her hands and joined him. "Find what you want?"

"Yes, but I can't have it."

"Why ever not? Jim is glad to have you use—" She caught her breath. They gazed at each other, and once again the effect of his passion and will stunned Norah. She struggled to control herself. "I said I was sorry. And I am! But I love Mason. I always have and always will. Can't you understand that, Eli?"

"Always is a long time. May I kiss you? Just once?"

"No, I'm afraid not."

"Just *once*? A Christmas present?"

It was dangerous, yet he had proffered the olive branch and been generous and cordial. Surely he wouldn't try anything with the men so near. "Okay. *One*." She pursed her lips and lifted her face, holding the empty sugar pail between them.

"That ain't good enough, Norah." He tossed the pail

onto the table, then put his arms around her. He wanted to do this right. It was his first kiss—and maybe the last. "I love you," he whispered, and put his lips on hers. Without meaning to, he crushed her so violently she fought for release.

"I'm sorry," she gasped, aware now that the delights of marriage and lovemaking with Mason had weakened her resistance.

He kissed along jawline and hairline and beneath an ear, feeling her relax a bit. "If you'd come to the EM for Christmas, I was goin' to seduce you so you'd have to marry me. Norah, don't say no. Be my wife. I love you more than—"

"Eli, I love Mason. You *know* that!"

"You kiss me as if you like me."

"Of course I like you. But I'm engaged. We plan to be married as soon as he gets back."

"Suppose he doesn't come back."

"Don't even *say* that!"

"Sorry." Eli put a finger under her chin. "One more for auld lang syne?" He kissed her hard, his erection large and demanding, obvious to her even through layers of cloth.

She knew she shouldn't be standing there in the gloom with a man's mouth bruising hers, their groins touching, a big hand smoothing her breasts. But her body betrayed her as she heard him moan her name. He swept her off the ground and hurried toward a corner of the barn with her in his arms.

"No," she tried to say against the voracious mouth. No. The image flashed back—Rose with her dress unbuttoned to the waist, skirts up, sprawling in the hay like a strumpet, a nipple in her lover's mouth and his fingers busy—"*No! Put—me—down!*" She kicked so hard he stumbled and fell, dumping her in a welter of petticoats.

"What the *devil*—!"

They were on their knees when Endicott entered the barn, and Norah glanced up in horror at being found there.

Eyebrows raised, he drawled, "Travelers comin' in. Mexicans, the boys say."

"I'll—I'll be right there. My brooch fell off. You know, the one that matches my ring. Must not have fastened it right. We can't find it. It'd be a shame if one of the animals stepped on it!"

Eli scrabbled in the shadows of Lovey's stall. "Here it is!" He jumped to his feet and pulled her up. Staring her in the eye, he repeated, "Here it is. A little dirty, that's all." He hastily handed her the brooch, and she realized he must have unpinned it trying to—she shut him out of her mind.

"Thank goodness! I'd die if I lost it!" She was grateful for his fib but anxious to be out of his presence. Holding the brooch tightly, she walked out with Endicott, talking a blue streak and lamenting her soiled dress. Eli turned to choose the hammer and nails they'd gone after, not sure whether to swear or laugh.

Intelligent and cultured, the visiting Mexican aristocrat was well dressed, well armed, and well supplied with gold to pay for food and lodging for himself and his men. They were riding to Tucson to fetch an orphaned niece and nephew sent from Spain.

"The latchstring's always out at the Double Bar F. No need to ask. No need to pay," Jim said stiffly.

"*Dispénsame*, señor, it was not my intention to insult you." Prickly as maguey, these Anglos! "Forgive my ignorance, I am unused to American customs." The traveler smiled deprecatingly.

Norah was heating leftovers for the travelers. "Where are you from?"

"The city of Chihuahua, señora." What a beauty wasted here!

"You own a cattle ranch down there?" Jim asked.

"No, I live in the city, being a lawyer and fond of my luxuries. My brother, Don Diego de Montaña, owns one of the biggest cattle ranchos in the world, however. Ah, *gracias*, señora, there is nothing like sweet hot *café*."

"Montaña. Yeah, I've bought cows from him," Jim remembered.

"I have just come from a big wedding there. That of Soledad, the last of his four daughters. She is a lovely young woman who married an Americano."

Norah dished up plates of food before settling down to chat. She exchanged smiles with Eli when he came in to hang the mirror. "Is he a cattleman from Texas?"

Jim laughed when the man paused in disbelief, fork halfway to his mouth. "A Montaña marry a Tejano? That—forgive me!—would be marrying an angel to a devil! No, no, this man wore a silver star. He had been badly injured and Don Diego rescued him from the Rio Yaqui. Soledad nursed him back to health—they fell madly in love—and now he is one of the family."

The room whirled. Norah leaned upon the tabletop and raised herself to a standing position, coughing nervously. Her heart thundered, and she had the sensation of blood draining from her face, emptying her heart. Forever. "What—does this American look like?"

"*Muy guapo*. Very handsome. He might pass for a Spaniard with his black hair and features. Much taller, of course. Golden eyes, most unusual. Tall, well formed, strong. But why do you ask? Do you know this hombre? Dear lady, are you ill?" The Mexican half-rose from his chair.

"His name. Tell me his name."

The man was visibly upset by the effect his information was having. "A strange one. Mason. Mason Fletcher."

"Why, that Christ-crucifyin' bastard!" Jim spat. "Done all right by himself, didn't he?"

When she fainted, Eli was there. His face was the last she saw going under, and he made sure it was the one she saw immediately upon regaining consciousness.

Fate had dealt him a winning hand that he meant to parlay into what he wanted most in life: a beautiful wife to help found the Martin dynasty.

26.

The girl tried to escape her customer's embrace, which in sleep tightened possessively. She liked Mr. Martin, who was generous and attractive and patronized her on most of his visits to Tombstone; she also knew she bore a strong physical resemblance to someone he was hopelessly in love with.

"Norah—Norah," he whispered, dreaming. The girl's back was to his front, and he squeezed a breast and cuddled it in his palm. His manhood swelled, but subsided as he muttered, sighed, and started to snore.

A tear slid down her cheek. She had managed to hide her sorrow the past two days, for the madam did not tolerate weeping or moods from her nymphs. Men paid to have fun, not listen to sad stories. The house motto was eat, drink, and make Mary, and if not Mary, there were plenty of others.

The young prostitute gulped, choking down grief that threatened to convulse her. *Billy! Oh, my darling Billy!* You were such a fool to tangle with the Earps and Doc Holliday. Now you and the McLaurys are lying dead in fancy caskets and store-bought clothes—how could you leave me?

Her customer, still half-asleep, pulled her over to face him and fumbled at her groin. He spoke the woman's name, begging her to spread her legs so he might plant seed and sire a son. Oh, let him in—ahhh, he had dreamed of that. He surged up into the girl.

Oh, Billy, if this were only you, your shaft filling me, bringing me real ecstasy. Christ, how many ceilings had she

272

looked at while she pretended some bastard was the greatest lover in the world?

Outside the parlor house, rip-snorting Tombstone blew off steam, kicked up its heels, and lived for the moment. But in the shadowed room smelling of spicy cologne, stale sweat, and the juices of sex, two people made love in melancholy frenzy—not to each other but to phantoms of the past.

"You heard about the fight back of Montgomery's O.K. Corral, Mrs. Beatty?" The Tombstone merchant's eyes gleamed with morbid curiosity. "Three men got killed."

Norah nodded, intent on a long shopping list. "I saw the crowd in front of the Ritter and Ryan Funeral Parlor." The dead men meant nothing to her, probably rustlers, smugglers, or thieves, as so many were in Arizona Territory. In the crowd someone had pointed out the tubercular Doc Holliday. She thought about his reputation, recalling the grief and pessimism the illness had inspired in her, and wondered if he was trying to get himself killed. And his friend, Wyatt Earp, was an adulterer, according to a gossipy dressmaker. He competed with Sheriff Behan for the affections of an "actress" and escorted her to the best restaurants, bold as brass. Earp's wife, Mattie Blaylock, was brokenhearted. Norah's lips thinned with anger. She'd suffered that sting of humiliation and rejection and felt sorry for poor Mrs. Wyatt Earp.

"Heard tell Doc's shotgun put a hole in Tom McLaury big as a man's palm—"

"Can we go on with my list? I'm anxious to get back to the rooming house."

"How's Mr. Fullerton feeling? Sure sorry to hear he's under the weather. Been a good customer ever since I opened." The man approved his invoice, a very nice order, and dated it: October 28, 1881.

She shook her head. "Not well at all, I'm afraid." In fact, the physician had warned her to be prepared. His heart was indeed bad, but she was to be sensible and not sit with him every minute. In fact, Jim himself insisted she shop and not hover; hang it, he did *not* require or want a deathwatch. Norah bit the inside of her upper lip. He had protested coming to Tombstone. Had the jolting seventy-mile trip by wagon made him worse? Had she and Joel been wrong insisting he seek medical treatment after a series of attacks over the past ten months?

"I'll get the perishable foodstuffs the day we leave."

"Of course, Mrs. Beatty, I'll put the usual order aside. Now, can I get you anything else?"

She consulted her notes. "No, I think that will be all. Oh, wait, add two dozen cans each of tomatoes, peas, peaches, and corn. Those are a real treat, not having to put them up myself."

"My pleasure, ma'am. Allow me to get the door. Thank you very much. Enjoy your stay in town, and my best wishes to Mr. Fullerton."

Norah smiled politely and stepped onto the boardwalk of Allen Street, Tombstone's main thoroughfare. Hard to believe this was Sunday, the way the town buzzed and hollered, yet she had attended morning Episcopalian service, held temporarily at the Presbyterian church, and had subscribed ten dollars toward the building fund in the children's names.

The hubbub reminded her of St. Louis—hard to believe how long it had been since she'd walked through a real town of any size! She knew that Ed Schieffelin's bonanza silver strike two years ago had catapulted Tombstone from a collection of shacks and tents to the biggest town between El Paso and San Francisco. Seat of the new county of Cochise, ironically named for the Chiricahua chieftain, it boasted a fluctuating population of seven to ten thousand, mostly men. Stagecoaches rumbled past, wild-eyed horses lathering their bits; schedules occasionally necessitated running them to death to stay on time. Wagon trains loaded with lumber from the Huachuca Mountains for the town's breakneck construction outdid the coaches in racket, as did sixteen-mule wagons headed from silver mines to stamping mills on the San Pedro River.

Hurrying toward the rooming house, Norah averted her gaze from the saloons but sniffed the mixture of malty fumes and free lunch buffets that emanated from them. Dice in chuck-a-luck boxes and ivory balls in roulette wheels beckoned those with money that burned holes in their pockets. "Around and around the little ball goes, and where it stops nobody knows," a voice called out in a bored singsong.

People streamed up and down both sides of the street beneath wooden canopies. She slowed her pace, intrigued by the color and drama of frontier humanity: cowboys, gamblers, mule skinners carrying coiled whips, miners in resin-stiffened hats, serape-draped Mexicans, Chinese, Indians, soldiers, fancy ladies from the brothels, proper family matrons, lawmen and outlaws, prospectors, ranchers, politicians, derbied drummers with sample cases of everything from liquor to girdles.

"Pardon, ma'am, you dropped a parcel." The man at her side picked it up. A chill went through Norah when their fingers touched. The stylish fringed jacket he wore was the trademark of Buckskin Frank Leslie, killer and notorious ladies' man.

"Th-thank you," Norah stuttered, frightened at being noticed, disturbed by the searing heat of his regard. "It's Studer's book on birds—"

"Have you met my fiancé, Frank?" a familiar voice chimed in.

She made no objection when Eli Martin drew her arm through his. He'd proposed three times since the disastrous Christmas almost four years ago when she learned Mason had married a Mexican cattle heiress. She'd refused each time but had grown more and more fond of Eli; Norah stepped closer, willing to be thought his bride-to-be rather than a woman alone.

Eli stood tall, hoping Leslie would back off, but sweat trickled from his armpits. Leslie was reputed to shoot flies off saloon ceilings to demonstrate his marksmanship, and Wyatt Earp considered him Doc Holliday's peer for speed and accuracy. Contrary to legend, law-abiding cowboys and ranchers such as Eli were not always quick on the draw, preferring rifles and shotguns to six-shooters; it was the peace officer and outlaw who had to be able to clear leather fast.

Leslie laughed, maliciously pleased with the effect he had had on them. "Congratulations, ma'am. And you're a lucky fellow, Martin." With that double entendre he tipped his hat and strolled in the direction of the Bird Cage Theatre.

Norah shivered. "He's cold as a snake!"

"Ain't nobody to cross."

" 'Isn't anybody,' " she corrected him absentmindedly, as she did Andrew, who was now four and a half and beginning to read. Brushing dirt off the package, she said, "Thanks for coming to my rescue."

Eli had not known she was in Tombstone, and when he saw her next to the badman, small and vulnerable as a heifer menaced by a wolf, his heart had faltered with love. "Wasn't me, somebody else would have stepped in. Nobody insults a lady like you and gets away with it." He pulled her aside as a drunk reeled past. "How've you been? Gretchen'll be sorry as the dickens she missed you. She almost came along."

"I'll miss her, too." Norah started walking and he put himself between her and the street. "I guess you don't know Jim's seriously ill with heart trouble. He'd be glad to see you, Eli, but only for a moment."

"Heard he'd been having spells. I'm powerful sorry to hear about this."

They entered the rooming house, Eli thinking she looked tired and drawn, but nonetheless prettier than the last time he had seen her. Her face was taut as if she never let up.

"How about a buggy ride? Fresh air'll do you good. Lots to see here."

"I—I really shouldn't." She unlocked the door, motioning for him to enter a room smelling of sickness and remedies. But it *was* a lovely day. The one Jim died on? Her eyes filled, and she put a handkerchief to them and then removed hat and gloves. "I'll see if he feels up to a visitor."

Eli went to sit by the bed, shocked at his neighbor's condition. "Howdy, Jim. You don't look so bad. Thought you were ready to kick the bucket."

Jim chuckled feebly. "Look poorly as all get out, you mean. Always were a lousy liar."

Norah left the room to get a prescription from her reticule, and Jim whispered, "Take care of her and the children. They need you." His face was ashen with pain.

"Okay, Jim, I'll do 'er. Set your mind at rest. Don't worry." Eli gripped a lax hand, touched by the other's fading strength.

Dark eyes, once quick and ardent, held his. "Promise."

"Promise. On my honor."

That was all that need be said. Jim closed his eyes, satisfied the woman he loved would not be left alone. Again. She had been so deeply hurt when Fletcher jilted her, he had feared for her sanity for several days. Martin had begged her to marry him and Jim had urged her to do so. But Norah had changed. A flower in full bloom, she closed herself up like a tightly furled bud into which no foreign element might intrude. The man she loved had made it plain. She was undesirable, unwanted. Jim almost preferred the sick, despondent, but plucky girl who had captured his heart that fall of 1875.

She stood over him. "Here. Two tablespoons. One at a time and a little water to wash it down."

"God! That's awful!"

"I'm sorry." The hand holding the spoon trembled.

"Thought I'd take Norah for a buggy ride, Jim, if you can spare her for a while."

"Yes, yes, you go. Been nursing me day and night. Go have a little fun."

"No." She glared at them both.

"Do as I say. The medicine's helped already. Now—get outa here." Jim moved his head back and forth. "Stubborn, stubborn."

"I'll pick you up in about fifteen minutes," Eli said.

Helpless between them, she finally shrugged. "Well, all right. But only if you feel—" When Jim waved his hand impatiently, she went into her room to get ready. Inserting a long pin through hat and hair, Norah unexpectedly felt more kindly toward herself; it was as if the city's tumult, vigor, and gusto had begun to melt the frozen shell in which her spirit was imprisoned. Norah welcomed the sudden hunger for the stimulation of an urban environment and, for the first time in a long while, a man's attentions.

When the rancher handed her into the buggy, he sensed the difference. She was whistling under her breath, her mouth puckered as though for kisses, and her eyes shone. Her hand even lingered in his, and he wet his lips nervously—maybe this time she'd say yes! He presented her with a box of French chocolates and arranged a wool throw over her knees before stepping into the vehicle. Flicking the horse's rump with the whip, he asked, "Jim all right?"

"He's sleeping. The medicine was strong and he's so weak—"

"Now, don't worry. He doesn't want you to. Eat your candy while I take you sight-seeing."

Norah gazed out at mountains in every direction that humped their backs to the sky like prehistoric beasts sculpted in stone. While the mountains dreamed, undisturbed, the hills of Tombstone thundered with underground blasting, shook with the passing of ore wagons, echoed with shouts and curses. Eli pointed out rich mines such as the Contention, Grand Central, Head Center, and Vizina. "Mills in operation got a hundred forty stamps going.

Stamps crush the ore, see? They get half a million in bullion every month.''

"How much do the miners make?"

"Schieffelin tells me top wages. Four dollars a day for a ten-hour shift mucking out ore from blasts set by the previous crew. Men who sink shafts earn six dollars, but that's more dangerous. Food costs a dollar a day, and they put up their own shanties or tents.'' Eli shook his head. "Ain't for me! Give me a good horse, cows, and the open air. Why, those fellows work by candlelight!'' He clucked to the horse. "No sirree, that's not for me!"

"Me, either!'' Norah ate two more chocolates, then covered the box, saving the rest for treats at the ranch. "Pretty country around here, but Vista Valley has it beat all hollow, don't you think?'' They agreed on that, too, and found plenty to talk about while they toured Tombstone. East on Allen Street past Chinatown, the O.K. Corral, the Occidental and Grand Hotels, the Oriental and Crystal Palace saloons, and Vogan's Bowling Alley. He hurried the buggy past the notorious Bird Cage Theatre and the red-light district.

He pulled the horse to a halt in front of the new Schieffelin Hall. "Biggest adobe building in the West, I've heard. Seats seven hundred, has a ceiling twenty-four feet high and a stage forty wide. There's a musical comedy tonight. How about dinner at the Palace Hotel and the theater after?'' His eyes sparkled with enthusiasm, and he bumped her shoulder with his.

"I can't.'' She looked at the office of the feisty *Tombstone Epitaph*.

"Why not?'' Eli said as they drove past C.S. Fly's Boarding House and Photograph Shop where pictures cost thirty-five cents.

"Wait! I want to look at that!'' Norah dove into her reticule and brought out field glasses. She focused on a bird up the street pecking at something in the middle of the road.

"What is it?" Her escort eyed the line of throat and bosom revealed by her uplifted arms.

"Just an old crow," she said with disgust. "I thought it was a new bird."

"Speaking of crow, how about dinner?"

"I don't think so." She didn't want to get involved or have to turn him down again.

"For Christ's sake, Norah, it's just *dinner*! I ain't askin' you to get in bed with me!" His face darkened with hurt.

It was hard for him to beg, and that he did revealed the depth of his feelings. Eli Martin would never throw himself at anyone's feet but hers. Still she hesitated. "Would you take me back now? I'm getting cold. I'm anxious about Jim, too. We've been gone so long."

Once there, he tied the reins to the hitching post. "Think I'll come in case there's anything I can do."

Norah peeked in the bedroom and whispered with relief, "He looks fine! Even has color in his cheeks. I'll light a lamp and turn it down low so he doesn't wake up in the dark."

"Those supper dishes on the tray?" Eli leaned close enough to touch her hair with his lips. He closed his eyes, overcome by her dearness. It wasn't lust—no, not that, but a yearning to shield and love in the purest husbandly fashion. Norah needed him as much as he needed her.

"Mrs. Patterson must have brought supper and given him his medicine, bless her." Norah turned to find herself face to face with her suitor. Suddenly she relented. Champagne, dinner, and the theater were just what she needed. Putting both palms on his chest, she said, "I'd like to freshen up and change. Half an hour?"

"Half an hour." He seized her hands and kissed them before hurrying away.

After bathing and redoing her hair, Norah buttoned up a white lace blouse with high scalloped neckband and long sleeves; this went with a new suit of royal-blue Sicilienne, a mixture of silk and wool. White ostrich plumes with cranberry and pink velvet roses adorned the matching felt bonnet. Norah pinched her cheeks and bit her lips, and eased on kid gloves after applying French perfume. Head tilted, she studied her reflection, seeing a woman there who hadn't existed a few days ago. Starved for nice clothes, she'd gone overboard at the dressmaker's. True, her savings had suffered, but it was worth it; she might not wear her purchases often, but their classical lines would require little renovation to keep them current. After all, it might be a long time before there was money to spend on clothes again.

Money. Anger stained her cheeks to think of the rude letter from Carleton's father some months ago in response to her belated and reluctant confession that Carleton was not Andrew's father. Shortly after she sent the letter, the Tucson bank notified her that the children's accounts had been closed.

The senator then wrote that, had his son not sent an intimate letter saying he was sure his wife had conceived shortly before his death, the Beattys would not even have corresponded with her. They found it shocking—as well as grievously disappointing—to learn Carleton had no male heir after all. Some funds had been settled on Rachel in the form of a monthly allowance, but Norah had to furnish a record or receipt for even the smallest expenditure. The senator planned to travel West when health permitted, at which time he'd decide, after meeting her, what amount—if any—should be allotted her as Carleton's widow.

Norah examined her teeth and made a face at the mirror. She and the children didn't need the Beattys' money. She was damned if they'd touch Rachel's allowance. They were getting along. Adjusting her bustle, she took a last loving glance at the sleeping patient and departed with the landlady's promise to look in on him. Eli waited in the parlor, wearing dinner clothes. "Why, how refined you look!" She smiled at well-worn high-heeled boots protruding from black broadcloth trousers.

"You mean I ain't—I'm not the rest of the time?" He handed her into the buggy, getting a flash of petticoat and small feet and ankles in light-gray leather.

"You know better. I'm just not used to seeing you in linen and a satin stock."

He directed the horse through the traffic. "I leave some duds here 'case I go to the capital at Prescott on business to wine and dine a legislator or two."

"Wining and dining legislators sounds impressive."

"Lot more so in the big cities. Sure like to have you with me. You'd knock their eyes out!"

"What do you do back there?"

"Oh, I dabble in politics, interest investors in Arizona mining properties, encourage lower cattle shipping rates, keep after congressmen to revise federal statutes so we can elect our own governor instead of having him appointed by the President as a favor to a friend. That type of thing."

Norah murmured preoccupied approval, savoring the noise and laughter coming from one of the better saloons. She peered in, avid for detail, knowing those on the ranch would want to hear all about it. Not ladylike, but who cared? Velvet draperies, polished brass and woodwork, and filigree ceiling lamps set the stage for black-garbed gamblers and fancy women in paint and powder.

"Naughty, naughty," Eli teased with a big grin, making her giggle. "Love to hear you giggle! Ever seen a boomtown before? A real sight, ain't—isn't it?" They laughed, light at heart, intoxicated with the town's vitality and boisterousness after their ranches' solitude and isolation.

At the restaurant Eli ordered a meal to make Norah's head spin. "We'll start with champagne—got an 1860?—oysters in bacon, chicken gumbo soup, lamb chops, french peas—"

"Eli! I'm not a harvest hand!"

"—lettuce and tomato salad, that nut bread I like, vanilla cream puffs for the lady, and apple pie with ice cream for me. Walnuts and almonds. Coffee with the meal." He pulled out a massive gold watch. "Schieffelin Hall comedy starts at eight. See we're served pronto."

"Yes, *sir*!" The waiter knew Mr. Martin. He tipped like Midas.

Decorative paper wrappers covered the ends of the chop bones. "Those are *papillon*. French for butterfly. Kinda fittin' for a certain lady rancher I know." They clinked glasses and drank, then drank again.

"I'm not much of a rancher lately, what with the children, Jim being sick, and Joel not tending to business. I don't even know how many cows I have."

"We just had the wettest summer I ever saw. Ought to be plenty of fat Mariposa calves come spring."

"I've been up to my ears in work, and my hands show it." She observed them ruefully, pink and chapped against snowy napkin and tablecloth.

He reached across the table to rub a thumb over her knuckles. "Don't have to be. I'd never let them do a lick of work."

"Don't spoil things, Eli, please."

"Can't blame a man for tryin'." Was she weakening? Her voice had been pleasant, not sharp, and her mouth curved as she repressed a smile. "How're Andrew and Rachel?" That was a safe subject. Goddamn, she was luscious with that flush on her cheeks from the champagne.

"Fine, growing like weeds. But I do wish Rachel would get over her fear of large animals."

"And my dandy boy?"

What an excellent father he'd be, she thought, with his love for animals and zest for living. "Endicott had him up on Lovey the other day. He was so thrilled his eyes popped. It gave me a twinge to see how fast he's shooting up." She had felt a twinge, too, at his resemblance to his father, a lifelong bittersweet reminder of false promises.

"You say Joel's not runnin' the ranch the way he should? Mind my cigar?"

"No, not at all. Well, I don't know what's happening.

He's capable enough, Lord knows, but he can't make decisions on his own. Since his father got sick, he's been at sixes and sevens. I guess he's an exemplary hand but a lousy owner."

Eli hailed the waiter and asked for the check. "He and Rose gettin' along?"

"Fairly well, but when they quarrel you can hear it all over the place. She's pregnant now, so maybe they'll calm down. It's obvious they love each other, but it's a case of—"

"Can't live with each other or without, eh?"

"That's about the size of it. I hope he straightens up pretty soon, because if it hadn't been for the boys ramrodding the spread, Jim would be out of business, I do believe."

"Better go. We want to get a good seat," he said later, giving the waiter gold coins, including a sizable tip.

"Oh, yes! I'm so looking forward to it! I've never been to a theater."

He stubbed out his cigar. "You're foolin' me." When she shook her head, he grabbed her arm and cried, "Come on then, darlin' girl, it's time you did!"

Norah laughed and leaned against him for an instant. She'd seen a vastly different individual in Eli here away from his great house and herds; he'd revealed unexpected sophistication with his fashionable clothes, dining, and interest in the arts. Eli was a complex and increasingly fascinating person who was rapidly worming his way into her affections. But he didn't know he couldn't breach the wall she had erected. No man could. She might love again—she would not be hurt again.

The musical comedy brought gales of laughter from a motley audience that included local celebrities such as John Clum, the *Epitaph* editor and friend of the Earps who sat with him; Nellie Cashman, angel of the mining camps; Dr. George Goodfellow, bon vivant, surgeon, and gunshot wound expert; Mr. and Mrs. Camillus Fly, the photographers. Afterward, when punch and sweetmeats were served in the lobby for the ladies, whisky and ice for the men, Eli proudly introduced his companion as an old and very dear friend.

"What a perfectly wonderful evening! I can't remember enjoying one more. Thank you!" Norah kissed him on the cheek as they stood outside the rooming house.

He fished in an inner pocket for an oddly shaped package. "Here's a little somethin'—just to cap the evening."

"You shouldn't have!" Unwrapping the gift, she held up tortoiseshell combs decorated with green stones and garnets. "Eli, how sweet!"

"Let me put them in your hair. They go at kind of an angle."

After she removed pin and hat, he settled the combs in her thick glossy hair, hardly able to touch it without hugging her. "Now. Look in the mirror 'fore you take 'em out."

"Then I'll know how to fix them next time. You're rough as bark outside and soft as your mice inside, aren't you?"

"Where you're concerned," he whispered, and brought her to him inch by inch. "May I kiss you good night?" Her lips parted in acquiescence, reserve and self-denial melted by his generosity and sincerity. They kissed and he held her close. "I never lived till this minute, Norah."

Her mind filled with images of Carleton. She had liked being married, and the children needed a father. Yet, was it fair to marry a man who loved you this much when your heart belonged forever to another, philanderer though he was?

"Getting cold?" She had stiffened in his embrace.

"A bit," she replied, pecking him on the cheek again and stepping away as the front door to the rooming house flew open.

The woman inside shaded her eyes to see the couple in the gloom beside the buggy. "Miz Beatty, that you? You better come! Mr. Fullerton's—well, you'd just better come!"

By the time they reached Jim he was dead. Norah

dropped down beside him, clasping his hands, breaking into tears of grief and disbelief. She had lost them one by one: her father, her mother, her aunt, Carleton, Mason, and now Jim. Oh, God, how she'd miss him! Father, brother, suitor, and friend, the first to kiss her as a lover. "I should have been here, not off gallivanting."

"Now, don't say that. He wanted you to go gallivanting." Eli helped her up and let the tears flow on his chest. He was too decent to feel triumph at his fellow rancher's death, but it did leave Norah bereft of support in a situation where she might be welcome no longer, now that Joel and Rose owned the ranch. He exulted in his improved position as refuge and giver of succor.

He patted her back when she started to cough and gave her a neatly ironed bandana. Norah laughed hysterically at the contrast with evening clothes. "A bandana! Eli, what am I going to do with you?"

"Marry me," he said promptly while she blew her nose. "Let me take care of you and the kids. You know how much I love you. How *long* I've loved you." He guided her to a chair and sat down beside her. "Will you be my wife, sweetheart?"

Norah put a hand along his cheek. "Don't push, my dear. We'll see, we'll see."

He slid off the chair onto his knees and laid his face in her lap, worship and desire feuding within him. She ran her fingers through his hair, murmuring softly, and Eli's heart burst with joy.

27.

Leg hooked around the saddle horn, the man lighted a Mexican cigarillo. It was pleasing to bask in the sun and look at the hacienda in the valley below. Like an oyster shell, the huge house enclosed and protected its pearls—the women and children who belonged to Don Diego de Montaña's family. In essence Don Diego owned them as he did his vaqueros and their families, the buildings, equipment, horses, and innumerable cattle, the several million acres dotted with ancient Indian villages—these comprised his empire in the wilds of Chihuahua.

The man rubbed an indentation in his forehead, an injury he hid by combing hair down to the eyebrow. Not that his wife, Soledad, cared. She kissed it, rubbed it with unguents, pressed it to her breast—when she was not having a spell of confusion and pain that sent her in search of even she knew not what.

A fiesta would be held tonight, a saint's day, probably. Such celebrations were common with so many children and brightened the endless days. He found the *niños,* whether noble or peasant, quite lovely with their ebony hair and limpid eyes, their skins that ranged from lily-white to coppery brown, their charm and laughter.

His hand fell upon his knee to finger black velvet pants. He affected the style of Don Diego, his father-in-law, who had once owned a princely domain in Alta California; shortly before the War of 1846 he had moved to Chihuahua with other members of the clan to get away from the damned gringos. He had carried with him the antiquated élan of that beautiful place, enlivened by a flair for Spanish theater.

The man brooding over these thoughts was himself dramatic, an American with silver-threaded black hair, cat's eyes, and a powerful physique only recently mended from multiple gunshot wounds and broken bones. His costume accentuated that quality: pants and vest decorated with pure silver buttons, white linen shirt and red silk scarf, black felt hat with gold silk sewn to the brim's underside, and a chin strap worn under the sensual lower lip.

He signaled to his horse with a gentle spur. He was constantly after the vaqueros to treat their mounts more kindly, to get better performance over a longer period and to save Don Diego's stock. Mason Fletcher would have done the same; he was sure of that for no reason in the world he could prove. Mason Fletcher. He often puzzled over the name engraved on the Colt .45 laid away in a drawer, beside a silver star. But it meant nothing, triggered no memory before his life on this rancho, created no images of the past. Perhaps it wasn't even his!

He owed Don Diego the greatest of debts, that of saving his life, of diving into raging waters and hauling him out more dead than alive. The hacendado joked he had made a double catch, for his men had lassoed a big mule in a bad way whose pack had shifted under its belly. Don Diego cherished the cantankerous animal, for an ancestor had raised the huge Andalusian jackass for which Spain was world-famous in the eighteenth century, stallions from which this excellent creature was surely descended. A strict embargo existed on blooded jacks, and the testicles of those released were, for political reasons, being crushed before shipment. Only for the great president, Jorge Washington, Don Diego said, had Charles III waived the embargo to present him with a fertile jack which the gentleman from Virginia named Royal Gift. While Mason recalled that Washington had been instrumental in starting the mule industry in the U.S., he could not, for the life of him, remember seeing this rescued mule before.

A young woman cantered toward the solitary horseman, riding astride with the grace of all Montaña children. Her father rode stirrup to stirrup, brown, wrinkled, and solemn. As they drew nearer, the younger man grinned and called out. "I am glad to see you well enough to be out of bed, my dove."

"I wanted to be with you." Pulling rein beside him, his wife leaned to touch his mouth with her fingertips.

It was her worst habit, this eternal touching. No matter whether at table or in chapel, Soledad could not keep her hands to herself. A man would be a fool to object, yet she overdid it, smothering him and causing many a raised eyebrow. But no one had the heart to reprimand the twenty-year-old Venus who was disdained by local bachelors. Blond hair and turquoise eyes made her the spitting image of a great-grandmother, a princess from northern Spain. A princess, unfortunately, who had been quite mad. Her descendants now carried this flaw, even down to the granddaughter's fourth daughter born on a New World frontier.

Don Diego had seized the opportunity when Soledad lost her heart to the gringo who did not remember who he was. A sorry pair, but from their physical beauty and the man's intelligence and strength, perhaps children would result in whom the taint of madness was reduced to the extent that great-grandchildren would be normal. He loved and cherished Soledad, but had she been a heifer she would have been slaughtered long ago for her genetic imperfections. Don Diego demanded perfection and blamed his wife, descended from the princess, for Soledad's affliction, although it seemed held at bay now by marriage. As yet the bridegroom had not had to scour the plains searching for his wife who sometimes saw zigzag lines of light and patches of color, went partially blind, vomited, and screamed in agony from mere headaches. But then he suffered them also from a blow to the head received either before or while being tumbled pell-mell down the river.

The hacendado was fond of this son-in-law who filled a void in his existence. For what in God's name was a man without sons! He blamed his wife for that also, although he honored her as a good woman with whom he had spent his life. Ah, but to have a son like this American! He had the virtues of ancient Spain: courtesy, bravery, and chivalry. He rode like an Apache and fought them with a grizzly bear's ferocity, but played with children like a kitten. He shot with deadly accuracy and handled men firmly but kindly. Don Diego fervently hoped he would never remember who he was, but should he do so, he would be kept here by force if necessary. The hacendado was not completely without sympathy, however. Not to know who you were, where you came from, what you had done, who your loved ones were—*Sangre de Cristo,* that could break your heart!

"Good morning, you are well?" Clever old eyes narrowed above the hawkish Castilian nose.

Mason nodded and smiled. It had been the same for almost four years. The next question, sure as the devil, was going to be—

"When will I have a grandchild to hold on my saddle? You, too, Soledad, are fit now and hopping here and there like a cricket."

"When God wills it, señor." Mason crossed himself. He now followed the Catholic religion to make the family happy; he had had no choice, as the chapel was part of the great house.

"You are right, my son." Don Diego studied the man. Twice Soledad's age, he had lived a hard life and been accustomed to exerting authority, had no doubt killed and more; crossing swords with this giant would be dangerous. "Come, my children, the new colt born to the black Arabian needs a name. Would you like to give him one, *mi corazón?*" When his daughter's face lit up at the prospect, he trotted down the incline toward the stables. The man with no past and the half-mad girl rode side by side behind him, drawing a measure of comfort from each other.

Exhausted from making love, the husband turned on his side. Surely they had made a child! It took Soledad a long time to come and then she usually whimpered and collapsed. But tonight had been different; she had opened to him as she had never done before. She was always enthralled with his privates, loved to squeeze and rub them against her, to kiss and mouth them. He remembered vividly an evening late in convalescence when he awoke to find himself uncovered and Soledad caressing his sleep erection with wide-eyed fascination as one might touch the stalk of an exotic flower. Her *dueña* had gone for water, and had any male family member entered at that moment he would have been shot out of hand.

Or would he? He now knew he had been an answer to a prayer, to a plea for a husband for the beauteous and strange Soledad. Maybe marrying her had been the best thing for him in the long run, despite his not being lucid at the time; in fact, the whole ceremony had happened in a haze with him drifting off, being shaken awake, and then finally being allowed to sink into sleep. He had awakened to find his new wife twined about him, eyes devouring, hands busy, legs spread. He had taken but one virgin in his life— Now, how did he know that? And who had it been? He concentrated until his head hurt, but nothing else surfaced.

Sighing with exasperation, he eased out of bed, pulled on his pants, and padded barefoot to the patio, where he paced back and forth, smoking one cigarrillo after another. He reminded himself of some poor bastard of a horse hooked on loco weed hanging over a water trough unable to drink. *Why, goddamn it, he couldn't remember worth spit!* Things flashed across his mind like greased lightning. He'd almost catch them but then they'd vanish.

Who in the world was he? An outlaw on the run with another's weapon? A lawman? The Marshal's badge was a mystery, possibly torn from the chest of a peace officer who'd been on his trail in the Sierra Madre. Had he killed him? Was that how the star came into his possession? Was he a murderer? He considered stealing the Arabian and heading for the border, but either Don Diego and his relatives would hunt him down or somebody up there might turn him in to the nearest sheriff. It was too big a chance to take, at least until his memory returned. If it ever did.

He came to an abrupt halt to gaze about the patio with its plants and vines and Spanish tile, at caged birds twittering sweetly at him in the moonlight. He put a finger through the bars for a cardinal to peck at. He loved birds. And they meant a lot to—to whom? Or was it simply that they were fellow prisoners? Tears trickled down stubbled cheeks, and he made no move to wipe them away.

It helped—*oh, Christ Jesus, hear me*—it helped to cry alone in the dark.

Norah removed them from their place of honor above the fireplace: the helmet, pistols, dress sword, and cavalry guidon, the daguerrotype taken back East before they met. She balanced on the chair to study the image and, with thickening throat, kissed the stern face, for she had truly loved him. She wrapped it in a cloth and put it in a box. As far as Andrew was concerned, his father had been a brave officer who died in hand-to-hand combat with an Apache warrior. He had to have a hero to cling to. Time enough to tell the truth—if she ever did.

"Well, think of the devil," she said as her son burst into the room. "Did you come to help me wash and paint the walls? Why, what's the matter, honey? You're white as a sheet!"

He gulped, trying to get his breath. "Joel! It's Uncle Joel and Rose! They're fighting!"

She stepped down and put the box on the table. "Is that all? They don't do anything else lately."

"But, Mama, she's got a knife! A big one this long!" He

measured with his hands. "He hit her and she said she'd *get* him!"

Norah gasped. A mature seven, Andrew did not lie. "Where are they?"

"Down by the pond."

She had lifted her skirts to run through the door when Joel staggered into the house, sinking to the floor at her feet. He had been stabbed in the back, and the knife point protruded from his breast. As he toppled onto his side, Endicott rushed in.

"Is he dead?" she cried. They knelt beside the young rancher, trying to remove the knife and staunch the flow of blood.

"Ain't far from it," Endicott muttered, rolling him onto his back after withdrawing the blade and tossing it aside.

"Uncle Joel?" Andrew asked timidly. "You okay, Uncle Joel?"

"Get him out of here," Norah commanded, and Endicott shouted for help to the hands gathered outside. Once the child had been removed, they lifted Joel and put him on her bed. Blood soaked the linens in a flood.

"Wild honey ain't gonna stop *that* bleedin'," Endicott remarked glumly. He wet a clean diaper and moistened Joel's lips as Emedio and John Smith entered, hats in hand.

"Norah—Norah—" Joel searched for her, mouth agape, eyelids fluttering.

"I'm here, darling, I'm here." She clasped his hand.

"Grace—take care—Grace." His tiny daughter with the Apache's cloud of hair and his mother's bluebonnet eyes, the dearest creature in the world beside which all else had paled into insignificance. His paternal love had driven him and Rose apart, for they had at last discovered physical attraction alone to be insubstantial as smoke.

"Like my own babies," Norah promised shakily.

"The ranch—witness—" he whispered, staring at the men around him. "Goes to Norah. Norah and baby. Hear?" They nodded. Endicott crossed his heart in a boyish gesture.

The dying man smiled. He felt so *light*. As if he could float! Float in the air like the time he sailed off the horse's back. "Pa. Pa? You see how I rode old Charlie's Britches? Man—I—" His eyes crossed and slid up into his head. Norah jumped, put a hand to his chest. He was gone. Just like that. She shut his eyelids.

"Joel? *Joel?*" A woman's voice 'cracked with anxiety. "Where'd you go, Joel?" Rose edged into the bedroom to stare down at her lover. "He is sleeping?"

Norah did not have it in her to be cruel, sure the girl had not meant to kill him. "I'm so sorry, Rose. He's—dead."

"No. Oh, no, he *can't* be. I didn't hurt him that much!"

Endicott snorted and strode from the room, returning with the knife which he shook in her face. "You sure weren't peelin' potatoes!"

"Endicott!" Norah frowned.

"S'truth," he growled.

Rose said nothing further, and in the stillness they could hear blood dripping from the mattress. She started as if remembering, left the room for a moment, and brought back a pan of ashes and scissors.

"Don't cut your hair. Please don't," Norah said.

Immobile, the Indian woman waited by the dead man for the privacy she needed. Deciding it would be beneficial, Norah pushed the men out and latched the door quietly. A wail rose as the death chant started.

Andrew and Rachel came running with pieces of corn-bread in their hands. "Somebody sick, Mama?" her daughter asked.

Bending to kiss them, Norah replied, "Yes, I guess you could say that. Rose is sick at heart for doing a bad thing she didn't mean to do."

"If you don't mean to do a bad thing, will Lord Jesus still love you?" Andrew wanted to know, upset by the situation.

"You *bet!*" Endicott assured him. "How 'bout a pony ride?" He tossed the boy onto one shoulder and his sister on the other when Rachel insisted on riding, too. "Land's sake," he grumbled amiably as they rode a cockhorse to Banbury Cross and into the barn.

Norah dismissed the men who milled in the yard, but John Smith lingered. "You gotta report this to the sheriff," he said.

"You know about such things, do you?" she said, her voice turning shrill and accusing.

He shrugged. "Just tellin' you what's got to be done. Rose'd better hit the trail, too. Be different if'n she'd been a white woman. But an Apache killin' a white man—well, folks might hang her."

"You—you're serious!" Norah sat down, stunned. Turn Rose in like a common criminal when it had been a—what did they call it? A crime of passion, that was it. "She didn't mean to kill him! She didn't!"

"You got to go to Tombstone, too, now you'n the baby own the Double Bar F. Get it all recorded." Smart girl as she was, with both Fullertons gone she needed a little nudge. She'd been right. He did know about things like this.

"Oh. Yes. I—didn't think of that. You and Emedio and Endicott, you're witnesses. Won't you have to come, too?"

"Can't, ma'am."

She rubbed her upper arms, cold and tense. "Why not? Are you wanted?"

"Some say so. But I got a little boy in Las Cruces needs me out workin', not doin' time." He swung into the saddle and headed for the corral.

He could have walked, she thought wildly, but cowboys mounted up to ride across the road. Norah had seen them do so, uneasy on the ground as sailors back from a long voyage. "My God!" she said aloud, realizing her mind was trying to avoid what happened. What on earth were they to do? Renegade Apaches had been marauding again this past year, necessitating General Crook's reassignment to Arizona. People wouldn't take kindly to Rose. Just another murdering Indian—she could hear them now. The girl would be condemned to die, or at the least sentenced to prison.

Her flesh crept at the lament coming from the house. Rose always reverted to race in time of crisis in spite of having lived with the Fullertons all her life. Was that the answer? Should she join a clan? Dissolve into it so no white could find her? Subject herself and Grace to miserable reservation life? Why, they'd never survive! What could she do, though, with a charge of murder over her head and the law after her? If she ran, she'd be a fugitive from justice—if she stayed, she might die. Norah coughed, glad it wasn't her choice to make.

That evening the women sat opposite each other in silence and fatigue. Hair shorn, pale beneath the peachy skin, Rose seemed smaller, thinner. She rocked her baby, glancing fiercely at Norah from time to time, then blurted, "The ranch should have been mine! But you always wanted it and now it's yours, damn you!"

Norah sighed, distraught from discussing the situation and preparing Joel for burial in the morning. "I wanted my own outfit, Rose, not this one. Besides, it was your husband's deathbed wish that it come to me—*and* Grace, remember. If I could change things, I would, but I didn't have anything to do with it. There were witnesses. Listen, dear—"

"Don't 'dear' me," Rose spat. Tears poured down her cheeks and fell upon her infant's wrappings. "I didn't mean to do it, Grace. I wouldn't kill your daddy, you know that, don't you?" She sobbed and rocked, sobbed and rocked.

With the corpse laid out in her bed, Norah slept in the chair, waking once to see Rose prowling to and fro, beating her breast. The next thing she knew it was almost dawn.

Rose came from her room, red eyed but dressed for travel. Food, blankets, cooking utensils, matches, binoculars, canteen, slicker, and extra clothing covered the table. "Will you help me pack the mule?"

"Of course. But where are you going? Will you be all right?"

"I have—friends. What do you care?"

"I care very much!"

The black eyes glowed with emotion akin to hate. "I don't believe you. Ever since you came here I've sucked hind tit. Now it's all yours. I hope you're happy."

"Rose! I never meant for it to be that way." Norah got to her feet. "Let's part friends. Tell me where you're going so we can keep in touch. We'll want to know whether you and Grace are all right." She looked around but didn't see the champagne basket anywhere, that ideal baby carrier Grace was toted about in.

Anguish twisted the girl's features and made her look old. "I've decided to leave her with you and the children. I can't take her where I'm going. When this blows over and they see me as a woman who killed the man she loved without meaning to, instead of a blood-thirsty Apache, I'll come for her." She put her shoulders back, tragically beautiful in her sacrifice. "Swear on your Bible you'll take good care of her."

"I swear," Norah whispered, touched beyond words by the young mother's decision.

The room grew brighter and the women started as if a peremptory knock had sounded at the door. "Do you have money? I'll get you some." Norah hauled a strongbox from under her bed, averting her gaze from the sheet-covered figure. She grabbed gold and silver coins and put them on the table. "You can't live without money. *Take* it! And medicine. Let me fix you a few things." Needles, scissors, thread, spirits of turpentine, a small container of goose grease, cloths for bandages, whiskey—that universal panacea—peppermint oil, quinine, calomel, laudanum, and, on impulse, a red scarf from her bureau. She wrapped the items in flannel, then gave them to Rose. "You needn't go so soon, you know. No one off the ranch has heard about Joel. The boys won't tell." She wasn't too sure of that, for there were new hands she didn't know. Norah dreaded to see Rose off on her own, friendless, in danger from all kinds of men, much too attractive for her own good.

"I might as well get it over with," Rose murmured and went outside to finish readying the animals—the mule and a steady, nondescript horse. Rose had no need for a mount like Steel, no need for haste, just stealth, Norah realized sadly. If Jim were only alive, he'd have known what to do. She felt so helpless and useless.

The final trip into the house to bid farewell to her daughter almost crushed Rose, and her shoulders heaved while she settled in the saddle and made a last check of equipment. The face she eventually turned to Norah was ravaged. Her voice was low and shaky. "Give my *day-den* lots of love for me."

Her girl-child. She was hardly more than a child herself! Norah's throat constricted. "Don't worry. Be careful. God bless you."

Rose didn't look back as she rode south, but Norah watched until she was no longer to be seen. Downcast, she started into the house, then stopped. The ranch was coming awake with sounds of the crew, animals, birds, a morning breeze that tousled her hair and took away the night. *This beloved place*. Hers now and tiny Grace's. Norah made a pattern in the dust with the toe of her boot—the Mariposa. A new ranch—born like a bull calf in blood and travail but destined to trample the range in triumph. Her chin went up—she was ready.

28.

"Gone to *Tucson*?" Eli growled at the old cowboy.

Doggedly braiding a horsehair rope with gnarled fingers, Shorty said, "Yep. Boss left yestiddy. Home in time for roundup, she said."

Eli struck his pommel with a big fist. "My God, the county's crawling with desperadoes and hostiles and she takes off in that buckboard like she's goin' to a tea party!"

Shorty chuckled. "Don't worry none. She ain't alone. Endicott and Emedio, they're ridin' shotgun. 'Sides, she shoots better'n most of us."

Gritting his teeth, Eli wondered if a more aggravating female had ever lived. Here it was October of 1884 already, three years since Jim died, almost two since Joel was killed, and whenever he mentioned getting hitched, she'd almost say yes then shy like a green filly from a hackamore and put him off. She'd gotten now so it was always either the ranch or the kids. Nothing else seemed to matter—yet he *knew* in his guts she wanted love and was still strongly inclined toward him.

He gazed about with interest at the spread which had taken precedence over him. The place bloomed with prosperity. But then, cattle were selling for boom prices of thirty to thirty-five dollars; the Mariposa brand was now seen at railroad construction sites, mining towns, government posts, and butcher shops throughout Arizona. Norah had more drive, imagination, and daring than many men he'd known. She'd also made a smart move in choosing John Smith as foreman despite her dislike; he was capable,

299

no one tried to take advantage of him, and he never cheated. Eli had a hunch the man idolized his boss. Yes, she had really gone to town. Paint, fences, more corrals, a vegetable garden, extra rooms on the house, two more milk cows, marigolds and geraniums planted in the shape of her brand, a windmill under construction, poultry houses, water piped into the kitchen. The ranch looked—loved. That was the right word. Loved.

"Bring in that bluegrass and clover she planted?" Supplemental feed, she called it, an idea gleaned from Hooker and livestock magazines. Of course, he'd forgotten Norah was raised in a bookstore. As natural for her to consult books as for him to go to an experienced hand like Shorty.

"Yep. Wanted it ready for them shorthorns and Herefords comin' in from Ioway. Sellin' off the Mexican stuff, the Texas, too, 'cept for Old Sugar. Says her younguns' futures depend on smaller herds, quality beef. Ain't sure but what that book larnin' jest might have somethin' to it."

"Do tell!" A woman's ideas about the cattle business making sense to this old-timer? Eli was impressed.

"Got a head on her shoulders, give 'er credit for that. Says too many folks bringin' herds into the valley. Won't be grass to go 'round, let alone water. Overstock and when drought comes, you got *big* trouble."

Norah Beatty had in fact astonished the ranching community by succeeding in this male-dominated business. In addition, she turned out to be a good judge of men, deferring to the crew's savvy about land, grass, browse, and cattle management; they had spent their lives soaking up such special knowledge. She expected honesty, fair dealing, and loyalty, and her crew, grown to ten men who were treated well and paid high, took perverse pride in working for a woman. The increasingly famous butterfly brand was vehemently defended by word and fist.

The rancher shifted in his saddle. "Old man, we gettin' married or not?"

Shorty cackled with glee. "You ain't hardly my type, Eli, dear."

"You know what I mean, you windy polecat."

"Shouldn't wonder. Ranchin's a lonely life fer a pretty gal. She's busy as a cat on a hot griddle, though."

"Been thinkin' about goin' into horses, gettin' rid of my herds. Think she'd go for that? Live on the EM, maybe lease out the Mariposa?"

"Cain't say. But she's powerful fond of the Mary Posee." Shorty's mind wandered to her current errand. Borrowing money from foreigners. He didn't like the sound of that at all. The headstrong woman had overextended herself, as she called it. Spent more'n she took in, he'd call it.

"Jesus! That's an Arabian!" Eli gasped as a man led a horse from blacksmith shed to barn. An extremely expensive horse! What was she up to?

"Yep, got some fancy name means drinkin' the wind."

"Where is she in Tucson? I want to talk to her!" She was in way over her head.

"Reckon she wouldn't mind my sayin'." The faded eye studied him as Shorty furnished the hotel's name. "Bring 'er home before she does somethin' she shouldn't, son."

Norah sat up ruler-straight, daintily grasping the handle of a bone-china cup. She and the three men had finished dinner and dessert at Tucson's finest hotel; they had asked for and received permission to smoke; now came business. She had dressed carefully, wavering between the royal-blue suit with its white lace waist or a bronze satin and black velvet copied from *Harper's Bazaar*. Deciding the black was more worldly, she made a matching hat, shirring and draping the materials, adding pheasant feathers and a rose fashioned from material the exact blue of her eyes.

Sipping tea, Norah studied the entrepreneurs about whom she had read and to whom she'd written, outlining expansion plans. Money was available in Arizona for two percent a month, but unspoken prejudice against women in a man's business barred her from it. To her delight the men had responded by setting an appointment on their way to Wyoming.

"We've had a look at your ranch, Mrs. Beatty. Our survey man advises it's a superior place." The Englishman was the first to speak, polite and enchanted.

"Ay, clean and well kept, he says, with bonny animals," the Scotsman added, approving good husbandry.

"And the water is—" The dandified Frenchman kissed his fingertips.

The trio was typical of foreign investors fascinated with the American West and fortunes to be made from industries peculiar to this virtually untouched country. Most so-called cattle barons had never sat a horse, branded a calf, or choused a mother cow but tracked down profits skillfully as Indians read tracks.

"A man looking at the Mariposa? Oh, was he the one interested in—pretending to—?"

"Well, lass, ye'd never expect us to talk wi' ye had we not known what we were talkin' about," the Scotsman said with a smile.

Norah put the cup down. "Of course not, gentlemen. I'm simply surprised he didn't identify himself. I'd have given him much more information had I known."

"No offense meant, Mrs. Beatty, a matter of procedure." The Englishman referred to papers taken from a breast pocket. "Let's see, now. Ownership in order. Range approximately fifteen miles square. Valley and mesa with excellent forage on which you presently run several thousand head, some of which drift below the border and must be driven back to home range in the spring."

"Besides reducing herd size to improve quality, I want to fence my holdings. I plan to produce tender beef for Eastern markets. Fences will keep my neighbors' scrub bulls away from the blooded heifers, keep *them* from straying, cut down on labor and theft."

The Frenchman raised a manicured finger. "Ah, the

rustlers. Cochise County, madame, is one of the worst in the West. Even President Arthur despairs of it! Tombstone? That is correct? A droll name but a den of thieves. Bandits preying on decent people. Not a good situation. To put money there—" He shrugged and raised his eyebrows.

Norah clenched a fist in nervous emphasis. "Open-range ranching is going to be a thing of the past. Everything points to it. Fenced range is easier to protect. And I have a topnotch crew."

"So we heard, lass, so we heard." Soft as silk but smart as a whip, the man from Glasgow thought. "But ye ken we've stockholders to account to when we invest their hard-earned money. A ranch in a lawless territory—a woman without a mon—cattle straying into another country—Indians stealing livestock and often burning ranches—"

"But southern Arizona's a stockman's dream! The climate's so good cattle stay in the open the entire year. It has marvelous feed—grama grasses never touched by buffalo. No chaparral. Natural springs. And as for law and order—it's coming!"

They glanced at one another. "We canna wait, lass."

Her eyes flashed disdain. "You're afraid to take a gamble! Afraid to dare!" she accused them. Damn it, she'd lost! Why not twist their tails a bit?

Lips quirked with suppressed amusement, but their gazes remained cool. Each answered in his soul, however, to her challenge and regretted for a moment the cold fact that small but courageous, innovative businessmen hadn't a snowball's chance in hell next to the bottom line: the mother lode to be mined from corporate enterprise.

"Something might be arranged. Would you sell?"

"No." Give up the Mariposa? *Never!* Soul, friend, lover, and enemy? No.

"Should we lend, we'd have to manage your affairs."

"No. Absolutely not. I can get along on my own hook, I think. I'm sorry to have wasted your valuable time,

gentlemen." Norah shuddered imperceptibly, despising rejection.

They murmured politely, but the Scotsman leaned forward to confide. " 'Twas no time wasted. You're a breath of
fresh air. Of the future. But ye ken, your ranch is tiny. Not
profitable enough. We own five million acres and run a
hundred fifty thousand cows in Wyoming alone." She
stared, stunned by the mighty figures and their potential.

The men rose, bade farewell, and departed. Norah
ordered more tea and a chocolate éclair, watching the dining
room fill for the evening meal. She put down her fork with a
surge of excitement when the Scotsman returned. They had
reconsidered!

They had not, but he brought a bouquet of late-summer
roses. "For a battle well fought. Th'art a braw lass. Had we
met thirty years ago—"

Touched, Norah slipped a flower in his buttonhole.
"We'd have built an empire together, I ken."

"Ay, I'll think on that wi' pleasure." He bowed and
joined his companions waiting at the men's bar entrance.

She smelled the flowers and for the first time longed for
Eli—for his strength and macho presence, his steadfast
affection and the comfort and security it brought. For his
kisses and hard, hungry body. For an end to celibacy.

A waiter appeared with champagne. "From the gentleman over there, madame."

"Eli!"

Startled, diners glanced up to see a radiant woman rush
into the arms of a man grinning with happiness. Shocking.
Unladylike! Yet there wasn't a person there who wouldn't
have traded places, for love filled the room like the scent of
the roses she held.

Norah paused to say good night at the door. They had
talked and talked over sherry, Eli scolding her for not asking
him for money and for investing in costly horses when all

her bills weren't paid. Not that he didn't understand the mystical attraction of a magnificent animal!

"See you at breakfast?" He waited for the usual kiss on the cheek.

His hot wanting beat against her like July winds off the grassland before the summer storms. Like a bolt of lightning, desire struck in her in answer, and she was almost sick with need. She stepped into the room. "Come in."

They waited in the near darkness. Then Eli tossed his Stetson aside, ran palms down her arms, and carried her hands to his lips. She had made the first move but could choose to go no farther. It was up to him to persuade her.

Gently, he started with the hat, unpinning it and placing the confection on a chair. "Let me——"

"Do it," she whispered, brushing the fly of his trousers. *"Do it.* Quickly!"

Stomach aflutter, Eli helped her undress. The room remained dark, for they'd lit no lamp, yet her white skin appeared to glow. Eli's lips parted in amazement to see Norah naked. *She was giving herself to him with no holds barred!* He swept his prize into brawny arms, peered down in triumph at the bare breasts pushed against his shirt, at dark red hair above feminine parts. He cleared his throat, unable to breathe without difficulty.

She pushed him onto the chair and hat, trying to open his clothing. "Christ, Norah, wait a minute. Wait a minute!"

She straddled him, gasping for breath, urging him to hurry. He lifted her under the arms, then slowly and excruciatingly impaled her upon him. Norah dug nails into his back as her body enveloped him. Her unexpected boldness—the culmination of his fantasies—his physical and spiritual loves—these elements combined to give him great strength, yet Eli thought he was going to pass out with sheer ecstasy. Now she came, putting a hand over her mouth to muffle a cry, and Eli shook in every muscle when he pressed her down on him and expelled his semen.

Norah was slick with sweat, head resting on his shoulder,

arms limp about his neck. They didn't move, emptied of
lust and cleansed for lovemaking to come, until he said
she'd catch cold and carried her to bed. He undressed and
got in with her. "You okay?" he asked.

"More okay than I've been in a long time." Norah didn't
meet his gaze. "Do you think I'm wicked?"

He shook his head, although he was truly astounded to
discover the passion in her. They fell silent and explored
each other, finding every crevice and sensitive spot. "You
are the most exciting woman in the world," he said with
reverence.

"Want me for better or worse?" Her mind was made up.
Why wait any longer?

He squeezed her waist hard enough to hurt. "You mean
it? Now, Norah, you don't mind havin' more kids, do you?"

"Let's make one tonight and get married tomorrow." She
bent down, took him in her mouth, let him quiver and
enlarge, received him there.

"It doesn't work that way," he said, gasping. Where had
she learned to make love like this? It was highly unusual for
a refined woman to be so forward, to insist on her pleasure,
too. His mind shoved the inevitable answer away. She was
his now; nothing else mattered. "Norah, I ain't got the
words to express what I feel, but I'll—I'll love you
forever."

"No more words." Words could be daggers. Mason had
promised to love her, too, but betrayed her instead; she
scorned the weakness that made her love him still.

They kissed, mouths tender but still starved, a signal for
their bodies to join and part throughout the night. And if a
ghost hovered in the dark, each thrust it away with thoughts
the other never knew.

They sat on their horses, smoking and studying the
Mariposa layout from the rise overlooking it. Beside the
recently completed two-story, thirty-room mansion of brick
and redwood, the old buildings appeared shabby. The

children played nearby at the artesian pond, and Endicott whittled under a tree. Yucca in bloom swayed in the breeze like enormous lilies-of-the-valley with spiny skirts; Mexicans called them candles of the Lord.

Eighteen eighty-five had come and gone, bringing homesteaders and barbed wire—the devil's hatband—drought and irreversible deterioration of the range; this was due mainly to overstocking, importation of cattle, and ignorance of conservation. Too many cattle destroyed vegetation that held soil intact and initiated erosion. Prairie dogs, which, like earthworms, crumbled subsurface soil so it retained moisture, were now being eliminated; new grass withered and wells ran dry. A cow drank up to thirty gallons of water a day—and it hadn't rained. The animals suffered and died, wiping out their owners in the process.

Prices dropped to less than ten dollars, and cattlemen drove herd remnants to Tucson to be shipped to Los Angeles; the dry, depleted range was soon swept clean of fat cattle. For most ranchers it had been a matter of sell or go under, and the drought, which would last for years, taught hard-earned lessons: raise fewer and better animals; sell two- and three-year-old steers but retain she stuff for breeding; develop artificial water with wells, windmills, natural tanks, and piping from foothill springs; pay to fatten cattle on alfalfa near Phoenix and Tempe in Maricopa County when necessary.

Norah and Eli had weathered the bust, for he had other financial interests, and she had learned from him to diversify. She had reduced herd size, concentrating on high-grade half-breeds and the surprisingly adaptable Herefords that were hardy as native stock. Like all ranchers, big or small, she had a heavy range mortality; by robbing Peter to pay Paul, she was able to offset the loss, but there was no getting around it. The cattle business was a poker game in which Nature always held the winning hand. To Eli's disgust she invested in a sheep-raising operation near Flagstaff, having learned that the sheep business didn't fluctuate as wildly as did the beef. It was the infant Arabian herd that kept her on a short tether financially yet wholly captivated her heart. One jump ahead of payments due and always a day late and a dollar short, Norah gradually built her empire.

"You like it?" Eli asked now.

"What?" Her mind was a million miles away.

"That goddam mausoleum down there that cost an arm and a leg. The EM has a perfectly good house, and the Fullerton place isn't bad. Why you wanted this is beyond me."

Norah took no guff from anyone, including her husband, who tried to run her life and business. She'd thought they'd be partners, but it hadn't worked that way. It wasn't that he thought her incapable of running the Mariposa spread, still her property after marriage under Arizona community property law; Eli simply wanted his wife home having babies and running a household instead of a bunch of tough cowboys. She hadn't the slightest doubt he loved her with every bone in his body; being bossy and domineering was just his way—but she wouldn't put up with it.

Her eyes darkened with pique. "You said once you'd give me the world on a silver platter. Well, that down there is what I want right now, and I'll probably want something else later!" She relighted her cigarillo. Smoking was a habit recently begun in defiance of him and convention.

Eli grunted. Her sass and resistance to his authority irritated him the way a burr under the saddle drove a horse berserk; conversely, he enjoyed those qualities. He admired the tendrils of hair sneaking from her hat onto lightly freckled cheekbones, the almost stern profile set against the arid mountains. His gaze dropped to her crotch snugged against the leather; her striped California pants wore like iron, fit like skin, and were the sexiest things Eli had seen her wear. His mind drifted back to the first time they went to bed and how she'd thrown herself at him—attacked him, by God! To his sorrow, that hadn't happened again. She didn't act reluctant about making love, far from it, but the spark that had electrified them that night in the hotel had not revived. Nor had she gotten pregnant, a frustration and sadness for Eli.

"Where's Grace? I don't see her anywhere."

"Wasn't she with Emedio and the dog, mending fence at the colt pasture?"

Norah scanned the spread with binoculars. "I don't—yes, thank goodness, there they are." She sighed with relief.

"You real sure Rose is with Geronimo's bunch? All you got is another Indian's word for it."

"He's a scout under Lieutenant Charles Gatewood's command." It had been as difficult for her as for other Arizonans to accept the premise of Apaches tracking down Apaches for the U.S. Army. She rather liked the young man, however, who had stood fingering the metal identification neck tag that was his safety guarantee among white men. He'd spoken to Rose when she and other women had come to Fort Bowie to beg supplies; she had mentioned a blue-eyed child on the Mariposa.

"Does being a scout make him truthful?" Eli recalled her speaking with affection of Fletcher's Apache companion; maybe that made her more comfortable with the scout's information.

"He has no reason to lie, and the lieutenant vouches for him. Oh, Eli, I can't bear to think of Rose with those brutes. The last time we heard—when was that? Last year? She was cooking for a Mexican merchant in Guadalajara. And why mention Grace? Do you think—do you suppose she wants Grace now?"

Her husband loved the charming four-year-old, too, hated to picture her crawling with lice and fleas, subsisting on mesquite beans, cactus fruit, piñon nuts, and berries after knowing milk and meat. "Now, don't worry. The men will watch her until Geronimo and his followers are caught."

"It's not that she doesn't have every right to have Grace

with her. But I can't bear—well, I'll try to keep her closer to me." Which was easier said than done considering her working day and the child's natural curiosity about things. Norah decided to go so far as to offer Rose a place on the Mariposa. No warrant had been sworn out for her arrest, after all. Anything to save the baby from a life on the run. It was hard to picture Rose with the Chiricahua escapees who had fled San Carlos in May of 'eighty-five. Forty-two braves and ninety women and children, including teen-age boys training for the warpath, had cut a path of death through Graham and Cochise counties and southwestern New Mexico. Big ranches with straight-shooting ranch hands and the manpower to guard them had not been bothered; smaller, more isolated families had not been so lucky during what was to be a fifteen-month period of terrorism.

Andrew and Rachel waved at them from the wide veranda before disappearing into the empty house. "They'll get lost in there, sure as heck," Eli suggested dryly. You'd think Norah planned to fill it with children. Was this what she'd been waiting for? He regarded the structure with a kindlier eye, though he still thought it pretentious for Vista Valley, and ranch folk despised pretense above all else. Yet Norah had a way with folks, so maybe it would work out in the end. But the cost! Dormer windows and chimneys, several fireplaces, brick-arched windows, a full basement with servants' quarters, a cool-room for fruits and vegetables, a dumbwaiter, storerooms, a drinking-water reservoir piped upstairs, fuel storage, and attic space galore. "You ordered the furniture yet?"

"Yes, most of it, and a few Navajo rugs, too. They'll just glow on that pine floor! I'll go to Tucson for sterling, crystal, and china later this month." She described details of the furniture, the designs and color schemes, hoping to infect him with her enthusiasm. "Then, as soon as I'm ready, we'll have the biggest housewarming you ever saw!" She had indeed come a long, long way from St. Louis sweatshops and waterfront rooms where walls dripped in dank air.

They reached out to clasp hands for a moment. "You get anything you want, you hear? I want my girl to be happy."

"Thank you, Eli. I love you." She squeezed his fingers.

"And I love you. But not very much."

"Oh, you! Bet you can't beat me back to the house!"

Her Arabian Kehilan stretched out and drank the wind into his nostrils, leaving Eli and his blooded Thoroughbred behind. But he didn't mind her little victory. His eyes were glued to that gorgeous ass that belonged to him, and his imagination seized on the night ahead. Yeah, he'd purely love to populate that monstrosity with kids fallin' out the windows! Maybe she'd changed—

29.

Stamping her foot, Soledad railed at her father, a privilege he permitted no one but her. "But Papa, why must *he* go? Send the vaqueros. I cannot live without him!" She wrung her hands, eyes starting slightly from her head.

Cutting into an onion and tomato omelette, Don Diego remonstrated in a mild tone. "*Silencio,* my golden dove. Your job is to rest and let the babe within you grow and flourish. You know how proud of you I am, don't you?" He chewed morosely. She had had three miscarriages already.

Blessed Savior, no more!

Soledad smoothed the slight rise of abdomen, mollified by praise. Another being lived in there. Imagine that. Then the old panic clawed at her. That being was feeding on her!

Sucking out her juices! She muffled a shriek, jamming the corner of her shawl into her mouth.

"Take Soledad to her room," Don Diego ordered his wife, who had delivered a plate of fresh tortillas. "She will remain there until I say. Is that clear?" No one spoke back to *el patrón,* and the women departed, awash in tears.

The hacendado finished breakfast, tossed his napkin down, and left for the corrals, where Mason and two men were preparing to track down a palomino mare and her filly. The animals had escaped through an unbarred gate and had been seen miles to the north. Swift and blessed with a rainy spring, they might be in Texas, New Mexico, or Arizona in a matter of days. Don Diego had beaten the peon responsible, and so he felt better; nevertheless, the horses were very dear to him, a link to the old life in Alta California; he was also deeply concerned lest they fall into the hands of Mangas, Geronimo, or old Nana.

"Ready, my son?" He trusted Mason, had taught him the cattle business during the more than seven years he had lived with them. His other sons-in-law were city men, uninterested in rural life and manure on their shoes.

Mason grinned and pulled the cinch strap tighter, kneeing the horse in the side; his mount had tried to outfox him by expanding its barrel so the strap would fall loose when it exhaled. Mason could hardly wait to be on his way, to be free of the stifling family atmosphere so typical of Latins, with its constant companionship, touching, and crowding. They had the best intentions of loving and sharing and found the gringo's need for privacy and space puzzling. And he was eager to be away from Soledad. He cared for her in many ways, but she drove him to distraction. His hands actually trembled with excitement! Horse-hunting in Apache country was no picnic, but he'd be closer to home, maybe across the border. No one would recognize him after all this time—if he *was* an outlaw. He'd grown heavier, had a beard, the hair at his temples had silvered, and his eyes grown darker.

"Buena suerte." The men embraced, pounding each other on the back. He'd need good luck to find the palominos before they were lassoed by Chiricahuas in some remote canyon; it would be a barbarity to find them killed and eaten. Don Diego leaned against the adobe barn and made the sign of the cross as the men disappeared in the distance, wearing faded clothes and riding dun horses so they'd blend into the landscape. He had an unexpected twinge of melancholy. He, too, wished to be on a good horse with the wind of adventure in his face. He crossed himself again, recalling what Apaches did to prisoners. Go with God, my son.

Rose squatted near the alligator juniper to which her daughter was tethered. They gnawed on deer bones, slavering with hunger, for food had been scarce among the escapees from San Carlos. Three groups had been formed. Rose was with the first, led by Nachez, the hereditary chief, and Geronimo, subchief and military tactician; Chihuahua and Hosanna headed a second, Chatto and Martine the third. Ordinarily, they existed on dried beef, mule or horse, water stored in horse intestine, and roasted agave leaves, a substitute for bread and sugar. The deer had been a gift from the gods.

The gods were fickle, Rose decided. The bands had been fleeing from desert to mountaintop, chased by American soldiers, Apache scouts from hostile clans, white civilians, Mexican troops, and Tarahumara Indian guides so fast and enduring they ran deer to death. The pursuit was like trying to catch hawks with butterfly nets, but despair now dogged the fugitives. Everyone was worn to a nubbin; they ate their ponies and risked death to secure supplies in Mexican villages. Surrender began to have advantages—but the very idea broke the heart. For centuries *Dineh*, the people, had ruled a vast kingdom, plundering, enslaving, and killing—a way of life practiced by men in other lands and centuries before them. Now they were the hunted, a valiant, vicious, and doomed remnant of the thousands who had once conducted a reign of terror from West Texas to western Arizona and hundreds of miles south into Mexico.

Rose was exhausted from carrying her plump daughter, who more often than not, spoiled and unused to hardship, had to be bound and gagged to keep her quiet. She was much like a new puppy: darling, huggable, wriggly, demanding, and an awful nuisance. Rose had kidnaped her easily—assuming correctly that Norah wouldn't give her up—by slithering through the grass on her belly and dangling the crystal necklace Norah had given her on a long-ago Christmas. She now regretted the maternal impulse that had driven her to reclaim the child. Rose wiped greasy fingers on her skirt and gave her daughter a piece of agave leaf to suck on.

She disliked the filth and constant travel, the women who accused her of not being worthy to associate with courageous chiefs. On the other hand, she was useful in eliciting information from villages, for though she had suffered abuse during her exile, Rose was still a handsome woman. She hardly recognized herself these days when, in mirror or stream, she saw a gypsyish hoyden in stolen finery from abandoned haciendas.

Her gradual downward journey to what she was now had accelerated as her temper worsened and laziness increased. The money had evaporated, for unaccustomed to handling it, she'd been wasteful. She'd had to work as lingerie embroiderer, corn grinder, nursemaid, cook, tortilla maker, mistress, and sheepherder, and this last job had been her entrée into the Apache bands which had killed the other herders and taken her and the sheep with them. At first she'd been frightened but soon thrived on the unfettered freedom these nomads enjoyed. She had a lover who fulfilled her; always sexually active, Rose found as she matured that she needed a man frequently.

Yes, there was much to dislike and quail from among these extremely dangerous men, not the least of which was their complete control over the women. They expressed anger and irritation alike with heavy blows or kicks or beatings. Still, Rose's soul was at rest at last among her own. She belonged and knew who she was.

She was adjusting a rag over Grace's face to lessen sunburn when her lover joined them. Bandoliers of ammunition crisscrossed his pink cotton shirt, and he sported a print four-in-hand tie and black-and-red silk vest. He came right to the point. "You cannot take this weakling child. Geronimo has spoken. We head for the main stronghold south of Janos and west of Río Casas Grandes. She'll never last. Only true Apache can stand the pace. I also have doubts about you."

Rose gestured at the landscape with concern. "Would a good mother abandon her here?" Leave Grace to certain death? She'd desert the band first. "The animals will eat her."

"Would a good mother have brought her along in the first place?" He ran a calloused hand along her thigh and led her into the nearby rocks. "Come, woman, we have a little time." The warrior counted himself fortunate to have a sweetheart in the midst of war, but if she faltered—for she was still soft from civilized living—he'd go it alone. She might even have to be killed to keep her from telling the Army their destination.

He scowled. Pressed to surrender, the chiefs had made a bad move in March at Skeleton Canyon; they had talked surrender with Crook even though Geronimo had broken his word twice before. Suspicious and jumpy, they'd gotten stinking drunk on a white renegade's whiskey and ridden for cover, mean as bears with sore paws. *Anh*—they had singed their own damned tail feathers and brought the wrath of the Great White Father down on them. Cavalry from Fort Huachuca had soon secured waterholes along the entire border, blocked plunder trails, and patrolled incessantly. The Army had too few men to cover the desert wastes, and it had always been awkward in guerrilla warfare and had difficulty pinning down a foe that moved in small, stealthy groups—but they were learning fast and time was running out.

He lifted his woman's skirt and entered her, shoving hard but not kissing, for Apache were not fond of that custom. She bucked, supple as a snake, climaxing with him. He was the most inexhaustible lover Rose had ever met; he wanted her for a wife and had promised they'd marry once safely in the Stronghold. She nuzzled his ear, vowing to teach him to kiss.

The warrior left then, eye caught by the flash of more of the "talking mirrors"; he and his fellow primitives had no way of knowing that a network of twenty-seven heliograph stations created solely for surveillance of Apache movement was now in operation. It blanketed a territory three hundred miles long and two hundred wide, covering in Arizona alone a twenty-thousand-square-mile area. In a land of eternal sun, the heliographs nagged the Apaches from mountaintop to mountaintop; one message traveled eight hundred miles in only four hours. Geronimo had thought them evil spirits, which might have been preferable to the elite pursuit force guided by the magic messages.

Rose paid no attention to the instruments of Apache downfall but rearranged her clothes and stretched out to nap. Time enough to decide about Grace tomorrow.

Perched on a slope overlooking the ranch, Norah had been engrossed in subtle differences between a Botteri's sparrow and a Cassin's and only inadvertently witnessed Grace's kidnaping. Too far away to prevent it, she vowed that the men assigned to guard the child had lost their jobs, and wouldn't find work anywhere in Arizona. Unfortunately, Eli had gone to Bisbee for a meeting of the new Territorial Stock Raisers' Association.

Norah knew it was foolhardy to hit the trail alone, but she had to follow Rose before she vanished. Kehilan showed he was worth every penny Norah had paid for him as they ascended into the mountains, following the little band as closely as possible. The child had to be rescued before disappearing forever into the fastnesses of the Mexican cordillera. Rose must not be allowed to ruin the child's life regardless of the fact she was Grace's mother.

The fugitives were apparently resting here just north of the border, readying themselves for the dash into Sonora. How cleverly they had eluded the patrol that had stopped at the Mariposa only hours earlier! Norah caught a glimpse of the women dipping water from a creek. She had no illusions. They could easily catch her, and they'd waste no pity, either killing her on the spot or selling her as a slave deep in Mexico. Hair on the back of her neck rose. Had Carleton been this apprehensive the night he tracked the warrior at Eagle Creek? Or, blinded by his obsession, had he gone to meet death eagerly? She waited for night, sipped water, and nibbled on jerky, dying for a smoke she dare not have. Again and again Norah checked the pearl-handled .45, Eli's gift to his little deadeye; he must be home by now and wondering where she was. He would be furious with her.

The sliver of moon cast no appreciable light as she inched toward the encampment on her stomach, praying she didn't encounter a timber rattler hunting mice or rabbit in her path. Dirt rubbed over face and hands; jacket buttoned to the chin to conceal a white shirt; hair in a bun to avoid branches; fear-sweat in her own nostrils. It was a hundred-to-one shot she would come up near Grace, but she did; still tied to the tree, the child was curled in a ball the same way she slept at home. Norah froze, blood beating in her ears, partially deafening her, motionless as a lizard paralyzed in the hawk's shadow. She peered at bodies cast about like ghostly logs and wondered where Rose Fullerton slept. Why was she on the run with these people? Did she matter to them? Whatever their crimes, did they matter to her? Was she no longer floundering in limbo between two worlds?

Norah reached out slowly. Slowly, slowly, untie the rope.

Grace slept as if dead, and Norah's scalp prickled with horror. *Sweet Jesus, don't let it be true!* She dropped the rope and crept forward, wincing when rocks jabbed her breasts. Darkness grew darker. She thought she was seeing things. Immediately before her eyes the dim outline of high Apache boots took shape. Someone hauled Norah to her feet. A bank of clouds obscuring the moon parted at that instant and reflected enough light for Norah to see who was holding her. Terror lanced through her stomach and heart.

Aboriginal bull, medicine man, killer, arsonist, thief, torturer, and symbol of Chiricahua defiance: Gokliya— Geronimo.

His stink assaulted her. An old dread stirred in her bowels, recalling their meeting years ago when he had tweaked her hair, and her near capture and rescue by Eli and his men a year later. They stood so close his breath fell on her cheek. No escape. *No escape.* Norah closed her eyes. His grip fell away. She grabbed for the .45 but he was quicker and disarmed her. Geronimo shifted position, and moonlight fell on the bear-trap mouth open and curved in amusement. He shoved the weapon in his belt, then reached around her head to unpin her hair. Norah almost fainted. Rape? Would they all ravish her and leave her corpse for the buzzards? Or do it as a periodic lesson until they found a rich hacendado partial to red hair and blue eyes?

The rumble that vibrated in the man's chest might have been a laugh. The Apache stooped, picked up the sleeping child, and put her in Norah's arms. She looked at him, mouth agape, unable to move and afraid to cause the slightest sound that might awaken Rose. Was he letting them go or playing a cruel game? Was this a gesture of compassion to make points at the next parley or was he ridding himself of an extra mouth to feed? Or could he be a hunted man whose heart had been touched by an unhappy baby who was part Apache? Norah realized with strange insight that she and Geronimo were a bit alike: arrogant, fiercely independent, stubborn, and brave, each struggling for what they loved.

He jerked his squarish head toward the forest, and she hefted the child, who instinctively clung to her neck. For a moment the adults stared at each other. Then, in the Apache way, she glanced skyward in unspoken thanks, received his nod in answer, and turned and ran.

"My God, Miz Martin, where you *been*?" Her foreman ran to seize the horse's foam-specked bridle. Chan Lee was at his heels, chattering excitedly in Chinese, and Endicott loped across the yard with worry etched on his face.

"Where's Eli?" Norah surrendered Grace to Endicott, assuring him they were both unharmed. "Are the children all right?"

"He's out with a search party," John Smith grumbled, afraid he might have revealed affection in his frantic greeting. "And the kids are sleepin' in the bunkhouse."

"Send a man to bring him back, and take care of Kehilan. He did a job and a half." Norah dismounted, so weary and unstrung by delayed shock her knees gave way and she slid to the ground. The men waited, uncertain what to do. Seeing her there in the dirt, clothing soiled and odorous, hair untidy, face and hands scratched—their hearts swelled with passion to think of this bitty woman bearding Apaches. She was a boss after their stamp.

"Help me up, John." Her legs shook, then steadied. "I need a bath!" The cook rushed away to heat water, and Endicott followed, bouncing Grace and cooing to her, relieved she seemed no worse for wear.

"What are the children doing in the bunkhouse?" Norah trailed after the foreman. He unsaddled Kehilan, threw a blanket over his back, and started walking him to cool him off.

"Didn't want to sleep in the big house alone with a stranger. Travelers come in the middle of the night. Big rancher from Sonora, think his men said. He and his vaqueros took back a mare and her filly from 'Paches, then got in a fracas with rustlers. The *jefe* got shot in the head. Put him in one of the extra bedrooms.''

"Is he dying?" She rubbed her eyes. Was it possible she had gone so far, been a hairbreadth from the infamous fugitive thousands of military were searching for? It seemed a dream, but Norah knew she was lucky to be alive.

Smith began to rub the horse down. "Don't think so. Bullet just creased him but knocked him out good."

"I see. Well, there's been enough killing." She yawned, smoothed the horse, whispering sweet words, then trudged toward the house. How nice it would be when the mansion was finally livable; having everything torn up gave her a sense of insecurity. One furnishing she had in mind was a big fancy scroll-foot tub in which to soak to her heart's content. One big enough for her and Eli. Her eyes sparkled with mischief. For the time being, though, the old washtub would serve as it had for so many Saturday nights.

The Mexicans who were hunkered down in front of the stranger's room jumped to their feet, pulling off sombreros, making jerky little bows of the head. They were able to make her understand that *el patrón* was still sleeping; beyond that Norah realized she'd need Emedio to translate. They studied her covertly. Dirt and fatigue failed to hide her loveliness, yet they had no doubt this was a shrewd, audacious *ranchera,* for jaw and eye revealed authority. Her smile comforted them, however; it was full of womanly kindness and compassion.

There was a shout outside. Oblivious to everyone, Eli ran into the house and grabbed her in his arms. Norah hugged him close before drawing back to see his face; she was touched and startled to see tears trickling down his cheeks. "You idiotic female! Why didn't you get help? Goin' off like that alone! I ought to beat you within a damned inch of your life!"

He shook her until her teeth rattled while the vaqueros gazed on with approval, but they stared in wonder when she started to laugh, bent over with uncontrollable mirth. He swore and shook her even harder. She collapsed against him, and Eli couldn't help joining in her hilarity. They staggered into the yard arm in arm and sank red faced into rustic chairs. Wiping his eyes, Eli gasped, "Look at you! What a sight! You smell like—No wonder the 'Pache didn't want you!" The friendly insult sent them into more laughter until they called a truce, holding their aching sides.

She noticed a knot of men by the barn, smoking and resetting saddles. "Your hands staying for supper? I'll have Chan Lee fix it."

"Nope. They're takin' you to the EM." Eli held up a hand to still the protest. "You and the kids go on, I'll be there in a couple hours. Time we stayed there anyway until this house is finished. I'm tired of camping out in half-empty rooms." He helped her rise, for her muscles had begun to stiffen from tension and from carrying Grace on the long ride back. They strolled down to join the others, greeting the children and watching them mount their ponies.

"Beat you to the EM, Momma!" Her son raced off, yelling like a Comanche, two cowboys not far behind him.

"You go with Endicott and Grace, Rachel. Your brother's not goin' to beat me anywhere!" Norah kissed her husband and was up on his Thoroughbred before he could say a word.

Seeing her gallop away, Eli smacked his hands together. The world was his oyster today! Then he went to check on the wounded man, who was tossing and muttering in delirium. When Eli came out of the house, shaken and afraid, he knew his world would never be the same again.

30.

Sitting beside the bed, hands in her lap, Norah absorbed his dark disheveled elegance and the unforgotten smell of him, an odor a lover always remembered. Outside a horse whinnied, a match was struck, a hummingbird's courtship dive made a muted whine. *Calypte costae*. Ascends a hundred feet, descends like a speeding bullet past prospective mate. Found in the Arizona sycamore strand. . . .

If Mason awoke and still did not know who he was—ah, God, how easy that would be for everyone! If he did, her life and the lives of those dear to her would be turned upside down. For she had not changed. She couldn't. She had always loved him far beyond reason. Norah rocked back and forth in a kind of mourning. She loved her husband, but Mason had held her soul in thrall since the day he boarded the stagecoach a decade ago.

Poor Eli. He had been subdued, almost melancholy, when he joined the family at the EM. He had made love to her later, coming but once and then softly; shortly after midnight he'd awakened her to say Mason Fletcher was back. In their new house. They had stared across at each other, and her tongue had been unable to form the consoling words Eli ached to hear. After saddling her horse in the morning and giving her a lift up, he'd stepped back, face pale and tight. He had slid his fingers under his belt at the small of his back, saying, "I love you. Come back."

Why hadn't he lost his temper, ranted and raved that no man was going to steal his wife? That she'd better behave herself, by God? Riding across the grassland, Norah decided it was because he wanted to trust her and felt helpless to compete with her love for Mason, despite his wealth and adoration. He didn't want to lose his temper and get her back up.

Now, at Mason's bedside, the power and impact of his personality abruptly knifed through Norah's reverie. He had opened his eyes, and they were luminous with recognition and love. He grinned, that rare, dazzling grin that gave her butterflies in the stomach and dissolved her bones. Was the attraction only physical? Had it always been? That would make things easier, too, help her retreat back to Eli and the life she had built.

"Norah!" He touched the bullet crease and winced. "What happened? What am I doing here? I've never seen this room."

"You *really* don't remember?"

"No. I—yes, Chico was killed. I exchanged gunfire with some Apaches and lost my prisoner—got shot before I fell off a cliff into a river. Somewhere in the Sierra Madre. Did you find me? No, that's impossible." He ran a hand along his beard, full and thick, certainly not the growth of a week or so. His eyes widened in alarm. "What the *hell*—"

Without thinking Norah rose to push him back onto the pillow as she did with the children. Touching his bare chest undid her resolve to remain at arm's length; she sank onto the edge of the bed. "It's been eight years, Mason. Your son is nine now."

Dismay and perplexity contorted his features. He sat up and grabbed her shoulders. *"Norah! What are you saying? Eight years! What happened? Where have I been? Eight years!"*

She repeated the story told Emedio by the vaqueros of his rescue and amnesia, his marriage and his important role as son-in-law and manager of Don Diego's rancho. Pain harshened her voice as she thought of time wasted and lost, and he put his arms around her. She gasped to find her mouth at the hollow of his throat, to feel the old magic engulf her. "Why, Lord Almighty, you must have thought I skipped out on you! I'm so sorry, Norah!"

"You couldn't help it."

"Eighteen eighty-five! I simply can't believe it! I'll be damned! A piece of my life cut out like a piece of pie and I don't know where it went." He kissed her lids, pale shells hiding the glory of her eyes. "Tell me what's happened. What can we do?"

"We're both married now. What *can* we do?" Except part forever. And that was a special kind of death.

Eli watched her dismount, then turned from the window. Downing his whisky in one gulp, he lit a cigar and went out to visit his baby animals. He let a young raccoon nibble his finger, withdrawing it in haste when the needle teeth drew blood. These were his children, who gave him solace. Eli cuddled a rabbit; it sneezed from the smoke of his cigar. Christ Jesus, *these* were his children! He pounded a roof support with a fist. Why, *why* hadn't they had kids of their own?

What was he to do now? He knew in his guts he came second to Fletcher. How to fight for her? With money? Norah had enough of her own to get by and the business savvy to make more. Marriage? It had been good, not too many quarrels, but only two short years. Lovemaking? It seemed wonderful to him, but children could have been the key, the cement to bind her to him. Jealousy coiled in him like a rattlesnake ready to strike. How *dare* that bastard show up after all these years? Eli's throat thickened, his chest hurt. He groaned aloud.

"You okay, Dad?" Andrew touched his sleeve, golden eyes lambent as an infant mountain lion's in the gloom.

Eli whirled and in his anguish almost struck his rival's child. The blow ended harmlessly on the boy's shoulder, although it rocked him so he almost fell. "No—son, I don't feel so good."

Concern washed across the boy's face. "You don't look

good, either. I'll feed the babies, you go on. Lay down or something."

"Yeah, or somethin'." Eli ruffled his hair and left the barn. Walking like an old codger, he thought ruefully. Maybe coffee and a tot of brandy to hit the spot. No! Whisky and lots of it. He didn't want to think anymore.

Norah entered while he was pouring a drink to report that one of the men had found Baron dead. "His throat was slit. He must have followed Rose, and either a warrior killed him or she did. I'm sick about it."

Eli lifted the glass. "Here's to Baron. He was a good dog. I'll miss him."

"So will the children. I dread telling them."

"Best to be right out in the open about it." He spoke not of the dead pet but of their situation. Eyes narrowed, he searched her face. She and Mason had not been together, for she didn't have that peculiar incandescence that shone from her after love. He reflected on her passion long ago in the hotel room and took a deep breath of optimism. Had the spell been broken? Were she and Fletcher strangers? Maybe he'd clear out now that his head was almost healed and he knew she was married.

"Isn't it early in the day to be drinking so much?" She piled sheets on the table and started to count them.

"You worried about me?" he growled.

Her face grew pink. "Of course. You ought to know that."

"Should I?" Hope flickered in his voice, and he turned away, unable to mask the naked love he felt.

"Don't be silly." Silence fell between them, lightened by sounds they loved—cattle lowing, the drumbeat of horses' hoofs, a clatter of pans in the kitchen, men laughing, someone hammering, the windmill's song. She frowned at his burly back. "I wish you'd stop treating me as if I'd done something wrong!"

"You damn well better *not* do anything wrong!" he burst out, immediately aghast at his mistake the moment he spoke. Now he'd gone and done it. He'd tried to play it cool, let her crush blow over like that of a schoolgirl for an older man. But now he'd really ruined things.

She tossed her head like an untamable mare, and hair flew about her shoulders. "Don't speak to me in that tone of voice! Don't tell *me* what to do!"

The rancher saw red, stumbling against the sideboard on his way across the room. He confronted Norah and yanked her to him, kissing her sloppily. She struggled to free herself and wiped her mouth on a shirt sleeve in disgust. They fell over the sofa and onto the floor. "Eli, you're drunk. Quit it! Let me go!" Panting, he fumbled for buttons, impervious to fists, words or threats. Norah opened her mouth and he stopped it with his, thrusting his tongue in so deeply she gagged. Arms capable of wrestling a steer to the ground held her while he pulled her lower garments down.

Mouth an inch from her lips, he snarled, "I'm gonna teach you a lesson, girl. Want a little screw with the man from Mexico? Shit, I'm a better man than he is any day and twice on Sunday." He forced his way in, not caring about her discomfort. "Know somethin'? I can do this any time. All day and all night. 'Cause I'm your husband. Now— ain't—that—the—fuckin'—truth!" he finished, emphasizing each word by surging up into her until he climaxed.

"Get off me, you son of a bitch," she hissed. "Get up before somebody comes."

His face turned darker red. "Somebody did come! And by God, I'm comin' again. I'll show you who's boss once and for all."

"Don't do this, Eli, I'm warning you." Her eyes flashed. "Eli, let me *go*! What if the children walk in here?" He ignored her pleas and he shuddered and collapsed, mouthing her with relief and drunken affection.

"Hey, Miz Martin, you want that bay shod today or—"

Norah stared past her husband's head into the crimson features of her foreman, John Smith, who wheeled and rushed from the room. Fury frothed through her veins like a flash flood. "Okay, you taught me a lesson. Now I'm going to teach you one," she snapped and pushed his limp form away, got to her knees, and fastened her garments. Only then did she rise to her feet.

Eli raised a hand in supplication, face gray beneath the bronze skin. What had he done? Stupid idiot, what had he *done*? "Norah?"

Her voice was unexpectedly soft. "You didn't have to do that, Eli. There was no cause. None at all. None whatsoever."

"I love you, Norah. I love you *so* much!"

Her tongue caressed her bitten lower lip. "Really?"

Eli scrambled to his feet and pulled up his pants. He didn't dare touch her standing there like an avenging angel, long hair streaming down. "Forgive me. Please! *Please*, Norah. I was so jealous I didn't know what I was doing. Let me make it up to you. I'll do anything you ask. Anything!"

She inspected him from head to toe, eyelids half lowered, mouth hard. "Do you realize what you just did? You raped your own wife! And don't tell *me* you didn't know what you were doing. You knew perfectly well, every single second you knew! You disgust me! I still love Mason Fletcher, Eli, I'll freely admit that, but it never entered my head to cheat on you. I've always respected you—until now—and been loyal to you." Norah folded her arms tightly against her stomach to still the nausea. "You've hurt me. And not just physically.

"I'm riding back to the Mariposa," she continued, "and when I want to see you again, mister, I'll let you know. But don't put a foot on that ranch or I'll have you thrown off. And I *mean* it, by God!"

"No, wait, Norah!" He grabbed her sleeve and she gave him such a glare he dropped his hand. Her perfume scented the air even when she was gone.

Eli poured a whisky, contemplated it, and then in blackest despair threw the glass at the nearest window, shattering it along with his heart.

"When are you going—home?" The word had such a final sound. The remains of a picnic lunch strewn on the tablecloth separated Norah and Mason. They had eaten little, giving the cheese sandwiches, hard-boiled eggs, and marble butter cake to the children, who were now busy collecting leaves and flowers. Their lesson tomorrow was identification of local flora; Norah had conducted classes around the kitchen table for years, occasionally netting a cowboy who wanted to learn to read.

She gazed about at the artesian pond, the old wagon, trees swaying in the spring breeze. It came to her with a little shock that Carleton had proposed on this spot. *And I will be the luckiest man in the world,* he'd said. And she had lied to him and borne a son to this man now sprawled across from her.

"Home? I guess it was home. Not now, though. I want to be here with you. But I can't."

"No, you can't. But I want you here. Need you here." She paused. "Do you know I can see your pulse in the vein on your temple?" His somber masculine beauty would be lost to her again—this time forever. Oh God, the *pain.*

"My thoughts are only of you. Always will be. Of the way your throat sweeps down to your bosom. Of your small feet and their lovely arch. Your hair glinting in the rays of sun stealing through the leaves."

"I'll think of your mouth, my darling, carved like that of a statue. And your hands, so graceful, so strong, capable of killing or caressing."

They made love by word and eye, constrained by decency and honor and years vanished into the past. By vaqueros who lounged nearby, mustachioed chaperons alert to their master's command to bring the Americano back. By Norah's realization that she might soon carry Eli's child. By Mason's pregnant wife, who desperately needed him and kept vigil, peering into empty distances.

Norah took the makings from her pocket and rolled a smoke skillfully as any cowhand. He leaned forward, took it, placed it between his lips, and lighted it with his own. Handing it back, he murmured, "At least my lips have touched yours."

She glanced away, eyes deep sapphire with feeling. "Are you happy?" How could he be, living among foreigners, sleeping with a mad wife?

"Are you?" His eyes grew melancholy, and his mouth curved down.

"I—thought I was. Now it's as if the eagle that lives on that mountain there has torn my heart out with its talons."

"Norah, don't. Don't make it any worse, for Christ's sake."

"Don't? Tomorrow you go back to Mexico to another woman. We'll never see each other again. And I love you so much I feel like dying."

Early the next day Mason gave her a bag of gold for Andrew while they waited for his horse. She dressed in black, tanned face wan, hair skinned back in a knot. "Take care of yourself. Let us hear from you. I don't want Andrew to lose track. He doesn't know yet, but I'll tell him who his father is when I think he can handle it."

"I'll mail my letters from El Paso. I go there on business now and then. I won't forget you, Norah." He kissed her cheek, aching to hold her, realizing that would devastate them both. "I'll always love you. Believe that."

Unable to respond, she nodded. Mason put a boot in the stirrup and the vaqueros mounted, anxious to be home. He put his foot back on the ground. The irresistible yearning in his face brought her to him in a rush. Girlishly, she hugged him about the waist and pressed her forehead to his shoulder, fighting for control. Mason imprinted the beloved form on his memory. A tear trickled down his bearded cheek and fell upon the hair he kissed so gently. Those present looked away or found things to examine at their feet. The vaqueros exchanged glances, comparing the woman to the young señora pining in Chihuahua. Understanding blossomed in their sentimental hearts. *Amor,* so sweet and so bitter.

The children came running with leafy bouquets, surprised to find their mother in the stranger's arms. "Brought an extra bandana, Mr. Fletcher," Andrew said. "Thought you might need it, being as you're going such a far piece."

Norah stepped away, and Mason took the kerchief, wiped his face, and blew his nose. "*Gracias, amigo.* Came in handy right off the bat." They smiled, image to image, their handsomeness so stunning that Norah caught her breath. "You take care of your mother, hear?"

"Yes, sir." The boy's fingers wormed their way into her clenched fist. Andrew wondered if this man had actually been crying, but that was ridiculous. Not a cool customer like him. He was puzzled about his mother, however, who shivered and gulped, unlike her brisk self.

Mason swung into the saddle, took a long look at Norah, his only love, and at Andrew, his boy. What sort of creature, cursed with her ancient lunatic blood, would emerge from Soledad's loins? He closed his eyes an instant, recalling past partings, then he leaned down for Norah's hand and kissed her fingertips. "*Vaya con Dios.*"

He touched his hat brim. Their eyes met one last time. Hers filled so that he seemed a dream under water. "*Vaya con Dios.*" She lifted her chin, determined not to cry. The eagle sank its claws into her heart again and Norah walked away, not watching his departure.

On the hillside Eli Martin observed their farewell through field glasses. He had his spy on the Mariposa and knew they had not been lovers, yet his heart sank to see his former friend ride away. He could have dealt with Mason better here, directly and with bullets. Gone, he became a phantom to haunt his wife. In fact, Eli had seen what he dreaded. A love so deep and pure that desire had been denied in the name of that love. They were so strong and he—he had ruined everything for nothing. Hatred for them gnawed at him and he bent his head and wept.

Part IV
MASON

But true love is a durable fire,
In the mind ever burning,
Never sick, never old, never dead,
From itself never turning.

> Sir Walter Raleigh:
> *As You Came from the Holy
> Land*

31.

The coppery-tailed trogon may be the most spectacular
and rare bird to enter our country along the Mexican
border. *Trogon elegans*'s brilliantly colorful appearance leads you to expect a nightingale's song, but he
disappoints; his call resembles that of a hen turkey.
This plebian feature is offset by an unique one: the toe
position, unusual in that the first and second toes are
turned backward.

Norah put down her pen. Rainbow Prince, Chico had
called him. How surprised she'd been to glimpse tenderness
in a feared Apache. Mind returning to her subject, she
continued with her first treatise; the prestigious institution in
Washington, D.C., to which she had sent information over
the past several years, had requested it.

The tail is long and broad, the rectrices occasionally
being squared at the tip; they are often overhung by
long tail-coverts. I examined a specimen (dead from
natural causes) and found a soft, loosely attached
plumage with no down; the bird frequents the tropics
and does not winter in Arizona, so perhaps down is not
needed for protection from the elements. I also noticed
loosely seated contour-feathers in very delicate skin;
these come off by the scores at a touch.

In J. Gould's second edition of his *Monograph*
(1875) he divides sixty-some species in the world into
seven genera and—

She glanced up to see her new foreman waiting at the entrance to the study. "What is it, Nelson?" she asked with mild annoyance.

"Sorry, Miz Martin, but it's mighty important."

She leaned back, cool, competent, and disciplined, accustomed to emergencies, ready to make decisions. She fastened her eyes on the man, waiting, not judging. John Smith had ridden out the day after Eli raped her, a serious loss for which she held her husband responsible. This new foreman had come highly recommended; he was cow-wise but still had to prove himself loyal to Norah's outfit.

"Spit it out," she said with a smile.

When he cleared his throat, a prominent Adam's apple bobbed. "I think Mr. Martin's burnin' the EM brand on Mariposa calves."

"*What?*" She jumped to her feet, knocking the chair over. "You must be mistaken!"

He bridled, not yet accustomed to working for a woman. "Know what I seen, ma'am."

"All right, I believe you. Saddle my Arabian, I'm heading for the EM. How many calves did you find? Where?" They discussed the problem while walking toward the corral, Norah's temper heating up with every step. As if she didn't have trouble enough.

The cattle business had declined since Geronimo and his people had at last surrendered to an unarmed Lieutenant Gatewood on August 25, 1886, just about a year ago. Twenty percent of the entire Army had been involved in Apache warfare on the Arizona frontier; with most of those troops now assigned elsewhere in the country, beef sales had plummeted. It was a relief to all that the entire Chiricahua nation had been settled in Florida; that they languished and died from heat and humidity at Fort Marion seemed to be of minor importance. Norah and many others thought it a blot on the national honor, though, that Apache scouts had been incarcerated along with those they had helped the Army hunt down—surely their bravery, tenacity, and fidelity were ashes in their mouths. And what, Norah wondered sadly, had happened to Rose? She must be dead after the relentless battle waged against the bands with whom she'd chosen to ally herself.

"Oh, almost forgot, Miz Martin. Soldier dropped this letter off." The foreman gave it to her and started to bridle Kehilan. "Gosh, hope it ain't bad news, ma'am!" She'd turned white as milk then scarlet as her geraniums at the sight of the El Paso postmark.

"A note from an old friend, that's all. Hurry up, will you? I want to get this over with. And bring the men." She folded the letter and stuck it in her shirt pocket.

"Yes, ma'am." It was common knowledge the Martins were always at each other's throats, especially since she'd lost their baby. The boss lived at the mansion with her kids while her husband stayed on the EM. Kinda too bad. Went to show bein' rich didn't mean bein' happy.

Norah tensed as they neared his great house. Why did they tear at each other this way? She had forgiven him the rape long ago, but had asked for a divorce on grounds of incompatibility. Eli had flatly refused to give her up, despite the fact they were no more than business partners now.

The Mariposa had its share of top-grade hands who handled six-shooters and rifles expertly, but Norah refused to hire any man unwilling to abide by rules: no gambling, drinking, or fighting. Faithful to their outfits, her crew and Eli's weren't any friendlier than the estranged couple. She spoke to Nelson now, riding stirrup to stirrup. "I don't want any trouble. See to it." She operated under an unwritten law Jim had followed; the foreman, or wagon boss, gave the orders, not the owner; many Americans, so much more independent than vaqueros, wouldn't work for a ranch unless that was the case.

Eli waited for her, leaning on the hitching rack. He was heavier in the paunch now, the once-clear eyes muddied by alcohol during the past year. "Hello, Norah. Long time no see."

She dismounted and approached, wasting no time. "I hear you're branding my cows with the EM iron. I won't have it, Eli."

He grunted. "Who told you that?"

"My foreman."

"New, ain't he?" He studied the hard men who backed her up.

"New or not, he knows his business. Why are you doing this? Just to get my goat? You ought to know by now I won't stand for anything like that."

She sniffed the shaving lotion he wore that reminded her of how immaculate he'd been when they were living together. He had tried to get back in her good graces, but Norah had made up her mind not to have him back. To be fair, one swallow didn't make a summer—the rape had been an unpremeditated thing—but shortly thereafter he had started to hit the bottle, which she couldn't abide. There had been rumors of women, too, although she had given them no credence until recently when the children reported a girl at the EM. It was as if her dwindling love had torn away his defenses, leaving him vulnerable to weaknesses he had once been able to control.

Now Eli came around the post and took her arm. Norah stiffened. "Oh, don't be like that. Let's have a brandy and talk about this. Your man's wrong, I'm tellin' you." She allowed him to escort her inside. The house reeked of Mexican cooking and a musky cologne.

"Still have your 'housekeeper'?" she asked with cool scorn.

"Lupita? Nah, got me a real chile pepper this time." Eli poured brandy into snifters and brought one to her. "Had a blue-eyed chile pepper once, but she lives like a nun now." He peered mockingly over the rim of his glass. "Sits over there, I hear, writin' about birds, dryin' up like a fall leaf."

"It's simply none of your business what I do on the Mariposa. And if you don't get rid of that woman, the children aren't coming here again. Listen, I didn't ride over here to argue. What about those EM brands showing up on my calves?"

He nipped the end of a cigar and spat. "Don't know anything about it. Why brand yours? Got plenty of my own. And mavericks belong to the range they're found on. You know that." He lighted the cigar. "Far as gettin' your goat, no, I don't want to do that. You know how I feel about you."

Eli had never lied to her. She'd give him the benefit of that. "Think it might be a mischief maker on your crew?"

"Better not be, by God! I'll horsewhip him where he lives!"

Tossing off the brandy, Norah put the glass down. "I was hasty. I apologize."

He coughed, a phlegmy sound, and poured another drink. "Stay awhile? Maybe have dinner?"

Norah hesitated. There had been good times, laughter, and camaraderie here. He lived alone now except for the woman; Gretchen and her husband were in Phoenix, where they raised hay; Mary, the cook, had died; the animal orphans had matured and been returned to the wild, not to be replaced. Only the mice remained to comfort him, including a fierce and carnivorous grasshopper mouse that slept in his shirt pocket. "I'm afraid not. I have work to do. Another time."

He shrugged, gazing into the liquor and swirling it. "Too bad."

"Don't forget what I said about the children," she reminded him sternly. Not waiting for an answer, she joined her crew waiting outside. Norah mounted, spun her horse on a dime, and cantered away, more or less satisfied that her husband was innocent of wrongdoing. Pigeonholing the branding problem for future action, her mind turned to the letter and what it might mean to her.

When Norah boarded the night train at Willcox, she noticed that the stationmaster was an old drinking buddy of

Eli's; no doubt the man would make sure Eli knew his wife had gone to El Paso, sneaking off in the dark instead of taking a day train. At this point, however, she didn't care. What she did with her life now was her own business, no one else's.

Maybe Eli had been hurt beyond reckoning by her confession that she loved Mason, but she'd been hurt, too, by their quarrels, the awkward situations arising from his drunkenness, and maybe most of all by his infidelity, which humiliated her before the Vista Valley families. He had turned their existence into a farce and made his bed—let him lie in it until he gave her the divorce she wanted.

Norah settled next to a window, removing her gloves and hat for the hours ahead. The train swayed and the wheels sounded like tiny hoofs on sun-baked earth: clockety-clock, clockety-clock. Like all lovers en route to clandestine rendezvous, she was scourged by anticipation, intense longing, shame, guilt, and a purpose that would brook no barrier.

Her reasons for meeting Mason were complex, far more than a tumble in the sheets. But it boiled down to adultery—bald, brutal word. Norah shuddered. God forgive her for being unfaithful, but she had to be with him who was—had ever been—her life. Star-crossed lovers they were, doomed to be apart, searching for joy in sorrow, surcease in despair, peace in loneliness.

"Coffee, madame?" The conductor offered a steaming cup.

"Thank you! That will hit the spot."

He'd seen her on horseback in Willcox wearing those scandalous pants, directing cowpunchers who goaded her cattle into cars for shipment to alfalfa country near Phoenix or to slaughterhouses. Tonight she was the perfect lady in a dark-gray twill traveling cloak lined with maroon silk to match her dress. The hat in her lap was smart and deceptively simple: a gray felt top hat around which a gray-and-pink scarf was wound. The conductor, who had an eye for clothes, approved the bustle, far more conservative than most, and whistled at her magnificent gold necklace with its opals, emeralds, and pearls.

"Pardon, madame, but may I suggest you put that necklace in the baggage-car safe? It's too much of a temptation to wear in the open."

"I appreciate your concern, but I do believe I'll wear it." He had a point though, she decided, concealing it under her dress so the only jewelry visible were jet earrings and a small watch pinned to her waist. The necklace grew warm, and she wondered about the Aztec woman who'd worn it centuries ago. Had it been a gift of love then, as it had been to her shortly after Andrew's birth?

She clenched the reticule with Mason's letter. *A year that's been a century, darling Norah. I can't stand never seeing you again when I can think of nothing but you. My marriage—God, what a laugh!—is killing my soul. I need you so! Come to me on the tenth of September. Save me—*

Save me! How miserable he must be! More so than she, for the children were her salvation. Optimistic, cheerful Andrew, ever ready to try anything. Rachel, prim, fastidious, and critical. Grace—dear little Grace!—trotting after the cook on plump legs, entranced with cooking and baking. Chan Lee and Endicott, bachelor fathers, were caring for them while she was on this trip.

Trip? An odyssey rather, a searching until she reached the journey's end in Mason's arms where it all began. It had been almost twelve years since he took pity on a dying girl in the night, held her to him, urged her to sleep and gather strength for the coming of day. They had been destined for one another from the beginning. Out of all the people in the world, what mysterious force had brought them together? She made knots in the scarf. Why was the train so *slow*?

Mason met her at the station, running down the platform to seize and hold her as she stepped from the car. They said nothing, immersed in each other. Finally, Mason released her and took the suitcase. As if in a spell they walked toward a carriage stand, where Norah chose the best-kept of the sorry nags. At a luxurious but discreet hotel they checked in separately, arranging to meet for dinner. It was unspoken they'd not go to bed right away, though each was on fire to do so. They'd journey instead through a courtly foreplay of dressing, dinner, and dancing, their discipline both punishment and delicious anticipation.

Norah wore a dinner gown, a smoke-blue velvet with folds of flesh-colored lace and coral roses across the bodice and trailing to the floor; it was the perfect foil for the Aztec necklace and earrings. She swept forward eagerly to meet him at the dining room entrance. She'd treasure this moment when his eyes widened with profound admiration and love. "You're my dream come true," Mason murmured over her gloved hand. "We're here, love. Here together." Her fingers clenched his, and his eyes glowed.

The maître d'hotel escorted them to a table, held Norah's chair, waved imperiously to waiters. She glanced around with a shyness that Mason found enchanting. Could anyone tell they were lovers? The Lord forbid, did anyone recognize her? She was taken aback to find men studying her openly and gorgeously gowned women smiling in an odd way. One couple lifted champagne glasses in salute and laughed.

A poignant knowledge dawned on her. "Mason. What kind of hotel is this?"

Anxiety tightened the bearded features. "I was afraid someone you know might see you if we went to an uptown hotel. Someone you'd done business with. This is a very expensive hotel and—"

"—these are kept women and philanderers." The thrill of being with him lessened.

He flushed, then drained his glass before confirming her suspicions. "And we are lost souls the same as they. Forgive me. I thought this best. Beggars, my dear, can't be choosers." He leaned forward, earnest and regretful.

"Surely you know it's no slur. Not on the mother of my son!"

Norah lifted her glass. The company of the wicked and unwise had an unsettling effect. Was she, in fact, no better than they? Well, she'd taken the plunge, why the devil not enjoy it to the hilt? "You did the right thing. Here we can blend into the crowd. A toast, my darling. A toast to the nights to come and the years behind us."

"Most of these women aren't even twenty. But you outshine them all. You're so exquisite I can't take my eyes off you for a second."

"Mason, you're embarrassing me. People are looking." Norah fluttered the fan, cooling her face. He laughed and settled back to order their meal.

When dinner was over, Norah sighed with satisfaction. "I haven't eaten much the last few days because"—she cleared her throat—"because I've been sick with love for you."

The orchestra was playing a waltz, and other couples swirled past, skirts and coattails flying. Mason pulled back her chair. "Do you know we've never danced before?" They glided onto the floor with mindless bliss, easily falling into the same rhythm. Although she had danced little, it was natural to yield to the guidance flowing from his hand and body to hers. At last they stopped of one accord. "Coffee and brandy, darling?"

"Please." She sat down, arranging the velvet train about her feet. "Did you know Talleyrand liked his coffee black as the devil, hot as hell, pure as an angel, and sweet as love?"

"You come up with the darndest things. It's all those books you read." They drank and she told him about Eli. Finally he sighed and whispered, "Shall we go?"

Norah panicked and froze. Her face was hot. Ashamed yet exhilarated by the unbridled desire racing through her veins, she rose with dignity, hampered by knees that were shaking. He signed for the check and now folded her arm into his. She jerked with the electric shock of his touch. His features grew taut and he led her from the dining room and up the marble balustrade to her second-floor suite. Once inside they wrapped their arms around each other, momentarily unable to speak. Then he whispered, "I couldn't wait another minute."

"Nor I," she agreed against his lips. The die was cast now. *She wanted him, oh, how she wanted him!* They undressed each other with feverish haste, fell upon the bed, and made love with the hunger of ascetics fallen and helpless before the onslaught of their appetites. She was almost virginal, offering herself so he might teach her once again what their bodies, mouths, and hands once understood. Paradoxically, Norah felt wanton, aroused by the dark pleasures being practiced in other rooms.

"This isn't all that I love about you. You know that, don't you?" He smoothed hair away from her face. "You're like the water of a river when the sun shines on it, and it sparkles and shimmers, forever changing and yet always the same."

"Thank you for saying that." She touched the scar on his forehead. "Does it still hurt?"

"Only when I'm under pressure. Know what I've done? I'm a lawman of sorts again. I ride with Colonel Emilio Kosterlitski of the Rurales. They're rogues and bandits, most of them, with officers who are the cream of the Mexican Army. But, God, I hate it! I feel so sorry for the peons under the heel of government, church, *and* military."

"Then why do it?" Norah remembered vividly how much his badge had meant to him.

"Because I can't live off my father-in-law now that I know who I am. And I go out of my mind—God forgive me—being with my wife all the time." Conscience— honor—responsibility: his bedrock and his millstones.

Norah traced his mouth with a fingertip. "I'm sorry. Truly I am. For you, for her, and the children. There are children?"

Mason shook his head. "Four miscarriages. And she grows more strange after each one. Even her father now admits he did me a grave injustice." He cupped Norah's breast, kissed it. "I should feel ashamed, but I don't. Soledad is—is a little wild animal."

"Then why make love to her?" Norah ran the flat of her hand down his hard belly.

"Let's not talk about it." Mason plunged hands deep in her hair, his mouth claiming hers. And this time their passion was like an earthquake. Tremors racked Norah, and she opened to him so her organs dissolved and his love consumed her like lava.

Waiting for the train, they huddled on a bench, bruised and spent but radiant. "Meet me before Christmas, Norah."

"Oh, I can't!" But they knew she would.

He held her close. "Don't decide now. But I'll be waiting at the hotel on the fifteenth."

"All aboard, please. All aboard!"

Mason's face turned haggard. "Jesus save me, I can't let you go! We only had two days!"

"You must. The children need me. The Mariposa needs me."

"More than you need me," he concluded, angry yet understanding.

"Never, never, never!" She balanced on the step, cloak moving in the slight wind of the train's increasing speed. "I love you! Don't ever forget how much I love you!" He ran alongside while she hurried to sit down, throwing a last kiss when he reached the end of the platform. Had passengers not been watching avidly, Norah would have broken down. Christmas! An eon away.

"Boss, found out who's been puttin' the EM on your wife's cows." Eli's top hand brandished a crude iron. "Funniest thing. A bunch a raggedy Injuns. Thought they were all in Florida. Had a woman with 'em, a real good-looker. I ain't so sure but it was that Apache what knifed Joel Fullerton."

Eli sealed a letter. "Wonder what the devil they're up to. Kill any of 'em?"

"Nope, took us by surprise. Scooted up into the hills. We'll keep an eye out from now on. Want I take that letter when I ride in for supplies?"

"Yeah, it goes to Philadelphia." The cowboy took it and strode out, spurs jingling faintly. Eli tapped a pencil on the edge of his teeth. He had a big surprise for Norah. She might fool others by pretending she'd gone to El Paso on business, but he knew she went to rendezvous with Mason Fletcher. Had been for almost three years. He'd had just about enough of this crap. He was going to take care of the bitch. As the word fled across his brain, his heart lurched with love but then turned back to stone.

The housekeeper strolled by, and Eli grabbed her around the waist. "Oh, stop it, man. You a rabbit?"

He pushed her away, calling her names. He had grown to dislike women, using them only for sexual release. Sometimes in the night he'd start thinking of his wife in bed and other pictures clear as paintings appeared: Norah's eyes shining with pleasure or solemn with thought while she worked on bird manuscripts; Norah stirring the laundry, ringlets on her moist forehead; Norah trying on a hat before the rosewood mirror; Norah pulling him down to her at night with that low delicious chuckle; Norah soothing a sick child, or galloping alongside, smiling and talking. Oh, Christ, he'd screwed up, all right, treating her like a whore. Now she'd turned into one. He hated her—*hated* her like poison! God damn her to hell! Eli poured a big whisky and cursed to envision her in another man's arms. The man she'd loved from the start, still loved when she married the cavalry officer and when she became Mrs. Martin. Eli shook himself like a horse coming out of a creek. He had lots to do before her train got in tomorrow night.

Norah woke with a bad taste in her mouth, coughing from the soot and gritty dust in the railroad car. She bought a wilted cheese sandwich and hot tea from a boy hacking refreshments. This last visit with Mason had been so exhausting and depressing she hardly wanted to think about it. Since the fall of 'eighty-seven, she'd endured sixteen-hour round trips, almost memorized the dreary New Mexico landscape, and, worst of all, lied to those she loved about cattle buying and real estate investment trips. It had to stop, for it had become obvious she and Mason had no future together. She had even made the supreme sacrifice of offering to sell the Mariposa and move away with him and the children. It didn't matter where, just so they were together.

Mason had refused, agony glinting in the honey-colored eyes. He couldn't desert his wife, who was at last, to the joy of the entire family, carrying a child to full term. Nor could he abandon the old hacendado, who had failed recently and depended on his son-in-law to keep his empire from disintegrating. He'd dropped to his knees to kiss the hem of her skirt. "I know what selling the ranch means to you. I'm—I'm humbled to think you'd even consider it, to know your love is so—ah, Norah, say you understand why I can't go. Tell me you do. You'll be the world to me until my dying breath. But I can't do it!"

"You think then that I'm so strong I can go on living the empty life I do, existing without you?" She also fell to her knees, so that they faced and clung to each other.

"Somehow—God knows how!—you must be." They made love then, half-weeping, their emotions so intense Norah fainted. After regaining consciousness, she decided not to meet him again, no matter how strong the heartache of separation. Carleton's obsession had killed him—she would not let hers destroy her.

When the train pulled into the little cow-town station, Norah was deeply relieved to be home, to climb into the buggy with its warm blanket and ten-gauge shotgun and head for the Mariposa in moonlight. She was afraid of nothing, they said, steel under velvet, but as the horse trotted south, Norah was deeply uneasy. She tried to cast it off, blaming it on fatigue and the pain she and Mason had suffered.

Once at the ranch she unharnessed the horse, turned it out in the corral, then hastened to the big house brooding in the darkness. I rattle around in these thirty rooms like dice in a cup, she thought, thankful for lamps Endicott had left burning. He slept in the basement servants' quarters now, while the children had rooms on the same floor as her bedroom. She trudged upstairs, dragging her cloak on the floor. Peeking in on Andrew and Rachel, she saw mounds under rumpled covers and decided not to disturb them. At the entrance to Grace's room, however, Norah heard crying. With a sigh she entered and gathered the girl in her arms. "What's wrong, Grace? A bad dream? Momma's home. Momma won't go away again."

The child knuckled her eyes. "Everybody's gone. I was afraid here alone."

Norah rocked her. "I love you. There's nothing to be afraid of." She wondered why Andrew had not come to quiet her, for he acted as Grace's protector. He was probably sleeping hard because of a busy, physical day; he worked beside the cowboys, anxious to prove his manhood at thirteen. "Want to sleep with me?" Grace nodded vigorously and wound her arms about Norah's neck, chuckling with glee when she was dumped on the bed hard enough to bounce.

Lighting a lamp and giving the girl her gloves to try on, Norah undressed down to petticoats and camisole. Suddenly there was a movement near the fireplace and Norah whirled, seizing and cocking the gun that always rested on the bedside table. A man rose from the chair. "*Eli!* What's the idea of scaring me that way? And how dare you enter my room unless I say so?" She put the gun down and hurriedly donned a wrapper, not liking his hungry gaze.

"My, my, ain't we unfriendly. Been too chummy with your lover to be nice to your husband?"

"Get out of here. I'm tired, and Grace has been frightened by something. Probably you. Come back in the morning, if you must." She was too used to him to notice the danger signs—twitching hands, bloodshot eyes, sweating face and underarms, protuberant veins on temple and neck. She only noticed the whiskey on his breath and stale smoke on his clothes and wished him gone.

"Nope, I'm here to stay."

"The devil you are!" she flared, eyes blazing with anger.

"You want to know where your kids are, you better be nice to me. *Real* nice!"

Her heart missed a beat. "What have you done, Eli? *What—have—you—done?* If you've hurt them, I'll see you hang from the nearest tree, so help me God!"

"Aw, you know me better'n that. I love those kids." He stepped closer, a great brown bulldog whose head settled into heavy jowls. "But you ain't no fit mother, so I sent them to Philadelphia."

"Since when are you judge and jury of my life? I ought to have my boys work you over."

Eli snorted. "Yeah? Take a look down there."

Norah edged to the window. Below in flickering lantern light every member of her household and crew stood with hands high in front of Eli's men, who were holding guns. Norah's mind raced. She forced herself to breathe slowly, to clear mind and spirit for battle. The iron will lifted her chin and slowed the runaway beat of her pulse. "All right. You've got the whip hand. What do you really want?" She sat on the bed and hugged Grace.

Eli grinned and wiped his mouth with the palm of his hand. She had class! "What I want is what I've always wanted—you." He coaxed her, drunk enough to be playful or cruel. "I ain't so bad. Never was. We could have good times again. Even sail over to Europe, see them statues 'n things."

"I'm not going to talk about it. You and I were all talked out long ago. I'm putting Grace to bed, and in the morning

I'm heading for Philadelphia to get my children back. You
dared take your anger at me out on them! Your lousy
revenge! Sending them away among strangers!" Loathing
closed her throat and she coughed.

"Grandparents ain't strangers. And the kids thought the
train ride was some punkins. Now, Grace, you go on to bed
in your own room, okay?" The child came to him
trustingly, for he had always been gentle. "Kiss," she
demanded. He complied, giving her a light slap on the
bottom. She exacted a second kiss from a distraught Norah
and walked out, yawning.

Eli sprang to the door, turned the key, and slipped it into a
pocket. "Oh, no, mister, we're not going through *that*
again. Oh, no!" Norah went for her gun but he leaped, lithe
as a youth, catching her wrist, catapulting them onto the
bed, which skidded into a corner. They fell heavily onto the
floor. He wrestled her weapon away, threw it out through the
window, and burrowed a stubbled face between her breasts.
She tried to knee him and he slapped her cheek hard enough
to make her cry out. His hate and her helplessness excited
him. She had to be raped, thrown, tied, and branded.

"Ain't this nice? Remember, last time was on the floor,
too." He slid a hand under her skirts and tried to insert it
between her thighs.

She struggled frantically, scratching, slapping, and biting. Then Norah realized her fighting only inflamed him, so
she forced herself to lie still. "Eli," she said calmly, hiding
her perturbation behind reasonable words, "this isn't going
to change things. It's been too long and we're different
people now. Please let me go before something happens
we'll both regret."

He grunted. "The hell with that shit. I'm gonna have
you."

Norah sighed as she might at a child's obstinacy. "Well,
for Heaven's sake, get it over with, then. But you ought to
know by now you'll never be the man Mason Fletcher is."

His whole body seemed to swell in size above her so her

vision filled with the fire in his eyes, the purplish-red flood beneath his skin, the grimace of rage and humiliation twisting his face. Eli got to his feet awkwardly and yanked her up by the hair. Sexual desire had soured beneath her insult. Hatred, until now diluted by true love, distilled into bitter wrath that surged through him. "You ain't gonna have another brat of his! I'll see you bleed it out on the carpet, you whore!" He punched her in the stomach and hurled her across the room. She smashed into the wall and slid dazed to the floor.

"Eli, don't—" She'd made a fatal mistake thinking she could handle him in this mood. He approached on unsteady legs, and she threw a stool that struck him on the chest, eliciting nothing but a laugh. Again he brought her to a standing position by hauling on her hair, and she screamed with pain. Outside someone shouted and gunfire shattered the quiet.

Where was her bag with the derringer in it? He slapped her face back and forth, back and forth. Her lips split; cartilage in her nose crunched. Norah turned icy with fear. *Good God, he was going to kill her!* She had to get to the other side of the room where she'd dropped that bag. She managed to grab an andiron and poke at his genitals. He released her hair to cover himself with his hands, and she hit him on the head hard enough to send him to his knees. But he was not too hurt to clutch her ankle when she ran past, causing her to fall headlong. He moaned in pain and drunken confusion. Norah reached up for the table lamp and pressed the hot glass to his hand. He yelled and let her go, sucking burned flesh. "You bitch, you bitch! You'll pay for that!"

Gasping for breath, shaking as if she had palsy, Norah fumbled inside her bag, found the short-barreled pistol, pulled back the hammer, and pointed it. Numbed by shock, she forgot the lamp was still in one hand. "Back off, Eli! I don't want to hurt you."

He lurched to his feet, pushing himself up on his

knuckles like an ape. He roared with amusement, big teeth gleaming in the soft light. "*Hurt* me? You can't even kill a damned bird, let alone a man. What makes you think you can hurt *me*? Gimme that pop gun." Eli made a pass and Norah stumbled backward, found herself in a corner. Eyes hard, mouth compressed with intent to maul and batter, confident of her womanly weakness when it came to death, he lunged at her. Hands that could snap a calf's neck like a twig went for her throat.

"*Eli, don't! For God's sake—*" She fired straight for the heart, shooting to kill, for shooting to injure meant being beaten to a pulp, and she was afraid for her life. The large-caliber bullet blasted his aorta to jelly; at the same instant his hand struck the lamp she was holding and knocked it to the floor. It broke on impact, flames darting out and setting fire to the draperies. Norah went down under him, cracking her head against the wall.

Groggily, she pushed at him. "Eli, get up! *Get up!* The drapes are on fire!" She shoved him away with the last remnant of her strength. Had she killed him? Of course she had. She seldom missed and at such short range—Norah shook him, tried to take a pulse, but her fingers were too clumsy. He stared at the ceiling, jaw slack as if in protest at being bested by a woman.

Voices sounded in the hallway, and the door creaked with pressure from without. The fire had spread rapidly by the time Endicott and John Smith burst into the room. They rushed to her, for she was almost overcome by smoke. Endicott picked her up in his arms, shouting for the other man to see if Eli was alive. "Nope, dead as a doornail! Look at her face! If she hadn't killed him, I would've!"

Her one-time foreman kicked the corpse before running from the room. That bastard had caused her trouble before. Good riddance. Smith, accompanied by his son and outlaw friends, had ridden in with hopes of quietly watering their horses; instead they had encountered a ranch under siege. Surprising Eli's crew, he and his gang had freed the

Mariposa men. His old job on the Mariposa had been a last chance; after quitting, he had reverted back to form, stealing horses and cattle—not from her, of course—and robbing an occasional bank.

"Grace! Grace!" Now Norah roused enough to call for the girl.

"Don't worry. She's with Chan Lee. Now hold still 'fore we fall down these stairs."

Outside, Eli's men reached for the sky, wanting no part of the desperadoes who had the drop on them. After being told that their boss was dead, they were allowed to ride out. John Smith and his gang then vanished to hole up somewhere near the Mariposa, while Norah watched the mansion burn to the ground. Birds in nearby trees fled in dismay and animals in the corral spoke restlessly of the smoke in their nostrils. The fire had been too hot for the men to retrieve Eli's body, and she was sorry about that. She shivered and pulled a blanket about her shoulders. Her mind reeled at what she had done—had been forced to do in self-defense. Thank God the children hadn't seen it.

The flames crackled as they consumed the house and the dreams it once represented. Eli had called it a mausoleum and hadn't been far wrong—it was his funeral pyre. Norah prayed for his soul and for youth and hope gone with the winds of time. A strange combination of emotions filled her in the smoky night: mourning, regret, relief, guilt, rejoicing—and a loneliness that crushed her like a vise.

32.

"He is a proper Spaniard, is he not?" Don Diego beamed at the grandson nestled in his daughter's arms.

Mason nodded, lips soft at the sight of his child: great black eyes, black hair, and olive skin, without a trace of Soledad's fair coloring. Only time would tell, he thought wearily, whether the boy was tainted with her madness. At least she had not delivered a monster. He knew he could not have borne that.

The señora bustled in to shoo them out. She was in her element, for here the authoritarian husband had neither place nor influence. Men planted seed, a simple and pleasurable procedure, but it was woman who blossomed, carried, and produced fruit of that seed—this was her eternal mastery. Mason bent to kiss his wife in whose white face the turquoise eyes snapped with excitement. "I love you," he said, without deceit. For he did love her as he might any vulnerable creature in his power.

She clutched his lapel. "You are pleased?"

"Of course! How could I not be? Have you not given us a son?"

The girl sank back with a calculating expression and lifted the infant to her doting mother. "Take him. I wish to sleep now and regain my strength." She gazed at her husband with open hunger before closing her eyes.

The men touched the infant's hair reverently, then strolled into the patio to be served wine and tiny tostadas heaped with mashed black beans, onion, tomato, and avocado. Mason sat in the sunshine, mind deliberately blank, turning his glass by its stem. He had learned to discipline himself, to flood his mind with a thousand trivialities. He stifled discouragement and disappointment, ignored the intellect starved for English books, newspapers, and conversation, blocked out the memories of hours with Norah. Only at night did his heart and mind take control and torture him with what might have been.

"You have not been to El Paso recently, my son." His father-in-law peered at Mason from the corner of his eye.

"No. It is a long ride."

"She no longer comes to meet you, then?"

Mason glanced at him sharply, face turning red. "What do you mean?"

"Ah, are we not men of the world? I have my little sweethearts in the city. I know of the American señorita. I have eyes and ears. And once I saw you together."

"You never mentioned it." Had they been spied on? He stiffened with fury. Hadn't it been bad enough to have to take Norah to that particular hotel?

Don Diego put a conciliatory hand on his shoulder. "Because I understood."

"How could you?" Mason cried in agony, pulling away and jumping to his feet. "How could you *ever* know what it is to lose years out of your life? Be chained to a crazy girl? And now, God forgive me, be trapped by an innocent child? *Understood?* Jesus Christ!"

The older man so shriveled within the theatrical clothes he affected that he appeared to be in masquerade. "At first I did not care about you. All I saw was a husband for my poor Soledad. I did wrong, but I did it in the name of love. I cannot apologize for that. But I have prayed many times for your forgiveness."

They stared at each other. The caged wild birds nearby whistled and chattered, oblivious to the men's misery. "You never *asked* for it," Mason accused.

"I do now. I do now." The hacendado bowed his head in repentance, gnarled hands clasped between the knees.

"When I die you will be one of the richest men in Mexico. I have seen to that. It was to be my penance—I do it now from love and respect for you."

Mason sighed, relenting. "All right, old man, we're both stuck with a bad bargain. And your heart's in the right place. I know that." He gulped down the wine, wheeled, and left the patio. In his room he opened a bottle of whiskey. After taking a hearty slug he wiped his mouth with his forearm. He hadn't been drunk for months, but today was a special occasion. How often did you bring new life into being? Wasn't he the father of a handsome, sturdy son? He slumped onto the bed, shirt gaping and hair uncombed. What more could a man want out of life? Several things: Norah—Andrew—his own country—freedom.

What a silly fool Mason Fletcher was, that sorry SOB who glared back at him from the mirror. Any other man would have ridden out, thumbed his nose at the whole clan after the lousy trick played on him, taken a chance on shooting it out with Montaña and his vaqueros. Then again they might let him go now that he'd done his husbandly duty. And what if they did? He'd still be a married man with nothing to offer his Norah. His—what a laugh. There hadn't been a letter for months. And no wonder. They'd both seen the handwriting on the wall. Mason drank thirstily and emptied a third of the bottle. At least he didn't have to go to bed with Soledad tonight. He shuddered with distaste. Faraway coyotes keened like voices from the past, and he longed to sleep under the stars alone and unfettered, to inhale wood smoke and pine, have a belly full of cowboy chow. He wanted to be up-to-date on happenings in Arizona and the United States, longed to use his brain again.

"What's the use, here's to honor and duty," Mason muttered in a bitter voice. "And here's to conscience." Mason finished off the whiskey and hurled the bottle at the mirror, nodding with solemn satisfaction when it broke and showered onto the floor. "There, you son of a bitch, now I don't have to look at your sanctimonious face." He collapsed on the bed and with a curse descended into restless sleep.

Ostriches minced across their compound like gigantic feather dusters on legs. Norah and Grace grinned at their haughty mien and at the chicks running behind, gray two-toed feet working frenziedly.

"Well, Gretchen, they are a sight, just as you wrote. I had no idea they were so droll! And imagine one three-pound egg being equivalent to thirty-three hen eggs. I can't believe it!"

Her friend regarded the birds with a raised eyebrow. "If only they weren't so profitable—I prefer to raise alfalfa."

"And children!" Norah smiled fondly at the blond, blue-eyed brood that ringed them, awed by their mother's guest in expensive fabrics and smelling of roses. "Go with them, Grace. They want to show you the new kittens in the barn." After they scampered off, Norah's attention returned to the ostriches. She had invested ten thousand dollars in fifteen pairs of breeding birds and realized a hundred percent gross profit in less than two years from selling chicks; the adults' feathers sold for seventy-five dollars a pound and were used on hats and garments all over the world.

Gretchen's husband considered ostriches a form of livestock superior in some ways to cattle: they ate but four pounds of alfalfa a day compared to the thirty to sixty consumed by cows; they required much less water; and they sold for much more—a hundred dollars for a chick and eight hundred for a four-year-old. "They kick like mules, the big buggers—forward, not backward. And look out when you cut their plumes! They can jump six feet high, grow to be eight feet tall, and weigh three hundred to four hundred pounds. The book says they run sixty miles an hour, faster than any animal on earth!"

"I have a hunch you like them more than you let on," Norah teased.

"How can you like a bird bigger than you are, with ears

in the back of his head, and a brain the size of a pea?"
Gretchen protested. Her eyes twinkled as they walked back
to the house for coffee and kuchen. "They are funny, I
admit."

The women settled in the handsomely furnished parlor.
"You've done well, Gretchen," Norah said with approval.
"You and Ernst will prosper even more now that Phoenix is
the capital. The summers here are awfully hot, though."
She leaned back with cup and saucer in hand, admiring the
wine, beige, and blue color scheme and the welcome
atmosphere.

"*Ja*, we have worked hard. Another piece of kuchen?
No? You are so skinny I can see you don't eat sweets much.
You are sure you won't stay the night, Norah? It will be so
good to talk about old times."

"I'd love to, but the train for Tucson leaves at three
twenty-five this afternoon. Grace starts spring semester in
two days. I want to get her settled in before I go back to the
ranch."

"Is so much education good for a girl? To be a wife—"

"She wants to 'learn everything in the world'! And I
want her to be well rounded and ready for the new century.
To be her own person because she has a head on her
shoulders."

"Give the child time to be a child." Gretchen bit her lip.
"I'm sorry, *liebchen*. You pour all your love into her
because you miss the others."

Norah paled and put fingertips to her tightly laced
midriff. "I miss them like something vital from inside me.
Do you know I went to Philadelphia, and they wouldn't let
me see my own children? Barred me from entering their
home? It almost killed me." She straightened, eyes cold
and distant. "My lawyers are working on it. The Beattys
have no right to do this. I'll hound them until they give in.
What Eli did was vicious and cruel."

"Now that Eli is dead, surely they—"

Norah waved her hand. "Makes no difference. They

believed Eli's story that I was an unfit mother. He even told my lawyers I probably murdered my husband and then set the house on fire to conceal the 'crime'!"

"But the inquest exonerated you. You had been beaten and threatened. Your nose was broken. Your men were held at gunpoint."

"There was some doubt in the jurors' minds even so, I'm sure of that. All men, of course. After all, the only witness I had was Endicott, who's prejudiced in my favor. John Smith couldn't testify. There are wanted posters out on him." The scar on his neck had surely been from an interrupted hanging. "Nevertheless, the finding was in my favor, thank goodness."

"Ah, this has been worrisome for you. And—Mr. Fletcher? What of him?"

Gazing out the window, Norah fought down the lump in her throat. "We haven't seen each other since last fall. I haven't written—what's the use?—but I had a letter telling me he has a son there now. Gretchen, we really must go! It's been so wonderful seeing you. Tell Ernst I'll be driving at least five thousand young steers up to him for pasturing before I put them on the San Francisco market. Southern Pacific raised tariff rates twenty-five percent to some California destinations, but a lot of us refuse to pay their blackmail. Besides, driving overland is about three dollars a head cheaper than shipping."

"It's a marvel how you know such things! You look as if you care only for fashions and parties." Gretchen fingered the lilac cashmere cloak with black beads and Persian wool cuffs and collar, coveted the lavender silk and jet bonnet. "Do you like being rich?"

"I'd trade it all for him, but I guess it isn't meant to be." The women embraced, kissed, and went outside for Grace. When Norah drove the rented buggy away, her heart was heavy with longing and envy. Money couldn't buy the happiness Gretchen had.

An ostrich followed along the fence with his odd camel-like gait, and the horse stared at him askance and broke into a faster trot. The girl hugged Norah's arm. "Aren't they big silly creatures, Momma?"

"Indeed they are, my dear." Norah looked at Grace closely as she laughed and made clucking noises at the bird. This child of an Apache and a Texas boy was going to be remarkable. Only eight, she was precocious and smart, mastering most subjects with ease and modesty; she also had a quality rare in females in that classmates took to her at once, sensing genuine warmth and sweetness. Grace would want for nothing in worldly goods, but Norah hoped above all that she'd be blessed with true love—for life had little meaning without it.

Mason pulled away in disgust. "That's enough, Soledad. Go to sleep. I have a hundred miles to ride tomorrow. I need my rest."

Her hands wandered over his bare body, pinching, stroking, rubbing. She threw herself on top of him, panting with lust. He turned his head away from her bad breath; it wasn't her fault she had decaying teeth, but the least she might do was chew cloves. Tired as he was, another erection swelled and she chortled. He let her slide down on him, tried to stay firm, and failed. She screeched with anger and slapped him.

"Shut *up*!" Mason knew her cries could be heard throughout the hacienda. Her tirades were nothing new, but it remained a mortifying fact that everyone knew when they were having intercourse.

"Do it again!" she demanded, turning around so her privates were poised in front of his face and his penis rested in her mouth.

"No, no, no. Now, quit it." Lovemaking had deteriorated into vulgar battles, wrestling matches with no tenderness or concern on her part, only constant attack and seldom assuaged hunger. He had long forced himself not to compare their joining to his and Norah's—Mason was afraid he might kill his wife in a fit of madness. She bit him without warning and he howled with pain and rage. He grabbed her by the waist and shoved her off the bed onto the floor. "What in Christ's name do you think you're doing? That was no love bite!" He held himself and rocked in anguish.

She nibbled a handful of hair that streamed over breast and thigh. Were her eyes wilder than usual? Chills knifed through his bowels and, breaking into a cold sweat, he turned up the lamp. Soledad was so lovely—until you stared into those whirlpools of confusion and cunning, aquamarine now as if flooded with seawater. "Oh, honey, what's the matter?" he asked in English. Pity scalded him as well as guilt at his increasingly frequent rejection of her. Resignedly he got out of bed and helped her to her feet, shrinking back to find he had a maniac on his hands. His wife moaned and screamed, struck and kicked, making such noises of hysteria and towering fury that the door burst open to admit Don Diego, his wife, and several servants, all in night-clothes. Their dark eyes bugged at the scene before them.

"What is *wrong*? *Dios,* are you—?"

"Trying to kill her?" Mason gasped. He struggled to bind Soledad with his arms and yet avoid being bitten on the face. He was pallid with shock. "No—I—I think she's— she's gone over the edge."

The mother screamed and her daughter answered with gibberish and shrieks of insane merriment. Saliva drooled down the pretty chin, and she grabbed Mason's hair and yanked with all her considerable strength. "Don Diego! For God's sake!" Mason jackknifed as her knee connected with his genitals. Ordered forward by Don Diego, the servants first crossed themselves, then approached the girl as they might a rabid animal. The hacendado shoved his wife from the room with orders to fetch laudanum and the cords from their bedroom draperies.

While they waited for the tincture of opium, those remaining did not speak. What was there to say? Shadows flickered in the lamplight, and the stench of the mad-woman's involuntary defecation fouled the close air. Soledad stopped fighting and sang strange melodies in a quavery voice; Don Diego recognized them as gypsy airs from Andalusia. His skin pebbled at the eerie voice—she was singing music she had never heard. At last the distraught señora returned. After a large dose of the drug was forced down Soledad's throat, she was wrapped in blankets and bound, then taken to an empty room at the far end of the house.

Completely exhausted and oblivious of his nakedness, Mason lowered himself onto the bed and held his head in shaking hands. Don Diego poured laudanum into a glass and put it beside him. "Drink this, my son. It will make you sleep." His son-in-law failed to respond, and the hacendado trudged away to see to his daughter's welfare and set a guard at his grandson's crib. They would need a wet nurse in the morning, too, for though Soledad had milk, she might hurt the baby. So this was the answer to his prayers, Don Diego mused bitterly. For the first time he spurned his Savior as he passed the chapel door.

Thunder boomed and lightning cracked, and horses sidestepped nervously in their stalls. Wrapped to the eyes in a striped wool serape, Mason lounged against grain bags, smoked, and watched the rain pour down. He had moved out of the house three months ago, unable to endure the pandemonium his wife created, and now ate with bachelor vaqueros and kept occupied with the ranch; he had quit the Rurales, unable to lower himself to their brutality. He saw his frail little son when permitted, and met with Don Diego once a week to discuss business matters. Aside from such brief visits he lived in the barn like a twenty-dollar-a-month cowpoke and finally had privacy, dignity, and peace.

Mason drowsed, pleasantly aware of his warm seat and back, of the familiar smells of horseflesh, dried corn, and leather. The downpour slackened and he wondered about riding to the west arroyo; it probably would flood soon, and a handsome heifer large with calf had been sleeping there. He moaned and pulled his hat brim over his nose but not before extinguishing a Bull Durham cigarette, the American tobacco his only link with home. Cows were savvy; she'd know the flash flood was on its way by the quaking of the sandy creekbed. His conscience jabbed him, and he knew he must make sure the heifer was safe. To a real cowman each cow was as different as people were, and she was a lady and one of his favorites.

He threw a saddle on his swimming horse, one of a string that included a night pony, a running horse for fast trips and occasional racing wagers, the calf roper used at branding time, the cutting horse that separated animals from the bunch, a few dependable all-purpose riding mounts. Mason swung aboard after donning slicker and gloves and was about to ride out when Don Diego stumbled into the stable. He was hatless, his face putty colored.

"*Mason, Mason!*" He leaned against a roof support, winded and anxious. "*She's gone! Mason, she's gone and taken the baby!* The wet nurse is dead, stabbed!"

Mason's head began to ache. "What direction? Where?"

"We don't know! My wife just found the wet nurse in a pool of blood and the crib empty! Sweet Savior, Sweet Savior, help us!" He sank to his knees in manure-saturated mud, brought a rosary from beneath his jacket, and prayed. He still had doubts, but one accepted all the divine intervention one could get.

"Get back in the house, you old fool! You'll catch your death of cold and then what'll your family do?" Mason shouted for the vaqueros and they came running from their humble houses, a few with tortillas still clenched in their teeth. He explained tersely what the trouble was and they saddled up without delay and followed him into the storm.

He tried to put himself in Soledad's mind. Was she just running away from confinement with her human doll? Did she contemplate another murder and then suicide? Did she

even know what she was doing? His stomach churned and a
sour taste rose in his mouth. He spat and in so doing saw a
tiny slipper being trampled beneath his horse's hoofs.
Whistling shrilly, he signaled the men to spread out along
the arroyo's bank. Even as he gestured, they heard the gut-
gripping roar of flash flood rumbling down from water-
logged mountain passes.

A vaquero rode up on his left and pointed to cattle a half
mile away milling uncertainly and lowing with terror. The
animals broke into a run as if galvanized by the lightning
that played along the steers' horns like St. Elmo's fire
dancing on ship spars. Wild-eyed heads tossed and
slammed into each other, left bloody stumps when horns
broke off. Don Diego had so many cattle that one stampede
was of small import; the farthest they'd go was five miles,
and the men who lived on that part of the range would move
them back. Mason decided to let them go. Then his heart
congealed in ice.

Between him and the enormous power of the bellowing,
galloping mass, Soledad darted from behind a huge boulder
that was a landmark on the desert plain. The vaqueros
exclaimed in horror and crossed themselves, spurred their
mounts, tried to turn the panic-stricken herd aside from
woman and child. Mason was ahead of them but it became a
nightmare in which his horse ran in place, Soledad grew
smaller and smaller, the cattle bigger and bigger. He was
conscious of white garments clinging to her body, of the
sodden bundle in her arms, of cows' tongues hanging out,
sharp horns shining with wet.

"Soledad! Soledad! Here!" He leaned down to catch her
about the waist. The vaqueros, unable to stem the tide, yet
loyal to him, whipped their mounts unmercifully, praying
aloud they would not trip and dump their riders before the
hoofed death.

Mason grabbed his wife and had her feet off the ground
when his horse slipped and went down. He heard its neck
crack as he was thrown into the air. Stunned but up on hands

and knees, Mason saw her not far away, smiling at him. The earth moved under his feet. He motioned to the nearest man to rope Soledad with his hundred-foot-long reata and drag her to safety. The brave Mexican reined in, twirled the big lariat, and cast—but Soledad had darted too far away, laughing and beckoning to the racing beasts. Her name stuck in Mason's throat and he scrambled to his feet, seeing the bovine juggernaut envelop her and his son. With strength born of crisis, a vaquero seized him by the upper torso and rode with him out of harm's way.

Mason remained for the memorial service. There was no funeral, for there had been nothing to bury after the maddened cattle passed. The entire family converged on the ranch from different parts of Mexico to comfort their parents and relatives, to mourn Soledad and her infant. Everyone agreed their deaths had been God's will—He knew best. They also offered their hearts to the husband who had never faltered in his duty, an often odious one, to be sure. *Sí,* he was a *verdadero caballero,* a true and chivalrous gentleman who made them wonder if there might not be good qualities in gringos after all.

"I suppose you must go? It will be like losing my right arm," Don Diego mourned.

"I've been here a long time. It's time to go. To build my life elsewhere." Mason fastened Grendel's bridle, departing with the big mule and little more than he brought with him over a decade ago. "Your nephew from Morelia can easily take my place. And he is young and eager to please."

The hacendado took a pack mule's reins. Holding them out, he said, "Once I promised you would be one of the richest men in Mexico. The gold in these panniers will make you the same in your country."

Mason shook his head. "I can't take it. You said when you *died* I'd be—"

"I insist. You earned it. Every single coin." Mason hesitated but a moment before accepting, noticing Don

Diego's old eyes were moist. "We will not meet again, my son?"

"I doubt it." Sadness washed over him at parting from these warmhearted, gentle folk who had shared his life: children, vaqueros, women, and Indian laborers. They had been his friends. Apprehension surfaced also, for he had been isolated here as if on an island, speaking only Spanish, adapting to Mexican rhythms with their subtle, ancient differences from the country across the border.

"Then *vaya con Dios*. May He bless you and may you find happiness with the lady from Arizona."

"Not hardly. She's married," Mason said glumly. "*Gracias*, Don Diego. *Hasta la vista*."

Three men, including the vaquero who had saved his life, escorted him to the border in case of bandits. After sharing a bottle of tequila, Mason rewarded each with a gold coin, his rescuer with two. Their figures dwindled away in the vastness as they headed home while he leaned on the saddle horn, brooding. Finally, he rode on to camp by a stream. He put bacon to fry, shaved off his beard, and trimmed his mustache. Later, tin cup of coffee in hand, he watched bats and nighthawks embroider the poppy, pearl, and amethyst sunset with ebony motifs as they wheeled and darted after insects. Apache kingdom once, held with fire, bullet, and blade, it was serene now.

Mason tried to sleep but was too keyed up with his new freedom. That Norah had not written since their last rendezvous about a year ago pricked him like a cactus needle. He could only surmise that she and Eli had reconciled. And perhaps that had been for the best. She and the children needed a stable life, a man there for them to depend on; Norah must have stopped wanting the impossible. Oh, how it hurt when you loved and that love could not be returned! Mason sat up to roll a smoke, listening to Grendel smack his lips over the grass.

Mason inhaled, then blew out slowly. He had absorbed a certain amount of fatalism from the Mexicans. *Jesucristo*, was he not one of the most fortunate of men? Back in his own country with a fortune of gold, able to do whatever appealed to him? If only he and Norah—well, it wouldn't hurt to ride past the Mariposa, maybe catch a glimpse of her and Andrew at a distance. Then he'd be on his way to California. Eli would never know he'd gone by, but if he did, he'd realize what a lucky man he was. Mason rubbed out his smoke and lay down again. That's what he'd have— one glance at what might have been.

33.

Mugs of hot chocolate in hand, Norah and Grace studied the globe of the world that had been one of the girl's birthday presents. Rain slashed across the window with gravelly sounds. The blaze in the fireplace was comforting, and Norah decided she had been right in not rebuilding the thirty-room mansion but renovating and expanding the old Fullerton house instead. She had not wanted to live on the EM after Eli died and had rented it to an English lord who hungered for Western game trophies.

"Let's start from the beginning, and if you get all the details correct I'll bake you a lemon pie with lots of meringue." She'd do it anyway because it was Grace's ninth birthday, but the girl adored a challenge. Norah wished her own children were here—but it hurt too much to think about that.

"You have her itinerary there?" Grace asked.

"I do. Okay, here we go. Nellie Bly left New York last year the morning of November fourteenth aboard the Hamburg Line steamer—"

"—the *Augusta Victoria* and reached Southampton six days and twenty-one hours later. She took a train to London, another to Calais—where she interviewed Jules Verne—imagine that, Momma! Then a train to Brindisi, Italy, where she boarded a steamer to get to Port Said, Egypt, continued to Ceylon and Singapore, and reached Hong Kong December twenty-second." She paused for breath and a sip of chocolate.

Norah liked to look at her. Tall for her age, a bit skinny and coltishly awkward, black hair curling over a broad forehead and cascading down the back, her mother's dusky apricot skin, features refined by Joel's blood. She must go to school in Switzerland, Norah decided, and when she was of marriageable age the family would tour the continent where Apache heritage would be exoticism, not a disadvantage.

"You're not listening, Momma."

"Sorry. My mind was wandering. Where is Nellie now?"

"Well, she was stuck in Hong Kong five days, so she visited Canton, China, then sailed for Yokohama, Japan, on the twenty-eighth. She reached there January second—no, the third—then sailed on the *Oceanic* the seventh, disembarked in San Francisco the twenty-first, hopped a special train the Atchison, Topeka and Santa Fe put together for her—it averaged seventy-eight and one-tenth miles per hour—and got into Jersey City January twenty-fifth."

"How far did she travel and how long did it take?"

"She said she could go around the world in seventy-five days—faster than Phineas Fogg in 'Around the World in Eighty Days.' She actually went 24,899 miles in seventy-two days, six hours, eleven minutes, and fourteen seconds, and I get a lemon pie!" Grace jumped up and down, eyes sparkling.

Norah applauded, impressed by the girl's recital. "I'll start on it right away, so it'll be ready for supper. You be sure to recite that at school. Geography, mathematics, memory—that was excellent."

Grace beamed. "Think I'll take a few apples out to the horses, Momma. Kind of a backward birthday."

"You'll get soaked."

"I'll change and then change back for supper." The girl pulled Norah to her feet and hugged her. "I love you, Momma."

"I love you, too, darling." Norah wondered if she would have discovered the girl's brilliance had her own children been here. She held Grace close, feeling privileged to witness her flowering. "Run along now. And be sure to put your old boots on."

"I will!" Grace skipped into the kitchen, anxious to visit her equine friends.

Norah thought of how many pies she'd made since she came to live with Jim. A couple thousand surely! Rolling dough, fluting edges, flouring her hands, sniffing grated lemon, whipping egg whites—this labor of love eased mind and heart. The simplest tasks were often the biggest lifesavers.

Norah laid out ingredients, mind busy. She had an extra surprise for Grace at supper—a stereopticon of her own with new slides. The Tower of London, the Coliseum and Eiffel Tower, Venetian canals, castles on the Rhine. Mademoiselle Carolista walking a tightrope over a Denver street, Bridal Veil Falls, Garfield Beach at Great Salt Lake in Utah, the William H. Seward sequoia in Mariposa Grove. Mariposa. Norah smiled with wry amusement. Butterfly. She was no longer such a fragile creature but then neither was she the usual rancher, either. She had always been grateful for her good fortune in being given part of the Fullerton ranch and inheriting Eli's wealth as well; she'd been spared much hardship because of those windfalls.

Norah pictured ranch wives she knew and deeply admired, many of whom had complexions turned to leather by the elements; eyes once luminous were now bracketed by squint lines from sun and dust; hands had turned raw from lye soap and potato starch and bodies had gone shapeless from childbearing; hearts had been broken by infant death, drought, fire, financial defeat. Yet she envied them, for they had their men and love to sustain them. As the Indian menace disappeared, the Vista Valley population had increased, and she'd joined the women at candy pulls, housewarming dances, barbeques, and quilting bees and envied the glow on their faces. Petticoats from flour sacks, shoes polished with stove soot, wedding dress cut into baby clothes, hats braided of straw from the threshing floor—all hardships forgotten for a few hours. Daring and gallant, *they* were the ones who made sense out of this winning of frontiers—always had, right from the first Englishwoman to disembark from a ship and step onto the alien soil of Roanoke Island.

She reflected on her life. Had she been shortsighted not to welcome Eli back? The night the house burned down he'd offered to take her "to see them statues 'n things." He'd been willing to go partway. Would it have been so bad? Maybe she could have weaned him off the bottle. Maybe they'd still be together. They hadn't all been rough times, not by a long shot.

Sunshine slanted into the kitchen, and Norah opened the hot oven. If it dried up tomorrow, she'd ride out with the crew to see how spring branding was going and get away from the house. She'd drifted again of late, reluctant to make decisions, to pull herself together. Correspondence had piled up. Even the museum bulletin enthusing over "N. Carlisle, a new and exciting name in ornithology among lay experts," was a hollow triumph. They didn't know the monograph's author was a woman. Her nostrils flared. Maybe it was time they did! Yet what did it matter? There was no one with whom to share successes or failures; that was one kernel of her discontent.

Norah washed the utensils over and over. Her children out of reach, Mason lost, a national financial panic in progress, beef prices plunging—thank goodness, wool was steady— rustlers getting to be a pain in the butt. This last surprised her, for they ordinarily left a woman's ranch alone. She disliked hiring guns for the Mariposa, but too many cattle had been disappearing. God, her mind was filled with cotton! If only Mason had left her pregnant the last time, she'd have a baby to care for. Even pushing thirty-eight she'd have handled it fine. It would have been a joy, a piece of him for her to cherish. "If only"—those words ought to go on her tombstone.

"Momma, I need more apples." The girl came into the kitchen, muddy but happy.

"Help yourself, but take the old ones first. Wait, I think I'll come along. Haven't said hello to Lovey or Steel or Kehilan for a few days."

"They asked about you," Grace chided with a serious face. She said horses talked to her, and no one scoffed. Maybe they did.

They walked from the house, arm in arm, voices rich and soft on the damp air. A woman up on the hillside watched for a moment, then angrily jabbed a knife into the tree behind which she crouched.

The acrid stink of burning hair and frying flesh was distasteful as ever. Norah thought back to the day Shorty had helped her brand her first calf and how she'd thrown up, much to his disgust and the cowboys' amusement. She had not done it again, preferring to brand inanimate objects like saddles, doors, and fireplace mantels; her mark was appliquéd on rugs, dresser runners, pillowcases, and towels; a Navajo silversmith repeated it in jewelry. Lollie Gates, living in Tucson, where Theo was now in private practice, presented Norah a quilt covered with butterflies of every description surrounding the Mariposa brand.

Her foreman muttered under his breath, and she glanced at him curiously. They sat side by side on horseback, watching ropers cast loops, lasso calves, and drag them to the ground crew busy near a bed of coals in which the branding irons were heated. "What's wrong, Nelson?"

Careful to hide her fondness for him, Norah approved the expertness and swiftness with which the men dehorned and castrated the bull calves. Both bulls and heifers had to be earmarked, branded, and doctored, but the latter kept their horns for protection against 'range predators.

"Ain't nothin'. Lost part 'a my finger takin' up a dally." Fingers caught between rope and saddle horn sometimes snapped off when a cowboy hurriedly wound his lariat a few turns around the horn to take up slack. He'd have quit before admitting it hurt like thunder.

"Need a stitch?" she shouted over the uproar of cows bawling for their babies. Like most ranchwomen, Norah's sewing skill extended to human flesh. She studied the bloody stump form the corner of her eye, started to speak, then decided against it. Old hands took injuries in stride and asked for no sympathy. It went with the territory.

"No, thanks, ma'am." He inhaled a pinch of snuff. "Stayin' for noon chow? Be proud to have you."

"Maybe so." Norah loved the male spectacle of roundup: counting, separating, and branding in spring, readying cattle for market in fall. It was so virile and earthy and in a peculiar way sexually attractive. Shirts taut over muscular shoulders. Teeth white in dusty faces. Trousers tight where it was most interesting. The unconscious arrogance of stance, the casual mastery of danger. The firmness with which their knees guided the horses, lean rumps snugged against the cantle, thighs pressing the animal's sides.

She adjusted a bandana tied over her face to cut dust kicked up by the herd; it had another purpose today—that of hiding reactions to the men working around her. Good Lord, she was getting randy as a cowpoke snowed into line camp for the winter! This business of being without a man was hard. She'd even considered asking one of the more handsome cowboys to bed down with her, but that would most certainly play hob with a good crew. She had no dearth of prospects; single ranchers, a sheriff's deputy, a mining engineer, and the Englishman at the EM, among others, had

made it politely plain they were available day or night—but
none of them appealed to her. Being a man had advantages,
all right. They could blow off steam in Tombstone or Bisbee
or even Cananea below the border, where twin lodestones of
temptation and trouble drew them like bears to honey. She
had only an occasional dream to relieve tension, or
frustrating fantasies of Mason.

"Miz Martin, Miz Martin! My God, looky there!" The
chuckwagon cook pointed toward the ranch. Black smoke
spiraled skyward, and Norah's solar plexus flinched as if
punched. Not again! Oh, please, *not again!* She spurred her
horse, weaving recklessly through the nearby cattle, the
men's shouts fading behind her. What had happened? The
stoves were out, the iron cold, the lamps unlit. *And, where
was Grace?* Her lovely house, newly painted and carpeted
and curtained. The stylish furniture and clothes. *Grace!* An
image of Eli's body sprawled on the floor and beginning to
smoke blazed across her mind, and Norah whipped Steel as
she had never done.

Looking down on the Mariposa, Mason rolled memories
of it around in his mind as he might candy in his mouth,
tasting and savoring them. How he'd slipped out of bed
before dawn that long-ago day to hit the trail for his last
manhunt. Studied Norah's beloved face and that of his son a
final time. A lot of water had gone under the bridge since
then. He shook himself mentally, bringing his thoughts back
to the present.

What a top-notch, well-kept spread, except for the ruins
of a large house that had burned. They must be proud of
what they'd accomplished in spite of Eli's shortcomings. A
sigh escaped him despite a determination not to be affected.
He raised binoculars as a man and woman, dark haired and
furtive, ran away from the largest barn; if he wasn't
mistaken, that's where Norah had told him she stabled the
racing stock and her Arabians.

Suspicious now, he watched the couple race into the

trees, then he glanced back at the barn. He glimpsed the first tendrils of flame and even at a distance heard horses calling in growing panic. A man on crutches and Chan Lee came out of the cookshack, and the Chinese rushed into the barn and came out with two bucking colts.

Grendel plowed through brush like a landslide all the way down, and the pack mule was hard put to keep up with its heavy load of gold. Mason hit the ground running, and raced into the barn, untying halter ropes and chasing animals outside so they'd not turn back into the inferno. Other men joined him, and it took several of them to handle the stallion, Kehilan, whose mane was afire. Horses bunched and parted, then joined together again in fright and confusion, and some broke away with cowboys in pursuit.

Norah dismounted before Steel slid to a halt, but recoiled from the heat. Color sprang back into her cheeks to see Grace standing in front of the house, and she signaled that she should stay there. The girl was safe, thank God. She seized a man's arm. "Did we lose any?" Her mouth dried to think of even a single horse burned to death. The sleek brood mares, swelling with foal. The three stallions, fierce and so magnificent. Each horse so dear to her heart she couldn't face—

"No, ma'am. Not a one. Ain't no injuries either. Close thing, though."

She breathed a silent thanksgiving. Nothing but a barn, then. "How'd this happen? If somebody was smoking in there and fell asleep, I'll kick him out of the county so fast he won't know what hit him!"

"Wasn't any of your crew, Norah. I saw a man and woman run away right before the fire started." Mason almost flinched when she swung around, eyes flashing, neck cords tense. The impact rocked him, for this was a side of her he'd never seen before, the drive, power, audacity, and fearlessness of a strong woman on her own.

"This here pilgrim got most of the horses out. Was poppin' brush good down that there hill 'fore we got here.

Good job, mister." One of Norah's men shoved out a calloused hand.

Mason gripped hard. "You, too, hombre." The cowboy hurried off to help form a lariat corral until each horse was roped and led to safety.

Norah closed her mouth, which had fallen open with amazement to find him standing before her as if dropped by a giant bird. "Thanks a lot for what you did." She coughed with smoke and shock at his reappearance; his presence actually distressed her deeply, for she had trained herself to think of him—when she allowed herself to do so—as being dead. It had been better that way, however painful. "What are you doing here?"

"Passing through on my way to the coast." She'd removed her Stetson and was slapping it nervously against her leg. Her hair had more golden glints than it had had in her youth, the color delicately lightened by sun.

How handsome he was without the beard. Dignified, aristocratic. Even princely. Yet he'd been through a tough time, she could tell from his mouth and eyes. "How about a brandy? Come on up to the house."

A sadness Mason was unable to dispel flooded his spirit. The offer of hospitality was automatic, expected on every ranch. And why should he expect more? She had made her life without him, as was proper and good for the children. Did he think he merited a lost lover's welcome? "No, think I'll mosey along after I water the mules. Don't want to cause any trouble."

"What more could you cause? Wait a minute, will you? I'd like you to see how Grace has grown." She went to the calmer horses, stroked them, and commiserated with them while they made soft, troubled noises. She spoke to Kehilan, who continued to be unruly, then ordered him to be put in a stall apart from the other stallions.

Mason approved the efficiency with which the situation was handled, smoking timbers raked apart and doused with water, mares and colts led quietly to temporary quarters, some men cantering back to the range with hot food in their bellies. She ran a good outfit.

"That's the second fire in a year," Norah said as they approached the house. She pointed to the charred ruins of the mansion. "I can do without another one for the rest of my life."

She held her arms out to Grace, who ran full tilt into them. "Are they all right? Are the colts okay? Was—"

"Whoa! Take it easy! They're nervous and upset, but nobody was hurt." She glanced at Mason and smiled. "Nobody! You'd think those horses were human!"

The girl choked back a sob. "Oh, I'm so glad! I've got to talk to them! Tell them they're safe!" She ran away before Norah had a chance to reintroduce Mason. A red ribbon slid off her long black hair, falling unheeded to the ground.

He picked it up and gave it to Norah. "Guess she loves horses."

They laughed, and she said, "That's an understatement! Strangely enough, she can't ride too well. Come on in. I'll get us that brandy. Don't know about you, but I need it!"

He approved of the cheerful and casually elegant rooms. "As I said, I don't want to be any trouble." Eli had to be far out on the range not to have noticed the smoke.

"You aren't. Refreshments are the least I can offer after you saved my stock. Make yourself comfortable. I'll be back shortly."

Listening to a grandfather clock in another room, he sat stiffly for a while, hat upon his knees, and finally consulted his pocket watch. Norah'd been gone half an hour. He'd better leave before Eli bulled his way in and raised the roof. Furthermore, Mason realized he was most unhappy in her house; there was too much of her all about—sewing, bird books, magazines, an unfinished letter, a pair of red leather slippers. He headed for the door.

"Wait! Where are you going?" Dressed in a blue silk blouse and navy wool skirt, she held a tray with brandy and fruitcake. Her hair was massed atop her head, and the slender neck was desirable and deceitfully fragile.

He caught his breath at her loveliness. "Look, Norah, I know how he is. I don't want Eli to lose his temper and make things bad for you. I wouldn't even be here if I hadn't seen those two run away from the barn." He paused, and his resolve not to touch her almost failed. "Take care of yourself."

She rushed to stop him, knowing she would have to let him go—but not so soon! She had to be with him a little while, be close to him before he rode out of her life again. Then it hit her, what he had said. "Mason! You couldn't know! I—I didn't write because it seemed so painful—and so useless. Eli died last year when the big house burned down." She stepped back, startled by the look on his face.

Dazed, he had to clear his throat, but even so the words emerged in a croak. "My wife and son died in a stampede not long ago, God rest their souls. And I didn't write to you, either. For the same reasons." Emotion akin to awe choked him into silence.

She gasped at the import of their words and dropped the tray with a crash. "Oh! Oh, look what I've gone and done!" Her knees gave way and she went to the floor. Lifting a shard of the broken china, she stared at it as if she'd never seen it before. "Pick up the pieces. That's what we'd have to do. Can we do it after all this time? *Can we?*" *Tell me we can or I shall die. I cannot bear to lose you again.*

He stumbled as he knelt and pulled her clumsily to him. They murmured incomprehensible love talk, smoothed, patted, and squeezed each other with disbelief and pleasure. "*Can* we?" he whispered in her ear, feeling her heart race against his. "After everything we've been through? You *bet* we can! We have so much to make up for it'll take the rest of our lives. Oh, darling, marry me, marry me right away! Don't leave me for a minute until the preacher ties the knot."

They kissed for the first time in many months, besotted

with joy believed lost forever, and each found in the other's eyes the paradise thought sacrificed and unattainable. Unheard and unnoticed, Grace entered to stare enthralled at two intelligent adults sitting in smashed cake, spilled brandy, and broken glass. Her mouth curved with affection and amused exasperation. Grown-ups were so silly sometimes.

34.

The room had been converted into a shrine to Carleton Madison Beatty. Mason stirred uneasily and hoped his mother would never be so maudlin. Pictures from babyhood to cavalry life. Little silver-backed hair brushes, a baby fork and spoon, bronzed baby shoes, a watercolor of the young student in dueling garb. A class ring, a college pennant, a watch, a straw hat with faded ribbons.

Mason felt sure the servant had made a mistake escorting him to this room. Surely Mrs. Beatty did not receive here. He walked back into the long hall and toward the front of the Georgian mansion. What was taking so long? His card had been taken up. They had no idea who he was, of course, nor were they aware he had married their granddaughter's mother. They were so cruel, not letting the children come home. Did they think they were God? He'd really flown off the handle when Norah told him what Eli had done and of her futile efforts to get Rachel and Andrew back. He had left for Philadelphia right after their honeymoon in San Francisco, which had taken place only a week after their meeting.

Mason had power she did not: he was a man—and he was rich as Croesus. His old Fort Guardian buddy, Eddie

Bertram, medically retired from the Army and now working for Pinkerton, put him in touch with certain parties privy to damaging information about Senator Beatty's private life. Use of this weapon went against Mason's grain, but he wanted his son and his wife's child. Now.

The couple's appearance surprised him—they were the reverse of what he expected. She, fair, tall, and heavy like her son and leaning on a cane; her husband dark, dapper, oily, and quick on his feet, literally and figuratively. They entered the parlor to which Mason had drifted, followed by servants with a tea cart. He smiled inwardly during introductions as they appraised his expensive clothes and jewelry. Had he arrived in rancher's garb, he'd have gotten short shrift and been sent to the tradespeople's entrance by the butler.

"Please sit down, Mr. Fletcher. Won't you have tea?"

"Thank you, I'd enjoy that, Mrs. Beatty. Two lumps, if you'd be so kind."

From California, the senator decided, or maybe Colorado. Filthy rich, tough, self-made. One look at mouth and shoulders told him so. He prided himself on his ability to read people. This haughty devil was seeking a political plum or passage of a bill—mining, timber, or shipping. A big fish who'd be properly grateful. "Cigar, sir? Allow me to light it for you. Now, sir, how can I be of service?"

Mason crossed long legs and sipped the tea. "I have a proposition for you."

"I seldom if ever join in business discussions," the woman said, reaching for her cane, "so if you gentlemen will—"

"You're involved in this, too, madame." Her large pale-blue eyes widened.

Her husband no doubt kept her ignorant of his shenanigans outside home and Senate Chamber. All the better for shock effect. She was surely from an important family desirous of avoiding scandal; the man wouldn't have chosen a nobody—he wasn't the type. What Mason had ferreted out could blow their world apart and topple the senator from his perch.

"Very well, sir, what is this proposition?"

Mason fixed the other man with an amber glare that nettled and almost frightened him. Lawless barbarians, these violent Westerners, Anglo-Saxon savages killing Indians, eating raw meat at campfires, riding wild horses, shooting anybody they pleased.

Mason relished the other man's anger and nervousness. This pompous bag of wind had caused Norah a great deal of suffering. "Either Andrew and Rachel leave this house with me today to go home to their mother—who is my wife—or the *Independence* will publish an article concerning peculiar incidents that occurred at houses on Hyatt Street, Concord Plaza, and especially Jackson Square. May I have a second cup, please?"

Mrs. Beatty automatically poured. She studied her husband with cold speculation, for his peccadilloes were hardly news to her; she was aware of every sordid detail about his mistresses and his reputation as a card shark. This visitor was so confident, however, that her heart sank. It must be—she blinked rapidly. Lose Rachel, the only link with their dear dead son? The very thought made her heart beat irregularly.

The senator poured a stiff glass of sherry and downed it before answering. He was not about to have his bizarre indiscretions made public. He wiped his brow, avoiding his wife's eye, wondering how this rich stranger had come by his information. The man could have the brat. "Go ahead. Take Rachel. I'll have a maid pack her things—"

"*Mr.* Beatty! Rachel isn't going *anywhere*!" she exclaimed.

The men turned. "My love—" her husband said in a warning tone.

"Don't you know it will break my heart to lose her? I have nothing else left of Carleton!"

"It broke Norah's heart, too, when Eli Martin stole the

children. And again when you refused to let her see them. She's their *mother*, madam!" Mason said impatiently.

Mrs. Beatty studied the carpet a moment and then told the maid to bring Miss Rachel to the parlor. "I must apologize, Mr. Fletcher. I was told the young woman—your wife—was a person of loose morals who was unfit to raise them. I admit I seized the opportunity to have them with me, even if Andrew was not really our grandson." Her eyes clouded with hurt and anger and beseeched Mason for understanding. "But I see now a man like you wouldn't marry such a woman."

"Where's Andrew? Is he all right?"

The senator refilled his glass. "He—he ran away. Two days ago."

Mason grabbed the pleated shirtfront and shook the man hard enough to spill wine over his hand and cuff and onto the carpet. "Why? You bastard, if you laid a glove on my son—!"

"No, no, he never did! We loved Andrew. He's a fine boy." Mrs. Beatty had limped to them and was trying to loosen his grasp. "He was unhappy here, that's all. He begged me to let him go home, but I could hardly allow him to go so far alone. I've been unable to travel and the senator—"

"—is always too busy," a girl's voice added tolerantly. Rachel entered the room, a duplicate of her grandmother in miniature. "Andrew said he'd get to Arizona by himself, and knowing him, I'm sure he will."

Mason released the man, aghast at the news. It was dangerous enough west of the Mississippi, but the big cities he'd pass through were cesspools. "How was he traveling? Did he have a horse?"

"Went on the freight trains. He'll get along. He's got the gift of gab," the girl said.

Mason put a hand on the girl's shoulder. "Do you remember me? I'm your stepfather now. Your mother and I were married not long ago, and I've come to take you home."

"I want to stay here with my grandmamma."

"Nonsense!" Mason flared. "Your mother's been sick about you being gone. Doesn't that mean anything? Don't you love her?" His scowl was thunderous, yet it didn't phase the girl a bit. Perhaps there was something of Norah in her after all.

The senator's wife hugged Rachel. "Of course she does. She loves her mother very much, but she doesn't love ranch life."

"I've got my own little pony and trap and pretty clothes and a maid and—"

"And you're a very selfish girl!"

"Is Mrs. Fletcher with you?" the senator's wife asked.

"No. We think she's expecting, and I forbade her to come such a long distance." Mason studied his stepdaughter and decided she had Norah's stubborn chin and the same way of tossing her head. He looked at Mrs. Beatty and recalled the memorial room where she communed with her son, and for some inexplicable reason he thought of the melancholy and despair Don Diego had expressed at his departure. Mason came to a decision.

"Very well, Rachel, I can't take you on the train screaming and dragging your heels, and to be truthful, I don't want to. I made a special trip back here expressly to get you, but I think we'll go at this another way. Senator, sit down at your desk over there. Write a letter stipulating that Rachel will visit the Mariposa ranch three months of every year, beginning this August, until she reaches eighteen or gets married. Naturally, she's welcome to remain there." He heard the grandmother sigh. "You and your wife will sign the letter which I'll deliver to our attorney. As for Andrew, I want every ounce of your political clout put into action within the hour. Call in every marker you have. Railroad yards are to be searched, train conductors, freight engineers, and station masters put on alert, police all along the line advised to watch for him."

"We haven't been insensible to his predicament. I already sent detectives out, but there's been no news."

Mason promised in a quiet voice, "If my son turns up dead, I'm going to ruin you."

The other man turned white and rubbed his dry lips. "I'll get busy as soon as I finish the letter. We'll find him. You can count on that."

"Rachel, you are excused," Mason said.

She flushed, turned to obey, then stopped in the doorway. "Will you let us know as soon as you can? I love Andrew too, you know." At his curt nod she curtsied and disappeared up a marble staircase.

Mason relit his cigar, laying odds she'd want to stay with Norah eventually. To be fair, she'd been in Philadelphia a year, during which time her every whim had been catered to; she'd been pampered, indulged, and spoiled rotten. Adults weren't the only ones who could be selfish.

When Mason rode onto Mariposa range, he saw Norah coming like a bat out of hell on her Arabian with Endicott and another hand not far behind. He shook his head and frowned. She shouldn't be riding now! "Sweetheart, what are you doing? You'll endanger the baby." They leaned to kiss each other, eyes shining with love.

"It's all right. Well, not exactly all right, but I'm not pregnant so it doesn't matter but what *does* matter is——"

"Whoa, back 'er up there. What are you trying to tell me?"

The men drew closer and she fairly bounced in the saddle. "He's here, darling. *Andrew's come home!*"

"God Almighty, what a load off my mind! I had visions of him cut to pieces under the wheels of a train, locked in some lousy jail, or working on a chain gang for stealing food to stay alive."

"So did I," she admitted with a catch in her voice, "but he's a man now. He can take care of himself."

"My father's father had his own clipper ship at twenty. A chip off the old block, eh? Listen! Before he gets here—does he know I'm his father?"

"I told him. He understands why I didn't tell him before. After all, he's fourteen, and he was always mature for his age." She laughed. "Besides all he has to do is look in the mirror!"

They trotted to meet him and reined in on either side of his horse. He put out a hand, intensely curious but wary of this man he resembled so closely. "Hello, Father."

Mason choked, alarmed by eyes suddenly gone wet. Their son. So straight and handsome, confident and strong. "Welcome home, son. Glad you got here in one piece," he managed in a husky voice. He gripped the hand so hard the youngster winced. "Took a lot of guts crossing the country alone. Have any trouble?"

"None I couldn't handle." Skinned knuckles and a black eye contradicted the boyish boast.

"Oh, this is wonderful!" Norah cried. They smiled and she fumbled for a handkerchief.

"Take it easy, honey." Mason reached out to pat her cheek.

She twisted her head to kiss his palm. "I'm okay. Honest. Now, if Rachel were only here!"

"She will be—in August."

"She *will*? Then the whole family can be together! We'll have a big party!"

Mason decided not to spoil the moment with explanations. "I'll tell you all about it later, but right now I'm hungrier than an old mountain lion who's lost his teeth. That train food is really bad."

"It's not too late for hotcakes, is it?"

Andrew gave an exuberant cowboy yell that made the horses jump with surprise, and laughing with the sheer pleasure of each other's company, they cantered toward the Mariposa.

They fell asleep immediately, exhausted from emotion and a busy day, relaxed by full stomachs and their bodies pressed together. Norah woke first in the warm dark, hungry for love. Running the flat of her hand down his chest and abdomen, she played with him while kissing his ear and neck.

"Mmmmm—if you're trying to seduce me, you're doing a good job of it." He pulled the nightgown over her head. "Why even wear this?"

"So you can complain."

Mason nibbled her lower lip. "The only thing I complain about is we don't do this often enough."

"You're kidding." Their desire was forever fresh, and they often met at the house during the day to make love, feeling kittenish and silly and wicked.

"Sure it's all right to try again so soon? Don't want to hurt you," he murmured, pulling her on top of him so that he might feel her on him from throat to toe.

"I want that baby before I'm too old." Thirty-eight was right on the edge, but she was willing to take the chance.

"You're *my* baby." He brought her down on him before rolling over. Norah groaned as she accepted the beloved burden of his weight, the thrust and rubbing that started her, the final fullness of him within her as they joined in climax.

"Did we make a little Fletcher?" Mason asked, snuggling down, her buttocks cupped in his loins.

She giggled drowsily. "Hard to tell. Might have to do it again."

"Tonight?" he asked in mock protest.

"Too much for you?"

"Try me," he said with a sigh.

Norah dismounted, tethered her horse, and crept to peer over the great rock overhang. The rustlers had not been quick enough this time in fleeing the place of butchering; thanks to a light snowfall, she and Andrew had been able to follow them without difficulty. Side by side on their stomachs, she and her son looked down upon a natural amphitheater of boulders where the outlaws had pitched their camp. It appeared to be permanent, with a pole corral and crude lean-tos under which blankets and personal possessions were piled. The smell of cooking meat rose to their nostrils and Norah's mouth watered. It was a cold dusk and way past suppertime.

She watched a man frying steaks, ladling up beans, tossing chunks of bread on tin plates. Or was it a woman in—Norah gasped, covering her mouth. That was Rose Fullerton in men's clothing, with her hair cut short! The tight shirt and pants emphasized a woman's figure running to fat but still superb. An outlaw ran a hand down her thigh in passing, and Rose whirled to jab him in the leg with a long-handled fork. He cursed but took his plate and sat down while the others jeered and kept their hands to themselves. The meal was over and the fire banked by the time a man with long blond hair rode in. Rose went to meet him and while he put saddlebags under the lean-to and tended his horse, she revived the fire to heat his food.

As Norah and Andrew rode the ten miles back to the Mariposa she wondered if Rose had had anything to do with a string of mishaps the ranch had suffered: her cattle branded with the EM when Eli was alive, the firing of the barn, cattle slaughtered and left to rot, cowboys fired at, a ripe coyote carcass dumped in an artesian pond. She had rescued Grace from Geronimo's camp in 1886—was it really seven years ago?—just before he and his band fled into Mexico for the last time. Rose must have carried that in her craw all this time.

Where had she been since then? Obviously she had fled when Geronimo surrendered, then taken up with that white trash back there. Maybe she was to blame for this serious mischief, although it could have been a jealous neighbor, failing and desperate. Norah overlooked an infrequent cattle kill, for hard times had descended on southern Arizona again during yet another long drought; it had only recently broken with heavy rains in July that were too late to halt a murderously high mortality on the range. If the kills were being made by outlaws, however, they had to be stopped pronto.

Mason was a stickler for the law. "Call in the sheriff, hon. Now that you've found their hideout, he'll form a posse and either run 'em out or wipe 'em out. And I do wish you and Andrew wouldn't take chances like that. You ride up the wrong canyon, you're liable to run into the Apache Kid." Cochise County cattlemen had been warned to go armed; the former Army scout had turned bad and was considered so dangerous the state legislature had passed a bill authorizing a five-thousand-dollar reward for him, dead or alive.

Norah finished her meal. "You know, I have to admit Rose's boyfriend was good-looking for a desperado. Shoulder-length hair the color of flax, dark bright eyes, and the biggest mouthful of teeth I ever saw. I'd guess he was part Indian to watch him walk."

Mason froze with fork poised in midair. "How old?"

"Your age or a little younger. Why? Do you know him?"

"Could be." Mike Ward come back from the grave? If it *was* that bastard, they still had a score to settle—and Ward had a long delayed meeting with the gallows.

A grimness settled on his features that startled Norah. "You *do* know him! Mason, don't do anything foolish. I'm sending a man to Tombstone in the morning to get the sheriff. Like you said, let the law handle it."

"Don't worry. I just want to scout their camp. Take a look-see for myself. Maybe I don't know him. A lot of lawless men in Arizona, you know." He rose from the table, kissed her after thanking her for supper, and sat down in the parlor to catch up on his reading. He loved having a home, a place to call their own, a haven where he could shed his cares, take a nap, or smoke by the fire, loved and content.

Andrew polished off his dessert. "I'll take care of him," he said in a low voice so his father wouldn't hear.

Norah smiled tremulously at the cub guarding the grizzly. "It's just that we were apart for so long I don't want the tiniest thing to happen to him."

Her son nodded gravely. "I understand." To him their love story was like a myth of old. Andrew was sixteen now and courting a rancher's daughter. Romance had flowered in his heart, and he had begun to see his parents not simply as adults but as lovers. The way they looked at each other sometimes made him blush.

"Going to the O'Connell ranch tomorrow?"

He fidgeted. "They asked me to go to church with them and stay for supper."

"Church! Is this that serious? If it is, bring the young lady home so we can meet her."

"She'll have to tell *me* if it's serious." There were other girls—but she was special.

"She must be very pretty." For my hawk-handsome son to choose.

"Purty as a speckled pup. Want me to help with the dishes?"

Norah teased, "You don't have to bribe me. Just be sure to do your chores before you leave."

He grinned and started to clear the table. "I don't mind. Say, Grace'll be home for Christmas vacation pretty soon, won't she?"

She stacked dishes in the sink, added soap, and poured hot water over them. "I can hardly wait until she opens the box with her new dress in it."

"The one on the dress form? Looks too tailored to me. I like her in lace and ruffles."

"It's a tennis dress." White hopsacking with ombré surah that had a lot of red in it. She liked red, just as her mother did. Norah scrubbed a frying pan vigorously. Where *had*

Rose gone? The posse had found the hideout deserted; careful as she and Andrew had been, a sentry must have seen them and given the alarm. It worried her, knowing Rose was out there somewhere, like a balanced rock ready to let go that you watched from the corner of your eye when you rode under it.

"You need a dress for tennis?"

Norah gave him a platter to dry. "Of course. You need one for the beach, for bathing, boating, yachting, fencing, traveling, ice skating, and visiting. Costumes for riding and bicycling and dresses for the four seasons as well as undergarments, stockings, shoes, boots, gloves, hats, jewelry, parasols, coats, capes—" She stopped and chuckled at his expression.

He had paled. "Do I have to buy all those when I get married?"

She took pity on him. "No, dear, only society women have enough money to buy such extensive wardrobes. Ranchwomen do with much, much less and look lots better in my opinion. Here, I'll finish. Endicott tells me you're awfully busy out there in the barn." Andrew was an artist at tooling leather and was making gifts for Christmas.

"Santa Claus is coming, you better be good!" He relinquished the dish towel and left the house whistling.

Mason came in for a dish of black walnuts and a nutcracker. "He sounds happy."

"Christmas may have a little to do with it, but it's mostly the girl, I imagine."

"Girl!" Mason exclaimed, pausing in the doorway.

"He's sixteen, darling."

"Where does time go?"

They settled in front of the fire, where they often played cards, made hand shadows on the wall or string figures stretched between the hands, looked at stereopticon slides or just talked, happy to be together. Mason thought his wife's grasp of affairs extraordinary and liked to advance ideas and theories for discussion. Tonight subjects ranged from 1894 being only weeks away to the depression and breadlines back East to the disastrous dive in silver prices from $1.25 an ounce to $.25; the drop had closed almost all Arizona silver mines but had inspired a surge in gold mining. While he rubbed her feet, they also debated whether the governor's yearly salary of $2,600 was too much.

Computing mentally, Norah said, "Too much! That's only fifty dollars a week, for goodness sake. Think what gamblers make. Think what saloon owners rake in!"

"But Hughes will ruin the Territory," Mason remarked. "He's against licensed gambling and strong drink, and remember he inspired a federal law that stipulates an eight-hour day. *And* he's as strong an advocate of women's suffrage as his wife is."

Norah cracked a nut with unnecessary force, winding up with a handful of fragments. Their marriage was exemplary except for two things. He was far too authoritarian, the result, she supposed, of bossing hundreds of vaqueros to whom his word had been law; this attitude had resulted in the loss of several good cowhands. She'd told him about this numerous times, and he was finally pulling back and giving the men more room.

She now attacked the second weakness. "The ladies in Wyoming have had the vote since 1869, and Arizona women should be able to vote, too. Remember that drunk in Fairbank who got thirty days for cussing in front of women? Just think! That old soak can vote, and *I can't*! Not only that, he can sit on a jury and I can't!" She rose to pace back and forth with impatience and scorn for the blindness of the opposite sex.

He closed his eyes, listened to her footstep, the rustle of starched petticoats, and the sly creak of a new corset. How he loved her! How grateful he was simply to be in the same room with her. "You know how most men feel. Women are made to be wives and mothers, not politicians."

"Voting on matters like a new road or another school is

hardly being a politician. Do you honestly think I'm incapable of being anything but a wife and mother?" She swished to a stop in front of him, arms akimbo.

Mason grabbed her by the waist and sat her down on his lap in a flurry of skirts. They tussled and she kicked his ankle. "My insufferable suffragette," he murmured while nibbling her ear. He forced her chin up so he could kiss her.

"Oh, *you*!" She giggled in spite of herself and put her arms around him. They'd come to an impasse on the voting question again, but she always won when it came to love.

35.

Grace understood about her monthlies, Momma had explained the whole thing. But it was still disquieting. Furthermore, it was topsy-turvy for Momma's to stop because she was pregnant and for hers to arrive with regular inevitability. They were supposed to last for years and years, a prospect she didn't relish. On the other hand, her bosom had pushed out a tiny bit more and her rump was rounding, exciting yet startling facts verified in the mirror, although Momma said she must not look at herself naked.

Today, for example, under the juniper, she sensed herself growing as if the sap of the young tree ran through her veins. She leaned against its scaly trunk and scanned the valley with binoculars. There was Andrew, herding cows and a few spindly calves. She adjusted the lenses to clarify his profile. How that girl he was sparking could resist him was a mystery. Something to do with a cavalry officer, Momma said. Grace smiled. The officers *were* divine with their tight uniforms and waxed mustaches, but her brother was even more so. Being twelve was hard. She hoped it wouldn't take too long to grow up so some young officer at Fort Huachuca would invite her to play tennis or croquet and watch the baseball games between cavalry and infantry teams.

Grace put the glasses down—and was instantly paralyzed by fear. Three rough-looking men sat watching her, resting forearms on their saddle horns. Gooseflesh rose on her body. *Danger, danger!* The need for privacy had been overwhelming today, too much so; she had gone far beyond boundaries specified for her by Mason. He had taken into consideration that she was not a good rider and that she didn't like firearms, refusing to carry even a single-shot .22, a boy's first weapon. To make matters worse, she had ridden her old friend, Lovey, who ran about as well as she shot. Grace waited, heart thumping, mind assessing the situation as if it were a chess move. She felt sick to her stomach. Checkmate.

"Wal, looky here," the oldest renegade drawled, spitting so accurately tobacco juice landed on the girl's knapsack beside her. "Ain't you the half-breed what lives on the Mary Posee? You're Rose's brat, aintcha?"

"Sure, that's her," the second outlaw confirmed. "Seen her once before."

The third man had a coarse but interesting face and black eyes that stripped her bare. He grinned and she shivered. "Mason Fletcher still livin' down there?"

Grace shook her head, vainly protecting the man she loved like a father. The desperado shook out his lariat and lassoed her so she fell sideways to the ground. Dragging her closer to the horses, he looked down and grinned again. "You ain't a good liar, missy. Is he there?"

She yelped with pain when he tightened the rope. "When he finds out what you did he'll—"

"He ain't gonna do nothin', 'cause he wants you back. Come on, let's go see your momma."

"Hey, wait a minute, Ward. When we get back to camp

we gotta share. Let's have some now. Roll the dice—see who gets her first." The younger man leered at Grace and licked his lips. "I ain't never had me one of them virgins before."

Ward studied his mistress's daughter, the heavy dark hair and pansy-blue eyes lifted to his, the trembling limbs that betrayed her fear. He dismounted. Hurting someone dear to Fletcher was a pleasure he had not anticipated. "Yeah. Oughta see if she's as good a lay as her ma."

The girl recoiled at a movement behind the pants fly. She knew how bulls and stallions did it, but Norah always sidled around the subject when asked how people did it. Deep in her heart Grace tried to prepare herself for violation and something even more dreadful that would damage her spirit. She prayed for strength and swallowed with difficulty, for her throat and mouth had dried. Then they were on her, yanking her clothes off, jesting at the bloody cloth she wore, feeling the nipples with hard fingertips. One of them confirmed she had not been entered, and they began to breathe faster. She struggled silently, crying but fighting with all her might.

Ward pushed her roughly back to the ground and started to unbutton his pants. "What the dash! Thought we were gonna toss." The other two edged closer.

"Shut up and watch how it's done." Ward went to his knees and pulled the girl's thighs apart, slapping her hard when she resisted.

"You awready got a woman, damn it. Give us a break," the younger complained with a hand poised over his gun.

"You make me tired," Ward said, and drew so fast his Colt blurred. Casually as drilling a target, he shot the man in the intestines and then the heart. Blood spattered onto the girl's exposed flesh, and she screamed in dread and revulsion. "You got anything else to say?" he asked the remaining man.

"No," a strange voice answered, "but I do. Get away from that girl. Slowly and carefully. And don't come up shooting unless you want to go through life without your pecker." The stranger's gray eyes were cold as the gun he held.

Billy Smith was in his teens and had known a life of wild adventure with his father, John. Mike Ward wouldn't fight him, in spite of his position as gang leader, for he knew Billy's draw was like lightning and he never missed. Had he wished to form his own band, rebels and malcontents would have flocked to him, for Billy had matured early and possessed a rare gift of mastery over men.

In the beginning Billy had been thrilled to ride thundering through the night, to have complete freedom, live in the open, outwit the law, feel the near madness of danger, intoxicating as liquor or women. Then his father had narrowly escaped hanging, and later died with a bullet in his belly while stealing a lousy two hundred bucks. That had been the turning point for the boy. Weary of fugitive life, Billy now wanted to settle down. And the girl who sat there on the ground so defiantly was going to be his wife when she grew up. He knew that as surely as he breathed.

"Okay, okay," the outlaw leader said sullenly. His woman would have knifed him anyhow had he harmed her kid. "Now what?"

Billy motioned with his weapon. "Mount up and ride out."

"Want this fresh stuff for yourself, is that it?"

"Ride out," Billy repeated, "and don't try anything." Taking the girl was the farthest thing from his mind; he had had sex, but forcing a girl on the verge of womanhood was odious. Once the riders were well on their way, leading the dead man's horse with his body over the saddle, he holstered his gun and dismounted. Grace tensed and pressed a torn shirt over budding breasts and the hair feathering above her privates. "Don't worry. I won't hurt you. Get dressed and I'll take you home."

Billy gathered up her garments and brought them to her. While she put her clothes on, he inspected the range below with the glasses. He planned to escort her as close to the ranch as possible, but he certainly didn't want to run across her mother's men and get shot.

The drought of 1892-93 had been brutally destructive to water supplies, vegetation, and herds. It had scoured the range clean of bulls and the spring calf crop had been pitiful. Maybe not as bad as in Pima County, where only about 250 calves had been branded instead of the usual thousands, but plenty bad, nevertheless. He'd seen skeletons in dry water holes and watched bone gatherers at the San Bernardino carting them off to sell to bone factories in the East.

He wouldn't raise cattle on his spread, the great dumb beasts. Blooded horses, that was his ambition, one inspired by many an animal that had passed through the rustlers' hideouts. Nothing expensive like Arabians either, but fine, flashy, daring Thoroughbreds with hearts full of courage. Beauties with fire in their eyes and thunderbolts in their hoofs, necks arching like rainbows and manes flying in the wind like silken banners.

"I don't know your name," Grace said, putting a hand on his arm, "but I want to thank you from the bottom of my heart." Billy turned, the hard lines in his face softening. She smiled at him. "My name is Grace Martin."

"Billy. Billy Smith. My father knew Mrs. Fletcher. Worked for her once." He smiled back. Intelligence radiated from those eyes that bloomed blue as mountain iris, and the impulse to have her for his own firmed into resolve. "You ready?" When she nodded, he untied Lovey's reins and cupped his hands so she might step into the stirrup more easily. His gallantry was natural, for he respected women; his father, a gentleman before taking a wrong turn in the trail, had taught him that a real man treated a lady not as a possession but as a cherished companion. He had never known his mother, but surely she must have been the most angelic individual ever—until this blossoming maiden entered his life today.

They descended to the valley floor and rode along the foothills in friendly silence. They stepped through coral-red mallow and minute yellow daisies, passed century plants like immense artichokes with phallic stalks twenty feet high, yucca with rhubarb-pink stems weighed down by pearly clusters of fragile waxen bells. A cardinal blazed by in scarlet splendor, caroling in flight. "*Richmondena cardinalis*," she said, well trained by Norah. "*Icterus parisorum*." *But Norah was not her momma after all.* Shock was wearing off, awareness and hurt creeping into its place. *Half-breed!* Rose's brat! She'd heard Norah speak of Rose, an Indian who had run away.

"You like living on a ranch?" he asked, hoping she'd say yes.

"Oh, I love it! I'd stay here all the time if I could, but I have to go to school. To seminary in Tucson." She glanced at him shyly. He was really quite attractive, with curly dark-brown hair and a light, stylish way of riding, as if he were a centaur, part horse, part man, yet also separate from the animal in the upright rhythm of his body. Her knight in shining armor, he had saved her virtue, as storybook heros did. The sun surrounded him with an aura of stern, chivalrous nobility, and although she didn't know it then, she had fallen in love. "Mr. Fletcher and—my mother will want to thank you for what you did."

Billy's mind raced. He knew what he wanted, and it was not the life his father had led. They had quarreled bitterly over his not being allowed to participate in raids and robberies, although he had been in a few shooting scrapes. Now Billy blessed his dead parent, for there wasn't a single wanted poster standing in his way. If he played his cards right, his dreams might come true. "I sure could use a job. Think they might take me on?"

"Kinda like that boy," Mason remarked. "But I'd bet a dollar he's got a wild streak. Closemouthed as the devil. He's been around, or I'll eat my hat." He had the girls to think about, and he was suspicious because Billy had come out of nowhere.

Norah took the last stitch in a darned sock. "Says he wants to raise horses and have a ranch here in Cochise County. That doesn't sound harum-scarum. And Andrew likes him. Think of him facing down this Mike Ward you told me about. I think that's wonderful!"

He bent to stroke her cheek. "He still may be three feet short of a yard. We'll have to see." She had shadows under her eyes. She was too thin for a pregnant woman and was tired in nothing flat. He had been right. They'd tried again too soon, before she'd regained her strength. "You feel all right, darling?"

"Perfectly," she chirped, biting a thread in two.

"Big fibber. Want me to fetch a doctor?"

She reached out to rumple his thick black hair. "Don't you think Grace acted odd when she came home? She pulled away when I put my arms around her."

"Wouldn't you act odd if you'd almost been raped?" Mason got to his feet to study his wife carefully. "Maybe she didn't want to be touched just then."

Norah's mind flashed back to the day Eli had attacked her, and she shrank from what might have happened to that jewel of a girl. "I suppose. But there was something else. I felt it in the way she *looked* at me."

"You're imagining things." He removed the sewing from her lap and pulled her to her feet. "I think you need more rest. You don't have to be busy every second. You're no spring chicken, you know." Norah made a face and poked him in the ribs. "Come on, take a nap for an hour." They walked to the bedroom, her head on his shoulder. "Love you," he murmured before kissing her eyelids shut and covering her with a light blanket.

As Mason walked past Grace's room, he heard weeping. His hands balled into fists. God, how he'd like to get those bastards in his sights! Not vigilante justice—he didn't believe in that except under unusual circumstances—but a showdown face to face. Rid this area of the scum that were putting decent men out of business. Sweeping down from mountain hideouts, the rustlers could run off a herd before a posse was even formed. The Chiricahua range offered fugitives a thousand gorges, hidden pine-rimmed meadows, fantastic rock formations, huge caverns, and forested labyrinths with passes leading into New Mexico.

He was about to walk on down the hall when the door was flung open. Grace poised there a moment, then ran out to throw herself against him. "Hey, there, hey, take it easy! You'll make yourself sick."

His face hardened, and he fingered his mustache nervously. Had she actually been raped and not told them? "Come back in here. I don't want to disturb your mother." Once the door was shut he looked her right in the eye. "Did those men do anything to you? Don't be ashamed to tell me if they did."

"No, I swear they didn't. Billy came before they could— could—oh, it was terrible!" Her face was strained and adult. "But that wasn't the worst of it. They said *Momma isn't my mother!* Did you know that? They said my mother's name is Rose. I'm a *half-breed!*" Her eyes, so blue Mason half-expected the tears to be blue, filled, but she wiped them dry.

He cleared his throat. For the Lord's sake, hadn't Norah told the kid long ago? Well, would he have? Not that there was any shame in Apache blood, but Grace hobnobbed with daughters of rich and educated white men who'd pillory her if they found out. It would be years before Indian blood was accepted socially. "Let's sit down, dear." He motioned to the bay window where she liked to read with the ranch's newest puppy or kitten beside her.

"I'll be honest—your mother was an Apache." He raised a hand at her gasp of dismay. "One of my best friends was an Apache, Grace." Good old Chico. It had been a while since he had thought of his compadre.

"Oh, Daddy! I've seen them at San Carlos! Remember

that time Momma took a wagon full of meat and blankets when the government rations didn't come in? I'm not like them. *I'm not!*" She ran to the mirror. It confirmed that she was a far cry from the broad-faced, thick-bodied women with their straight coarse hair, black eyes, and coppery skin.

Straight from the shoulder. She was smart enough and strong enough to hear. "You're right. You're not. Although there you're seeing them at their worst. Now, I remember your mother very well, Grace. She is—or was—one of the best-looking girls I ever saw. You have her lovely hair and that peachy complexion, and it looks like you're going to have her figure. Norah has a daguerreotype somewhere. I'll try to find it for you.

"Your father was Joel Fullerton. You've heard Norah speak of him and his father. He was a tall, dark Texas man with a smile like yours that lights up a room. And he was the best bronc buster who ever came down the pike." He took her hands in his. "I can only imagine what a shock this has been, but do you know exactly what half-breed means? In your case, it simply means a girl who's the child of a white man and an American Indian woman." He tried desperately to think of someone to compare her with. "Remember Sacajawea, who guided Lewis and Clark? Her children were half Shoshone and half French. There was no shame in that and you have nothing to be ashamed of in your mother, I swear on the Bible." He crossed his heart.

"But why didn't she *tell* me?" His boylike gesture, oddly enough, comforted her.

"Maybe Norah was waiting until you were old enough to really understand the situation. Maybe she didn't want to tell you your mother had—uh—strayed from the path, for fear you'd hate her."

"Is she—a wicked woman?" Grace asked in a pained voice.

Mason sweated. "Not wicked. Hotheaded and foolish maybe. Like lots of people."

"Then why can't we help her? It must be awful living with men like those!"

"She can take care of herself," Mason assured her, "as well as any man." He decided not to mention that Rose had killed Joel accidentally. The girl had plenty on her plate now. "Believe me, she's doing what she wants to do."

Grace looked out the window at Billy Smith shoeing a horse. He knew where Rose was. She'd make him take her there. "I want to meet her."

"I don't think—Tell you what, let's ask Norah."

"I'm her daughter. I want to meet her!" See if there's anything of her in me or me in her. Had her mother known where she was all these years? Why hadn't she come? It must have been because she was poor. She had denied herself the company of a child so it might have what she could not give it. Yes, that had to be it. Perhaps she and Norah had even made some agreement.

He sighed. "When Norah wakes up, we'll discuss this. But *don't*—please, sweetheart—don't make the mistake of going back there alone to see her. They're stronger than she is, and they'll sell you into Mexico so far from home you'll never get back. Believe me, Grace, I've seen American women like that, bought from Comancheros."

Despite the wind of rebellion in her, Grace agreed, for she respected his judgment and experience. He wouldn't lie and neither would she, so she gave her word. When he left, she put her forehead against the glass and continued to watch Billy working. Who was she now? Two girls in one. A stranger—and the Grace everyone else knew.

She turned to gaze about her room, feminine, charming, filled with things she had once thought important—the wardrobe with its many dresses, a German music box, her stereopticon, books, the four-poster and dresser, the velvet-covered chair with its big doll. All false, all unreal. The Grace Martin who owned them no longer existed. The girl shuddered as if she were very cold and buried her face in her hands.

How would she ever face the girls at school? Surely her Apacheness would show now? And how could she face herself every morning, not knowing whose blood ran in her veins? That of some warrior who scalped women and dangled their hair from his lance, or that of a medicine man, revered by his tribe and full of ancient wisdom? She knew so little about Indians, only the bad parts, really, that she'd gleaned from adult conversation. Surely there was good in them, too. There had to be—else she'd hate herself.

Grace wound the music box that played "Home Sweet Home" and sat down in the bay window, listening with half an ear. Her mind raced furiously, grasping for straws. She gazed out over the ranch—it had not changed. She had. Billy crossed the yard, leading the horse, glanced up at her and grinned, admiration plain on his face. Grace waved and the pain in her heart eased a trifle. Maybe things weren't so bad after all.

36.

The outlaw slumped comfortably in the saddle while giving the Mariposa layout a good once-over. He wanted those horses down there so bad he could taste it, especially that dark chestnut mare. The Fletchers had a big crew, but he had more than enough men to pin them down in the bunkhouse. Nevertheless he had been waiting until Fletcher was away. He had finally headed for Bisbee two weeks after Billy left the gang and went to work for him. Ward did not plan to take or harm the two females—he didn't want the whole territory on his back.

"*Qué piensa*, Mike?" The Mexican who spoke had

saved his life years ago when the wounded mule fled with
Ward bound to its back. They had traveled together ever
since, friends without an ounce of conscience or honor
between them. He was the only one with whom Ward
shared his woman—when she had the hankering. "A big
rancho. How many hombres? I don't want—what is it?—a
rope necktie."

"We can handle it. Tell the men to get some grub and be
ready to ride about midnight." The grin that unnerved his
men now creased his vicious face. "I'm gonna fix him
good, and then I'm gonna gut-shoot him while he's riding
home."

"The señora carries his child, I hear." The Mexican
rolled a cigarette without wetting the paper, pinched the
ends, and placed the unlit cylinder between his lips.

His amigo took the smoke from his friend's mouth and lit
it for himself. "Now, ain't that plumb cozy? I know
somebody'd like to look into that."

It was almost one in the morning when Grace and Norah
went to bed, exhausted by an evening of recrimination and
explanation. By mutual unspoken consent they had postponed any confrontation until Mason departed on an
overnight trip with Billy; Andrew, who was headed to visit
his girl, would accompany them partway. At Grace's door
Norah reached out to draw her close, distressed by the stiff,
resentful body. "If you'd known, it wouldn't have made any
difference," she repeated, noting how tall Grace was, how
fast she was shooting up and maturing.

Grace wanted to remain hurt and angry, but she was tired
and the other's abdomen pressed to hers disarmed her. An
infant lived within, adorned perhaps with Mason's mouth
and the mother's large expressive eyes, features of the two
people she loved most and best in the world. Grace
wondered what her natural mother had thought while she
was carrying her. Had she wanted her? Dreamed of her?
Wished she were a boy? Ached to caress the baby flesh? Or

had she hated the burden and later the living barrier that wrenched her and her husband apart?

"Oh, Momma, I'm so mixed up," she said plaintively. Norah stroked her back and uttered comforting sounds. "Suppose a boy proposes? What do I *tell* him?"

"Well, you're pretty young to be thinking about *that*! But when one does, tell him the truth. If he loves you, he'll treasure that part of you just as he does the rest. It wasn't your fault, for goodness sake."

"What about my friends in school?" The question emerged a whisper. Blond, blue-eyed, white-skinned friends who shrieked in mock terror and pointed in disdain at Indians come to Tucson accompanied by missionary or Army escort.

"It's simply none of their business!" Norah snapped. "I wouldn't say boo to any of them, unless she's a special friend. Besides, you're prettier and smarter than all of them in a bunch. Now, go along to bed. You must be worn out. I know I am." She kissed Grace and shoved the girl gently into her room.

"Momma, I know you don't approve—but I really do have to see her."

They had opposed each other on this from the start, but now Norah capitulated and nodded. "Very well. I'll ask Mason to arrange it." She had been blinded by concern. After all, wouldn't she, too, wonder all her life what her mother had looked like, thought like? Better get it out of her system, maybe arrange for Rose to visit now and then, an arrangement such as Rachel had. Her heart still hurt to think her own daughter preferred grandparents and a big city to her mother, brother, and the ranch. Now it bothered her more deeply than she cared to admit that Grace, too, might abandon her. Would she go off with Rose into a life of being hunted, hungry, dirty, and cut off from society in the belief she belonged with her natural parent? Yet—how could a whole life spent with her on the Mariposa stack up against a single meeting with Rose? Norah nodded again. "When he comes home . . ."

They had barely put out the lamps and pulled up their covers when the rustlers attacked. Gunfire splintered the dark, and hoofbeats and shouts played counterpoint to its savage staccato. Horses in the corral whinnied with fright, and their lustrous eyes shone white-rimmed in the torches' flare. A light went on in the bunkhouse and then winked out with a crash of glass; flashes lit the night as cowboys fired at the intruders, their marksmanship hampered by a hail of bullets from the dark.

Rushing to the window, Norah saw men roping her horses. Such rage filled her for a moment that she was unable to breathe. *"Momma! Momma! Did you see—"* Grace rushed in to peer over Norah's shoulder.

"Stay here!" Norah yanked a coat out of her wardrobe and jammed her feet into old slippers. "Whoever that is has got the boys pinned down!" Her voice trailed off as she seized the gun from the bedside table and ran out of the room and downstairs. Norah took a loaded rifle from the gun rack and jacked a shell into the chamber. She slipped out the door and off the porch, trotting crouched from one place of concealment to another. Hurry, but take it easy, Mason counseled in emergencies. Keep cool. Think straight—and if necessary shoot first and ask questions afterward.

Hiding behind a shed, Norah aimed the rifle and fired. A Mexican in a sombrero cried out and clapped a hand to his breast. He dropped his reata on the dark chestnut mare, gasping with pain and holding on to his horse's neck. She fired at the man who rode up to take the Mexican's place but missed. Startled by the closeness of the shot, the rustler spurred his mount forward only to have it drop, killed by a stray bullet. His hat fell off, releasing a torrent of black hair. Some men did wear their hair woman-long, but this wasn't a man. God, no! It was Rose. Then it *was* Mike Ward's gang! And Mason miles away! The mare reared over the dead horse, front feet working, and Rose released the rope and rolled away as the animal wheeled and ran.

The women now faced each other on either side of a flamelit arena, for one side of the barn nearby had been torched. They stared across the years, their eyes glittering with dislike.

"You still got my girl?" Rose spat dirt and tossed hair back from her face.

"She's here. You know that."

The Apache snugged down her gun belt. "I wanted to come for her, but ain't no place for little girls where I been. Mike don't like kids anyhow, and I do what he wants. He's my man."

"Did you stay with Geronimo long?" Inane to converse as if no chaos reigned in the background.

"Too long. I damned near starved to death." Rose leaned forward to hiss, "If I'd known you was in camp after Grace that night, I'd have ripped you from belly to brisket."

Norah felt faint and supported herself against a wagon awaiting repair. "I took Grace for her own good. She'd be dead by now if she'd stayed with you. Look at *this*! You're so right. There's been no place in your life for your daughter."

"That's for me to decide," Grace interrupted in a firm voice. Dressed in boots, pants, and shirt, she put a shawl around Norah's shoulders and then walked toward Rose with curiosity and a touching eagerness.

Dismay and disbelief stunned Norah. The girl was ready to ride! Words failed her, and the weapons she held were cold and strange in her hands. Rose crossed the arena, still lithe despite added flesh. Mother and daughter stood inches apart. The Indian woman searched her soul for maternal instincts but found it barren as wind-scoured rock. The girl waited for acknowledgment, but her heart sank. She'd expected a display of frustrated love and warm acceptance, but obviously her mother didn't care at all. Grace was too young to realize that her mother did—but she cared about the girl's budding beauty and its effect on the outlaw chieftain. Norah recognized the look, however, and stepped between them a moment before Ward swooped down from behind to grab her weapons.

"Jesus, ain't this dandy? Another chestnut mare and a blue-eyed filly." Although he had decided against kidnapping as too dangerous a crime, the ranch's prosperity had aroused his greed. Let Fletcher come for his women—and trade them for that fortune in gold rumor said he'd brought from the Montaña hacienda.

"Rose!" Norah appealed. "Don't let them do this to Grace! Don't let them take her!"

The woman glanced at the girl and motioned to one of the gang. "Leave her behind but bring Mrs. Fletcher." She stepped into her lover's stirrup and swung up behind him. "Let's get out of here. You got what you come for."

Grace protested. "She's pregnant. She might lose the baby. Take me and leave her!" She tried without success to keep Norah from being hauled up onto a man's saddle.

"Ain't that noble?" Rose gave her daughter a malicious smile. "I've waited a long time for this. She stole Jim Fullerton from me, you know. That was your daddy's pa. I never loved *your* pa. That's right, kid. You was an accident. And then she kept the ranch that oughta've been mine 'cause half went to you."

"I didn't *keep* it, Rose, you know that." Norah turned to Grace. "Your father willed it to me and you on his deathbed."

"It was mine, you whey-faced bitch!"

"If you hadn't murdered Joel, you'd be standing here, not me," Norah reminded her grimly.

"*Murdered?*" the young girl moaned.

"I didn't mean to kill him. It was an accident. You know that!"

"Shut up!" Ward growled. "That's enough of that crap."

Bitter sadness mixed with pity and compassion washed through Grace. She might have emerged from this woman's loins, but that was the only link between them. Now she understood why Norah had protected her. Norah, who was her real momma, held by the waist there in front of a bearded ruffian. Norah, her darling mother, so white and disheveled. Suddenly her blood boiled with hate, and before anyone could intervene, she pounced upon a fallen rifle. Its metal, still warm from firing, excited her and the heady power of being able to kill energized her. Irrationally, the old saying popped to mind: God created all men but Mr. Colt made them equal. The muzzle yawned at Ward. "Tell that man to put Mrs. Fletcher down, mister, or you'll have a hole in your chest big enough to drive the spring herd through! I mean it!"

"Will you look at this child throwin' down on me?" Ward exclaimed. He fully respected her dominance, for although the gun wavered, the hammer was back and the finger firm on the trigger. They all gaped at the scholarly little female who dared defy one of the most famous outlaws in the Arizona Territory.

Ward thought quickly. They had the horses. But he wanted to hurt Fletcher more! Stolen stock was nothing— ah, but dead women were something else again. His hand drifted down toward the holster, but Rose stopped it. "Look at that pretty little thing," she muttered, "ain't she somethin'?"

"Put—her—down," Grace repeated shakily. Ward jerked his head and the man holding Norah threw her to the ground, the crack of an arm breaking plain to the ear. She screamed in agony and Grace ran to her, whirling to fire over their heads again and again in sheer fury. *"Go away! Go away!"*

Rifle fire erupted behind them as cowhands burst out of the bunkhouse and rustlers tried to regroup. Endicott snapped off a shot as he raced toward the girl, who was covering Norah's body with her own. "Jesus Sufferin' Christ! Are you hurt?"

"Never mind me!" Norah commanded. "Just get those

sonsabitches! And bring my horses back!'' She groaned and put her good hand to her abdomen, tears trickling down her cheeks. *"Oh, Grace, I'm losing the baby!"*

Mason and Billy Smith trotted toward the ranch at a steady pace, collars up and shoulders hunched against the spring chill. The older man silently recalled the time he'd first guided Norah there, coughing and scared to death of dying, yet gutsy as the bravest man in her gentle way. How meaningless life would have been had they not at last come together after Eli's and Soledad's violent deaths. He had often doubted God while he was living in Chihuahua, yet how else could he account for their reunion? It gave a man a heap to think about.

"I'm sure glad you decided to go back tonight, Mr. Fletcher, 'stead of morning.'' Billy turned his head, but the big hat completely darkened his face.

"Why's that?'' The kid was still on probation, but Mason, like Norah and Andrew, was fond of him. He never shirked, knew cows, and better yet, knew horses like no man Mason had met. Billy had an almost mystical way of working them, of getting them to do what he wanted while allowing them to retain their dignity. "I got a feeling we should be there. That we're needed—if that doesn't sound too foolish, sir.''

Mason grunted, having had the same feeling. Nothing to put a finger on but keen enough to turn him back when halfway to his destination. "Worried about the outfit, Billy?''

Billy had been picturing Grace, with a book in hand, the smile in those spectacular eyes. "Oh, yes, sir, but about Miss Martin, too.'' Then in a youthful confidence he was incapable of containing, he blurted, "I plan to ask her to be my wife, sir!''

"Wife!" Mason growled. "Why, she's—she's still a baby. You'll marry her over my dead body! And Mrs. Fletcher's!''

The boy was chagrined he had not made himself clear.

"When she's sixteen, sir, not *now*! And with your permission. I'll have something to show by then." He straightened in the saddle and stared ahead. "I plan to be governor some day."

Mason chuckled. Not a bad ambition. Then abruptly he pulled rein. "Listen! That's gunfire!" They sat motionless for an endless moment, glanced at each other wildly, then spurred their mounts along the road leading to the Mariposa.

They emerged from the night like dark avenging angels, teeth bared in vengeful grimace, eyes wide and furious. Both knew a stealthy approach would be more sensible—to get the bastards in a crossfire between them and the cowboys. But the sight of their beloved women, white and prostrate on the ground, inflamed the man and youth past caution or logic.

Momentarily confused, the rustlers milled like trapped cattle until Ward yelled, "Forget the fuckin' broncs! Let's get our asses outa here!" He reared his horse in an attempt to dump Rose for flight, to relieve the animal of her weight. She fell off but leaped quickly to her feet, ready to mount again. "Mike, here! *Mike!*" Rose reached for his hand. He kicked her brutally in the breast, sending her reeling. Crimson rage exploded in her brain. Drawing her gun, she sank to one knee, drew a bead, and fired.

The tableau of death and destruction sprang into vivid life before Mason as he thundered past the house and into the melee, eyes fixed on his old enemy. Hair tinged red by firelight, black gaze demonic, Ward swore as Rose's shot pinked him in the neck. Before she could shoot again, he deliberately murdered her, shooting her in the middle of the forehead.

Glancing up from his deadly handiwork, the outlaw saw the ex-lawman headed right for him, an alarming sight even to the hardened criminal. This was the avenger, the vindicator, reins in his teeth, both six-shooters spitting flame. The outlaw dropped like a stone to the far side of his horse, gripping a loop braided in its mane; he swung under its neck Comanche fashion, offering no target and using its body as protection.

Unaware of the older men's vendetta, Billy only remembered Ward's attempted rape of his intended; Ward's assault on the ranch was the last straw. He got to Ward before Mason and launched out of the saddle, clinging to the man like a puma to a deer. They struggled and the horse staggered, pulled off balance by the moving mass that clung to its side. Caught by surprise when the animal sat down, the men fell free. Billy was a crack shot but freely admitted being no prize when it came to bare knuckles, and Ward remembered this weakness. He hammered on the boy, frantic to get away so he might remount and flee, but Billy hung on, blood pouring down his face. Mason dismounted, and Ward jerked his opponent in front of him, forcing the rancher to fire high in order to miss Billy. Ward seized Billy's gun and shot him. Red blossomed on the youngster's back and he poised stock-still then collapsed, clutching his midriff.

From the corner of his eye Mason glimpsed his wife and the girl as they embraced, and an anvil lifted from his heart. He breathed more freely as he confronted Ward. "So it's you. I might have known."

"Well, if it ain't the big bull of the wood hisself," Ward jeered. "Ain't this like old times, though?" His eyes flicked back and forth. If he had had a few minutes more he would have been gone. Now it was too late. Mariposa men had caught most of his bunch, and he heard shots in the distance as the others defended themselves. He stared at his adversary and wet his lips, afraid of the showdown held in limbo these many years.

The glow from dying flames lit their faces, and the outlaw's stomach muscles tightened with tension. It seemed only yesterday Fletcher's cold eye had sighted along a gun barrel down there in the Sierra Madre. "I ain't goin' back to prison, Marshal."

"I'm not a peace officer anymore, you know that. But have it your own way." Mason drew himself in, ready for hair-trigger action. "You owe me." Owed time and heartache and years of not knowing who he was.

"You got all the cards here," Ward complained. He slid his weapon into the tied-down holster with the greased lining. He meant what he said, for he would die before languishing in solitary again. His heart fluttered. He was going to die in the next few minutes. His Indian blood told him that.

Billy groaned as his friends lifted and carried him to the bunkhouse. Chan Lee had cleared the table, brushing all the dishes onto the floor. A wounded rustler, coughing blood, begged for help; the men passed him by in stony, hurried silence. A bird scolded the world for disturbing its slumber, and a dog barked far off in the valley. The aged Judas longhorn, Old Sugar, partially blind, lumbered out of the shadow and spooked a few of the men.

Norah sensed rather than saw the beginning of Ward's draw. She breathed her husband's name like a prayer. Shots rang out only seconds apart, and the longhorn snorted and trotted back into the night. Ward sprawled in the trampled dirt, gun clutched so tight they would have to pry it loose before burial. Brute handsome and defiant, he grinned up at Mason. *"Unhuh,"* he choked in Apache, blood and sputum dribbling down his chin. "Yeah, goddamn it, the hell with it—"

"Is Daddy—all right, Momma? I can't look! *Is* he? *Is* he?" Grace's voice quavered and broke.

"Look for yourself!" Norah sobbed in gladness as her husband ran toward them. *"Oh, my darling!"*

Mammoth thunderheads seethed and muttered ominously over southern Arizona as masses of jungle air rolled up from Mexico. They dwarfed the two riders, who grew smaller in the distance. The four young people watched with varying emotions as the older couple disappeared from view.

"Where are they going?" Andrew's slim brown sweet-heart, mind long made up to capture him, moved closer. Her fingers crept into his hand. "Her arm's barely healed." Nor was Norah recovered from losing the baby. Or maybe she was, for Norah Fletcher was a legend. How romantic that they should go off together like that with no practical reason in view such as checking water holes or looking for cattle with screwworms. It was as if a special madness possessed them. Was Andrew that way? She hoped so.

His golden eyes sparkled with amusement and affection. "Oh, they have some secret place, I think." He had packed the mule with bedrolls, bird-watching materials, and food and camp gear, hiding a smile at the perfume and after-shave in their personal bundles. Would he and his betrothed remain so in love at that age, their feelings incandescent, white-hot as a branding iron left in the coals? He gripped her fingers so hard she tried to get loose. "Momma said something about tracking down the Rainbow Prince."

"Who's he?" Grace asked defensively. "Apache roy-alty?"

"Nah, Apaches don't have princes like you read about in books. They had some sort of royal blood system though. I think it's some kind of a bird. You ever listen to her talk about birds? Uses the darndest words. Barbules, mandibles, tibiotarsus—"

"I know what they are," Grace boasted, relieved no one had commented about her Apache blood, yet in a strange way disappointed, too. Maybe it wasn't so bad after all. Maybe her mother's parents had been royalty.

"Want to watch me put the black filly through her paces, Miss Grace?" Billy knew when unpleasantness bothered her. He was, in fact, as closely attuned to the girl as he was to horses; he often knew what she was going to say. It would be wonderful watching her grow up, sure of her place in his life, waiting until the time was right. "Thought I'd call her Rosa Negra, if you don't mind."

Grace flushed, then smiled tentatively. Black Rose. She rather liked that. "Is she pretty?"

"Wouldn't call her that if she wasn't." He walked slowly, still recuperating from his gunshot wound, then called over his shoulder, "Coming, Miss Grace?"

She started to follow him, eager now to see the baby horse perform. Then she stopped, shaded her eyes from a radiant shaft of sun, and peered down the grass-bronzed valley that panted for rain. Where *were* they going? Grace missed the times before Mason and Andrew had come when Norah belonged solely to her. Rosa Negra. That *was* nice! She ran after Billy, calling to him to wait for her.

Norah had been in the ranch cemetery, tending the flowering plants on each plot. Aunt May, Jim, Joel, Charlie the cook, a cowboy dead from snakebite, Shorty, Chan Lee's wife and stillborn infant. So many. And now Rose, at peace at last, buried as close to the Fullertons as possible. Norah scraped a depression in the soil and flicked out a rock. She'd have felt better had she been able to bury the child, but it had not been formed when she miscarried.

Spurs jingled behind her and Norah stood, patting at her eyes with a folded handkerchief. He came toward her, chaps moving winglike with his stride. "You all right? You were gone so long."

Mason put his arm around her shoulders, and she leaned on him. "I'm fine. Just had a lot to do." She studied the rowdy sky with growing interest. "Mason, do you know where I'd like to go for a few days? You and me?"

He ruffled her hair. "No, where? Tucson? San Francisco?"

"No. Guess."

A chuckle rumbled through his frame. He grinned and then laughed aloud. "That's a dangerous place for a gorgeous woman. Your husband's liable to make love to you from the minute we get there."

She ran her hands over the big chest and up behind his

ears and into the thick black hair. "Let's go and do nothing but eat and drink and sleep and make love."

Mason pulled her close and kissed her long and hard. "You're the love of my life," he whispered, "ever since that day in the stagecoach you've been my only reason for living. You know that, don't you?"

"I know I can't live without you. Oh, darling, there's so little time!" She gestured at the cemetery and her eyes filled once again.

"There's all the time in the world. Let me take you and take you," he invited huskily, kissing her throat, moving down to the upper bosom.

"Oh, Lord, you always could make me melt like butter on a hot stove."

"Melt," he murmured urgently, "melt like the night in El Paso—the first visit, remember?—when you almost fainted with love. By God, I'd like you to do that again!"

Returning to the house, flushed and skittish as newly-weds, they fended off a spate of questions, had Andrew pack, and rode south side by side. Once the prairie dogs' barking would have lent a mournful quality to the rising wind that swept butterflies helplessly along before them. She had been blown about that way, but no more. Mason was the tree among whose leaves and branches she hid when life frayed her wings and dulled her colors. Mason and the Mariposa. The two great loves that had ruled her heart and shaped her destiny.

Like other kindhearted ranchers, they often put cow ponies out to pasture after lives of hard work, and now several animals raised their heads from browsing to watch them go by. "Hello, my friends," Norah greeted them, eliciting a whicker from Steel, the blue roan. They had given love, loyalty, and service, unspoken and without deceit. Man had much to learn from animals.

Mason said, *"Buenas dias, amigos!"* They exclaimed in joyous companionship when Grendel trotted out to join them for a short distance, long ears twitching at their voices.

Ah, it was mighty fine to be riding down the range, free as a bird and twice as flighty, with no one to answer to or be responsible for. It was true the world had changed, and they would never again be lords of an unmeasured domain with no law but their own. Yet the future lifted before them like the mountains beginning to dissolve in the fading light.

Norah recalled the last time she had visited the ancient cliff house. It had been a day much like this with clouds devouring the sky, her horse laboring to climb to a higher altitude. Young stags with velvet-covered antlers watched from cover in winsome majesty. Gray foxes slipped by, narrow noses twitching; they hurried to their dens, these rufous and silver descendants of those animals she'd seen years ago. The ranch dog that accompanied them angled in the foxes' direction as Baron had once done, but Norah called to him sweetly, unwilling to have creatures harassed in her Eden.

They unsaddled their mounts and tied them to the old tree, leaving them standing in the cave mouth safe from rain and falling limbs. They commanded the dog to stay with the horses, then carried supplies and equipment up the incline and down into the enclosure. "Hasn't changed," he said with quiet delight, enchanted by the prospect of leisurely days alone with his wife.

She removed hat and scarf. "I'm so glad no one else found it." How often she had pictured the little Indian wife here centuries ago weaving a basket, nursing her infant, snuggling under furs with her mate. And it was here, too, that Mason had made her a woman.

"Think our songster will drop by?" Mason had started a fire. It would be chilly soon and they'd be hungry. He unpacked the food.

Norah said with glee, "Imagine you remembering that! He was *Hylocichla guttata*, the hermit thrush. Mmmm."

She breathed deeply of pine and sun-warmed trees. "Listen! There comes the rain!"

They climbed up to the ledge and stood in the open at the mercy of the elements. They waited arm in arm while the rain traveled through the forest, the sound like that of a waterfall, growing louder as it approached. In the pause preceding the storm, an ethereal melody rose not far away, and the man and woman glanced at each other in awe to think the bird had joined them in this precious moment. Like a paean of hope and renewal, the birdsong swelled until at last the wind lashing the treetops swallowed it up.

Lightning cracked yellow as creek columbine and pink as a primrose. Norah cried out when the bolts struck, so mighty was the noise, but Mason tilted his head and roared back at the tempest, at fate and the past that they had conquered. Primitive forces raced through his veins, invigorating and cleansing him. Teeth gleaming in the half-light, he swept her up in his arms as if to offer her to the gods of the sky and shouted between claps of thunder, *"I love you! I love you!"*

Hair loose, damp and streaming in the wind, she kissed him and made him shiver with desire. *"And I love you to the end of time!"*

They fled the driving rain and clambered down into their private place. Mason put her down, but Norah clung to him, knowing he sought in her as she did in him safety from the tumult, from life itself. She raised her eyes to his and caught her breath at what she saw there, only faintly aware of the howling wind that clawed at the cliff house and made the flames waver.

He wrapped a blanket about her shoulders, and they sat and toasted their feet. Norah rested her head on his shoulder. Here in their rocky refuge, needs pared down to barest essentials, far from man and enclosed in the living mountain, they drowsed with heartbeats blending, part of their environment like rain absorbed into the thirsty valley. He turned his head so he might put his cheek to hers, and she lifted her face with ardor and longing.

Their mouths met and clung and thunder shook the mountain, but Norah was unafraid. She would never be afraid again with Mason to cherish her.

For their love would shield and nourish them forever.

PALOMINO

Danielle Steel

Beautiful, dynamic, an award-winning advertising executive and wife of a nationally known TV anchorman, Samantha is a woman who has everything—until the morning her husband leaves her. After fleeing to California, Samantha must choose between her New York career and the rugged cowboy who promises a new world full of endless, irresistible passion. She will risk everything, lose everything, to find a rare courage equal to the untamed spirit of the proud Palomino stallion who carries her toward her wildest dreams!

A DELL BOOK   16753-1 $3.50